QUEEN OF CANDESCE

TOR BOOKS BY KARL SCHROEDER

Lady of Mazes
Permanence
Ventus
Sun of Suns
Queen of Candesce

KARL SCHROEDER

QUEEN OF CANDESCE

Virga | BOOK TWO

A TOM DOHERTY ASSOCIATES BOOK **TOR®** NEW YORK

This is a work of fiction. All of the characters, organizations, and events portrayed in this novel are either products of the author's imagination or are used fictitiously.

QUEEN OF CANDESCE: BOOK TWO OF VIRGA

Copyright © 2007 by Karl Schroeder

Edited by David G. Hartwell

A Tor Book
Published by Tom Doherty Associates, LLC
175 Fifth Avenue
New York, NY 10010

www.tor.com

Tor® is a registered trademark of Tom Doherty Associates, LLC.

Library of Congress Cataloging-in-Publication Data

Schroeder, Karl, 1962–
    Queen of Candesce / Karl Schroeder.—1st. ed.
       p. cm. — (Virga ; bk. 2)
    "A Tom Doherty Associates book."
    ISBN-13: 978-0-7653-1544-1
    ISBN-10: 0-7653-1544-0
    I. Title.
    PR9199.3.S269Q84 2007
    813'.6—dc22
                                                              2007012908

First Edition: August 2007

Printed in the United States of America

0 9 8 7 6 5 4 3 2 1

QUEEN OF CANDESCE

Prologue

GARTH DIAMANDIS LOOKED up and saw a woman in the sky.

The balcony swayed under him; distant trees wavered in the hot afternoon air though there was no breeze. A twist of little clouds pirouetted far overhead, just beneath the glitter and darkness of the city that had exiled Garth, so many years ago, to this place. Well below the city, only a thousand feet up at this point, a single human form had appeared out of the light.

She rotated up out of Garth's view and he had to wait several minutes for her to come back around. Then, there she was: gliding with supernatural grace over the tall, ragged wall that rimmed the world at its nearer end. Behind her, infinite air beckoned, forever out of reach of Garth and the others like him. Ahead of the silent woman, a likely tumble into quickly moving trees, broken limbs, and death. If she wasn't dead already.

Someone tried to escape, he thought—an act that always ended in gunshots or bloody thrashing beneath a swarm of piranhawks. This one must have been shot cleanly by the day watch for she was spiraling across the sky alone, not attended by a retinue of blood droplets. And now the spin-gale was teasing the fringes of her outlandish garment, slowing her; bringing her down.

Garth frowned, for a moment forgetting the aches and pains that bedeviled him all day and all night. The hovering woman's clothes had been too bright and fluttered too easily to be made of the traditional leather and metal of Spyre.

As the world turned the woman receded into the distance, frustrating Garth's attempt to see more. The ground under his perch was rotating up and away along with the whole cylindrical world; the black-haired woman was not moving with it but rather sailing in majestically from one of the world's open ends. But Spyre made its own winds as it turned, and those winds would pull her to its surface before she had a chance to drift out the other side.

She would have sped up by that time, but not enough to match Spyre's rotation. Garth well knew what happened when someone began clipping the treetops and towers at several hundred miles per hour. He'd be finding pieces of her for weeks.

The ground undulated again. Frantic horns began echoing in the distance—an urgent conversation between the inner surface of Spyre and the city above.

Watching the woman had been an idle pastime, since it looked as though she was going to come down along the rail line. People with more firepower and muscle than Garth owned that; they would see her in a few moments and bring her down. Her valuable possessions and clothes would not be his.

But the horns were insistent. Something was wrong with the very fabric of Spyre, an oscillation building. He could see it in the far distance now: the land heaved minutely up and down. The slow ripple was making its way in his direction; he'd better get off this parapet.

The archway opening onto the balcony had empty air behind it and a twenty-foot drop to tumbled stones. Garth hopped over the rail without hesitation, counting as he fell. "One pilot, two pilot, three—" He landed among upthrusts of stabbing weed and the cloudlike brambles that had taken over this ancient mansion. Three seconds? Well, gravity hadn't changed, at least not noticeably.

His muscles creaked as he stood up, but climbing and jumping were part of his daily constitutional, a grim routine aimed at convincing himself he was still a man.

He stalked over the crackling grit that painted a tiled dance floor. Railway ties were laid callously across the fine pallasite stones; the line cleaved the former nation of Arbath like a whip-mark. Garth stepped onto the track daringly and stared down it. The great family of Arbath had not reached an accommodation with the preservationists and had been displaced or killed, he couldn't remember which. Rubble, ruins, and new walls sided the tracks; at one spot an abandoned sniper tower loomed above the strip. It now swayed uneasily.

The tracks converged in perspective but also rose with the land itself, a long graceful curve that became vertical if he followed it far enough. He didn't look that far but focused on a scramble of activity taking place about a mile distant.

The Preservation Society had planted one of their oil-soaked sidings there like an obscene graffito. Some of the preservationists were pouring alcohol into the tanks of a big turbine engine that squatted on the tracks like an idol to industrialism. Others had started a tug and were shunting in cars loaded with iron plating and rubble. They were responding to the codes brayed out by the distant horns.

They were so busy doing all this that none had noticed what was happening overhead.

"You're crazy, Garth." He hopped from foot to foot, twisting his hands together. When he was younger he wouldn't have hesitated. There was a time when he'd lived for escapades like this. Cursing his own cowardice, Garth lurched into a half-run down the tracks—in the direction of the preservationist camp.

He had to prove himself more and more often these days. Garth still sported the black cap and long sideburns that rakes had worn in his day—but he was acutely aware that the day had come and gone. His long leather coat was brindled with cracks and dappled with stains. Though he still wore the twin holsters that had once held the most expensive and stylish dueling pistols available in Spyre, nowadays he just carried odd objects in them. His breath ratcheted in his chest and if his head didn't hurt, his legs did, or his hands. Pain followed him everywhere; it had made crow's-feet where once he'd outlined his eyes in black to show the ladies his long lashes.

The preservationist's engine started up. It was coming his way so Garth prudently left the track and hunkered down beneath some bushes to let it pass. He was in disputed land, so no one would accost him here, but he might be casually shot from a window of the train and no one would care. While he waited he watched the dot of the slowly falling woman, trying to verify his initial guess at her trajectory.

Garth made it the rest of the way to the preservationist camp without attracting attention. Pandemonium still reigned inside the camp, with shaven-headed men in stiff leather coats crawling like ants over a second, rust-softened engine under the curses of a supervisor. The first train was miles up the curve of the world now and if Garth bothered to look down the length of Spyre, he was sure he would see many other trains on the move as well. But that wasn't his interest.

Pieces of the world fell off all the time. It wasn't his problem.

He crept between two teetering stacks of railway ties until he was next to a pile of catch-nets the preservationists had dumped here. Using a stick he'd picked up along the way, he snagged one of the nets and dragged it into the shadows. Under full gravity it would have weighed several hundred pounds; as it was he staggered under the weight as he carried it to a nearby line of trees.

She was going by again, lower now and fast in her long spiral. The woman's clothes were tearing in the headwind and her dark hair bannered behind her. When Garth saw that her exposed skin was bright red he stopped in surprise, then doubled his efforts to reach the nearest vertical cable.

The interior of Spyre was spoked by thousands of these cables; some rose at low angles to reattach themselves to the skin of the world just a few miles away. Some shot straight up to touch down on the opposite side of the cylinder. All were under tremendous tension and every now and then one snapped; then the world rang like a bell for an hour or two, and shifted, and more pieces fell off of it.

Aside from keeping the world together, the cables served numerous purposes. Some carried elevators. The one Garth approached had smaller lines draped and coiled around its frayed black surface—some old, rusted, and disused pulley system. The main cable was anchored to a corroded metal cone that jutted out of the earth. He clipped two corners of the roll of netting to the old pulley. Then he jogged away from the tracks, unreeling the net behind him.

It took far too long to connect a third corner of the huge net to a corroded flagpole. Sweating and suffering palpitations, he ran back to the flagpole one more time. As he did she came by again.

She was a bullet. In fact, it was the land that was speeding by below her and pulling the air with it. If she'd been alive earlier she might be dead now; he doubted whether anyone could breathe in such a gale.

As soon as she shot past Garth began hauling on the pulleys. The net lurched into the air a foot at a time. Too slow! He cursed and redoubled his effort, expecting to hear shouts from the preservationist camp at any moment.

With agonizing slowness, a triangle of netting rose. One end was anchored to the flagpole; two more were on their way up the cable. Had he judged her trajectory right? It didn't matter; this was the only attachment point for hundreds of yards, and by now she was too low. Air resistance was yanking her down and in moments she would be tumbled to pieces on the ground.

Here she came. Garth wiped sweat out of his eyes and pulled with bloody hands. At that moment the shriek of a steam whistle sounded from the preservationist camp. The rusted engine was on the move.

The mysterious woman arrowed in just above the highest trees. Garth thought for sure she was going to miss his net. Then, just as the rusted engine sailed by on the tracks—he caught snapshot glimpses of surprised preservationist faces and open mouths— she hit the net and yanked it off the cable.

A twirling screw hit Garth in the nose and he sat down. Sparks shot from screaming brakes on the tracks and the black tangling form of the falling woman passed between the Y-uprights of a jagged tree, the trailing net catching branches and snapping them as she bounced with astonishing gentleness into a bed of weeds.

Garth was there in seconds, cutting through the netting with his knife. Her clothes marked her as a foreigner, so her ransom potential might be low. He probably couldn't even get much for her clothes; cloth like that had no business being worn in Spyre. Oh well; maybe she had some adornments that might fetch enough to buy him food for a few weeks.

Just in case, he put a hand on her neck—and felt a pulse. Garth cursed in astonishment. Jubilantly he slashed away the rest of the strands and pulled her out as a warning shot cracked through the air.

Unable to resist, he teased back the wave of black hair that fell across her face. The woman was fairly young—in her twenties—and had fine, sharp features with well-defined black eyebrows and full lips. The symmetry of her face was broken only by a star-shaped scar on her jaw. Her skin would have been quite fair were it not deeply sunburnt.

She only weighed twenty pounds or so. It was easy to sling her over his shoulder and run for the deep bush that marked the boundary of the disputed lands.

He pushed his way through the branches and onto private land. The preservationists pulled up short, cursing, just shy of the bushes. Garth Diamandis laughed as he ran, and for a precious few minutes he felt like he was twenty years old again.

1

A LOW BEAMED ceiling swam into focus. Venera Fanning frowned at it, then winced as pain shot through her jaw. She was definitely alive, she decided ruefully.

She was—but was Chaison Fanning also among the living, or was Venera now a widow? That was it, she had been trying to get back to her husband, Chaison Fanning. Trying to get home—

Sitting up proved impossible. The slightest motion sent waves of pain through her; she felt like she'd been skinned. She moaned involuntarily.

"You're awake?" The thickly accented words had the crackle of age to them. She turned her head gingerly and made out a dim form moving to sit next to her. She was lying on a bed—probably—and he was on a stool or something. She blinked, trying to take in more of the long low room.

"Don't try to move," said the old man. "You've got severe sunburn and sunstroke too. Plus a few cuts and bruises. I've been wetting down the sheets to give you some relief. Gave you water too. Don't know what else to do."

"Th-thanks." She looked down at herself. "Where are my clothes?"

His face cracked in a smile and for a second he looked much younger. He had slablike features with prominent cheekbones and piercing gray eyes. Eyes like that could send chills through you, and from his confident grin he seemed to know it. But as he shifted in the firelight she saw that lines of care and disappointment had cut away much of his handsomeness.

"Your clothes are here," he said, patting a chair or table nearby. "Don't worry, I've done nothing to you. Not out of virtue, mind; I'm not a big fan of virtue, mine or anyone else's. No, you can thank arthritis, old wounds, and age for your safety." He grinned again. "I'm Garth Diamandis. And *you* are a foreigner."

Venera sighed listlessly. "Probably. What does that mean around here?"

Diamandis leaned back, crossing his arms. "Much, or nothing, depending."

"And here is . . . ?"

"Spyre," he said.

"Spyre . . ." She thought she should remember that name. But Venera was already falling asleep. She let herself do it; after all, it was so cool here. . . .

When she awoke again it was to find herself propped half-upright in a chair. Her forehead, upper body, and arms were draped with moist sheets. Blankets swaddled her below that.

Venera was facing a leaded-glass window. Outside, green foliage made a sunlit screen. She heard birds. That suggested the kind of garden you only got in the bigger towns—a gravity-bound garden where trees grew short and squat and soil stayed in one place. Such things were rare—and that, in turn, implied wealth.

But this room . . . As she turned her head her hopes faded. This was a hovel, for all that it too seemed built for gravity. The floor was the relentless iron of a town foundation, though surprisingly she could feel no vibration from engines or slipstream vanes through her feet. The silence was uncanny, in fact. The chamber itself was oddly cantilevered, as though hollowed out of the foundations of some much larger structure. Boxes, chests, and empty bird cages were jammed or piled everywhere, a few narrow paths worn between them. The only clear area was the spot where her overstuffed armchair sat. She located the bed to her left, some tables, and a fireplace that looked like it had been clumsily dug into the wall by the window. There were several tables here and the clutter had infected them as well; they were covered with framed pictures.

Venera leaned forward, catching up the sheet at her throat. A sizzle of pain went through her arms and shoulders and she extended her left arm, snarling. She was sunburned a deep brick red that was already starting to peel. How long had she been here?

The pictures. Gingerly, she reached out to turn one in the light. It was of a young lady holding a pair of collapsible wrist-fins. She wore a strange stiff-looking black bodice, and her backdrop was indistinct but might have been clouds.

All the portraits were of women, some two dozen by her estimation. Some were young, some older; all the ladies seemed well-off, judging from their various elaborate hairdos. Their clothes were outlandish, though, made of sweeping chrome and leather, clearly heavy and doubtless uncomfortable. There was, she realized, a complete absence of cloth in these photos.

"Ah, you're awake!" Diamandis shuffled his way through the towering stacks of junk. He was holding a limp bird by the neck; now he waved it cheerfully. "Lunch!"

"I demand to know where I am." She started to stand and found herself propelled nearly to the ceiling. Gravity was very low here. Recovering with a wince, she coiled the damp sheet around her for modesty. It didn't help; Diamandis frankly admired her form anyway, and probably would have stared even if she'd been sheathed in plate armor. It seemed to be his way, and there was, strangely, nothing offensive about it.

"You are a guest of the principality of Spyre," said Diamandis. He sat down at a low table and began plucking the bird. "But I regret to have to inform you that you've landed on the wrong part of our illustrious nation. This is Greater Spyre, where I've lived now for, oh . . . twenty-odd years."

She held up the picture she had been looking at. "You were a busy man, I see."

He looked over and laughed in delight. "Very! And why not? The world is full of wonders, and I wanted to meet them all."

Venera touched the stone wall and now felt a faint thrum. "You say this is a town? An old one . . . and you've turned gravity way down." Then she turned to look at Diamandis. "What did you mean, 'regret to inform me'? What's wrong with this Greater Spyre?"

He looked over at her and now he seemed very old. "Come. If you can walk, I'll show you your new home."

Venera bit back a sharp retort. Instead, she sullenly followed him through the stacks. "My temporary residence, you mean," she said to the cracked leather back of his coat. "I am making my way back to the court at Slipstream. If ransom is required, you will be paid handsomely for my safe return . . ."

He laughed, somewhat sadly. "Ah, but that it were possible to do that," he murmured. He exited up a low flight of steps into bright light. She followed, feeling the old scar on her jaw starting to throb.

The roofless square building had been built of stone and steel I-beams, perhaps centuries ago. Now devoid of top and floors, it had become a kind of open box, thirty feet on a side. Wild plants grew in profusion throughout the rubble-strewn interior. The hole leading to Diamandis's home was in one corner of the place; there was no other way in or out as far as she could see.

Venera stared at the grass. She'd never seen wild plants under gravity before. Every square foot was accounted for in the rotating ring-shaped structures she called towns. They were seldom more than a mile in diameter, after all, often built of mere rope and planking. There was no other way to feel gravity than to visit a town.

She scanned the sky past the stone walls. In some ways it looked right: the endless vistas of Virga were blocked by some sort of structure. But the perspective seemed all wrong.

"Come." Diamandis was gesturing to her from a nearly invisible set of steps that ran up one wall. She scowled, but followed him up to a level area just below the top of the wall. If she stood on tiptoe, she could look over. So she did.

Venera had never known one could feel so small. Spyre was a rotating habitat like those she had grown up in. But that was all she could have said to connect it to the worlds she had known. Diamandis's little tower sat among forlorn trees and scrub grass in an empty plain that stretched to trees a mile or more in each direction. In any sane world this much land under gravity would have been crammed with buildings; those empty plazas and tumbled-down villas should have been awash with humanity.

Past the trees, the landscape became a maze of walls, towers, open fields, and sharp-edged forests. And it went on and on to a dizzying, impossible distance. Diamandis's tower was one tiny mote on the inside surface of a cylinder that must have been ten or twelve miles in diameter and half again as long.

Sunlight angled in from somewhere behind her; Venera turned quickly, needing the reassurance of something familiar. Beyond the open ends of the great cylinder, the reassuring cloudscapes of the normal world turned slowly; she had not left all sense and reason behind. But the scale of this town wheel was impossible for any engineering she knew. The energy needed to keep it turning in the unstable airs of Virga would beggar any normal nation. Yet the place looked ancient, as evidenced by the many overgrown ruins and furzes of wild forest. In fact, she could see gaps in the surface here and there through which she could glimpse distant flickers of cloud and sky.

"Are those holes?" she asked, pointing at a nearby crater. Leaves, twigs, and grit fogged the air above it, and all the topsoil for yards around had been stripped away, revealing a stained metal skin that must underlie everything here.

Garth scowled as if she'd committed some indiscretion by pointing out the hole. "Yes," he said grudgingly. "Spyre is ancient and decaying, and it's under an awful strain. Tears like that open up all the time. It's everyone's nightmare that one day, such a rip might not stop. If the world should ever come to an end, it will start with a tear like that one."

Faintly alarmed, Venera looked around at the many other holes that dotted the landscape. Garth laughed. "Don't worry, if it's serious the patch gangs will be here in a day or two to fix it—dodging bullets from the local gentry all the while. They were out doing just that when I picked you up."

Venera looked straight up. "I suppose if this is Greater Spyre," she said, pointing, "then that is Lesser Spyre?"

The empty space that the cylinder rotated around was filled with conventional town wheels. Uncoupled from the larger structure, these rings spun grandly in midair, miles above her. Some were "geared" towns whose rims touched, while others turned in solitary majesty. A puff of smaller buildings surrounded the towns.

The wheels weren't entirely disconnected from Greater Spyre. Venera saw cables standing up at various angles every mile or so throughout the giant cylinder. Some angled across the world to anchor in the ground again far up Spyre's curve. Some went straight past the axis and down to an opposite point; if you climbed one of these lines you could get to the city that hung like an iron cloud half a dozen miles above.

She didn't see any elevator traffic on the nearest cables. Most were tethered inside the mazelike grounds of the estates that dotted the land. Would anyone have a right to use those cables but the owners?

When Diamandis didn't reply, Venera glanced over at him. He was gazing up at the distant towns, his expression shifting between empty adoration and anger. He seemed lost in memory.

Then he blinked and looked down at her. "Lesser Spyre, yes. My home, from which I am exiled for life. Always visible, never to be achieved again." He shook his head. "Unlucky you to have landed here, Lady."

"My name," she said, "is Venera Fanning." She looked out again. The nearer end of the great cylinder began to curve upward less than a mile away. It rose for a mile or two then ended in open air. "I don't understand," she said. "What's to prevent me—or you—from leaving? Just step off that rim yonder and you'll be in free flight in the skies of Virga. You could go anywhere."

Diamandis looked where she was pointing. Now his smile was condescending. "Ejected at four hundred miles per hour, Lady Fanning, you'll be unconscious in seconds for lack of breath. Before you slow enough to awake you'll either suffocate or be eaten alive by the piranhawks. Or be shot by the sentries. Or be eviscerated by the razor-wire clouds, or hit a mine. . . .

"No, it was a miracle that you drifted unconscious through all of that, to land here. A once-in-a-million feat.

"Now that you're among us, you will never leave again."

DIAMANDIS'S WORDS MIGHT have alarmed Venera had she not recently survived a number of impossible situations. Not only that, he was manifestly wrong about the threat the piranhawks represented; after all, hadn't she sailed blithely through them all? These things in mind, she followed him down to his hovel where he began to prepare a meal.

The bird was pathetically small; they would each get a couple of mouthfuls out of it if they were lucky. "I'm grateful for your help," Venera said as she lowered herself painfully back into the armchair. "But you obviously don't have very much. What do you get out of helping me?"

"The warmth of your gratitude," said Diamandis. In the shadow of the stone fireplace it was impossible to make out his expression.

Venera chose to laugh. "Is that all? What if I'd been a man?"

"I'd have left you without a second thought."

"I see." She reached over to her piled clothes and rummaged through them. "As I suspected. I've not come through unscathed, have I?" The jewelry that had filled her flight jacket's inner pockets was gone. She looked under the table and immediately spotted something: it looked like a metal door in the floor, with a rope loop as its handle. Her feet had been resting on it earlier.

"No, it's not down there," said Diamandis with a smile.

Venera shrugged. The two most important objects in her possession were still inside her jacket. She could feel the spent bullet through the lining. As to the other—Venera slipped her hand in to touch the scuffed white cylinder that she and her husband had fought their way across half the world to collect. It didn't look like it was worth anything, so Diamandis had apparently ignored it. Venera left it where it was and straightened to find Diamandis watching her.

"Consider those trinkets to be payment for my rescuing you," he said. "I can live for years on what you had in your pockets."

"So could I," she said levelly. "In fact, I was counting on using those valuables to barter my way home, if I had to."

"I've left you a pair of earrings and a bracelet," he said, pointing. There they were, sitting on the table next to her toeless deck shoes. "The rest is hidden, so don't bother looking."

Seething but too tired to fight, Venera leaned back, carefully draping the moist sheet over herself. "If I felt better, old man, I'd whip you for your impudence."

He laughed out loud. "Spoken like a true aristocrat! I knew you were a woman of quality by the softness of your hands. So what were you doing floating alone in the skies of Virga? Was your ship beset by pirates? Or did you fall overboard?"

She grimaced. "Either one makes a good story. Take your pick. Oh, don't look at me like that, I'll tell you, but first you have to tell me where we are. What is Spyre? How could such a place exist? From the heat outside I'd say we're still near the sun of suns. Is this place one of the principalities of Candesce?"

Diamandis shrugged. He bent over his dinner pot for a minute, then straightened and said, "Spyre's the whole world to those of us who live here. I'm told there's no other place like it in all of Virga. We were here at the founding of the world, and most people think we'll be here at its end. But I've also heard that once, there were dozens of Spyres, and that all the rest crumbled and spun apart over the ages. . . . So I believe we live in a mortal world. Like me, Spyre is showing its age."

He brought two plates. Venera was impressed: he'd added some cooked roots and a handful of boiled grains and made a passable meal of the bird. She was ravenous and dug in; he watched in amusement.

"As to what Spyre is . . ." He thought for a moment. "In the cold-blooded language of the engineers, you could say that we live on an open-ended rotating cylinder made of metal and miraculously strong cables. About six miles from here there's a giant engine that powers the electric jets. It is the same kind of engine that runs the suns. Once, we had hundreds of jets to keep us spinning, and Spyre's outer skin was smooth and didn't catch the wind. Gravity was stronger then. The jets are failing, one by one, and wind resistance pulls at the skin like the fingers of a demon. The old aristocrats refuse to see the decay that surrounds them, even when pieces of Spyre fall away and the whole world becomes unbalanced in its turning. When that happens, the Preservationist Society's rail engines start up and they haul as many tons as needed around the circle of the world to reestablish the balance.

"The nobles fought a civil war against the creation of the Preservation Society. That was a hundred years ago, but some of them are still fighting. The rest have been hunkered down on their estates for five centuries now, slowly breeding heritable insanities in the quiet of their shuttered parlors. They're so isolated that they hardly speak the same language anymore. They'll shoot anyone who crosses their land, yet they continue to live, because they can export objects and creatures that can only be made here."

Venera frowned at him. "You must not be one of them. You're making sense as far as I can tell."

"Me? I'm from the city." He pointed upward. "Up there, we still trade with the rest of the principalities. We have to; we've got no agriculture of our own. But the hereditary nobles own us because they control the industries down here." The bitterness in his voice was plain.

"So, Garth Diamandis, if you're a city person, what are you

doing living in a hole in the ground in Greater Spyre?" She said it lightly, though she was aware the question must cause him more pain.

He did look away before smiling ruefully at her. "I made the cardinal mistake of all gigolos: I cultivated popularity among women only. I bedded one too many princesses, you see. I was kindly not killed nor castrated for it, but I was sent here."

"But I don't understand," she said. "Why is it impossible to leave? You said something about defenses . . . but why are they there?"

Diamandis guffawed. "Spyre is a treasure! At its height, this place was the equal of any nation in Virga, with gravity for all and wonders you couldn't get anywhere else. Why, we had horses! Have you heard of horses? And dogs and cats. You understand? We had here all the plants and animals that were brought from Earth at the very beginning of the world. Animals that were never altered to live in weightlessness. Even now, a breeding pair of house cats costs a king's ransom. An orange is worth its weight in platinum. We had to defend ourselves and prevent our treasures being stolen. So, for centuries now, Spyre has been ringed with razors and bombs to prevent attack—and to prevent anyone smuggling anything out. And believe me, when all else has descended to madness and decadence, that is the one policy that will remain in place." He hung his head.

"But surely one person, traveling alone—"

"Could carry a cargo of swallowed seeds. Or a dormant infant animal in a capsule sewn under the skin. Both have been tried. Oh, travel is still possible for nobles of Lesser Spyre and their attendants, but there are body scans and examinations, interrogations and quarantines. And anyone who's recently been on Greater Spyre comes under even more suspicion."

"I . . . see." Venera decided not to believe him. She would be more cheerful that way. She did her best to shrug off the black mood his words had inspired, and focused on her meal.

They ate in silence for a while, then he said, "And you? Pirates or a fall overboard?"

"Both and neither," said Venera. How much should she tell? There was no question that lying would be necessary, but one must always strike the right balance. The best lies were built of pieces of truth woven together in the right way. Also, it would do her no good to deny her status or origins; after all, if the paranoid rulers of Spyre needed money then Venera Fanning herself could fetch a good price. Her husband would buy her back or reduce this strange wheel to metal flinders. She had only to get word back to him.

"I was a princess of the kingdom of Hale," she told Diamandis. "I married at a young age—he is Chaison Fanning, the admiral of the migratory nation of Slipstream. Our countries lie far from here—hundreds or thousands of miles, I don't know—far from the light of Candesce. We have our own suns, which light a few hundred miles of open air that we farm. Our civilizations are bounded by darkness, unlike you who bask in the permanent glory of the Sun of Suns . . ."

Some audiences would need more—not all people knew that the whole vast world of Virga was artificial, a balloon thousands of miles in diameter that hung alone in the cosmos. Lacking any gravity save that made by its own inner air, Virga was a weightless environment whose extent could easily seem infinite to those who lived within it. Heat and light were provided not by any outside star but by artificial suns, of which Candesce was the oldest and brightest.

Even the ignorant knew it was a man-made sun that warmed

their faces and lit the crops they grew on millions of slowly tumbling clods of earth. But the world itself? One glance up from your own drudge-work might encompass vast, cloud-wreathed spheres of water, miles in extent, their surfaces scaled with mirror-bright ripples; thunderheads the size of nations, which made no rain because rain required gravity but rather condensed balls of water the size of houses, of cities, then threw them at you; and a glance down would reveal depths of air painted every delicate shade by the absorption and attenuation of the light of a dozen distant suns. How could such a place have an end? How could it have been made by people?

Venera had seen the outer skin of the world, watched icebergs calve off its cold black surface. She had visited the region of machine-life and incandescent heat that was Candesce. The world was an artifact, and fragile. In her coat pocket was something that could destroy it all, if you but knew what it was and how to use it.

There were things she could tell no one.

A thing she could tell was that her adopted home of Slipstream had been attacked by a neighboring power, Mavery. Missiles had flashed out of the night, blossoming like red flowers on the inner surface of the town-wheels of Rush. The city had been shocked into action, a punitive expedition mounted with her husband leading it.

She explained to Diamandis that Mavery's assault had been a feint. He listened in mesmerized silence as she described the brittle dystopia known as Falcon Formation, another neighbor of Slipstream. Falcon had conspired with Mavery to draw Slipstream's navy away from Rush. Once the capital was undefended, Falcon Formation was to move in and crush it.

The true story was that Venera's own spy network had alerted them to this plot. Chaison and Venera Fanning had taken seven ships from the fleet and left on a secret mission to find a weapon powerful enough to stop Falcon. The story she told Diamandis now was that her flagship and its escort were pursued by Falcon raiders, chased right out of the lit air of civilization into the darkness of permanent winter that permeated most of Virga.

That had been a month ago.

After that, more things she could tell: a battle with pirates, being captured by same; escape, and more adventures near the skin of the world. She told Diamandis that they had sailed toward Candesce in search of help for their beleaguered country. She did not tell him that their goal was not any of the ancient principalities that ringed the sun. They were after a pirate's treasure, in particular the one seemingly insignificant piece of it that now rested in Venera's jacket. They had come seeking the key to Candesce itself.

In Venera's version, the Slipstream expedition had been met with hostility and chased into the furnace-like regions around Candesce. Her ships had been set upon and half of them destroyed by treacherous marauders of the nation of Gehellen.

In fact, she and her husband had orchestrated the theft of the pirate's treasure from under the noses of the Gehellens and then fled with it—he back to Slipstream and she into the Sun of Suns. There she had temporarily disabled one of Candesce's systems. While it was down, Chaison Fanning was to lead a surprise attack on the fleet of Falcon Formation.

Slipstream's little expeditionary force was no match for the might of Falcon—normally. For one night, the tables should have been turned.

Venera had no idea whether the whole gambit had been successful or not. She would not tell Diamandis—would not have told anyone—that she feared her husband was dead, the force destroyed, and that Falcon cruisers ringed the Pilot's palace at Rush.

"I was lost overboard when the Gehellens attacked," she said. "Like much of the crew. We were close to the Sun of Suns and as dawn came, we burned. . . . I had foot-fins, and at first I was able to fly away but I lost one fin, then the other. I don't remember anything after that."

Diamandis nodded. "You drifted here. Luckily the winds were in your favor. Had you circulated back into Candesce you'd have been incinerated."

That much, at least, was true. Venera suppressed a shudder and sank back in her chair. She was infinitely weary all of a sudden. "I need to sleep."

"By all means. Here, we'll get you to the bed." He touched her arm and she hissed in pain. Diamandis stepped back, concern eloquent on his face.

"There are treatments—creams, salves . . . I'm going to go out and see what I can get for you. For now you have to rest. You've been through a lot."

Venera was not about to argue. She eased herself down on the bed and, despite being awash in burning soreness, fell asleep before hearing him leave.

2

NEAR DAWN, THE lands of Greater Spyre were lit only by the glitter of city lights high overhead. In the faint glow, the ancient towers and forests seemed as insubstantial as clouds. Garth paused in the black absence beneath a willow tree. He had run the last hundred yards and it was all he could do to keep his feet.

Silhouettes bobbed against the gray outline of a tower. Whoever they were, they were still following him. It was unprecedented: he had snuck through the hedgerows and fields of six hereditary barons, each holding no more than a square mile or so of territory but as fanatical about their boundaries as any empire. Garth knew how to get past their guards and dogs, he did it all the time. Apparently, these men did also.

It must have been somebody at the Goodwill Free Clinic. They'd waited until he was gone and then signaled someone. If that was so, Garth would no longer be able to count on the neutrality of the kingdom of Hallimel—all six acres of it.

He moved on cautiously, padding quietly onto a closely cropped lawn dotted with ridiculously heroic statues. It was quiet as a tomb here, and certainly nobody had any business being out. He allowed himself a little righteous indignation at whoever it was that was following him. They were trespassers; they should be shot.

It would be most satisfying to raise the alarm and see what

happened—a cascade of genetically crazed hounds from the doorway of yon manor house, perhaps, or spotlights and a sniper on
the roof. The trouble was, Garth himself was a known and tolerated ghost in only a few of these places, and certainly not the one
he was passing through now. So he remained discreet.

A high stone wall loomed over the garden of statues. Its
bricks were crumbling and made an easy ladder for Garth in
the low gravity. As he rolled over the top he heard voices behind
him—someone exclaiming something. He must have been visible against the sky.

He landed in brambles. From here on the country was wild.
This was disputed territory, owned by now-extinct families, its
provenance tied up in generations-old court cases that would
probably drag on until the end of the world. Most of the disputed
lands were due to the railway allotments created by the preservationists; they had needed clearances that ran completely around
the world, and they had gotten them, for a price of blood. This
section of land had been abandoned for other reasons, though
what they were Garth didn't know. He didn't care, either, as long
as the square tower he called home was left in peace.

His intention was to reach it so that he could warn the lady Fanning that they had company—but halfway across the open grass-
land he heard thuds behind him as half a dozen bodies hit the
ground on his side of the wall. They were catching up, and quickly.

He flattened and rolled to one side. Grass swished as dark figures passed by, only feet away. Garth cursed under his breath,
wishing there were some way to warn Venera Fanning that six
heavily armed men were about to pay her a visit.

VENERA HEARD THEM coming. The darkness wasn't
total—Diamandis had left a candle burning—so she wasn't

completely disoriented when she awoke to voices saying "Circle around the other side" and "This must be his bolt-hole." A flush of adrenaline brought her completely awake as she heard scratching and scuffling just outside the hovel's door.

She rolled out of bed, heedless of the pain, and ran to the table where she snatched up a knife. "Down here!" someone shouted.

Where were her clothes? Her jacket lay draped across a chair, and on the table were the bracelet and earrings Diamandis had left her. She cast about for her other things, but Diamandis had apparently moved them. There they were, on another table—next to the opening door.

Venera's first inclination would normally be to draw herself up to her full five foot seven and stare these men down when they entered. They were servants, after all, even if they were armed. If she could speak and make eye contact, Venera was completely confident in her ability to control members of the lower classes.

At least, she used to be. Recent events—particularly her unwelcome dalliance with Captain Dentius of the winter pirates—had made her more cautious. Plus which, she was sore all over and had a pounding headache.

So Venera snatched up the candle, her jacket, and the jewelry and knelt under the table. The rope ring scraped her raw skin as she yanked on it; after a few tugs the mysterious hatch lifted. She felt down with her foot, making contact with a metal step. As men blundered into Diamandis's home she billowed the damp sheet behind her, with luck to drape over the hatch and hide it.

The candle guttered and nearly went out. Venera cupped a hand around it and cautiously felt for the next step. She counted seven before finding herself standing in an icy draft on metal flooring. A constant low roar made it hard to hear what was going on above.

This small chamber was oval, wider at the ceiling than at the floor, and ringed with windows. All the panes were flush with the wall, but a couple vibrated at a high speed, making a low braying sound. They seemed to be sucking air out of the room; it was the walls that soaked cold into the place.

Diamandis evidently used the room for storage because there were boxes piled everywhere. Venera was able to make her way among them to the far end, where a metal chair was bolted to the floor. The windows here were impressive: floor-to-ceiling, made of some resilient material she had never seen before.

The candlelight seemed to show a dense weave of leaves on the other side of the glass.

She was going to freeze unless she found something to wear. Venera ransacked the boxes, alternately cursing and puffing out her cheeks in wonder at the strange horde of broken clocks, worn-out shoes, rusted hinges, frayed quills, moldy sewing kits, left socks, and buckles. One crate contained nothing but the dust jackets of books, all their pages having been systematically ripped out. It was a small library's worth of intriguing but useless titles. Another was full of decaying military apparel, including holsters and scabbards, all of it bearing the same coat of arms.

At least the activity was keeping her warm, she reasoned. The faint clomp of boots above continued, so she moved on to a new stack of boxes. This time she was rewarded when she found it packed with clothing. After dumping most of that onto the floor she discovered a pair of stiff leather pants, too small for Diamandis but sufficient for her. Getting into them wasn't easy, though—the material scoured her already-raw skin so that it hurt to move. The leather cut out the wind, however.

Once she had donned the flight jacket Venera sat down in the metal chair to wait for whatever happened next. This was much harder; it wasn't in Venera's nature to remain still. Staying still made you think and thinking led to feeling, which was seldom good.

She drew her knees up and wrapped her arms around her shins. It came to her that if they took away Diamandis and she couldn't get out of here, she would die and no one would ever know what had happened to her. Few would care, either, and some would rejoice. Venera knew she wasn't well liked.

More stomping up above. She shivered. How far away was her home in Slipstream? Three thousand miles? Four? An ocean of air separated her from her husband and in that ocean gyred the nations of enemies, rising, lowering, drifting with the unpredictable airs of Virga. Awaiting her out there were the freezing abysses of winter, full of feathered sharks and pirates. Before the Sun of Suns had roasted her into unconsciousness, she had been determined and sure of her own ability to cross those daunting distances alone. She had leaped from the cargo nets of Hayden Griffin's jet and soared for a time like a solitary eagle in the skies of Virga. But the sun had caught up to her and now she was here, trapped and in pain hardly any distance from where she'd started.

She climbed off the chair, fighting a wave of nausea. Better to surrender herself to whoever waited above than die here alone, she thought—and she almost ran up the steps and surrendered. It was a pulse of pain through her jaw that stopped her. Venera drew her fingertips across the scar that adorned her chin, and then she backed away from the steps.

Her heel caught the edge of a box she'd dropped, and she stumbled back against the icy windows. Cursing, she straightened up, but as she did she noticed a gleam of light welling up through the glass. She put her cheek to it—which dampened the pain a bit—and squinted.

The windows were covered with a long-leafed form of ivy. The stuff was vibrating with uncanny speed—so quickly that the leaves' edges were blurred. Diamandis had said that Spyre rotated very fast; was she looking into the air outside?

Of course. This oval chamber stuck out of the bottom of the world. It was an aerodynamic blister on the outside of the rotating cylinder, and that chair might have once fronted the controls of a heavy machine gun or artillery piece mounted outside. It still might. Frowning, Venera clambered over the mounds of junk back to the metal seat and examined it.

There was indeed a set of handles and levers below the chair, and more between the windows. She didn't touch them but peered out through the glass there, as light continued to well through the close-set leaves.

Candesce was waking up. The Sun of Suns lit a zone hundreds of miles in diameter here at the center of Virga. Past the trembling leaves Venera could see a carousel of mauve and peach-painted cloud tumbling past with disorienting speed; but she could also see more.

The oval blister was mounted into a ceiling of riveted metal, as she'd expected. That ceiling was the hull of Spyre, and a few feet above it was soil, trees, and the foundations of the buildings she had seen yesterday. Covering this surface in long runnels and triangles was the strange ivy. Its leaves were like knives, sharp and long, and they all aligned in the flow of the wind. Venera had heard of something called speed ivy; maybe that was what this was.

The ivy seemed to prefer growing on things that projected into the airstream. Sheets of metal skin were missing here and there—in fact, there were outright holes everywhere—and the ivy clustered on the leading and trailing edges of these, smoothing the airflow in those places. Maybe that was what it was for.

This view of Spyre was not reassuring. The place was showing its age—dangling sheets of titanium whirred in the wind and huge I-beams thrust down into the dawn-tinted air, whole sagging acres just waiting to peel off the bottom of the world. It was amazing that the place kept itself together.

Next to the blister, a rusted machine gun was mounted on the surface. It faced stoically into the wind and didn't move when Venera tried the controls in front of the chair.

Well. All this was interesting, but not too interesting. She headed back to the stairs, but the light coming through the ranked leaves was considerable now and she could see more of the blister's interior. So the little passage that opened out behind the stairs was now obvious.

Venera gnawed her lip and rolled her eyes to look at the closed hatch overhead. One hand was on her hip; even here, with no audience, she posed as she thought.

She needed shoes—but she'd recovered the important items, the key to Candesce and her bullet. Venera was quite aware that she was obsessed with that bullet, and who wouldn't be, she usually reasoned, if one like it had flown a thousand miles or more across Virga to randomly spike through a window and into their jaw? This particular projectile had been fired in some distant war or hunting party and missed its target; since there was no gravity nor solid ground to stop it the thing had kept going and going until it met her. From that encounter Venera had gained a scar, regular crippling headaches, and something to blame for her own meanness. She'd kept the bullet and over time had become consumed with the need to know where it had come from. It was not, she would admit, a healthy need.

She patted the jacket, feeling the heavy shape inside it; then she slipped past the steps and into the narrow passage, and left Diamandis and his invaders to their own little drama.

IT WAS MORE of a crawlway than a corridor. Venera walked bent over, gasping as the old leather chaffed her hips and knees. Why didn't these people dress sensibly? Lit only by intermittent portholes, the passage wormed its way a hundred yards or so before ending in a round metal door. It was all so obviously abandoned—stinking of rust and inorganic decay—that Venera didn't bother knocking on the door, but turned the little wheel in the middle of it and pushed.

She stepped down into a mirror image of the blister she had just left. She half-expected to find another maze of boxes on the other side of the steps, with another junk-framed hovel and another Garth Diamandis waiting for her above. But no, the blister was empty save for a half-foot of stagnant water and a truly revolting gallery of fungus and cobwebs. The windows were hazed over but provided enough light for a tiny forest that was trying to conquer the metal chair at the far end. The stairs were jammed with soil and roots.

The prospect of dipping her bare feet into that horrid water nearly made her turn back. What stopped her was a tiny chink of light visible in the midst of the soil plug. After wading cautiously and with revulsion through the stinking stuff, she reached up and pulled at the roots. Gradually, in little showers of dirt, worms, and fibrous tubers, she widened a hole big enough for her to shimmy through. A minute later she dragged herself up, out, and into the middle of a grassy field.

Too bad about Diamandis, but with luck he was still off on his errand and the interlopers wouldn't be there when he got back. Anyway, he'd been more than compensated for taking care of her; that had been a Pilot's ransom of gems and faience he'd taken from her jacket. She half-hoped those loud burglars found the stuff—it would serve him right.

Venera's own destination was clear. Spyre being a cylinder, it had ends and one of those was only half a mile away. There, the artificial land curved up hundreds of feet in a gesture that would close off the end if continued. The curve ended in a broad gallery above and beyond which the winds of Virga shuddered. Venera had only to make it up that slope and hop off the edge and she would be in free flight again. She would take her chances with the piranhawks and snipers. She doubted any of them could hit one small woman leaving Spyre at four hundred miles per hour.

In this case, wearing leather would serve her well.

Between Venera and the edge of the world lay a chessboard of estates. Each had its tottering stone walls, high hedges, towers, and moats to defend its two or three acres from the ravages of greedy neighbors. Constrained by space and what Venera sensed was deep paranoia, the estates had evolved into similar designs—the larger ones walled, with groves surrounding open fields and a jumble of towers, annexes, and greenhouses at the center; small ones often just a single square building that took up the entire demesne. These edifices were utterly windowless on the outside, but higher up the curve of the world she could see that most contained courtyards crammed with trees, fountains, and statuary.

The walls of some estates were separated by no more than twenty feet of no-man's-land. She ran through these weed-choked alleys, dodging young trees, past iron-faced pillbox gates that faced one another across the minor space like boxy suits of armor. The footing was treacherous, and she suspected traps.

Venera was used to higher gravity than Spyre's. Tired and sore though she was, it was easy for her to leap ten feet to the top of a stone wall and run its length before dropping to the grass beyond. Her feet barely felt brick, root, and stone as she wove in and out of the trees, sprinted around open ponds under windows that were just beginning to gleam yellow in the light of Candesce. As she ran she marveled that such distances could exist; she had never run so far in a straight line and could hardly believe it possible.

The birds were the only ones making sound, but as she ran Venera began to notice a deep rushing roar that came from ahead of her. It was the sound of the edge of the world, and with it there came the beginnings of a breeze.

She heard surprised shouts as she crossed one fanatically perfect lawn, bare feet kissing wet grass. Glancing to the side, Venera caught a glimpse of a small party of men and women sitting on curlicued iron chairs in the morning light. They were sipping tea or something similar.

They stood up—stiff ornamented garments ratcheting into their standing configurations like portcullises slamming down—and the three men howled "Intruders!" as if Venera were an entire army of pirates. After a moment sirens sounded inside the looming stone pile behind them.

"Oh, come on!" She was panting with exhaustion now, her head swimming. But there were only two more estates to pass and then she would be on the slope to the world's edge. With a burst of speed she raced by more lighting windows and opening doors, noting abstractly that the considerable mob of soldiers who had spilled out of the first place's doors had stopped at the edge of their property as if they'd slammed into an invisible fence.

So she had only to outrace the alarm in each particular property. It could be a game and Venera actually would have enjoyed the chase if she hadn't been on the verge of fainting from exhaustion and residual heatstroke. If only she had the breath to taunt the idiots on the way by!

Gunshots cut the air as she passed the last estate. This was one of the big single-building affairs, all gray asteroidal stone drizzled with veins of bright metal. Its only external windows were murder slits that started fifteen feet up, and she saw no doors. Empty upward-curving fields beckoned on the other side of the edifice; she staggered onto what Diamandis had called "disputed territory" and paused to catch her breath. "Ha! Safe!"

The wind was now a harsh constant moan, flickering past her in gusts. It spun in little permanent tornadoes over gaps and holes in Spyre's skin. There were more and more such holes as the slope rose to the edge. The edge itself was ragged, a crenelation of collapsed galleries, upthrusting spars, and flapping plates that added to the din.

She heard something else too. A regular creaking sound seemed to be coming from overhead. Venera looked up.

Six wooden platforms had been lowered over the top of the stone cube and were being winched down. Each was crowded with men in tall steel helmets and outlandish spiked armor. They clutched pikes and rifles with barrels longer than they were tall. Several were pointing at her excitedly.

Venera swore and took off up the rubble-strewn slope. The wind was at her back and it became stronger the closer she got to the edge. Several gusts lifted her off her feet. Venera noticed that the metal skin of Spyre was completely exposed in the final yards leading up to the edge. Only fair-sized rocks inhabited the area behind it. As she watched, a stone the size of her foot rolled up the metal and spun off into the air. A few more yards and the wind would take her too.

Her foot sank into the slope and Venera fell in ridiculous slow-motion. As she pried herself upright again she saw that the metal plate bent by her foot was vibrating madly in the square hole it had made. Then with a loud pop it disappeared and suddenly a hurricane was howling into the bright aperture it had left.

Venera was sucked down and slid forward until she was right over the hole. She reached out and braced her hands on either side of it while the air screamed past her. It was trying to escape Spyre with even more passion than hers. For a few seconds she could only stare down and see what faced her if she made it to the edge and jumped.

Many long flagpole-like beams thrust out below the edge of the world. They trailed wire nets into the furious wind; anyone caught on those nets would suffocate before they could be pulled up. Far beneath the nets, where scudding clouds spun past, Venera glimpsed thousands of black specks and grayish veins in the air. Mines? More razor wire? Diamandis had not been lying, after all.

"Damn! Shit!" She tried to scream more curses—every one she could think of—but the air was being pulled out of her lungs. She was about to faint into the hole and die.

Strong hands took her by the arms and legs and hauled her back. Venera was hoisted onto someone's back and unceremoniously toted back down the slope. With every jolting step escape, home, and Chaison receded past the frame of her grasping fingers.

3

ALTHOUGH HE WAS her favorite uncle, Venera never saw much of Prince Albard. He was a mysterious figure on the periphery of the court, sweeping into Hale in his yacht to regale her with tales of strange cities and the outlandish women he'd met there (always sighing when he spoke of them). His face was split down the center by a saber scar, putting his lips into a permanent twist that made it look like he was smirking. Unlike most of the people who encountered him, Venera knew that he *was* smirking—laughing inside at all the pointless desperation and petty recrimination of life. In that regard he was the polar opposite of her father, a man with a mind focused by a single lens of suspicion; maybe that was why she clung to Albard's knees when he did appear, and treasured the odd-shaped dolls and toys he brought.

They recognized each other, this vagabond prince in his motley and the pouting princess in clothes she systematically tattered as soon as she was in them. So maybe it was natural that when the time came, it was in her bedroom that Albard barricaded himself.

He only noticed her after he had dragged her wardrobe in front of the door and piled some chairs and tables around it. "Damn, girl, what are you doing here?"

Venera had cocked her head and squinted at him. "This is my room."

"I know it's your room, damnit. Shouldn't you be at lessons?"

"I bit the tutor." Banished and bored, she had (not out of anger but a more scientific impulse) been beheading some of her dolls when Albard swept in. Venera had assumed that he was there to talk to her and had politely waited, limp headless body in one hand, while he proceeded to move all the furniture. So he wasn't there to see her? What, then, was this all about?

"Oh, never mind," he said irritably, "just stay out of sight. Things could get ugly."

Now she could hear shouting outside, sounds of people running. "What did *you* do?" she asked.

He was leaning back against the pile of furniture as though trying to propel it out of the room. "I bit someone too," he said. "Or, rather, I was about to, and they found out."

Venera came and sat down on the fuschia carpet near him. "My father, right?"

His eyebrows rose comically. "How did you guess?"

Venera thought about this for a while. Then she said, "Does that mean that everybody who makes Father mad has to come to this room?"

Albard laughed. "Niece, if that were true, the whole damn kingdom would be in here with us."

"Oh." She was slightly reassured.

"Give it up, Albard!" someone shouted from outside. It sounded like her father. There was some sort of mumbling discussion, then: "Is, uh . . . is Venera in there with you?"

"No!" The prince put a finger to his lips and knelt next to her. "The one thing I absolutely will not do," he said gently, "is use you as a bargaining chip. If you want to leave I will tear down this barricade and let you go."

"What will they do to you?"

"Put me in chains, take me away . . . then it all depends on your father's mood. There's a black cloud behind his eyes lately. Have you seen it?" She nodded vigorously. "It's getting bigger and bigger, that cloud, and I think it's starting to crowd out everything else. That worries me."

"I know what you mean."

"I daresay you do." There followed a long interval during which Albard negotiated with the people on the other side of the furniture. Venera retreated to the window, but she was far from bored now. At last Albard blew out his cheeks and turned to her.

"Things are not going well," he said. "Do you have a pen and some writing material?" She pointed to the desk that perched on top of the barricade. "Ah. Much obliged."

He clambered up and retrieved a pen and some paper. Then, frowning, he dropped the paper. He went to his knees and began hunting around for something, while Venera watched closely. He came up with one of her dolls, a favorite that had a porcelain head and cloth body.

"Do you mind if I borrow this for a minute?" he asked her. She shrugged.

Albard rubbed the doll's face against the stone floor for a while, while crashing sounds started from the hallway. The barricade shook. Holding the doll up critically, the prince grunted in satisfaction. Then he hunched over and began delicately pressing the pen against its face.

He was standing in the center of the room with his hands behind his back when the barricade finally fell. A dozen soldiers came in and they marched him out; he only had time to look back and wink at Venera before he was gone.

After they'd taken him away some members of the secret police ransacked her room. (That it looked substantially the same when they left as before Albard had arrived was a testament to her own habits.) They seized everything that could write or be written on, even prying the plaster off the wall where she'd scribbled on it. Venera herself was frisked several times and then they swirled out, all clinking metal and bandoliers, leaving her sitting in the exact spot where he had been standing.

Neither she nor anyone she would later meet would ever see Albard again.

Eventually she moved over to the window and picked up a particular doll. Its tunic was ripped where the secret policemen had cut it open looking for hidden notes. Venera held it up to the window and frowned.

So that was what he'd been doing. Albard had rubbed its eyebrows off against the stone. Then, in meticulous tiny lines and curls, he had repainted them. From a distance of more than a few inches they seemed normal. Up close, though, she could see what they were made of:

Letters.

THE NATION OF Liris curled around its interior courtyard as though doubled up in pain. Every window stared down at that courtyard. Every balcony overhung it and the six towers that surmounted the building were built to overlook it as well. The bottom of this well would be in permanent shadow if not for the giant mirrors mounted on the roof, which were aimed at Candesce.

Venera could plainly see that the courtyard was the focus of everything—but she couldn't see what was down there. For the first two days of her stay she was shuttled from small room to small room, all of them lined up in a short hallway painted institution green. After a brief interview in each chamber she was taken back to a drab waiting room, where she sat and ate and slept fitfully on the benches. She was startled awake every morning by a single gunshot sounding somewhere nearby. Morning executions?

It seemed unlikely; she was the sole inhabitant of this little prison. Prison it clearly was. She had to fill out forms just to use the one washroom, a cold cube with wooden stalls defaced by centuries of carven graffiti. Its high grated windows gave her a view of the upper stories of the inner courtyard. They hinted at freedom.

"B-b-back to waking?" Venera sat up warily on the third morning and tried to smile at her jailor.

He was tall, athletically muscled, and possessed the sort of chiseled good looks one saw in actors, career diplomats, or con artists. As dapper as could be expected for a man dressed in iron and creaking leather, he might have melted any lady's heart—provided she never looked in his eyes or heard him speak. Either of those maneuvers would have revealed the awful truth about Moss: his mind was damaged somehow. He seemed more marionette than man and, sadly, appeared to be painfully aware of his deficit.

Just as he had yesterday, Moss carried a stack of forms in one hand, bearing it as though it were a silver platter. Venera sighed when she saw this. "How long is it going to take to process me into your prison?" she asked as he clattered to a stop in front of her.

"P-p-prison?" Moss gaped at her. Carefully, as though they

were gold, he placed the papers on the peeling bench. His metal clothing gnashed quietly as he straightened up. "You're n-not in p-p-prison, my lady."

"Then what is this place?" She gestured around at the sound-deadening plaster walls, the smoke-stained light sconces, and the battered benches. "Why am I here? When do I get my things back?" They'd gone through her jacket and taken its contents— jewelry, key, and bullet. She wasn't sure which loss worried her most.

Moss's face never changed expression as he spoke, but his eyes radiated some sort of desperate plea. They always did, even if he was staring at the wall. Those eyes seemed eloquent, but Venera was beginning to think that nothing about Moss's looks or demeanor meant anything about his inner state. Now he said, in his intensely flat way, "This is the im-immigration department of the g-g-government of Liris. You were brought here to t-t-take your citizenship-ip exams."

"Citizenship?" But now it all made sense—the forms, the sense of being processed, and the succession of minor officials who'd taken up hours of her time over the past days. They had grilled her mercilessly, but not about how or why she had come here, or about what her plans or allegiances might be. They didn't even want to know about her peeling sunburns. No, they'd wanted to know the medical histories of her extended family, whether there was madness in her line (a question that had made her laugh), and what was the incidence of criminality among her relatives.

"Well, my father stole a country once," she had answered. She had of course asked them to let her go, in perhaps a dozen different ways. Her assumption was that she would be ransomed or otherwise used as a bargaining chip. With this in mind she had sat anxiously for hours, wondering about her value to this or that state or person. It had never occurred to Venera that she might be adopted by Liris as one of its own.

Now as she realized what was going on, Venera had one of the strangest moments of her life. She felt, for just a second, relief at the prospect of spending the rest of her life hidden away here, like a jewel in a safe. She shook herself, and the moment passed. Disturbed, she stood and turned away from Moss.

"B-b-but the news is good," said Moss, who looked like he was begging for death as he said it. "D-don't fret. You have p-p-passed all the t-t-tests so far. J-just one set of forms to g-go."

Venera gnawed at her knuckle, each bite sending little pulses of pain up her jaw. "What if I don't want to be a citizen of Liris?"

Moss proceeded to laugh, and Venera swore to herself she would do anything to avoid seeing *that* again. "F-Fill these out," he said. "A-and you're done."

It wasn't eagerness to become a citizen of a nation the size of a garden that made her sign the papers. Venera just wanted to get her things back—and get out of the waiting room. What she'd felt a moment ago was just a craving for anonymity, she told herself. Citizenship of any nation meant nothing to her, except as a sign of lowly status. Her father was hardly a citizen of Hale, after all; he *was* Hale and other people were citizens of him. Venera had grown up believing she too was above such categories.

"Come" was all Moss said when she was finished. He led her out into the hallway and at its end he unlocked the great metal door with its wire-mesh window. Before pushing the portal open, he picked up an open-topped box and held it out to her.

Inside were the necklace and earrings he'd confiscated from her jacket when she arrived. Rolling next to them was her bullet.

The key to Candesce was not there.

Venera frowned but decided not to press the matter just now. Moss gestured with one hand and she edged past him into her new country.

Shafts of dusty sunlight silhouetted tall stone pillars. Their arched capitals were muted in shadow, but the polished floors gleamed like mirrors. Save for a wall where the edge of the courtyard should be, the whole bottom floor of the great cubic building seemed open. Filling the space were dozens and dozens of cubicles, desks, worktables, and stalls.

Indeed, it seemed as if all the roles of a midsized town were duplicated here—tailor over here, doctor there, carpenters on this side, bricklayers on that—but all gathered in one room. Bolts of cloth were stacked with bags of cement. Drying racks and looms had been folded up under the ceiling to make way for chopping blocks and flour-covered counters. And working in determined silence throughout this shadow-cut space was a small army of silent, focused people.

Each was isolated at some chair or desk, and Venera had the startled impression that these workstations had grown up and around some of the people, like shells secreted around water creatures. It must have taken years for that man there to build the small ziggurat of green bottles that reared above his desk; nearby a woman had buried herself in a miniature jungle of ferns. Mirrors on stands and hanging from strings cunningly directed every stray beam of light within ten feet at her green fronds. Each position had its eruption of individuality or downright eccentricity, but their limits were strictly kept; nobody's keepsakes and oddities spilled beyond an invisible line about five feet in radius.

Moss led her to an outer wall, where he opened a dim chamber that reminded her of Diamandis's warren. Here were crates and boxes full of what looked like armor—except she knew it for what it was. "You are required to wear four hundred fifty p-p-pounds of mass during the day," said Moss. "That will offset our r-reduced g-gravity and maintain the health of your bones." He stood back, arms crossed, while Venera rooted through the mess looking for something suitable.

It seemed that Spyre's tailors were an unimaginative lot. The room contained an abundance of blouses, dresses and skirts, pants, and jackets, but all were done in intricately tooled and hinged metal. Only undergarments—those directly in contact with the skin—were made of suppler materials, mostly leather, though to her relief she did find some cloth. Venera tried on a vest made of verdigrised copper scales, added a skirt made of overlapping iron plates and weighed herself. Barely a hundred pounds. She went back and found greaves and wrist bracers, a platinum torque, and a steel jacket with tails. Better, but still too light. Moss waited patiently while she layered herself like a battleship. Finally when she topped the scales at one hundred pounds weight—five hundred pounds mass—he grunted in satisfaction. "B-but you need a h-h-hat," he said.

"What?" She glared at him. He had something like a belaying pin tied to his head; it wobbled when he moved. "Isn't all this humiliating enough?"

"We m-must put p-p-pressure on the s-spine. For l-long-term health."

"Oh, all right." She hunted through a cache of ridiculous alternatives, ranging from flowerpots with chin straps to a glass fishbowl, currently empty but encrusted with rime. Finally she settled on the least offensive piece, a chrome helmet with earflaps and crow's wings mounted behind the temples.

With all of this on her, Venera's feet made a satisfactory smack when they hit the ground. She could feel the weight and it was indeed nearly normal, but spread all over her surface instead of internally. And she quickly discovered that it took a good hard push to start walking and that turning or stopping were not operations to be taken lightly. She had a quarter-ton of inertia now. After walking into several walls and doorjambs she started to get the hang of it.

"N-now," said Moss in evident satisfaction, "you are f-fit to see the b-b-botanist."

"The what?" He threaded his way among the pillars without further comment. Venera nodded and smiled at the men and women who were putting down their work to openly stare as she passed. She tried to unobtrusively discern what they were working on, but the light here was too uneven. Shadow and glare thwarted her.

Sunlight reflecting off the polished floor washed out whatever was ahead. Venera glanced back one more time before entering the lit area. Blackness and curving arches framed a dozen white ovals—faces—all turned toward her. On those faces she read every emotion: amazement, curiosity, anger, fear. None avoided her gaze. They goggled at her as though they'd never seen a stranger before.

Maybe they hadn't. Venera's scalp prickled, but Moss was waving her ahead. Blinking, she stepped from the dark gallery into the courtyard of Liris.

For a moment it seemed as if she'd entered one of the paintings on the ceiling of her father's chapel. This one came complete with scented pink clouds. She reached out a hand to touch one of these and heard the sharp click of a weapon being cocked. Venera froze.

"It would be very unwise of you to complete that gesture," drawled a voice from somewhere ahead. Slowly, Venera retracted her hand. As her eyes adjusted to the brightness she saw the barrels of three antique-looking rifles aimed her way. Grim men in iron held them.

The soldiers made a shocking contrast to their setting. The entire courtyard was full of trees, all of one type, all in full flower. The scent and color of the millions of blossoms was overwhelming. It took Venera a moment to notice that the branches of many of the trees were hung with jewels, and gold rings encircled some of the trunks. It took her another moment to realize that a throne sat in the sole bare patch at the center of the courtyard. The woman lounging there was watching her with obvious amusement.

Her gown was of gold, silver, and platinum; on her head was a crown touched with gems of all shades that flashed in the concentrated light of Candesce. She appeared to be in early middle age, but was still beautiful; a cascade of hair dyed the same color as the blossoms wound down her shoulders.

"You seem reluctant to step into sunlight," she said with evident amusement. "I can see why." She tapped her own cheeks, eyes twinkling.

Venera eyed the soldiers, thought about it, and walked over. Since this was evidently a throne room of sorts, she bowed deeply. "Your . . . majesty?"

"Oh. Oh no." The woman chuckled. "I am no queen." She waved a hand dismissively. "We are a meritocracy in Liris. You'll learn. My name is Margit, and I am Liris's resident botanist."

"Botanist . . ." Venera straightened and looked around at the trees. "This is your crop."

"Please." The lady Margit frowned. "We don't refer to the treasure of Liris in such prosaic terms. These beings *are* Liris. They sustain us, they give us meaning. They are our soul."

"Pardon, m'lady," said Venera with another bow. "But . . . what exactly *are* they?"

"Of course." Margit's eyes grew wide. "You would never have seen one before. You are so lucky to gaze upon them for the first time when they are in flower. These, Citizen Fanning, are cherry trees."

Why was that word so familiar? There'd been a ball once, and her beloved uncle had approached her with something in his hand. . . . A treat.

"What are cherries?" she asked as guilelessly as she could.

"An indulgence of the powerful," said Margit with a smile. "A delicacy so rare that it evidently never made it to your father's court."

"About that," said Venera. "The court, I mean. My family are fantastically rich. Why make me a . . . citizen of this place, when you could just ransom me back? You could get a boatload of treasure for me."

Margit scoffed. "If you were the princess of a true nation then perhaps we would consider it. But you're not even from the principalities! By your own admission during the interviews, you come from the windswept wastes of Outer Virga. There's nothing there, and I find it hard to believe your people could own anything that would be of interest to us."

Venera narrowed her eyes. "Not even a fleet of battle cruisers capable of reducing this place to kindling from twenty miles away?"

Not only Margit laughed at this; the soldiers did as well. "Nobody threatens Spyre, young lady. We're impregnable." Margit said this so smugly that Venera swore she would find a way to throw her words back at her.

Margit snapped her fingers and Moss stepped forward. "Acquaint her with her new duties," said the botanist.

Moss stared at her, slack-jawed. "W-what are those?"

"She knows the languages and cultures of other places. She'll

be an interpreter for the trade delegation. Go introduce her."
Margit turned away, lifting her chin with her eyes closed so that
a beam of sunlight flooded her face.

ON HER SEVENTEENTH birthday, Venera snuck out of
the palace for the first time, acquired the means to blackmail her
father, killed her first person, and met the man she was destined
to marry. She would later tell people that "it all just sort of happened."

The capital of Hale was a collection of six town-wheels—
spinning rings, each two thousand feet in diameter—surrounded
by an ever-shifting cloud of weightless buildings and smaller
rings. The main sound in the city was the rumbling of jet engines,
as various rings and large municipal structures struggled to keep
their spin and to avoid colliding. The scent of kerosene hung in
the air; underlying it were other industrial and biological odors,
just as under the rumbling of the engines you could hear shouts,
horns, and the laughter of dolphins.

Venera had grown up watching the city life from afar. When
she traveled between the town-wheels it was usually in a closed
taxi. Sometimes one or another of the nobility hosted weightless balls; then, she and the other ingenues donned fabulous
wings that were powered by stirrups, and flew intricate dances
in the warm evening air. But that flight always took place within
careful limits. Nobody strayed.

She was of marriageable age now—and had recently come to
realize that in Hale, marriageable also meant murderable. Venera
had three sisters and had once had three brothers. Now she had
two of those, and the once-close girls of the family were starting
to actively plot against one another. With the boys, it was all
about succession; with the girls, marriage.

Someone had used a marvelous word at a dinner party just a few days before: *leverage*. Leverage was what she needed, Venera had decided. And so her thoughts had turned to old family tragedies and the mysteries that had consumed her as a girl.

Today she was dressed in the brown blouse and pantaloons of a servant girl and the wings on her back were not butterfly orange or feathered pink, but beige canvas. Her hair was tied down with a drab cloth and she soared the air of the city barefoot. In her waist bag she carried some money, a pistol, and a porcelain-headed doll. She knew where she was going.

The bad neighborhoods started remarkably close to the palace. This fact might have had something to do with the royal habit of simply dumping waste off the palace wheel without regard to trajectory or velocity. The upper classes couldn't be entirely blamed for the stench that wafted at Venera as she flapped toward her destination, however. She wasn't disgusted; on the contrary the smell and the sound of arguing, shouting people made her heart pound with excitement. Since she was little she'd sat for hours with her eye glued to a telescope, watching these citizens and this neighborhood roll by as the palace turned past it. She knew the place—she had simply never been here.

What Venera approached looked like nothing so much as an explosion frozen in time. Even the smoke (of which there was plenty) was motionless, or rather it moved only as quickly as the air that oozed slowly between the hundreds of cubes, balls, and disheveled shapes that counted as buildings here. Anything not tied down hung in the air and drifted gradually, and that meant trash, animal hair, balls of dirty water, splinters, and scraps of cloth all contributed to the cloud. When the doldrums of summer broke and a stiff wind finally did snake through the place, half the mass of the neighborhood was going to simply blow away, like chaff. For now it roiled around Venera as she ducked and dove toward the gray blockhouse that was her destination.

Her business in the building was brief, but every detail of the transaction seemed etched in extraordinary detail—for here were people who didn't know who she was. It was marvelous to be treated like servants and ordinary folk treated one another, for a change—marvelous and eye-opening. Nobody opened the door to the place for her; she had to do it herself. Nobody announced her presence, she had to clear her throat and ask the man behind the counter to help her. And she had to pay, with her own money!

"The contents of locker six-sixty-four," she said, holding out the sheet of paper she'd written the information on. The paper was for his benefit, not hers, for she'd memorized the brief string of letters and numbers years ago. Deciphering the letters Uncle Albard had penned on her doll's forehead had been one of her primary motivations to learn to read.

The keeper of the storage lockers merely grunted and said, "Get 'em yourself. If you've got the combination, you get in, that's the rule." He pointed to a doorway at the end of the counter.

She made to go that way and he said, "Back pay's owing on that one. Six hundred." He grinned like a shark. "We were about to clear it out."

Venera opened her bag, letting him see the pistol as she rummaged for the cash. He took it without comment and waved her through the door.

The only thing in the dingy locker was a water-stained file folder. As she stood in the half-light flipping through it, Venera decided it was all she needed. The documents were from the College of Succession at the University of Candesce, two thousand miles away. They included DNA analyses that proved her father was not of the royal line.

She barely saw the tumbled buildings as she left the block-house; maybe that was why she got turned around. But suddenly Venera snapped to attention and realized she was in a narrow chute formed by five clapboard structures, on her way down, not up toward the palace. Frowning, she grabbed a handy rope to steady herself and turned to go back the way she'd come.

"Don't." The voice was quiet, and came from above and to the left. Venera flipped over to orient herself to the speaker. In the gray reflected light from shingle and tar paper she saw a youth—perhaps no older than herself—with tangled red hair and the long bones of someone raised in too little gravity. He smiled toothily at her and said, "Bad men coming behind you. Keep going and take your first hard right, and you'll be safe."

She hesitated, and he scowled. "Not shittin' ya. Get going if you know what's good for you."

Venera flipped again, planted her feet on the rope, and kicked off down the chute. As she reached the corner the boy had indicated she heard voices coming from the far end of the chute—opposite the way he'd said the bad men were coming from.

This side way led quickly to well-traveled airspace and had no niches or doors out of which someone could spring. Feeling momentarily safe, Venera peeked around the corner of the chute. Three men were flying slowly up from the left.

"I really think you've gotten us lost this time," said the one in the lead. He was in his late twenties and obviously noble or rich from his dress and demeanor. One of his companions was simi-larly dressed, but the third man looked like a commoner. She couldn't see much more in the dim light. "The palace is defi-nitely not this way," continued the leader. "My appointment is at two o'clock. I can't afford to be late."

Two o'clock? She remembered one of the courtiers telling her that an admiral from some neighboring country would be calling on her father in the early afternoon. Was this the man?

Suddenly one of the other men shouted, "Hey!" He had barely writhed out of the way of a sword that had suddenly appeared in the third one's hand. "Chaison, it's a trap!"

Four men shot down the chute from the right. They were rough-looking, the sort of thugs Venera had watched roaming the neighborhood through her spyglass and sometimes fantasized about. All had drawn swords and none spoke as they set upon their two victims.

The one named Chaison whirled his cloak into the air between himself and the attackers and drew his sword as his friend parried a thrust from their erstwhile guide. After the initial warning from Chaison's friend, nobody spoke.

In a free-fall swordfight, the blade was as much propulsion as weapon. Each of the men found purchase in wall or rope or opponent with hand, foot, shoulder, or blade as they could. Each impact sent them in a new direction and they tumbled and spun as they slashed at one another. Venera had watched men practice with swords and had even witnessed duels, but this was totally different. There was nothing mannered about it; the fight was swift and brutal. The men's movements were beautiful, viscerally thrilling, and almost too fast to take in.

One of the attackers was hanging back. As his face intersected a shaft of light she realized it was the boy who had warned her. He held his sword up, wavering, in front of his face and ducked away from the embattled older men.

It took Venera a few seconds to realize that two of the men bouncing from wall to wall were now dead. There were black beads dotting the air—blood—and more was trailing the bodies, which continued to move but only languidly, from momentum.

One was the guide who had brought the two noblemen here; another was one of the attackers.

"Stand down!" Chaison's voice startled Venera so much that she nearly lost her grip on the wall. The remaining three attackers paused, holding onto ropes and bent shingles, and stared at their dead compatriots. The boy looked sick. Then one of his companions grabbed his arm and, with a roar of anger, jumped.

He spun away, slashed in the face by Chaison's companion. The other man had his sword knocked out of his hand by Chaison, who finished the uppercut motion with a blow to his jaw.

The boy was hanging in midair with his sword held out in front of him. Chaison glimpsed him out of the corner of his eye, spun and—stopped.

The blade trembled an inch from the boy's nose. He went white as a sheet.

"I'm not going to hurt you," said Chaison. His voice was soft, soothing—in total contrast to the bellow he had given moments ago. "Who sent you here?"

The boy gulped and, seeing that he still held his sword, he let go it spasmodically. As it drifted away he said, "B-big man from palace. Red feather in his hat. Didn't give a name."

Chaison made a sour face. "All right. Now off with you. Find another line of work—oh, and some better friends." He reached for his companion's wrist and they locked arms to coordinate their flight. Together they turned to leave.

The man who'd been struck in the chin suddenly snapped his head up and raised his arm. A snub-nosed pistol gleamed in his grimy fist. The boy gasped as he aimed it point-blank at the back of Chaison's head.

Bang! A spray of blood filled the air and the boy shrieked.

Venera peered through the blue cloud of gunsmoke. Chaison's

would-be assassin was twitching in the air, and both noblemen were staring past him, at her.

She returned the pistol to her carrying bag. "I-I saw you were in trouble," she said, surprised at how calm she sounded. "There was no time to warn you."

Chaison glided over. He looked impressed. "Thank you, madam," he said, graciously ducking his head. "I owe you my life."

In her fantasies Venera always had a perfect comeback line at moments like this. What she actually said was, "Oh, I don't know about that."

He laughed.

Then he extended his hand. "Come. We'll need to explain ourselves to the local police."

Venera flushed and backed away. She couldn't be caught out here—quite apart from the scandal, her father would ask too many questions. The papers she had just recovered might come to his attention and then she was as good as dead.

"I can't," she said and, turning, kicked off from the corner as hard as she could.

She heard him shouting for her to stop, but Venera kept on and didn't look back until she had passed through three crowded markets and slipped down five narrow alleys between soon-to-collide buildings. Cautiously, she worked her way back to the palace and changed in the guardroom while the man she'd bribed to let her out and in again waited nervously outside.

The next time she saw Chaison Fanning it would be two nights later, over the rim of a wineglass. He told her much later that his astonishment when he recognized her completely drove out all thoughts of the new treaty with Hale that he was celebrating. Certainly the expression on his face was priceless.

Venera had her own reason to smile, as she had learned who had tried to have this handsome young admiral killed. And as she danced with Chaison Fanning, she mused about what exact words she would use when she confronted her father. She already knew what it was she would be asking him for in exchange for her silence regarding his non-royal origins.

For the first time in her young life, Venera Fanning began to conceive of an existence for herself away from the intrigue and cruelty of the Court of Hale.

4

A THICK CABLE rose from the roof of the nation of Liris. Venera squinted at it, then at the blunderbusses the soldiers cradled. Another, larger blunderbuss was mounted on a pivot under a little roof nearby. That must be the damnable gun whose firing kept waking her up in the morning.

None of those ancient arms looked very accurate. She could probably just jump off the roof and run for it . . . but run where? Chances were she'd be snapped up by some neighbor worse than these people.

She decided—for the tenth time today—to remain patient and see what happened. No one in Liris seemed to have any immediate desire to harm her. Her best strategy was to play along with them until the moment came when she could escape.

"Now pay attention," whined Samson Odess. The fish-faced little man had been introduced yesterday as her new "boss." The very idea of a commoner giving her orders without an immediate threat to back them up struck Venera as both bizarre and funny. She had so far done the things he had asked but Odess seemed to sense that she wasn't taking him seriously. He was becoming ever more defensive as the morning wore on.

"This is our lifeline to Lesser Spyre," Odess said, slapping the cable. Venera saw that he stood on a low platform, at the center of which was a boxy machine that clamped the cable with big ratchet wheels. "By means of this engine, we can rise to the city above, where the Great Fair is held once a week. Visitors from everywhere in the world come to the Fair. It is the trade delegation's sacred task to ensure that we conduct the most advantageous transactions in the name of Liris." As he spoke the rest of the delegation popped up through the roof's one hatch. Four heavily armed men bracketed an iron box that must have held pithed cherries. Flanking them were two men and two women, the women veiled like Venera and dressed in ceremonial robes of highly polished silver inlayed with crimson enamel.

"Is the gravity the same up there as it is here?" Venera asked. If it was a standard g, they wouldn't be able to move. Odess shook his head vigorously.

"You can see the spin rate from down here. We'll shed our heavy vestments for city clothes once we're up there."

"Why not change down here?" she asked, puzzled.

Odess goggled at her in astonishment. He'd stared exactly that way yesterday, when he was first introduced. Moss had taken Venera to Odess's office, a glorified closet that made her wonder if Diamandis's pack-rat ways might not be the rule here, rather than the exception. Odess had filled the small space over the years, perhaps his whole lifetime, with oddments and souvenirs that likely made sense to no one but him. What was the significance of that single shoe, mounted as though it were a trophy and given its own little niche in the wall? Could anyone read the faded text on those certificates hung behind his chair? And was that some sort of exotic mobile that drooled from the dimness overhead, or the hanging mummified remains of some sort of animal? Books were stacked everywhere, and a pile of dishes three feet tall teetered next to a rolled-up mattress.

Odess's first words were addressed to Moss, not Venera. "You expect us to accept this . . . this *outsider* in our midst?"

"Is th-that not what you d-do?" Moss had asked. "G-go *out-side*?" Startled, Venera had sent him a sidelong look. Was there somebody home behind those glazed eyes, after all?

"B-besides, the b-botanist commanded it."

"Oh, God." Odess had put his head in his hands. "She thinks she can do anything now."

Any slight deviation from routine or custom threw Odess into a panic. Venera's very presence was upsetting him, though the rest of the delegation had been pathetically happy to meet her. They would have partied until dawn if she hadn't begged off early, pointing out that she had not yet seen the room where she was expected to sleep for the rest of her life.

Eilen, Mistress of Scales and Measures, had shown Venera to a closet just outside the delegation's long, cabinet-lined office. The closet was seven feet on a side—its walls of whitewashed stone—and nearly twelve feet high. There was room for a bed and a small table, and there was no window. "You can put your chest under the bed," Eilen said, "when you get one. Your clothes you can hang on those pegs for now."

And that was all. If Venera were inclined to sympathy with other people, she would have been saddened at the thought that Eilen, Odess, and the others accepted conditions like these as the norm. After all, they had likely been born and raised in such tiny chambers. Their playgrounds were dusty servants' ways, their schoolrooms window niches. Yet of all the citizens of Liris, they were the privileged ones, for as members of the delegation they were allowed to see something of the world outside their walls.

While Odess sputtered and tried to explain why tradition demanded that they rise to Lesser Spyre in full ceremonial gear, Venera watched the soldiers deposit their precious cargo on the platform. After the rest of the delegation was on board, they flipped up railings on all sides (to her relief) and one bent to examine the archaic engine. This was what really interested her.

"If we're all ready, we will sing the 'Hymn of Ascension,' " said Odess portentously.

Venera looked around. "The what?"

He looked as though he'd been slapped—but Eilen put a hand on his arm. "We didn't tell her about it, so how would she know?"

"Anyone in Spyre could see us arise, hear the . . ." He realized his mistake. "Ah yes. A true foreigner." Shaking himself, he put both hands on the rail and puffed out his cheeks. "Listen, then, and learn the ways of a civilized society."

While they sang their little ditty Venera watched the soldier spark the hulking rotary engine into life. Its chattering roar immediately drowned out the miniature choir, who didn't seem to notice. The wheel turned, gripping the cable, and the platform inched slowly into the air.

The purpose of the railings soon became clear. Only a few yards above the rooftop they caught the edge of the howling gale that swept toward the open end of Spyre. This steady hurricane was produced by the rotation of the great wheel, Venera knew; she'd seen its like in smaller wheels like those of Rush. A wind came in at the cylinder's axis of rotation and shot out again along the rim. If she simply jumped off the platform at this point, she would be propelled out of Spyre entirely, and at goodly force.

The four soldiers were here to shoot anyone who tried that. And now that they were higher up she could see other guarantors of obedience: gun emplacements were suspended in the middle air by more cables, and some of them were visibly manned. Hanging in the sunny clouds beyond the wheel were more bunkers and turrets. It seemed a miracle now that she had, unconscious, threaded her way between them all to land here.

"Father would love this place," she muttered.

Chaison Fanning, her missing husband, would probably consider Spyre a moral obscenity and would want to blow it up.

They rose some miles, through filigrees of cloud, puffballs that hovered like anxious angels between the incoming and outblowing gales; past houses and pillboxes, bolted to other cables, whose glittering windows revealed nothing of what might be taking place inside them. The lands of Greater Spyre widened and widened below Venera, its patchwork estates becoming a mesmerizing labyrinth: the blockhouses of a dozen, a hundred and more nations of Liris, it seemed, painted the inside of the cylinder. Slicing through these, leaving ruin and wildflowers on their sidings, were the railways of the preservationists.

All the while, Lesser Spyre came closer.

Venera had seen a geared town once before—in the dead hollow heart of Leaf's Choir Chaison Fanning's ships had moored next to the asphyxiated city of Carlinth. But Carlinth's pale grandeur couldn't match the wonder of Lesser Spyre because that other city had been motionless in death, and Lesser Spyre lived. Its great wheel-shaped habitats, each a half-mile or more in diameter, turned edge to angled edge like the meshwork of a vast clock. The citizen of one wheel could stroll to its edge and simply step onto the surface of another as their rims came within touching distance. The wheels were kept in configuration by a lattice of giant spars and thick cables, from which black banners fluttered.

The cable car eluded gravity entirely after a while, and its passengers clipped their metal costumes to the railing and waited until their destination hove into sight. The cable terminated in a knot of dozens of others, at a complicated cagework that threaded the axle of a town-wheel. Venera could see other people embarking and disembarking there. They moved in small groups that gave one another a wide berth.

She saw something else, though, that gave her hope for the first time in days: ships were berthed here. Sleek yachts, for the most part, of many different designs and flying diverse colors—but all foreign. They signaled the possibility of escape, real escape, for the first time since her arrival.

She tapped Odess's tin shoulder and pointed. "Our customers?"

He nodded. "Pilgrims from all the principalities of Candesce come to us, hoping to leave again with some trinket or token of ours. Do you recognize any of those ships?"

Venera nodded. "That one is from Gehellen." It was the only one she knew, but Odess was obviously impressed. "I know that we'll trade them cherries," she went on. "But what do the rest of Spyre's countries sell?"

He laughed, and just then the platform came to rest at its terminus. As they clambered over to the axle like so many iron spiders, Odess said, "What do they trade? You ask that with refreshing innocence. If we knew what half our neighbors traded, we might arrange some extra advantage for Liris. The fame of many of Spyre's commodities is spread far and wide—but not all. There are sections of the Fair no stranger can enter without providing a guarantee of circumspection."

"A what?"

"A hostage, sometimes," said Eilen. They had entered a long cylindrical chamber with many small doors spiraling up its interior. Odess found one of these and, producing a massive key, unlocked it. Inside was a slot-shaped locker, its walls encrusted with rust and cobwebs, with one incongruously bright mirror at the far end. Odess and the others proceeded to strip off their metal shells, trading them for ornately tooled leather equivalents—

except that in place of veils, each costume came with an elaborate mask. Odess passed a kit to Venera and she turned her back
modestly to change. Her mask had a falcon's beak.

"There are nations," Odess said, "that average one customer
every ten years. Whatever it is they trade, it is so fabulously valuable that the whole country lives off the sale for a generation.
That's an extreme example, but there are many others who
guard the nature of their produce with their lives. Liris used to
be one such. Now everyone knows what we produce, but that's
actually worked to our advantage."

"But what can those others be selling?" Venera shook her
head in incomprehension. She was stretching a black jacket
over a silver-traced vest, admiring herself in the mirror. With
the mask in place she looked intimidating. She liked the effect.

"*She* is from one of them." It was one of the soldiers who said
it. He didn't have to say who *she* was; Venera knew he meant the
botanist.

Venera raised an eyebrow. "She wasn't born in Liris?"

The soldier shook his head, glancing uneasily at Odess. "Our
previous botanist . . . the trees were languishing, m'lady. They
were dying, until she came." Odess was scowling in obvious
warning but the soldier shrugged. "Five years now, she's brought
them back to health."

"And you don't know anything about where she came
from?"

"Of course we do!" Odess laughed loudly. "She's a lady of the
nation of Sacrus. We know the families and lineage of Sacrus, we
know who she is . . . even if we don't know what it is that Sacrus
does."

"You need better spies," said Venera. Nobody laughed, but
the thought intrigued her. Spyre, it seemed, was an investigator's

playground. She would love to develop a network here, the way she had in secret in her adopted home of Slipstream.

They moved from the locker cylinder to the axle of the town-wheel. Here, dozens of yin-yang stairs and elevator shafts ran down to the copper-shingled roofs of the vast building lining the wheel. Odess showed their letters of transit to a succession of inspectors and gradually they worked their way over to one of the elevators.

"Stay alert, everyone," Odess said as the wrought-iron doors grumbled shut behind them and they began to move down. "Watch for any signs of change. In particular, our new inter-preter"—he nodded at Venera—"is going to cause a stir. We need to stick to our agreed story. You," he said to Venera, "must only speak to the customers and then only when we ask you to. We don't want to give our rivals any clues about our capabilities or what's been going on inside Liris."

This paranoia reminded Venera of Hale and the darkened cor-ridors of her father's palace. "But why?" she asked in irritation. "Why this skulking?"

"Questions might be asked," said Odess darkly. "About where you came from. About why our people might have ventured outside our walls. Where we might have gone, what we might have seen. What you might have seen." He shook his head. "Your story is that you were born and raised in Liris."

"But my accent—"

"Is why you will only speak to the customers."

There was silence for the rest of the ride. Venera adjusted her mask, glanced around, and noted the tightening of shoulders, straightening of stances as gravity rose until it neared the level she was used to. And then the elevator clunked to a halt, and the doors opened.

The trade delegation of Liris edged cautiously into the Great Fair of Spyre.

FABULOUS BEASTS SWEPT across the dance floor, their skirts wheeling in time to the deep drumbeat of Spyre's music. The beasts had the faces of monsters, of animals, of gods. They danced in pairs, sometimes pausing in midpose as the music paused. It was during those pauses that business was transacted.

One slender figure with a hawk's face stood at the foot of a gold-chased pillar, her backdrop a blue trompe l'oeil vista of wheeling towns. She watched the dancers alertly, aware of the deep strains of paranoia and deceit that must run through Spyre for it to have developed this custom. For this filigreed and gleaming ballroom and its whirling dancers was the Great Fair itself.

True, there were display rooms. Out of the corner of her eye she saw Odess emerging from the doorway that led to Liris's. He was alone, and doubtless his errand had been to check on the disposition of the glass cases and lights there. No customers had passed that door since she had been here.

Venera had spent some hours in the display room, helping the others set up. A solitary cherry tree dominated the marbled parlor; it sat in a broad stone bowl, the glow of its pink blossoms the first sight that greeted a visitor. It was a fake, made of silk and common woods.

While Liris's soldiers played cards behind a screen in the display rooms, the rest of the delegation danced. The music was loud, the dances fast and close; so conversation consisted of quick whispers in your partner's ear, quips at arm's length, or brief nose-to-nose exchanges. Eavesdropping was impossible in these circumstances—and the soldiers of Spyre watched carefully for any sign of it. Venera had been told that visitors were carefully screened, and the penalty for revealing secrets here was death. Ironically, the whole setup seemed designed for cheating, for who could tell what any two dancers were telling one another?

She had heard that the dances were occasionally interrupted by spontaneous duels.

The denizens of Spyre took their masque very seriously. Not all the visitors did; most eschewed disguises, and so Venera was able to tell how many principalities were represented here. She even recognized one or two of the national costumes they wore.

A gavotte ended and the dancers broke up. Gorgon-headed Eilen headed Venera's way. A waiting footman handed her a drink as she paused, panting. "Is it always like this?" Venera asked her. "Interested customers seem a bit thin on the ground."

"We have our regulars," said Eilen. "It's not the season for any of them. Oh, this gravity! It pulls at my stomach."

Venera sighed. These people were so immersed in their traditions that they couldn't see the insanity of it all. In the brief pause between dances, some of the customers had drifted off with outlandishly masked delegates—salesmen, really. Venera had been keeping track of who went through which doorways. Many of the portals around the vast chamber had never opened. They might be locked or even bricked up on the other side, for all she knew.

She couldn't figure out the architecture of the fair. It seemed that the sprawling, multiwinged building had been renovated, rebuilt, and reimagined so many times over the centuries that it had lost any sense of its original logic. Corridors ran into blank walls; stairwells led nowhere; elevator shafts opened onto roaring air where lower floors had once been. Behind the public walls countless narrow passages twisted their ways to the offices, storage lockers, and panic rooms of the trade delegations. Liris's domain extended several floors above and below their public showroom; Venera had glimpsed in passing a huge chamber, like a collapsing ballroom, its dripping casements lost in gloomy shadows. Eilen had told her that this was where they met customers back when their cherries were a state secret. The ballroom was on one of the high-security levels of the Fair; Liris still owned title to it but had no use for it now.

Venera had scoffed at this. "Has no one had the courage to drill spy holes in the walls to find out what your neighbors are up to?" Odess had sent her one of his disapproving, frightened looks, but nobody had said anything.

—Oh, something was happening—Capri, Eilen's apprentice, was leading four people in rich clothes toward the Liris door. The little surge of excitement was absurd, and Venera nearly laughed at herself. Now Odess was bowing to them. He was opening the door. Venera imagined cheering.

"Who are they?" she asked Eilen.

"Oh! Success! That's . . . let's see . . . the delegates from Tracoune."

Venera ransacked her memory; why was that word familiar? Ah, that was it. It was only a couple of weeks ago that Venera and her husband had attended a soiree in the capital of Gehellen. The event had been unremarkable up until the shooting started, but she did remember a long conversation with a red-faced admiral of the local navy. He had mentioned Tracoune.

"Excuse me, I'd like to watch this," she said to Eilen. The woman shrugged and turned back to the dance. Venera threaded her way around the outskirts of the ball and pushed open the door to the Liris showroom. It was at the end of a long hallway, seventy feet at least in length. Random words echoed back at her as Venera walked down it.

Odess was showing them the tree. Now he was opening a lacquered box to reveal the cherries. Capri hovered nervously in the background.

The visitors didn't seem too impressed. One of the four—a woman—wandered away from the others to stare idly at the paintings on the walls. They seemed to be marking time here, perhaps taking a break from dancing. Even Venera, with no experience in sales, could tell that.

She approached the woman. "Excuse me . . . ," said Venera. She deliberately did not stand or move the way Odess and Capri were—clasping their hands in front of them, darting hesitantly like servants. Instead, Venera bowed like an equal.

"Yes?" The customer looked surprised, but not displeased, at being approached in this way.

"Do I have the pleasure of addressing a citizen of Tracoune?" The woman nodded.

"I had the most illuminating conversation recently," Venera continued, "at a party in Gehellen. We talked about Tracoune."

An edge of calculation came into the woman's gaze. "Oh, really? Who were you talking to?"

"An admiral in the Gehellen navy, as it happens." Venera saw Odess notice that she had accosted a customer (his expression said, "The new one's loose!") and then he started trying to make eye contact with her while pretending to give his full attention to his own people.

Venera smiled. "I'm so sorry that you've had to cancel the Feast of St. Jackson this year," she said to her prospect. "The Gehellenese are speculating that you won't be able to afford to feed your own people this time next year. Gauche of them, really."

"They said that?" The woman's face darkened in anger. "The Incident at Tibo was hardly that serious!"

"Ah, we thought not," said Venera in a conspiratorial way. "It's just that appearance is so important to international relations, isn't it?"

Ten minutes later the visitors were signing on the dotted line. Venera stood behind the astounded trade delegation of Liris, her arms crossed, inscrutable behind her beaked mask.

Odess stepped back to whisper furiously to her. "How did you do it? These people have never been customers before!"

She shrugged. "You just have to know people's weaknesses. In a few weeks Tracoune will throw some minor party for visiting officials, and among other things they'll give away a few cherries . . . as if they could afford boatloads of them. A very discreet message, on a channel so private that almost no one on either side will know why when the Gehellens decide not to call in their outstanding loans to Tracoune. . . . Which they've been thinking of doing."

He glared at her. "But how could—"

She nodded. "The levers of diplomacy are very small. The art lies in knowing where to pry."

Venera chatted with the clients while a soldier loaded a carrying case with dry ice and Odess measured out the pithed cherries. ". . . Speaking of Gehellen," Venera said after a while, "we heard about some sort of commotion there a couple of weeks ago."

The head of the Tracoune expedition laughed. "Oh, that! They're the laughing stock of the principalities!"

"But what happened?"

He grinned. "Visitors from one of the savage nations . . . Oh, what was the name?"

"Slipstream," said the woman Venera had first dealt with.

"Slipstream, that was it. Seems an admiral of Slipstream went mad and took to piracy with some of his captains. They fought a

pitched battle with the Gehellen navy in the very capital itself!
Smashed their way out of the palace and escaped into Leaf's
Choir, where it's rumored they found and made off with the
hoard of Anetene itself!"

"But that part's too preposterous, of course," said the woman.
"If they'd found the hoard, they would have a key to Candesce as
well—the last one is supposed to be the centerpiece of the
hoard. With that they could have ruled all of Virga from the Sun
of Suns itself!"

"Well." The man shrugged.

"What happened to them?" asked Venera. "Did they escape?"

"Oh, they evaded the Gehellen navy right enough," he said
with another laugh. "Only to be cut to ribbons in some bar-
barous nation near the edge of the world. None escaped, I hear."

"None . . ." Venera's pulse was racing, but she chose not to
believe this man. His story had too many of the facets of rumor.

"Oh, no, I've been following this one," said the woman with
evident enjoyment. "It seems the Slipstreamers ran afoul of a
place called Falcon Formation. The admiral suicidally rammed
his flagship into some sort of dreadnaught of Falcon's. Both
ships were obliterated in the explosion. Of his six other ships,
only one got away."

"Its name?" Venera put her hand out to steady herself. Her
fingers met the false bark of the fake cherry tree.

"What name?"

"The . . . the ship that escaped. Did you hear which one escaped?"

The woman looked affronted. "I didn't follow the story that
closely." Now it was her turn to laugh. "But they foolishly ran
for home, and the Pilot of Slipstream had them arrested the instant they came into port. For treason! What foolishness of them
to even try to go home."

Venera was glad of the mask she wore. It felt like her heart was slowing and would stop at any second. It was all she could do to keep up appearances until the Tracoune delegation left with their first consignment of cherries. Then she rushed back to the screened alcove, ignoring the jubilant congratulations the others were lavishing on her.

Even though the mask would have hid them, she shed no tears. Venera had learned many years ago never to do that in the presence of another human being.

5

THAT EVENING THERE was a celebration in a gallery overlooking the cherry trees. Amber light poured into the blued central shaft, glinting off windows and outlining shutters and balconies above and below, while small gusts of air still warm from Candesce's light teased the diaphanous drapes. Like everywhere else in Liris, the party room was small, crammed with memorabilia and eccentric furnishings, and reachable only through a labyrinth of stairs and corridors. It reminded Venera of her childhood bedroom.

She had not wanted to come. All she wanted to do was sit alone in her closet. But Eilen insisted. "Why so gloomy?" she asked as she leaned hipshot in Venera's doorway. "You did great service to your country today!" Venera didn't speak as they walked; and she did her best to be the ghost at the wedding for the remainder of the night.

Her sorrow wasn't catching. Most of Liris turned out for the event, and a dizzying parade of strange and neurotic characters passed in front of Venera as she systematically drank herself into a stupor. There were the hereditary soldiers with their peaked helmets and blunderbusses; the gray sanitation men who spoke in monotones and huddled together near the drinks table; the seamstresses and chandlers, carpenters, and cleaners who all spoke a secret language they had developed together in their childhood.

And there were children too—grave, wide-eyed gamins who skirted around Venera as though she had stepped out of one of their fantasy books.

She watched them all go by, numb. *I knew that this might happen,* she told herself. *That he might die.* Yet she had gone ahead with her plan, dragging Chaison reluctantly into it. It had been necessary if they were to save Slipstream; she knew that. But the decision still felt like a betrayal.

"It's so *electric,*" said Eilen now, "having a new face in our world!" Quite drunk, she balanced on one foot near Venera, waving excitedly at people she had seen every day of her life. Of those people, a few had approached and introduced themselves, halting and stammering; most stayed back, muttering together and eyeing Venera. Foreigner. Strange beast. New darling of the botanist.

And yes, the botanist was here too. She glided through the celebrants as though on rails, nodding here and there, speaking strategic words on the outskirts of discussions, the same mysterious smile as always hovering just behind her lips. Eventually she made her way over to Venera. She hove to just this side of Eilen. Eilen herself moved away, suddenly quiet.

"I've always said that it pays to know your customers," the botanist said. "I judged your potential rightly."

Venera eyed her. "Is that what you feel you do? Judge people's potential? Like the buds of flowers that might bloom or whither?"

"How apt. Yes, that's exactly right," said the botanist. "Some are to be encouraged, others cut from the branch. You nod as though you understand."

"I've done a certain amount of . . . pruning . . . in my day," said Venera. "So I've achieved a great victory for your tiny nation. Now what?"

"Now," said the botanist in a breathless sort of sisterly way, "we talk about what to do next. You see, you've vindicated my methods. I believe Liris needs to be more open to the outside world. We need to send our delegates farther, even outside Spyre itself."

The fog of Venera's sorrow lifted just a bit. "Leave Spyre? What do you mean?"

"I would like to send a trade mission to one of the principalities," said the botanist. "You, of course, would lead it."

"I'd be honored," said Venera with a straight face. "But isn't it Odess's job to arrange such things?"

"Odess?" The botanist waved her hand dismissively. "Prattling whiner. Take him if you'd like, but I can't see what good he'll do you. No, I picture you, perhaps Eilen, and one or two loyal soldiers. And a consignment of our treasure to tempt potential customers."

"That sounds reasonable." Venera couldn't believe what she was hearing. Did the woman seriously believe she would come back if she got out of this place? But then, everyone in Spyre seemed dangerously naive.

"Good. Say nothing of this to the others," instructed the botanist severely. "It won't do to let old wounds fester."

What did that mean? Venera thought about it as the botanist strolled away; but then Eilen returned and spilled her drink on Venera's shoes. The evening went downhill from there, and so she didn't really ponder the botanist's unlikely offer until she got back to her closet, near dawn.

She had just closed the ill-fitting door and was about to climb under the covers when there was a polite knock on the jamb. Venera cracked the door an inch.

Moss leaned like a decapitated tree outside her door. "Citizen F-F-Fanning," he said. "I j-just wanted to give you th-th-these."

In the faint lamplight of the hallway, she could just make out a tiny bouquet of posies in his hand.

The juxtaposition of his chiseled features with the emptiness of his eyes made her skin crawl. Venera slipped her hand out to snatch the little bundle of flowers from his nerveless fingers. "Thanks. You're not in love with me, are you?"

"I'm s-s-sorry you're so s-sad," he murmured. "T-t-try not to be so s-s-sad."

Venera gaped at him. His words had been so quiet, but they seemed to echo on and on in the silent corridor. "Sad? Why do you think I'm sad?"

Nobody else had noticed—not even Eilen, who had been watching Venera like a mother hawk all evening. Venera narrowed her eyes. "I didn't see you at the party. Where were you?"

"I w-w-was there. In the c-corner."

Present yet absent. That seemed to sum Moss up. "Well." Venera looked down at Moss's present. Somehow she had clenched her fist and had crushed the little white blossoms.

"Thank you," she said. Moss turned away with a muted clattering noise. "Moss," she said quickly. He looked back.

"I don't want you to be sad either," said Venera.

He shambled away and Venera closed the door softly. Once alone, she let loose one long shuddering sigh, and tumbled face-first onto the bed.

THE NEXT MORNING, Venera wore the half-crushed posies on the breast of her jacket. If anybody noticed they said nothing. She ate her breakfast with the members of the delegation in their designated dining room—a roofed-over air shaft lined floor to invisible ceiling with stuffed animals—and followed them silently to their offices. She had discerned the routine by now: they would sit around for the rest of the day, occasionally engaging in desultory, short-lived dialogs, have lunch and then supper, and turn in.

If she had to live like this for more than a couple of days, Venera knew she would snap. So, at ten o'clock, she said, "Can't we at least play cards?"

One of the soldiers glanced over, then shook his head mournfully. "Odess always wins."

"But I'm here now," said Venera. "What if I were to win?"

Slowly, they roused into a state resembling the attentive. With much cajoling and brow-beating, Venera got them to reveal the location of the cards, and once she had these she energetically pulled a table and some chairs into the center of the room. "Sit," she commanded, "and learn."

This was her opportunity to grill her compatriots properly— the party last night had been too hectic and strange, with everyone playing pal in transparent ways—and Venera made the best of it. After ten minutes Odess emerged from his office, looking bleary and cross, but his eyes lit up when he saw her shuffling the cards. Venera grinned sloppily at him and he drew up a chair.

"So," she said as the others examined their cards. "Tell me about the botanist."

THE PANTRY WAR had been dragging on for five years. Liris and the Duchy of Vatoris both claimed a five- by seven-foot room off one of the twisting corridors of the fair. The titles went back a hundred years, and the wording was ambiguous. Neither side would back down.

"War?" said Venera as she peered over her cards. "Don't you mean feud?"

The other players all shook their heads. No, explained Odess, a feud was a family thing. This was a conflict between professional soldiers, and it took the form of pitched battles. —Even if those battles were between a dozen or so soldiers on either side, which was all the manpower the tiny nations could muster. After years of ambushes, raids, firefights, and all manner of other mayhem, it had settled into a war of attrition. Barricades had been thrown up in the disputed corridor; a no-man's-land of broken furniture and cracked tile stretched for thirty feet between them. The entrance to the closet beckoned only yards away, and either side could capture it in seconds. The trick was to hold it.

The two sides dug in. The barricades were ramified and reinforced, then backed up with cannon and rifles. Days might pass without a shot fired, but the other tenants of the Fair got used to sudden flurries of gunfire. Rarely was anyone actually hurt. The loss of a single man would constitute a disaster.

These things happened. Even now, the Fair was riddled with strange tensions—empty passages paved in dust where no one had walked in generations because of just such disputes as this; neighbors who would think nothing of murdering one another in quiet corners if they had the chance; victims walled up in alcoves; and everywhere, conspiracies.

It was a random bullet that had changed everything. The walls around the disputed hallway had never been strong, but the combatants had hired a neutral third party to shore them up at regular intervals. Perhaps it was inevitable, though, that chinks and cracks should develop. One day, a bullet fired from the Vatoris barricade slipped through such a crack, ricocheted sixty feet down an abandoned air shaft, and killed the heir of a major nation as he stood at a punch bowl.

Venera rubbed her jaw. "I can imagine the reaction."

"I'm not sure you can," said Odess portentously. The nation in question was the mysterious Land of Sacrus, a country of "vast size," according to Eilen.

"How vast?"

"Fully three square miles!"

Sacrus traded in power—but exactly how, no one was quite sure. They were one of the most secretive of countries, their fields being dotted with windowless factories, the perimeter patrolled by guards with dogs and guns. Small airships bristling with guns bobbed above the main complex. The Sacrans emerged from their smoke-wreathed towers only once or twice a year, and then they spoke almost exclusively to their customers. They were one of the few nations that had withstood the full force of the preservationists—in fact, nobody in the preservationist camp would talk about just how badly that particular battle had gone.

Sacrus was enraged at the death of their heir. Three days after the incident, the Vatoris barricade fell silent. The soldiers of Liris fired a few shots and got no response. When they cautiously advanced on the Vatoris position, they found it abandoned.

Discreet inquiries were made. No one had seen any of the Vatorins since the day of the fateful gunshot. In a moment of supreme daring, Liris sent its troops directly to the Vatoris apartments. They were empty.

At this point, rumors of a great stench rising from Vatoris itself reached Odess's ears. "I was sitting in our showroom," he said. "I remember it like it was yesterday. One of the scions of a minor nation entered and told me that his people were walking up and down along the border with Vatoris, sniffing the air and exchanging rumors. The smell was the smell of death."

Odess returned home that night to warn his people. "But it was too late. As I lay down to sleep that evening, I heard it—we all did." A hissing sound filled the chambers of Liris. It was faint, but for someone like Odess who had lived behind these walls his whole life, it had the effect of a siren.

"I stood, tried to run to the door. I fell down." The others related similar experiences, of sudden paralysis, landings behind desks or next to wavering doors. "We lay there helpless, all of us, unable to even focus our eyes. And we *listened*."

What they heard, after an hour or so, was a single set of footsteps. They moved smoothly from room to room, up stairs and down, not as if seeking anything, but as though whoever walked were taking inventory—committing every passage and chamber of Liris to memory. Eventually, they came to a stop. Silence returned.

The paralysis faded near dawn. Odess rose, retched miserably for a few minutes, and then—trembling—crept in the direction those footsteps had taken. As he went he saw others emerging from their rooms, or rising from where they had fallen in midwalk. They converged on the place where the footsteps had halted: in the cherry tree courtyard.

"And there she sat," said Odess, "exactly as she sits these days, with the same damned smile and the same damned air of superiority. The botanist. Our conqueror."

"AND NO ONE has challenged her?" Venera barked a laugh of disbelief. "You fear reprisals, is that it?"

Odess shrugged. "She ended the war, and under her leadership the cherries bloom. Who else are we going to have lead us?"

Venera scowled at her cards. A pulse of pain shot up her jaw. "I thought you were a meritocracy."

"And so we are. And she is the best botanist we have ever had."

"What happened to the one she replaced?"

They exchanged glances. "We don't know," confessed Eilen. "He disappeared the day Margit came."

Venera discarded one card and took another from the deck. The others did the same, then she fanned out her hand. "I win."

Odess grimaced and began to shuffle.

"She came to me last night," said Venera. She had decided that she needed information more than discretion at this point. "Margit was pleased with the work I did." Odess snorted; Venera ignored him and continued. "She had a proposal."

She told them about Margit's idea of an extended trade expedition into the principalities. As she did, Venera watched all movement around the table stop. Even Odess's practiced hand ceased its fanning of the cards. They were all staring at her.

"What?" She glanced around defensively. "Does this violate some ancient taboo? —I'm sure; everything else does. Or is it something you've been trying to get done for years, and now you're mad that the newcomer has achieved it?"

Eilen looked down. "It's been tried before," she said in a quiet voice.

"You must understand," said Odess; then he fell silent. Knitting his brows, he started furiously shuffling.

"What?" Now Venera was seriously alarmed. "What's wrong?"

"To travel outside Spyre . . . is not done," said Odess reluctantly. "Not without safeguards to guarantee one's return. Hostages, if one is married . . . but you're not."

Venera was disgusted. "The pillboxes, the guns, and razor wire—they really aren't to keep people *out*, are they? They're to keep them in."

"Yes, but you see if Margit is willing to send you out despite you having no ties here, no hostages, or anything she could hold over you . . . then she's obviously willing to try it again," said Odess. He slammed the deck down on the table, kicked his chair back, and walked away. Venera watched him go in startled amazement.

The soldiers were standing too, not making eye contact with anyone.

Venera pinned Eilen with her gaze. "Try *what?*"

The woman sighed deeply. "Margit is a master of chemistry and biology," she said. "That's why she is the botanist. Three years ago she conceived the idea of sending an expedition like the one you're describing. She chose a man who was competent, intelligent, and brave, but one whom she didn't completely trust. To guarantee that he would return, she . . . injected him. With a slow poison that was not supposed to begin to act for ten days. If he returned within those ten days, she would give him the antidote and he would be fine."

Venera eyed the splayed cards. "What happened?"

"The return flight was delayed by a storm. He made it back on the eleventh day."

Venera hesitated—but she already knew the answer when she asked, "Who was it that Margit sent?"

"Moss," said Eilen with a shudder. "She sent Moss."

6

"I HAVE TO admit I was expecting this," said Margit. Venera stood in the doorway to her apartment, dressed down in close-fitting black leathers. Two soldiers hulked behind her, their meaty hands resting heavy on her shoulders.

"In retrospect," Venera said ruefully, "I should have anticipated the trip wires." The inside walls of the courtyard were just too enticing a surface; freed of her metal clothing, Venera weighed only twenty pounds or so and she could easily clamber hand over hand up the drainpipe that ran next to Odess's little window. "There's no other way in or out of the building but up that wall. Naturally you'd have alarms."

". . . I just wasn't anticipating it so soon," said Margit. She twitched a housecoat over her lavender nightgown and lit another candle off the one she was holding. Even in the dimness of midnight Venera could see that her apartment was sumptuous, with several rooms, high ceilings, and tiled mosaics on the floor beneath numerous tapestries.

Of course Margit wouldn't live like the people she ruled. Venera wouldn't have either. She understood Margit enough by now that staying here in Liris had not been an option. So, after bidding her coworkers good night, she had retired to her closet and waited. When the building was silent and dark, Venera had

crept out and jimmied open a window that led onto the courtyard.

She hadn't been thinking clearly. The revelation about Moss
had shaken her and she had acted rashly. If she didn't regain
control of this situation she would be in real trouble.

"Come in, sit down. We need to talk," said Margit. "You may
leave us," she said to the soldiers. They lifted their hands off Venera's shoulders and retreated past the heavy oak door. They
would have a long walk down the winding steps that led down
to Liris's ground floor. *Good*, thought Venera.

She sat down on a decadent-looking divan; but she kept her
feet braced against the floor, ready to leap up instantly if that
was required.

The first step to taking control of the situation was taking
control of the conversation. Margit opened her mouth but Venera
spoke first: "What is an heir of Sacrus doing running a minor
nation like Liris?"

Margit narrowed her eyes. "Shouldn't I be asking the questions? Besides, what's your interest?" she asked as she gracefully
sat opposite Venera. "Professional curiosity, perhaps? —You are a
noble daughter yourself, are you not? A nation like Liris would
be an interesting playground for someone learning how to use
power. Are you interested in rulership?"

"In the abstract," said Venera. "It's not an ambition of mine."

"Neither is assisting your new countrymen, I gather. You
were trying to escape us."

"Of course I was. I was press-ganged into your service. And
you admit yourself you expected me to try it." She shrugged.
"So what could we possibly have to talk about?"

"A great deal, actually," said Margit. "Such as how you came
to be here at all."

Venera nodded slowly. She had been thinking about that, and

the conclusions she had come to had motivated her to run as much as the facts about Moss. "I arrived here through an odd chain of events," she said. "At the time I wasn't prepared to wonder why there were armed troops sneaking over the lawns of Spyre during the nighttime. I was mostly concerned with evading them. I didn't know enough to ask the right question."

Margit raised an eyebrow and sat back.

"It's my father, you see," said Venera in a confessional tone. "He's flagrantly paranoid and he wanted his daughters to be as well. He raised me to disbelieve coincidence. So if I was herded here, what could the reason be? The troops who were following me weren't from Liris. In fact, I assumed they weren't after me at all but were chasing down another trespasser whom I had met. It wasn't until today that I realized that those other soldiers had been from Sacrus."

Margit laughed. "That truly is paranoid. You would implicate my nation in every one of your misfortunes?"

"No, just this one." She sat forward. "Since we're talking, though, I'd like to ask you a couple of questions." Smiling her maddening smile, Margit nodded. "The first question is whether you maintain constant contact with your nation. I've been told you don't, but I don't believe that."

Margit shrugged. "It would be easy. So what if I did? Can't a daughter talk to her parents?"

"The second question," said Venera, "is whether Sacrus itself travels regularly into the principalities." Seeing Margit's suddenly guarded expression, Venera nodded. "You do, don't you?"

"So what?"

"Someone guessed where I had come from," marveled Venera. "More than likely the Gehellens have circulated descriptions of myself and my husband throughout the principalities. They seek us, and it's an open secret why."

Margit grinned in obvious delight. "Oh, you are smart! I was right to bring you into Liris in the way I did."

Venera cocked her head. "What other way was there?"

"Oh, I think you can guess."

"Under duress. Tortured," said Venera. "Why do you think I tried to flee just now? It suddenly made no sense to me that I was walking around freely. And your offer to let me travel outside Spyre . . . made even less sense."

"You became alarmed. That's understandable. I was told to learn everything you know about the key to Candesce," said Margit. "You figured that out, of course."

Venera looked innocent. "Sorry, the what?"

Margit stood up and paced over to a side table. "Drink?" Venera shook her head.

"Something happened a short time ago," said the botanist. She stood with her back to Venera and in those seconds Venera looked around quickly for anything that might give her an advantage. There were no handy hat pins, letter openers, or pistols lying on the pillowed furniture. She did spot a battered wooden cabinet that looked markedly out of place compared to the rest of the pieces, but had no time to get to it before Margit turned again, drink in hand.

"Something happened," Margit repeated. "A fight in the capital of Gehellen, rumors of a stolen treasure, and then an event that our scientists are starting to refer to as the *outage*."

Venera tensed. She hadn't expected Margit to know this part of the story.

"Candesce does many things besides light our skies," said the botanist. "We watch the Sun of Suns closely; we have to, our very lives depend on it. So when one of Candesce's many systems shuts down, even for a moment, we know about it. Even though such an event has not occurred in living memory."

She sat down again. "Only someone with a key could enter Candesce and manipulate it. And the last key was lost centuries ago. You can imagine the uproar that the outage has caused, here and abroad. The principalities are mobilizing, and agents of the Virga home guard have been seen nosing around, even here."

Home guard? Venera had never heard of them. But she wanted to kick herself for failing to realize that the gambit she and her husband had played would alert all the powers in the world. *Hit another trip wire,* she mused.

"It was only a matter of days before we had your name and description, and that of your husband and others in your party," said Margit. "We pay our spies well. So when a woman fitting that description miraculously appeared in the skies of Greater Spyre, we mobilized."

"Clearly I've been a fool," said Venera bitterly. "Then it was Sacrus troops who drove me here?"

"I actually don't know for sure," Margit admitted. "Our men were out that night, I know that much. But there may have been others as well. In any case, once I communicated that I had you, I was told to hand you and the key over. I couldn't very well refuse my masters the key—but you, I declined to part with."

Venera felt a pulse of anxious anger as she realized what Margit was saying. "Then the key is—"

"Locked away in the Grey Infirmary, where Sacrus keeps all their new acquisitions," said Margit with some smugness. She drained her wineglass and tilted it at Venera. "But you're here. I took Liris in order to have a base from which to grow my own power. You provide potential leverage. Why should I give you up?"

"And the offer to let me travel . . . ?"

"I increase my leverage and buy some insurance by getting you out of Spyre and to a safe place that only I know about," said Margit. "But you should really be happy that I haven't tortured you for what you know. I'd prefer to have you on my side. You must admit, I've treated you well."

Cautiously, Venera nodded. "It was too risky to keep the key to Candesce for yourself. But a lesser piece of leverage . . ."

". . . Who knows something vital about it that I can trade . . . that's useful to me at the moment." Margit smiled, catlike.

It still didn't quite add up. "Why did you let me go up to Lesser Spyre?" Venera asked. "Why risk exposing me at the Fair?"

"That was to prove that I had you," said Margit with a shrug. "While I was negotiating what to give up. Sacrus was at the Fair. I told them to watch for you, but with the guards and defenses that surround the Fair they couldn't snatch you from me. It was the safest place in Spyre to display you."

Someone unused to being used as a political pawn might have been surprised at these revelations. For Venera, discovering that she had been played was almost reassuring. It placed her in a familiar role.

She knew exactly what Sacrus was going to do now. Venera had fantasized about it herself: you took the key and entered Candesce, and then shut down the Sun of Suns. As the darkness and cold began to seep into the principalities, you made your demands of the millions whose lives depended on Candesce. You could ask for anything—power, money, hostages, or slaves. Your leverage would be total.

It would help to have enough experienced men to crew a navy, though, because one of your first demands would be that the principalities deliver up their own ships. "Sacrus doesn't have any ships, do they?" she asked. "Surely not enough to run the blockade that the principalities would put in place."

Margit shrugged. "Oh, we have several. Sacrus is a big nation.

But in terms of weapons . . ." She laughed, and it wasn't a pleasant laugh. "I doubt we would have to worry much about any fleet of the principalities."

Her confidence was suddenly unnerving. Margit sauntered over to the battered wooden cabinet and opened the top. "Since you're here," she said, "let's talk about the key to Candesce."

"Let's not." Venera stood up. "My knowledge is my only bargaining chip, after all. I'm not going to squander that."

This time Margit didn't answer. She pulled a bell rope that hung next to the cabinet.

The gravity was low enough and Venera still strong enough that she could probably make it to the window in one leap. Then, she could scale the stonework by the tips of her fingers if she had to and make it to the roof in under a minute. Not, however, faster than the soldiers could climb a flight of stairs to retrieve her.

Margit was watching her calculate her options. The botanist laughed as the door opened behind Venera and a large, heavily armored soldier entered.

"I'm not going to hurt you," said Margit. Something glittered in her hand as she approached Venera. "I just want to guarantee your compliance from now on."

"The way you tried with Moss?" Venera nodded at the syringe Margit held. "Is that the same stuff you used on him?"

"It is. His outcome was an accident," said the botanist as the soldier stepped forward and grabbed Venera's wrists from behind. "I'll be more careful with you."

His outcome was an accident. Venera was familiar with that sort of logic; she often blamed others for the things she did to them. For some reason, the argument didn't work this time.

Margit had to round a large couch as she approached Venera. She took a step to do so, and Venera made fists, bent her forearms forward, and then raised her arms in an egg-shaped curve that Chaison had once showed her. The startled soldier clung tightly to her wrists but suddenly found himself pulled forward and off-balance as Venera lifted his hands over her head. And then she turned and her hands were over his as he lost his grip and she pushed down and he thumped onto his knees.

She kicked him in the face. His helmet ricocheted across the room as Margit shouted and Venera hopped the couch, snatching up the open wine bottle and swinging it at the botanist's head.

Margit slashed out with the syringe, nicking Venera's sleeve. They circled for a second, then Venera grabbed for her wrist and they tumbled onto the floor.

The wine bottle skittered away, gouting red. Venera pulled Margit's arm up and bit her wrist. As the botanist let go Venera made a grab for the syringe. Margit in turn lunged for the bottle.

"I was just going to kill you," hissed Venera. She landed on Margit's back as the botanist closed her fingers on the bottle. "I've changed my mind!" She jammed the needle into Margit's shoulder and pushed the plunger.

Margit shrieked and rolled away. Venera let her. The botanist had let go of the wine bottle and Venera took it and upended it over the wooden cabinet.

Cursing and holding her shoulder, Margit ran over to the soldier, who was sitting up. When she saw Venera reach for one of the lit candles she screamed "No!" and backpedaled.

It was too late, as Venera touched the candle flame to the wine-soaked cabinet and the whole thing caught. In the orange light of the fire Venera ran through a nearby arch. She wanted to know whether that cabinet was all there was to Margit's power.

"Ah . . ." She stood in a large private pharmacy—dozens of

shelves covered in glass bottles of all sizes and colors hung above long worktables crowded with beakers, petri dishes, and test tubes. Venera joyfully swept her arm across a table and tossed the candle into the cascading glasswork as Margit clawed at her from behind.

There was fire behind them, now fire ahead, and smoke wafting up to the ceiling as Margit pushed and kicked at Venera and tried to get past her. When the soldier finally appeared out of the smoke, Venera stood over the botanist, her nose bleeding but a grin of utter savagery on her face. She brandished a long knife she'd found on the table.

"Back away or I'll cut her throat!" Venera's backdrop was flames. The soldier backed away.

Shouts of alarm and clanging bells were waking the house. Venera dragged Margit out of the inferno and threw her to the floor in front of the smouldering cabinet.

"Ten days." She pointed to the door. "You have ten days to convince your people to save you. I have no doubt that Sacrus has the antidote to your poison, but you'll have to go to them on bended knee to get it. For your sake I hope they're in a forgiving mood."

People were crowding in the doorway—men and women carrying buckets of sand and water, all shouting at once and all clattering to a halt at the sight of Venera standing over the all-powerful botanist.

"You are no longer the botanist of Liris!" Venera raised her arm, summoning everything she had learned from her father about how to intimidate a crowd. "Let no one here ever grant entry to this woman again! Run! Run home to Sacrus and beg for your life. This place is closed to you."

Margit staggered to her feet, clutching her shoulder. "I'll kill you!" she hissed.

"Only if you've a mind to do it," said Venera. "Now go!"

The botanist ran for the door, pushing aside the stunned fire-fighters.

"Get with it!" Venera yelled at them. "Before the whole house goes up!"

She walked through them and as more came up the stairs she politely eased to the side to let them pass. She reached the main floor of Liris to find all the lights lit and a confused mob swirling around the strangely decorated desks and counters.

"What's happened?" Odess emerged from the rush of faces. The rest of the trade delegation were behind him.

"I've deposed the botanist," said Venera. They gaped at her. She sighed. "It wasn't *that* hard," she said.

"But—but how?" They crowded around her.

"But *why?*" Eilen had grabbed her arm.

Venera looked up at her. Suddenly she felt tears in her eyes. "My . . . my husband," she whispered through a suddenly tight throat. "My husband is dead."

For a while there was silence, it seemed, though Venera knew abstractly that everyone was shouting, that the news of Margit's sudden departure was spreading like fire through Liris. Eilen and the others were speaking to her but she couldn't understand anything they said.

Strangely calm, she looked through the rushing people at the one other person who seemed still. He was giving orders at the foot of the stairs to Margit's chambers, putting out his arm to prevent people without firefighting tools from going up, pointing out where to get sand or buckets to those just arriving. His face was impassive but his gestures were quick and focused.

"What are we going to do?" Odess was literally wringing his hands, something Venera had never actually seen anyone do. "Without the botanist, what will happen to the trees? Will

Sacrus forgive us for what you did? Could we all be killed? Who is going to lead us now?"

Eilen turned to Odess, shaking his shoulder crossly. "Why shouldn't it be Venera?"

"V-Venera?" He looked terrified.

Venera laughed. "I'm leaving. Right now. Besides, you already have your new botanist." She pointed. "He's been here all along."

Moss looked up from where he was directing the firefighting. He saw Venera, and the perpetually desperate expression around his eyes softened a bit. She walked over to him.

As shouts came down the stairs saying that the fire was under control, she laid a hand on the former envoy's arm and smiled at him. "Moss," she said, "I don't want you to be sad anymore."

"I-I'll t-try," he said.

Satisfied, she turned away from the people of Liris. Venera traced the steps Margit had taken only minutes before, pausing only to arm herself in Liris's barracks. She walked up the broad stone steps over which towered row after row of portraits—centuries of botanists, masons, doctors, and scholars, all of whom had been born here, lived here, and died here leaving legacies that might have been known only to a handful of people but were meaningful nonetheless. She trod carefully patched steps whose outlines were known intimately by those who tended them, past arches and doors that figured as clearly as heroes out of myth in the dreams and ambitions of the people who lived under them—people to whom they were the very world itself.

And on the dark empty roof, cold fresh air blowing in from the abandoned lofts of winter.

She threw back the trapdoor and stalked to the roof's edge. These were the final steps of her old life, she felt. Venera was about to mourn, something she had never done and did not know how to do. She stepped onto a swaying platform and began winching it down, feeling the uncoiling certainty of her husband's death in her gut. It was like a monster shaking itself awake; any moment now it would devour her and who knew what would happen then? Her only defense was to keep turning the wheel to winch herself down. She focused her eyes on the tall grass that swayed at the foot of Liris, willing it closer.

In the dim light cast by Lesser Spyre, Venera Fanning walked into the wild acres of the disputed territories. She moved aimlessly at first, admiring the glittering lights overhead and the vast arcs of land and forest that swept up and past them.

When she lowered her eyes it was to see the black silhouette of a man separate itself from a grove of trees ahead of her. Venera didn't pause but turned slightly toward the figure. He came out to meet her and she nodded to him when he offered his arm for her to lean on.

"I've been waiting for you," said Garth Diamandis.

They strolled into the darkness under the trees.

7

VENERA DIDN'T REALLY notice the passage of the next few days. She stayed with Diamandis in a clapboard hut near the edge of the world and did little but eat and sleep. He came and went, discreet as always; his forays were usually nocturnal and he slept when she was awake.

Periodically she stepped to the doorway of the flimsy hideout and listened to the wind. It tore and gabbled, moaned and hissed incessantly, and in it she learned to hear voices. They were of people she'd known—her father, her sisters, sometimes random members of the crew of the *Rook* whom she had not really gotten to know but had heard all about during her adventures with that ship.

She strained to hear her husband's voice in the rush, but his was the only voice she could not summon.

One dawn she was fixing breakfast (with little success, having never learned to cook) when Garth poked his head around the doorjamb and said, "You've disturbed a whole nest of hornets, did you know that?" He strolled in, looking pleased with himself. "More like a nest of whales—or capital bugs, even. There's covert patrols crawling all over the place."

She glared at him. "What makes you think they're after me?"

"You're the only piece out of place on this particular board," said Diamandis. He let gravity settle him into one of the hut's two chairs. "A queen in motion, judging by the furor. I'm just a pawn, so they don't see me—and as long as they don't, they can't catch you either."

"Try this." She slammed a plate down in front of him. He eyed it dubiously.

"Mind telling me what you did?"

"Did?" She gnawed her lip, ignoring the stabbing pain in her jaw. "Not very much. I may have assassinated someone."

"*May* have?" He chortled. "You're not sure?" She simply shrugged. Diamandis's expression softened. "Why am I not surprised?" he said under his breath.

They ate in silence. If this day were to follow the pattern of the last few, Diamandis would now have fallen onto the cot Venera had just vacated, and he would immediately commence to snore in competition with the wind. Instead, he looked at her seriously and said, "It's time for you to make a decision."

"Oh?" She folded her hands in her lap listlessly. "About what?"

He scowled. "Venera, I utterly adore you. Were I twenty years younger you wouldn't be safe around me. As it is, you're eating me out of house and home and having an extra mouth to feed is, well, tiring."

"Ah." Venera brightened just a little. "The conversation my father and I never had."

Hiding his grin, Diamandis ticked points off on his fingers. "One: you can give yourself up to the men in armor who are looking for you. Two: you can make yourself useful by going with me on my nightly sorties. Three: you can leave Spyre. Or, four—"

"I thought you said I could never leave," she said, frowning.

"I lied." Seeing her expression, he rubbed at his chin and looked away. "Well, I had a beautiful young woman in my bed, even if I wasn't in there with her, so why would I let her go so easily? Yes, there is a way out of Spyre—potentially. But it would be dangerous."

"I don't care. Show me." She stood up.

"Sit down, sit down. It's daytime, and I'm tired. I need to sleep first. It's a long trek to the bomb bays. And anyway . . . don't you want to hear about the fourth option?"

"There is no other option."

He sighed in obvious disappointment. "All right. Let me sleep, then. We'll visit the site tonight and you can decide whether it's truly what you want to do."

THEY PICKED THEIR way through a field of weeds. Lesser Spyre twirled far above. The dark houses of the great families surrounded them, curving upward in two directions to form a blotted sky. Venera had examined those estates as they walked; she'd hardly had the leisure time to do so on her disastrous run to the edge of the world. Now, as the rust-eaten iron gates and crumbling battlements eased by, she had time to realize just how strange a place Spyre was.

On the steep roof of a building half-hidden by century oaks, she had seen a golden boy singing. At first she had taken him for some automaton, but then he slipped and caught himself. The boy was centered in bright spotlights and he held a golden olive branch over his head. Whether there was an audience for his performance in the gardens or balconies below, whether he did this every night or if it were some rare ceremony she had chanced to see—these things she would never know. She had touched Garth's shoulder and pointed. He merely shrugged.

Other estates were resolutely dark, their buildings choked in vines and their grounds overgrown with brambles. She had walked up to the gate of one such to peer between the leaves. Garth had pulled her back. "They'll shoot you," he'd said.

In some places the very architecture had turned inward, becoming incomprehensible, even impossible for humans to inhabit. Strange cancerous additions were flocked onto the sides of stately manors, mazes drawn in stone over entire grounds. Strange piping echoed from one dark entranceway, the rushing sound of wings from another. At one point Venera and Garth crossed a line of strange footprints, all the toes pointed inward and the indentations heavy on the outside as if the dozens of people who had made them were all terribly bowlegged.

It did no good to look away from these sights. Venera occasionally glanced at the sky, but the sky was paved with yet more estates. After each glance she would hunch unconsciously away, and each time, a pulse of anger would shoot through her and she would straighten her shoulders and scowl.

Venera couldn't hide her nervousness. "Is it much farther?"

"You whine like a child. This way. Mind the nails."

"Garth, you remind me of someone but I can't figure out who."

"Ah! A treasured lover, no doubt. The one that got away, perhaps? —Wait, don't tell me, I prefer to wallow in my fantasies."

". . . A particularly annoying footman my mother had?"

"Madam, you wound me. Besides, I don't believe you."

"If there really is a way off of Spyre, why haven't you ever taken it?"

He stopped and looked back at her. Little more than a silhouette in the dim light, Diamandis still conveyed disappointment in the tilt of his shoulders and head. "Are you deliberately provoking me?"

Venera caught up to him. "No," she said, putting her fists on her hips. "If this exit is so dangerous that you chose not to use it, I want to know."

"Oh. Yes, it's dangerous—but not that dangerous. I could have used it. But we've been over this. Where would I go? One of the other principalities? What use would an old gigolo be there?"

"Let the ladies judge that."

"Ha! Good point. But no. Besides, if I circled around and came back to Lesser Spyre, I'd eventually be caught. Have you *been* up there? It's even more paranoid and tightly controlled than this place. The city is . . . impossible. No, it would never work."

As was typical of her, Venera had been ignoring what Garth was saying and focusing instead on how he said it. "I've got it!" she said. "I know why you stayed."

He turned toward her, a black cutout against distant lights— and for once Venera didn't simply blurt out what was on her mind. She could be perfectly tactful when her life depended on it but in other circumstances had never known why one should bother. Normally she would have just said it: *You're still in love with someone.* But she hesitated.

"In there," said Diamandis, pointing to a long low building whose roof was being overtaken by lopsided trees. He waited, but when she didn't say anything he turned slowly and walked in the direction of the building.

"A wise woman wouldn't be entering such a place un-escorted," said Venera lightly as she took his arm. Diamandis laughed.

"I am your escort."

"You, Mr. Diamandis, are why escorts were invented."

Pleased, he developed a bit of a bounce to his step. Venera, though, wanted to slow down—not because she was afraid of him or what waited inside the dark. At this moment, she could not have said what made her hesitate.

The concrete lot was patched with grass and young trees and they scuttled across it quickly, both wary of any watchers on high. They soon reached a peeled-out loading door in the side of the metal building. There was no breeze outside, but wind was whistling around the edges of the door.

"It puzzles me why there isn't a small army of squatters living in places like this," said Venera as the blackness swallowed Diamandis. She reluctantly stepped after him into it. "The pressures of life in these pocket states must be intolerable. Why don't more people simply leave?"

"Oh, they do." Diamandis took her hand and led her along a flat floor. "Just a bit farther, I have to find the door . . . through here." Wind buffeted her from behind now. "Reach forward . . . here's the railing. Now, follow that to the left."

They were on some sort of catwalk, its metal grating ringing faintly under her feet.

"Many people leave," said Diamandis. "Most don't know how to survive outside of the chambers where they were born and bred. They return, cowed, or they die. Many are shot by the sentries, by border guards, or by the preservationists. I've buried a number of friends since I came to live here."

Her eyes were starting to adjust to the dark. Venera could tell that they were in a very large room of some sort, its ceiling ribbed with girders. Holes let in faint light in places, just enough to sketch the dimensions of the place. The floor . . .

There was no floor, only subdivided metal boxes with winches hanging over them. Some of those boxes were capped by fierce vortices of wind that collectively must have scoured every grain of grit out of the place. Looking down at the nearest box, Venera saw that it was really a square metal pit with clamshell doors at its bottom. Those doors vibrated faintly.

"Behold the bomb bays," said Diamandis, sweeping his arm in a dramatic arc. "Designed to rain unholy fire on any fleet stupid enough to line itself up with Spyre's rotation. This one chamber held enough firepower to carpet a square mile of air with bombs. And there were once two dozen such bays."

The small hurricane chattered like a crowd of madmen; the bomb bay doors rattled and buzzed in sympathy. "Was it ever used?" asked Venera.

"Supposedly," said Diamandis. "The story goes that we wiped out an entire armada in seconds. Though that could all be propaganda. If true, I can see why people outside Spyre would despise us. After all, there would have been hundreds of bombs that passed through the armada and simply kept going. Who knows what unsuspecting nations we strafed?"

Venera touched the scar on her chin.

"Anyway, it was generations ago," said Diamandis. "No one seems to care that much about us since the other great wheels disintegrated. We're the last, and ignored the way you pass by the aged. Come this way."

They went up a short flight of metal steps to a catwalk that extended out over the bays. Diamandis led Venera halfway down the long room; his footfalls were steady, hers slowing, as they approached a solitary finned shape hanging from chains above one of the bays.

"That's a bomb!" It was a good eight feet long, almost three in diameter, a great metal torpedo with a button nose. Diamandis leaned out over the railing and slapped it.

"A bomb, indeed," he said over the whistling gale. "At least, it's a bomb casing. See? The hatch there is unscrewed. I scooped out the explosives years ago; there's room for one person if you wriggle your way in. All I have to do is throw a lever and it will drop and bang through those doors. Nothing's going to stop you once you're outside; you can go a few hundred miles and then light out on your own."

She too leaned out to touch the cylinder's flank.

"So you'll go home, will you?" he asked with seeming inno-cence.

Venera snatched her fingers back. She crossed her arms and looked away.

"The people who ran this place," she said after a while. "It was one of the great nations, wasn't it? One of the ones that specialize in building weapons. Like Sacrus?"

He laughed. "Not Sacrus. Their export is *leverage*. Means of po-litical control, ranging from blackmail to torture and extortion. They have advisors in the throne rooms of half the principalities."

"They sell torturers?"

"That's one of the skills they export, yes. Almost nobody in Spyre deals with them anymore—they're too dangerous. Keep pulling coups, trying to dominate the council. The preservation-ists are still hurting from their own run-in with them. You met one of theirs in Liris?" She nodded.

Diamandis sighed. "Yet one more reason for you to leave, then. Once you're marked in their ledgers, you're never safe again. Come on, I'll give you a boost up."

"Wait." She stared at the black opening in the metal thing. The thought came to her: this won't work. She could not return to Slip-stream and pretend that things that had been done had not been done. She could not in silence retire as the shunned wife of a dis-graced admiral. Not when the man responsible for Chaison's death—the Pilot of Slipstream—still sat like a spider at the center of Slipstream affairs.

Thinking this made her fury catch like dry tinder. A spasm of pain shot up her jaw, and she shook her head. Venera turned and walked back along the catwalk.

Diamandis hurried after her. "What are you doing?"

Venera struggled to catch her breath. She would need re-sources. If she was to avenge Chaison, she would need power. "Yesterday you said something about a fourth choice, Garth." She rattled down the steps and headed for the door.

"Tell me about that choice."

YOU MUST BE ready for this, Garth had said. It is like no place you have ever been or ever imagined. Near dawn, as they approached the re-gion of Spyre known as the airfall, she began to understand what he meant.

The great estates dwindled as they threaded their way through Diamandis's secret ways; even the preservationists avoided this sector of the great wheel. Ruins dotted the landscape and strange trees lay nearly prone like supplicants.

The ground shook, a constant wavering shudder. The motion reminded her with every step that she stood on thin metal sheeting above an abyss of air. She began to see patches of speed ivy atop broken cornices and walls. And the loose soil thinned until they walked atop the metal of the wheel itself.

Wind pushed at her from behind; Venera had to consciously set her feet down, grinding them into the grit to prevent herself start-ing to run. Giving into that run would be fatal, Diamandis assured her. The reason why emerged slowly, horribly, from around the collapsed walls and tangled groves of once-great estates.

She clapped Diamandis on the shoulder and pointed. "How long ago?"

He nodded and leaned in so that she could hear him over the

roar. "A question important to our enterprise. It happened generations ago, in a time of great unrest in the principalities. Back
when the great nations of Spyre still traveled—before they began
to hide in their fortresses."

A hundred yards or so of slick decking extended past the last
broken stones, then the first tears and gaps appeared. Long
sheets of humming metal extended out, following the lines of
the girders that underlay Spyre's upper skin. Soon even they disappeared, leaving only bright shreds and the girders themselves.
A latticework of metal beams was all the ground there was for
the next mile.

Below the plain of girders dark clouds shot past with dizzying speed. Propelled by Spyre's centrifugal force, a ceaseless hurricane roared in and down and through the empty windows of
the broken ruins and leaped out of a vast hole in the world.

"Behold the airfall!" Diamandis gestured dramatically; but
there was no need. Venera stood awestruck at the sheer savagery
of the permanent storm that warred about her. If she lifted one
foot or straightened her back she might be caught and yanked
out and then down, and shot out of Spyre through this screaming, gouting wound.

"This—this is insane!" She hunkered down, clutching a
boulder. Her leathers flapped up around her ears. "Am I expected to run into that?"

"No, not run! Crawl. Because up there—do you see it? There
is your fourth alternative!" She squinted where he pointed and
at first didn't see anything. Then she blinked and looked again.

The skin of Spyre had been stripped away for at least a mile in
every direction. The hole must have unbalanced the whole
wheel—towers, farms, factories, and even perhaps whole towns
being sucked out and flung into the depths of Virga in a catastrophe that threatened to destroy the entire structure. For some rea-

son the peeling and collapse had propagated only so far and then stopped—but the standing cyclone of exiting air must have unbalanced Spyre so much as to threaten its immediate destruction.

This, if anything, explained the preservationists and the fierce war they had fought to lay their tracks around Spyre. The unstable wobble of the wheel could only be fixed by moving massive weights around the rim to balance it. There was no patching this hole.

Everything above had been sucked out as the skin peeled away—except in one place. One solitary tower still stood a quarter mile into the plain of girders. It had the great fortune to have been built overtop a main intersection point for Spyre's skeletal system. Also, the place might once have been a factory with its own reinforced foundation, for Venera could see huge pipes and tanks splayed like the roots of a tree below the girders. The tower itself was dark as the clouds that framed it, and it slowly swayed under the force of the winds. The girders bounced it like an acrobat in a net.

Just looking at it made her nauseated. "What is that?"

"Buridan Tower," said Diamandis. "It's our destination."

"Why? And how are we going to get there through . . . through that?"

"Using our courage, Lady Fanning—and my knowledge. I know a way, if you'll trust me. As to why—that is a secret that you will reveal, to both of us."

She shook her head, but Venera had no intention of backing out now. To do anything else but go forward in this mad adventure would be to invite relaxation—and thought. Grief drove her on, an active refusal to think. She waited, eyes tearing from the wind, and eventually Diamandis nodded sharply and gestured come on.

They crept across the last acre of intact skin, grabbing onto every rock and jammed tree branch that might offer purchase. As they approached a great split in the metal sheeting, Venera saw where Diamandis was going, and she began to think that this passage might be possible after all.

Here, a huge pipe ran under Spyre's topsoil and skin. It was anchored to the girders by rusting metal straps and had broken in places but extended out below the skinless plain. It seemed to head straight for swaying Buridan Tower.

Diamandis had found a hole in the pipe that was sheltered by a tortured dune. He let himself down into the black mouth and she followed; instantly the wind subsided to a tolerable scream.

"I'm not even going to ask how you found this," she said after dusting herself off. He grinned.

The pipe was about eight feet across. Sighting down it she beheld, in perspective, a frozen vortex of discolored metal and sedimented rime. Behind her it was ominously dark; ahead, hundreds of gaps and holes let in the welling light of Candesce. In this new illumination, Venera eyed their route critically. "There's whole sections missing," she pointed out. "How do we cross those?"

"Trust me." He set off at a confident pace.

What was there to do but follow?

The pipe writhed in sympathy with the twisting of the beams. The motion was uncomfortable, but not terrifying to one who had ridden warships through battle, walked in gravities great and small throughout Virga, and even penetrated the mysteries of Candesce. —Or so Venera told herself, up until the tenth time her hand darted out of its own accord to grip white-knuckled some peel of rust or broken valve rim. Rhythmic blasts of pain shot up her clenched jaw. An old anger, born of helplessness, began to take hold of her.

The first gaps in the pipe were small and thankfully overhead. The ceiling opened out in these places, allowing Venera to see where she was—which made her duck her head down and continue on with a shudder.

But then they came to a place where most of the pipe was simply gone, for a distance of nearly sixty feet. Runnels of it ran like reminders above and to the sides, but there was no bottom anymore. "Now what?"

Diamandis reached up and tugged a cable she hadn't noticed before. It was bright and strong, anchored here and somewhere inside the black cave where the pipe picked up again. Near its anchor point the line was gathered up and pinched by a huge spring, allowing it to stretch and slacken with the twisting of the girders.

"You did this?"

He nodded; she was impressed and said so. Diamandis sighed. "Since I've had no audience to brag to, I've done many feats of daring," he said. "I did none in all the years when I was trying to impress the ladies—and none of them will ever know I was this brave."

"So how do we . . . Oh." Despite her pounding headache, she had to laugh. This was a zip line; Diamandis proposed to clip rollers to it and glide across. Well, at least the great girder provided a wall to one side and partial shelter above. The wind was not quite so punishing here.

"You have to be fast!" Diamandis was fitting a pulley-hold onto the cable. "You can't breathe in that wind. If you get stranded in the middle you'll pass out."

"Wonderful." But he'd strapped her in securely, and falling was not something that frightened people who lived in a weightless ocean of air. When the time came she simply closed her eyes and kicked off into the white flood of air.

They had to repeat this process six times. Now that he had someone to give up his secret to, Diamandis was eager to tell her how he had used a powerful foot-bow to shoot a line across each gap, trusting to its grip in the deep rust on the far side to allow him to scale across once. After stronger lines were affixed it was easy to get back and forth.

So, walking and gliding, they approached the black tower.

In some places its walls fell smoothly into the abyss. In others, traces of ground still clung tenaciously where sidewalks and outbuildings had once been. They clambered out of the pipe onto one such spot; here, thirty feet of gravel and plating stretched like a splayed hand up to the tower's flank. Diamandis had strung more cables along that wall, leading toward a great dark shadow that opened halfway around the wall's curve. "The entrance!" Battered by wind, he loped over to the nearest line.

The zip lines in the pipe had given Venera the false impression that she was up for anything. Now she found herself hanging onto a cable with both hands—small comfort to also be clipped to it—while blindly groping with her feet on the side of a sheer wall, above an infinite drop now illuminated by full daylight.

Only a man with nothing to lose could have built such a pathway. She understood, for she felt she was in the same position. Gritting her teeth and breathing in shallow sips in vortices of momentary calm caused by the jutting brickwork, she followed Diamandis around Buridan Tower's long curve.

At last she stood, shaking, on a narrow ledge of stone. The door before her was strapped iron, fifteen feet tall and framed with trembling speed ivy. Rusting machine guns poked their snouts out of slits in the stone walls surrounding it. A coat of arms in the ancient style capped the archway. Venera stared at it, a brief drift of puzzlement surfacing above her apprehension. She had seen that design somewhere before.

"I can't go back that way. There has to be another way!"

Diamandis sat down with his back to the door and gestured for her to do the same. The turbulence was lessened just enough there that she could breathe. She leaned on his shoulder. "Garth, what have you done to us?"

He took some time to get his own breath back. Then he jabbed a thumb at the door. "People have been pointing their telescopes at this place for generations, all dreaming of getting inside it. Secret expeditions have been mounted to reach it, but none of them ever came via the route we just took. It's been assumed that this way was impossible. No . . ." He gestured at the sky. "They always climb down the elevator cable that connects the tower to Lesser Spyre. And every time they're spotted and shot by Spyre sentries."

"Why?"

"Because the nation of Buridan is not officially defunct. There are supposed to be heirs, somewhere. And the product of Buridan still exists, on farms scattered around Spyre. No one is legally allowed to sell it until the fate of the nation is determined once and for all. But the titles, the deeds, the proofs of ownership and provenance . . ." He thumped the iron with his fist. "They're all in here."

Her fear was beginning to give way to curiosity. She looked up at the door. "Do we knock?"

"The legend says that the last members of the nation live on, trapped inside. That's nonsense, of course, but it's a useful fiction."

It began to dawn on her what he had in mind. "You intend to play on the legends."

"Better than that. I intend to prove that they are true."

She stood up and pushed on the door. It didn't budge. Venera looked around for a lock, and after a moment she found one, a curious square block of metal embedded in the stone of the archway. "You've been here before. Why didn't you go in?"

"I couldn't. I didn't have the key and the windows are too small."

She glared at him. "Then why . . . ?"

He stood up, smiling mysteriously. "Because now I do have the key. You brought it to me."

"I . . . ?"

Diamandis dug inside his jacket. He slid something onto his finger and held it up to gleam in the light of Candesce.

One of the pieces of jewelry Venera had taken from the hoard of Anetene had been a signet ring. She had found it in the very same box that had contained the key to Candesce. It was one of the pieces that Diamandis had stolen from her when she first arrived here.

"That's mine!"

He blinked at her tone, then shrugged. "As you say, Lady. I thought long and hard about playing this game myself, but I'm too old now. And anyway, you're right. The ring is yours." He pulled it off his finger and handed it to her.

The signet showed a fabulous ancient creature known as a horse. It was a gravity-bound creature and so none now lived in Virga—or were they the product that Buridan had traded in? Venera took the heavy ring and held it up, frowning. Then she strode to the lockbox and placed the ring into a like-shaped indentation there.

With a mournful grating sound, the great gate of Buridan swung open.

8

GUNNER TWELVE-FIFTEEN WRAPPED his fingers around the dusty emergency switch and pulled as hard as he could. With a loud snap, the red stirrup-shaped handle came off in his hand.

The gunner cursed and half-stood to try and retrieve the end of the emergency cord that was now poking out of a hole in his canopy. He banged his head on the glass and the whole gun emplacement wobbled, causing the cord to flip out into the bright air. Meanwhile, the impossible continued to happen outside; the thing was now a quarter mile above him and almost out of range.

Gunner Twelve-fifteen had sat here for sixteen years now. In that time he had turned the oval gun emplacement from a cold and drafty purgatory into a kind of nest. He'd stopped up the gaps in the metal armor with cloth and, later, pitch. He'd snuck down blankets and pillows and eventually even took out the original metal seat, dropping it with supreme satisfaction onto Greater Spyre two miles below. He'd replaced the seat with a kind of reclining divan, built sunshades to block the harsher rays of Candesce, and removed layers of side armor to make way for a bookshelf and drinks cabinet. The only thing he hadn't touched was the butt of the machine gun itself.

Nobody would know. The emplacement, a metal pod suspended above the clouds by cables strung across Greater Spyre, was his alone. Once upon a time there had been three shifts of sentries here, a dozen eyes at a time watching the elevator cable that ran between the town-wheels of Lesser Spyre and the abandoned and forlorn Buridan Tower. With cutbacks and rescheduling, the number had eventually gone down to one: one twelve-hour shift for each of the six pods that surrounded the cable. Gunner Twelve-fifteen had no doubt that the other gunners had similarly renovated their stations; the fact that none were now responding to the emergency meant that they were not paying any attention to the object they were here to watch.

Nor had he been; if not for a random flash of sunlight against the beveled glass of a wrought-iron elevator car he might never have known that Buridan had come back to life—not until he and the other active sentries were hauled up for court-marshal.

He pushed back the bulletproof canopy and made another grab at the frayed emergency cord. It dangled three inches beyond his outstretched fingers. Cursing, he lunged at it and nearly fell to his death. Heart hammering, he sat down again.

Now what? He could fire a few rounds at the other pods to get their attention—but then he might kill somebody. Anyway, he wasn't supposed to fire on rising elevators, only objects coming down the cable.

The gunner watched in indecision until the elevator car pierced another layer of cloud and disappeared. He was doomed if he didn't do something right now—and there was only one thing to do.

He reached for the other red handle and pulled it.

In the original design of the gun emplacements, the ejection rocket had been built into the base of the gunner's seat. If he was injured or the pod was about to explode, he could pull the handle and the rocket would send him, chair and all, straight up the long cable to the infirmary at Lesser Spyre. Of course, the original chair no longer existed.

The other gunners were startled out of their dozing and reading by the sudden vision of a pillowed divan rising into the sky on a pillar of flame. Blankets, books, and bottles of gin twirled in its wake as it vanished into the gray.

THE DAY-WATCH LIAISON officer shrieked in surprise when Gunner Twelve-fifteen burst in on her. The canvas she had been carefully daubing paint onto now had a broad blue slash across it.

She glared at the apparition in the doorway. "What are *you* doing here?"

"Begging your pardon, ma'am," said the trembling soldier. "But Buridan has reactivated."

For a moment she dithered—the painting was ruined unless she got that paint off it right now—then was struck by the image of the man standing before her. Yes, it really *was* one of the sentries. His face was pale and his hair looked like he'd stuck it in a fan. She would have sworn that the seat of his leather flight suit was smoking. He was trembling.

"What's this about, man?" she demanded. "Can't you see I'm busy?"

"B-Buridan," he stammered. "The elevator. It's rising. It may already be here!"

She blinked, then opened the door fully and glanced at the rank of bellpulls ranked in the hallway. The bells were ancient and black with tarnish and clearly none had moved recently. "There was no alarm," she said accusingly.

"The emergency cord broke," said the gunner. "I had to eject, ma'am," he continued. "There was, uh, cloud; I don't think the other sentries saw the elevator."

"Do you mean to say that it was cloudy? That you're not sure you *saw* an elevator?"

He turned even more pale; but his jaw was set. As the liaison officer wound up to really let loose on him, however, one of the bellpulls moved. She stared at it, forgetting entirely what she had been about to say.

". . . Did you just see . . ." The cord moved again and the bell jiggled slightly. Then the cord whipped taut and the bell shattered in a puff of verdigris and dust. In doing so it managed to make only the faintest tinking sound.

She goggled at it. "That—that's the Buridan elevator!"

"That's what I was trying to—" But the liaison officer had burst past him and was running for the stairs that led up to the elevator stations.

Elevators couldn't be fixed to the moving outer rim of a town-wheel; so the gathered strands of cable that rose up from the various estates met in a knotlike collection of buildings in freefall. Ropes led from this to the axes of the towns themselves. The officer had to run up a yin-yang staircase to get to the top of the town (the same stairway that the gunner had just run down); as her weight dropped the steps steepened and the rise became more and more vertical. Puffing and nearly weightless, she achieved the top in under a minute. She glanced out one of the blockhouse's gunslits in time to see an ornate cage pull into the elevator station a hundred yards away.

The gunner was gasping his way back up the steps. "Wait," he called feebly. The liaison officer didn't wait for him, but stepped to the round open doorway and launched herself across the empty air.

Two people were waiting by the opened door to the Buridan elevator. The liaison officer felt an uncanny prickling in her scalp as she saw them, for they looked every bit as exotic as she'd imagined someone from Buridan would be. Her first inclination (drummed into her by her predecessor) that any visitation from the lost nation must be a hoax, faded as one of the pair spoke. Her accent wasn't like that of anyone from Upper Spyre.

"They sent only you?" The woman's voice dripped scorn. She was of medium height, with well-defined brows that emphasized her piercing eyes. A shock of pale hair stood up from her head.

The liaison officer made a midair bow and caught a nearby girder to halt herself. She struggled to slow her breathing and appear calm as she said, "I am the designated liaison officer for Buridan-Spyre relations. To whom do I have the honor of addressing myself?"

The woman's nostrils flared. "I am Amandera Thrace-Guiles, heir of Buridan. And you? You're nobody in particular, are you . . . but I suppose you'll have to do," she said. "Kindly direct us to our apartments."

"Your . . ." The Buridan apartments existed, the officer knew that much. No one was allowed to enter, alter, or destroy Buridan property until the nation's status was determined. "This way, please."

She thought quickly. It was years ago, but one day she had met one of the oldest of the watch officers in an open gallery on Wheel Seven. They had been passing a broad stretch of crumbling wall and came to a bricked-up archway. "Know what that is?" he'd asked playfully. When she shook her head he smiled and said, "Almost nobody does, nowadays. It's the entrance to the Buridan estate. It's all still there—towers, granaries, bedrooms, and armories—but the other nations have been building and renovating around and over it for so long that there's no way in anymore. It's like a scar, or a callus maybe, in the middle of the city.

"Anyway, this was the main entrance. Used to have a sweeping flight of steps up to it, until they took that out and made the courtyard yonder. This entrance is the official one, the one that only opens to the state key. If you ever get any visitors from Buridan, they can prove that they are who they say they are if they can open the door behind that wall."

"Come with me," said the officer now. As she escorted her visitors along the rope that stretched toward Wheel Seven, she wondered where she was going to get a gang of navvies with sledgehammers on such short notice.

THE DEMOLITION OF the brick wall made just enough of a delay to allow Lesser Spyre's first ministers to show up. Venera cursed under her breath as she watched them padding up the gallery walk: five men and three women in bright silks, with serious expressions. Secretaries and hangers-on fluttered around them like moths. In the courtyard below, a crowd of curious citizens was growing.

"This had better work," she muttered to Diamandis.

He adjusted his mask. It was impossible to read his expression behind it. "They're as scared as we are," he said. "Who knows if there's anything left on the other side of that?" He nodded to the rapidly falling stones in the archway.

"Lady Thrace-Guiles!" One of the ministers swept forward, lifting his silk robes delicately over the mortar dust. He was bejowled and balding, with a fan of red skin across his nose and liver spots on his lumpish hands. "You look just like your great-great-great-grandmother, Lady Bertitia," he said generously. "Her portrait hangs in my outer office."

Venera looked down her nose at him. "And you are . . . ?"

"Aldous Aday, acting chairman of the Lesser Spyre Committee for Public Works and Infrastructure," he said. "Elected by the Upper House of the Great Families—a body that retains a seat for you, kept draped in velvet in absentia all these years. I must say, this is an exciting and if I do say so, surprising, day in the history of Upper—"

"I want to make sure our estate is still in one piece," she said. She turned to Diamandis. "Master Flance, the hole is big enough for you to squeeze through. Pray go ahead and tell me that our door is undamaged." He bowed and edged his way past the workmen.

He and Venera wore clothing they had found preserved in wax paper in the lockers of Buridan Tower. The styles were ancient, but for all that they were more practical than the contraptions favored by Spyre's present generation. Venera had on supple leather breeches and a black jacket over a bodice tooled and inscribed in silver. A simple belt held two pistols. On her brow rested a silver circlet they had found in an upstairs bedchamber. Diamandis was similarly dressed, but his leathers were all a deep forest green.

"It's a great honor to see your nation again after so many years," continued Aday. If he was suspicious of her identity, he wasn't letting on. She exchanged pleasantries with him through clenched teeth, striving to stay in profile so that he and the others could not see her jaw. Venera had done her best to hide the scar and had bleached her hair with some unpleasant chemicals they'd found in the tower, but someone who had heard about Venera Fanning might recognize her. Did Aday and his people keep up on news from the outside world? Diamandis didn't think they did, but she had no idea at this point how far her fame had spread.

To her advantage was the fact that the paranoid societies of Spyre rarely communicated. "Sacrus won't want anyone to know they had you," Diamandis had pointed out one evening as they sat huddled in the tower, an ornate chair burning merrily in the fireplace. "If they choose to unmask you, it's at the expense of admitting they have connections with the outside world—and more important, they won't want to hint that they have the key to Candesce. I don't think we'll hear a peep out of them, at least not overtly."

The workmen finished knocking down the last bricks and stepped aside just as Diamandis stuck his head around the corner of the archway. "The door is there, ma'am. And the lock."

"Ah, good." Venera stalked past the workers, trying to keep from nervously twisting the ring on her finger. This was the proverbial moment of truth. If the key didn't work . . .

The brick wall had been built across an entryway that extended fifteen feet and ended in a large iron-bound door similar to the one at Buridan Tower. The ministers crowded in behind Venera, watching like hawks as she dusted off the lockbox with her glove. "Gentlemen," she said acidly, "there is only so much air in here. —Though I suppose you have some natural skepticism about my authenticity. Put that out of your minds." She held up the signet ring. "I am my own proof—but if you need crass symbols, perhaps this one will do." She jammed the key against the inset impression in the lockbox.

Nothing happened.

"Pardon." Diamandis was looking alarmed and Venera quashed the urge to make some sort of joke. She must not lose her air of confidence, not even for a second. Bending to examine the lock, she saw that it had been overgrown with grit over the years. "Brush, please," she said in a bored tone, holding out one hand. After a long minute someone placed a hairbrush in her palm. She scrubbed the lock industriously for a while, then blew on it and tried the ring again.

This time there was a deep click and then a set of ratcheting thumps from behind the wall. The door ground open slowly.

"You are the council for . . . infrastructure, was it not?" she asked, fixing the ministers with a cold eye. Aday nodded. "Hmm," she said. "Well." She turned, preparing to sweep like the spoiled princess she had once been, through the opened door into blackness.

A loud *bang!* and fall of dust from the ceiling made her stumble. There was sudden pandemonium in the gallery. The ministers were milling in confusion while screams and shouts followed the echoes of the explosion into the air. Past Aday's shoulder Venera saw a curling pillar of smoke or dust that hadn't been there a second ago.

With her foot hovering over the threshold of the estate, Venera found herself momentarily forgotten. Sirens were sounding throughout the wheel and she heard the clatter of soldiers' boots on the flagstones. In the courtyard, someone was crying; somebody else was screaming for help.

Expressionless, she walked back to the gallery and peered over Aday's shoulder. "Somebody bombed the crowd," she said.

"It's terrible, terrible," moaned Aday, wringing his hands.

"This can't have been planned," she said reasonably. "So who would be walking around on a morning like this just carrying a bomb?"

"It's the rebels," said Aday furiously. "Bombers, assassins . . . This is terrible!"

Someone burst into the courtyard below and ran toward the

most injured people. With a start Venera realized it was Garth Diamandis. He shouted a command to some stunned but otherwise intact victims; slowly they moved to obey, fanning out to examine the fallen.

It hadn't occurred to Venera until this moment that she could also be helping. She felt a momentary stab of surprise, then . . . was it anger? She must be angry at Diamandis, that was it. But—she remembered the mayhem of battle aboard the Rook when the pirates attacked, and the aftermath. Such fear and anguish, and in those moments the smallest gesture meant so much to men who were in pain. The airmen had given of themselves without a moment's thought—given aid, bandages, and blood.

She turned to look for the stairs, but it was too late: the medics had arrived. Frowning, Venera watched their white uniforms fan out through the blackened rubble. Then she lit her lantern and stalked back to the archway.

"When my manservant is done, send him to me," she said quietly. She strode alone into the long-sealed estate of Buridan.

IN AN ABANDONED bedchamber of the windswept tower while the floor swayed and sighs moaned through the huge pipes that underlay the place, Diamandis had told Venera histories of Buridan, and more.

"They were the horse masters," he said. "Theirs was the ultimate in impractical products—a being that required buckets of food and endless space to run, that couldn't live a day in freefall. But a creature so beautiful that visitors to Spyre routinely fell in love with them. To have a horse was the ultimate sign of power, because it meant you had gravity to waste."

"But that must have been centuries ago," she'd said. Venera was having trouble hearing Diamandis, even though the room's door was tightly closed and there were no windows in this chamber. The tower was awash with sound, from the creaking of the beams and the roaring of the wind to the deep basso-profundo chorus of drones that reverberated through every surface. Even before her eyes had adjusted to the darkness inside the building, before she could take in the clean stripped smell of chambers and corridors scoured by centuries of wind, the full-throated scream of Buridan had nearly driven her outside again.

It had taken them an hour to discover the source of that basso cry: the nest of huge pipes that jutted from the bottom of Buridan Tower acted like a giant wind instrument. It hummed and keened, moaned and ululated unceasingly.

Diamandis slapped the wall. This octagonal chamber was filled with jumbled pots, pans, and other kitchen utensils; but it was quiet compared to the bedchambers and lounges of the former inhabitants. "Buridan's heyday was very long ago," he said. He looked almost apologetic, his features lit from below by the oil lamp they'd brought. "But the people of Spyre have long memories. Our records go all the way back to the creation of the world."

He told her stories about Spyre's ancient glories that night as they bedded down, and the next day as they prowled the jumbled chaos of the tower. Later, Venera would always find those memories entwined within her: the tales he told her accompanied by images of the empty, forlorn chambers of the tower. Grandeur, age, and despair were the setting for his voice; grandeur, age, and despair henceforth defined her impressions of ancient Virga.

He told her tales of vast machines, bigger than cities, that had once built the very walls of Virga itself. Those engines were alive and conscious, according to Diamandis, and their offspring included both machines and humans. They had settled the cold black spaces of a star's outskirts, having sailed for centuries from their home.

"Preposterous!" Venera had exclaimed. "Tell me more."

So he told her of the first generations of men and women who had lived in Virga. The world was their toy, but they shared it with beings far more powerful and wiser than themselves. It was simple for them to build places like Spyre—but in doing so, they used up much of Virga's raw materials. The machines objected. There was a war of inconceivable ferocity; Virga rang like a bell, its skin glowed with heat, and the precarious life forms the humans had seeded inside it were annihilated.

"Ridiculous!" she said. "You can do better than that."

Spyre was the fortress of the human faction, he told her. From here, the campaign was launched that defeated the machines. Sulking, they left to create their own settlement on the far side of the solar system—but some remained. In faraway, frozen, and sunless corners of the world, forgotten soldiers slept. Having accumulated dust and fungus over the centuries, they could easily be mistaken for asteroids. Some hung like frozen bats from the skin of the world, icebergs with sightless eyes. If you could waken them, you might receive powers and gifts beyond mortal desire; or you could unleash death and ruin on the whole world.

The humans slowly rebuilt Virga's ecology, but they were diminished from their original, godlike power. Nations were spawned by the dozen, hot new suns springing into life in the black abyss. They turned their backs on the past.

Then, rumors began of something strange approaching across the cold interstellar wastes . . . a new force, spreading outward like ripples in a pond. It came from their ancient home. It had many names, but the best description of it was *artificial nature*.

"Ah," said Venera. "I see."

They made their rounds as Diamandis talked. Each foray they made began and ended in the central atrium of the old building. Here, upward-sweeping arches formed an eight-sided atrium that rose fifteen stories to the glittering stained-glass cupola surmounting the edifice. Lozenges of amber and lime, rose and indigo light outlined the dizzying succession of galleries that rose to all sides.

On the second day, as they were exploring the upper chambers, they came across traces of a story Garth Diamandis did not know. As Venera was poking her head in a closet she heard him shout in alarm. Running to his side she found him kneeling next to the armored figure of a man. The corpse was ancient, wizened and dried by the wind. A sword lay next to it. And in the next chamber were more bodies.

Some dire and dramatic end had come to the people here. They found a dozen mummified soldiers, all lying where they had fallen in fierce combat. Guns and blades were strewn about among long-dried pools of black liquid. The disposition of the bodies suggested attackers and defenders; curious now, Venera followed the path the interlopers must have taken.

High in the tower, behind a barricaded door, a blackened human shape lay on the moldering coves of a vast four-poster bed. The white lace dress the mummy wore still moved in the wind, causing Venera to jump in startlement whenever she glanced at it.

She systematically ransacked the room while Diamandis stood contemplating the body. Here, in desk drawers and cabinets, were all the documents and letters of marque Venera needed to establish her identity. She even found a genealogy and photos. The best of the clothes were stored here as well, and that evening, rather than listening to a story, Venera began to make up her own—the story of a generations-long siege, a self-imposed exile broken finally by the last member of the nation of Buridan, Amandera Thrace-Guiles.

THE DARKNESS YIELDED detail slowly. Venera stood in what had once been a cobblestoned courtyard overlooked by the pillared facade of the Buridan estate. Black windows looked down from the edifice; once, sunlight would have streamed through them into whatever grand halls lay beyond. At some point in the past dark buttresses had been leaned onto the smooth white flanks of the building to support neighboring buildings— walls and arches that had swathed and overgrown it in layers, like the accumulating scales of some vast beast. For a while the estate would have still had access to the sky, for windows looked out from many of the encircling walls. All were now bricked up. Stone and wrought-iron arches had ultimately been lofted over the roofs of the estate, and at some point a last chink must have let distant sunlight in to light a forlorn cornice or the eye of a gargoyle. Then that too had been sealed and Buridan encysted, to wait.

It was understandable. There was only a finite amount of space on a town-wheel like this; if the living residents couldn't demolish the Buridan estate, they'd been determined to reach other accommodations with it.

Two glittering pallasite staircases swept up from where Venera stood, one to the left, one to the right. She frowned, then headed for the dark archway that opened like a mouth between them. Her feet made no sound in the deep dust.

Certainly the upstairs chambers would be the luxurious ones; they had probably been stripped. In any case she was certain she would learn more about the habits and history of the nation by examining the servants' quarters.

In the dark of the lower corridor, Venera knelt and examined the floor. She drew one of her pistols and slid the safety off. Cautiously she moved onward, listening intently.

This servants' way ran on into obscurity, arches opening off it to both sides at regular intervals. Black squares that might once have been portraits hung on the walls, and here and there sheet-covered furniture huddled under the pillars like cowering ghosts.

Sounds reached her, distorted and uncertain. Were they coming from behind or ahead? She glanced back; silhouettes were moving across the distant square of the entranceway. But that sliding sound . . . She blew out the lantern and sidled along the wall, moving by touch.

Sure enough, a fan of light draped across the disturbed dust of the corridor revealed a shadow play of figures moving against the opposite wall. Venera crept up to the open doorway and peered around the corner in time to meet the eye of someone coming the other way.

"Hey! They're here already!" The woman was younger than Venera and had prominent cheekbones and long stringy hair. She was dressed in the dark leathers of the city. Venera leaped into her path and leveled the pistol an inch from her face.

"Don't move."

"Shills!" somebody else yelled.

Venera didn't know what a shill was, but yelled "No!" anyway. "I'm the new owner of this house."

The stringy-haired woman was staring cross-eyed at the gun barrel. Venera spared a glance past her into a long low chamber that looked like it had originally been a wine cellar. Lanterns burned at strategic points, lighting up what was obviously somebody's hideout: there were cots, stacks of crates, even a couple of tables with maps unrolled on them. Half a dozen people were rushing about grabbing up stuff and making for an exit in the opposite wall. Several more were training guns on Venera.

"Ah." She looked around the other side of the stringy-haired head. The men with the guns were glancing inquiringly at one of their number. Though of similar age, with his flashing eyes and ironic half-smile he stood out from the rest of these youths as a professor might stand out from his students. "Hello," Venera said to him. She withdrew her pistol and holstered it, registering the surprise on his face with some satisfaction.

"You'd better hurry with your packing," she said before anyone could move. "They'll be here any minute."

The guns were still trained on her, but the confident-looking youth stepped forward, squinting at her over his own weapon. He had a neatly trimmed moustache and what looked like a dueling scar on his cheek. "Who are you?" he demanded in an amused upper-class drawl.

She bowed. "Amandera Thrace-Guiles, at your service. Or perhaps, it's the other way around."

He sneered. "We're no one's servants. And unfortunate for you that you've seen us. Now we'll have to—"

"Stow it," she snapped. "I'm not playing your game, either for your side or for Spyre's. I have my own agenda, and it might benefit your own goals to consider me a possible ally."

Again the sense of amused surprise. Venera could hear voices outside in the hall now. "Be very quiet," she said, "and snuff those lights." Then she stepped back, grabbed the edges of the doors, and shut them.

Lanterns bobbed down the corridor. "Lady Thrace-Guiles?" It was Aday.

"Here. My lantern went out. In any case there seems to be nothing of interest this way. Shall we investigate the upper floors?"

"Perhaps." Aday peered about himself in distaste. "This appears to be a commoner's area. Yes, let's retrace our steps."

They walked in silence, and Venera strained to hear any betraying noise from the chamber behind them. There was none; finally, Aday said, "To what do we owe the honor of your visit? Is Buridan rejoining the great nations? Are you going to restart the trade in horses?"

Venera snorted. "You know perfectly well there was no room to keep such animals in the tower. We had barely enough to eat from the rooftop gardens and nets we strung under the world. No, there are no horses anymore. And I am the last of my line."

"Ah." They began to climb the long-disused steps to the upper chambers. "As to your being the last of the line . . . lines can be rejuvenated," said Aday delicately. "And as to the horses . . . I am happy to say that you are in error in that case."

She cast a sidelong glance at him. "What do you mean? Don't toy with me."

Aday smiled, appearing confident for the first time. "There *are* horses, my lady. Raised and bred at government expense in paddocks on Greater Spyre. They have always been here, all these years. They have been awaiting your return."

9

VENERA WAS NINE-TENTHS asleep and imagining that the pillow she clutched was Chaison's back. Such feelings of safety and belonging were so rare for her that by contrast the rest of her life seemed a wasteland. It was as though everything she had ever done, every school lesson and contest with her sisters, every panicky interview with her father, all the manipulations and lies, had been erased by this: the quiet, his breathing, his scent, and his neck against her chin.

"Rise and shine, my lady!"

Garth Diamandis threw back the room's curtains, revealing a brick wall. He glowered at it as scraps of velvet tore away in his fingers. Dust pillared around him in the lantern light.

Venera sat up and a knife blade of pain shot up her jaw. "Get out!" She thrashed about for a second, looking for a weapon. "Get out!" Her hands fell on the lantern and—not without thinking, but rather with malicious pleasure—she threw it at him as hard as she could.

Garth ducked and the lantern broke against the wall. The candle flame touched the curtains and they caught fire instantly.

"Oh! Not a good idea!" He tore down the curtains and, fetching a poker from the fireplace, began beating the flames.

"Did you not hear me?" She cast the musty covers aside and

ran at him. Grabbing up a broken splinter of a chair leg, she brandished it like a sword. "Get *out!*"

He parried easily and with a flick of the wrist sent her makeshift sword flying. Then he jabbed her in the stomach with the poker.

"Ooff!" She sat down. Garth continued beating out the flames. Smoke was filling the ancient bedchamber of the Buridan clan.

When Venera had her breath back she stood up and walked to a side table. Returning with a jug of water, she upended it over the smouldering cloth. Then she dropped the jug indifferently—it shattered—and glared at Garth.

"I was asleep," she said.

He turned to her, a muscle jumping in his own jaw. She saw for the first time that his eyes were red. Had he slept?

"What's the matter?" she asked.

With a heavy sigh he turned and walked away. Venera made to follow, realized she was naked, and turned to don her clothing. When she found him again he was sitting in the antechamber, fiddling with his bootstraps.

"It's her, isn't it?" she asked. "You've been looking for her?"

Startled, he looked up at her. "How did you—"

"I'm a student of human nature, Garth." She turned around. "Lace me up, please."

"You could have burned the whole place down," he grumbled as he tugged—a little too hard—on her corset strings.

"My self-control isn't good when I'm surprised," she said with a shrug. "Now you know."

"Aye." He grabbed her hips and turned her around to face him. "You usually hide your pain as well as someone twice your age."

"I choose to take that as a compliment." Conscious of his hands on her, she stepped back. "But you're evading the question—did you find her? Your expression suggests bad news."

He stood up. "It doesn't concern you." He began to walk away.

Venera gnawed her lip, thinking about apologizing for attacking him. It got no further than thinking. "Well," she said after following him for a while, "for what reason did you rouse me at such an ungodly . . ." She looked around. "What time is it?"

"It's midmorning." He glanced around as well; the chambers of the estate were cast in gloom save where the occasional lantern burned. "The house is entombed, remember?"

"Oh! The appointment!"

"Yes. The horse masters are waiting in the front hall. They're mighty nervous, since neither in their lifetimes nor those of their line stretching back centuries has anyone ever audited their work."

"I'm not auditing, Garth. I just want to meet some horses."

"And you may—but we have a bigger problem."

"What's that?" She paused to look at herself in a faded mirror. Somewhere downstairs she heard things being moved; they had hired a work gang to clean the building, just before fatigue had caught up with her and forced her to take refuge in that mildewed bedchamber.

"There's a second delegation waiting for you," Diamandis explained. "A pack of majordomos from the great families."

She stopped walking. "Ah. A challenge?"

"In a manner of speaking. You've been invited to attend a confirmation ceremony. To formally establish your identity and tites."

"Of course, of course . . ." She started walking again. "Damn, they're a step ahead of us. We'll have to turn that around." Venera pondered this as they trotted down the sweeping front steps. "Garth, do I smell like smoke?"

"Alas, my lady, you have about you the piquant aroma of a flaming curtain."

"Well, there's nothing to be done about it, I suppose. Are those the challengers?" She pointed to a group of ornately dressed men who stood in the middle of the archway. Behind them, a motley group of men in work clothes milled uncertainly. "Those would be the horsemen, then."

"Gentlemen," she said to the horsemen with a smile as she walked past the officials. "I'm so sorry to have kept you waiting."

"Ahem," said an authoritative voice behind her. Venera made herself finish shaking hands before she turned. "Yes?" she said with a sweet smile. "What can I do for you?"

The graying man with the lined face and dueling scars said, "You are summoned to appear—"

"I'm sorry, did you make an appointment?"

"—to appear before the—what?"

"An appointment." She leaned closer. "Did you make one?"

Unable to ignore protocol, he said "No" with sarcastic reluctance.

Venera waved a hand to dismiss him. "Then take it up with my manservant. These people have priority at the moment. *They* made an appointment."

An amused glint came into his eye. Venera realized, reluctantly, that this wasn't some flunky she was addressing, but a seasoned veteran of one of the great nations. And since she had just tried to set fire to her new mansion and kill her one and only friend in this godforsaken place, it could be that her judgement wasn't quite what it should be today.

She glanced at Diamandis, who was visibly holding his tongue.

With a deep sigh she bowed to the delegation. "I'm sorry. Where are my manners. If we conduct our business briefly, I can make my other appointment without ruffling feathers on that end as well. Who do I have the honor of addressing?"

Very slightly mollified, he said, "I am Jacoby Sarto of the nation of Sacrus. Your . . . return from the dead . . . has caused quite a stir amongst the great nations, lady. There are claims of proof that you must provide before you are accepted for who you are."

"I know," she said simply.

"Thursday next," he said, "at four o'clock in the council offices. Bring your proofs." He turned to go.

"Oh. Oh dear." He turned back, a dangerous look in his eye. Venera looked abjectly apologetic. "It's a very small problem—more of an opportunity, really. I happen to have become entangled in . . . a number of obligations that day. My former debtors and creditors . . . but I'm not trying to dodge your request! Far from it. Why don't we say eight o'clock P.M. in the main salon of my home? Such a date would allow me to fulfil my obligations and—"

"Whatever." He turned to confer with the others. The conference was brief. "So be it." He stepped close to her and looked down at her, the way her father used to do when she was young. Despite herself, Venera quailed inside—but she didn't blink, just as she had never reacted to her father's threats. "No games," he said very quietly. "Your life is at stake here." Then he gestured sharply to the others and they followed him away.

Garth leaned in and muttered, "What obligations? You have nothing planned that day."

"We do now," she said as she watched Sarto and his companions walk away. She told Garth what she had in mind, and his eyes widened in shock.

"In a week? The place is a shambles!"

"Then you know what you're going to be doing the rest of the day," she said tartly. "Hire as many people as you need—cash in a few of my gems. And Garth," she said as he turned to go. "I apologize for earlier."

He snorted. "I've had worse reactions first thing in the morning. But I expected better from you."

For some reason those parting words stung far more than any of the things she'd imagined he might say.

"YOU HAVEN'T TALKED about the horses," he said late that evening. Garth was pushing the far end of a hugely heavy wine rack while Venera hauled on the near side. Slowly, the wooden behemoth grated another few inches across the cellar floor. "How—oof!—what did you think of them?"

"I'm still sorting it out in my own mind," she said, pausing to set her feet better against the riveted iron decking that underlay her estate. "They were beautiful, and grotesque. Dali horses, the handlers called them. Apparently, a Dali is any four-legged beast raised under lower gravity than it was evolved to like."

Garth nodded and they pushed and pulled for a while. The rack was approaching the wall where the little cell of rebels had made their entrance—a hole pounded in the brickwork that led to an abandoned air shaft. Garth had explored a few yards of the tunnel beyond; Venera was afraid the rebels might have left traps behind.

"It was the smell I noticed first," she said as they took another break. "Not like any fish or bird I'd ever encountered. Foul but you could get used to it, I suppose. They had the horses in a place called a paddock—a kind of slave pen for animals. But the beasts . . . they were huge!"

Voices and loud thuds filtered in from the estate's central

hallway. Two of the work gangs Garth had hired that day were arguing over who should start work in the kitchens first.

Shadows flickered past the cellar door. The estate was crawling with people now. Lanterns were lit everywhere and shouted conversations echoed down, along with hammering, sawing, and the rumble of rolling carts. Venera hoped the racket would keep the neighbors up. She had a week to make this place fit for guests and that meant working kitchens, a ballroom with no crumbling plasterwork and free of the smell of decay—and, of course, a fully stocked wine cellar. The rebel gang had removed all evidence of themselves when they retreated but had left behind the hole by which they'd gained entrance. Because the mansion had only one entrance—the back doors had not yet been uncovered—Venera had decided it prudent to keep this bolt-hole. But if she was going to have a secret exit, it had to *be* secret; hence the wine rack.

"Okay," she said when they had it about three feet from the wall. "I'm going to grease the floor under the hole, so we can slide the rack to one side if we need to get out in a hurry." She plonked down the can she'd taken from one of the workmen and rolled up her sleeves.

"We'll have to survey for traps sometime," he said reasonably.

Venera squinted up at him. "Maybe, but not tonight. You look like you're about to collapse, Garth. Is it the gravity?"

He nodded, wincing. "That, and simple age. This is more activity than I've had in a long while, when you factor in the new weight. I thought I was in good shape, but . . ."

"Well, I hereby order you to take two days off. I'll manage the workmen. Take one day to rest up, and maybe on the second you tend to the . . . uh, that matter that you won't talk to me about."

"What matter?" he said innocently.

"It's all right." She smiled. "I understand. You've been in exile for a long time. Plenty of time to think about the men who put you there. Given that much time, I'd bet you've worked out your revenge in exquisite detail."

Garth looked shocked. "Revenge? No, that's not—oh, I suppose in the first few months I thought about it a lot. But you get over anger, you know. After a few years, perspective sets in."

"Yes, and that's the danger, isn't it? In my family, we were taught to nurture our grudges lest we forget."

"But why?" He looked genuinely distressed for some reason.

"Because once you forgive," she said, as if explaining something to a small child, "you set yourself up for another betrayal."

"That's what you were taught?"

"Never let an insult pass," she said, half-conscious that she was reciting lines her father and sisters had spoken to her many times. She ticked the points off on her fingers. "Never let a slight pass, never forget, build realistic plans for your revenges. You're either up or down from other people and you want always to be up. If they hurt you, you *must* knock them down."

Now he looked sad. "Is that why you're doing all this?" He gestured at the walls. "To get back at someone?"

"To *get back*, at all," she said earnestly, "I must have my revenge. Else I am brought low forever and can never go home. For otherwise—" Her voice caught.

For otherwise, I have no reason to return.

His expression of compassion on anyone else would have maddened her. "You were telling me about the horses," he said quietly.

"Ah. Yes." Grateful of the distraction, she said, "Well, they have these huge barrel-shaped bodies and elegant long necks. Long heads like on my ring." She held it up, splaying her fingers. "But their legs! Garth, their legs are twice the length of their bodies—like spider's legs, impossibly long and thin. They stalked around the paddock like . . . well, like spiders! I don't know how else to describe it. They were like a dream that's just tipping over to become a nightmare. I'm not sure I want to see them again."

He nodded. "There are cattle loose between some of the estates. I've seen them; they look similar. You have to understand, there's no room on the city wheels to raise livestock."

Venera pried open the lid of the grease can and picked up a brush. "But now that the nation of Buridan has returned, the horses are our responsibility. There are costs . . . it seems a dozen or more great nations have acted as caretakers for one or another part of the Buridan estate. Some are tenants of ours who haven't paid rent in centuries. Others are like Guinevera, who've been tending the horses. There's an immense web of relationships and dependencies here, and we have a little under a week to figure it all out."

Garth thought about it for a while. "First of all," he said eventually, "you need to bring a foal or two up here and raise it in the estate." He grimaced at her expression. "I know what I just said, but it's an important symbol. Besides, these rooms will just fill up with people if you give them a chance. Why not set some aside for the horses now?"

"I'll think about that."

They cleared out the space behind the rack and slid it against the wall. It fit comfortably over the exit hole. As they stood back to admire their work, Garth said, "It's a funny thing about time, you know. It sweeps away anger and hate. But it leaves love untouched."

She threaded her hand through his arm. "Ah, Garth, you're so sentimental. Did it ever occur to you that's why you ended up scrabbling about on Greater Spyre for the past twenty years?"

He looked her in the eye. "Truthfully, no. That had never occurred to me. If anything, I'd say I ended up there because I didn't love well enough, not because I ever loved too well."

She sighed. "You're hopeless. It's a good thing I'm here to take care of you."

"And here I thought it was I taking care of you."

They left the cellar and reentered the bedlam of construction that had taken over the manor.

THE HEADACHE BEGAN that night.

Venera knew exactly what it was; she'd suffered these before. All day her jaw had been bothering her; it was like an iron hand was inside her throat, reaching up to clench her skull. Around dinner a strange pulsating squiggly spot appeared in her vision and slowly expanded until she could see nothing around it. She retired to her room and waited.

How long was this one going to last? They could go on for days, and she didn't have days. Venera paced up and down, stumbling, wondering whether she could just sleep it off. But no, she had mounds of paperwork to go through and no time.

She called Garth. He exclaimed when he saw her and ran to her side. "You're white as a new wall!"

"Never mind," she said, detaching herself from him and climbing into bed. "Bring in the accounts books. It's just a headache. I get them. I'm sick but we need to go through these papers."

He started to read the details of Buridan's various contracts. Each word was like a little explosion in her head. Venera tried to concentrate, but after ten minutes she suddenly leaned over the edge of the bed and retched.

"You need to sleep!" Garth's hands were on her shoulders. He eased her back on the bed.

"Don't be ridiculous," she mumbled. "If we don't get this stuff straight, we won't convince the council and they'll cart us both away in chains." A blossom of agony had unfurled behind her left eye. Despite her brave words Venera knew she was down for however long the migraine decided to hold her.

Garth darkened the lamps and tiptoed around while she lay sprawled like a discarded doll. Distant hammering sounded like it was coming from inside her own head, but she couldn't hold up the renovations.

Sleep eventually came, but she awoke to pain that was abstract only until she moved her head and opened one eye. *This is how it's going to be.* These headaches were the bullet's fault; when it smashed her jaw it had tripped some switch inside her head and now agony ambushed her at the worst times. Always before, she'd had the safe haven of her bedroom at home to retreat to— her time on the Rook had been mercifully free of such episodes. She used such times to indulge in her worst behavior: whining, accusing, insulting anyone who came near her, and demanding that her every whim be catered to. She wallowed in self-pity, letting everyone know that she was the sad victim of fate and that no one, ever, had felt the agonies she was enduring so bravely.

But she really was going to die if she let the thing rule her this time. It wasn't that there was nobody around to indulge her; but in a moment of clarity she realized that all the sympathy in the world wasn't going to save her life if she didn't follow through on the deception she and Garth had planned. So, halfway through morning, Venera resolutely climbed out of bed. She tied a silk sash over her eyes, jammed candle wax in her ears, and picked up an empty chamber pot. Carrying this, she tottered out of the room. "Bring me a dressing gown," she said in reply to a half-heard question from a maid. "And fetch Master Flance."

Blindfolded, half-deaf, she nonetheless managed to make her

rounds of the work crews, while Garth followed her and read from the books. She told him what points to underline for her to look at later; inquired of the work and made suggestions; and, every now and then, she turned aside to daintily vomit into the chamber pot. Her world narrowed down to the feel of carpet or stone under her feet, the murmur of words in her ear, and the cataclysmic pounding that reverberated inside her skull. She kept going by imagining herself whipping, shooting, stomping on, and setting fire to Jacoby Sarto and the rest of this self-important council who had the temerity to oppose her will. This interior savagery was invisible from without, as she mumbled and queried politely, and let herself be led about.

All of this busywork seemed to be getting her somewhere, but that evening when she collapsed onto her bed, Venera realized that she had no memory of anything she had said or done that day. It was all obscured by the angry red haze of pain that had followed her everywhere.

She was doomed. She'd never be ready in time for the interrogation the council had planned. Venera rolled over, cried into her pillow, and finally just lay there, accepting her fate. The bullet had defeated her.

With that understanding came a kind of peace, but she was in too much pain to analyze it. She just lay there, dry-eyed, frowning, until sleep overcame her.

10

"WHAT IS *THIS?*" Jacoby Sarto glared at the rickshaws clustering in the courtyard below the Buridan estate's newly rebuilt entrance. It was seven P.M. and Candesce was extinguishing itself, its amber glories drenching the building tops. Down in the purpled courtyard the upstart princess's new footmen were lighting lanterns to guide in dozens of carts and palanquins from the crowded alley.

Someone of a minor noble nation had heard him and turned, smirking. "You didn't receive an invitation?" asked the impertinent youth. "It's a gala reception!"

"Bah!" Sarto turned to his companion, the duke of Ennersin. "What is she up to? This is a feeding frenzy. I'll wager half these people have come to gawk at the legendary Buridans, and the other half to watch us drag her out of the place in chains. What does she gain out of such a spectacle?"

"I'm afraid we'll find out shortly," said the duke. He was as stocky as Sarto, with similarly graying temples and the sort of paternal scowl that could freeze the blood of anyone under forty. Together the two men radiated gravitas to such an extent that the crowds automatically parted for them. True, most of those assembling here knew them, by sight and reputation at least. The nations of Sacrus and Ennersin were feared and respected by all. —All, it seemed, save for newly reborn Buridan.

These two were here tonight to make sure that this new situation didn't last.

"In any case, such entertainments as this are rare, Jacoby. It's sure to attract the curious and the morbid, yes. But it's the third audience that worries me," Duke Ennersin commented as they strode up the steps to the entrance.

Sarto glared at a footman who had the temerity to approach them at the entrance. "What third audience?"

"Do you see the Guineveras there? They've been keeping Buridan's horses for generations. Make no mistake, they'd be happy to be free of the burden—or to own the beasts outright."

"Which they will after tonight."

"I wouldn't be too sure of that," said Ennersin. "Proof that this Amandera Thrace-Guiles is an imposter is not proof that the real heirs aren't out there."

"What are you saying, man? She's been in the tower! Clearly it's empty after all. There are no heirs to be had."

"Not there, no . . . But don't forget there are sixteen nations that claim to be related by blood to the Thrace-Guileses. The moment this Amandera's declared a fake the other pretenders will pounce on the property rights. It'll be a legal free-for-all—maybe even a civil war. Many of these people are here to warn their nations the instant it becomes a possibility."

"Ridiculous!" Sarto forgot what he was going to say next, as they entered the lofting front hall of the Buridan estate.

It smelled of fresh paint and drying plaster. Lanterns and braziers burned along the pillared staircases, lighting a frescoed ceiling crawling with allegorical figures. The painted blues, yellows, and reds were freshly cleaned and vibrant to the point of being nauseating, as were the heroic poses of the men and half-clad women variously hanging off, riding, or being devoured by hundreds of ridiculously posed horses. Sarto gaped at this vision for a while, then shuddered. "The past is sometimes best left buried," he said.

Ennersin chuckled. "Or at least strategically unlit."

Sarto had been expecting chaos inside the estate; after all, nobody had set foot in here in centuries, so Thrace-Guiles's new servants would be unfamiliar with the layout of their own home. They would be a motley collection of rejects and near-criminals hired from the dregs of Lesser Spyre, after all, and he fully expected to see waiters spilling drinks down the decolletage of the ladies when they weren't banging into one another in their haste to please.

There was none of that. Instead, a string quartet played a soothing pavane in the corner, while men and women in black tails and white gloves glided to and fro, gracefully presenting silver platters and unobtrusively refilling casually tilted glasses. The waitstaff were, in fact, almost mesmerizing in their movements; they were better than Sarto's own servants.

"Where did she get this chattel?" he muttered as a man with a stentorian voice announced their arrival. Lady Pamela Anseratte, who had known Sarto for decades and was quite unafraid of him, laughed and trotted over in a swirl of skirts. "Oh, she's a clever one, this Thrace-Guiles," she said, laying her lace-covered hand on Sarto's arm. "She's hired the acrobats of the Spyre Circus to serve drinks! I hear they rehearsed blindfolded."

Indeed, Sarto glanced around and realized there was a young lady with the compact muscled body of a dancer standing at his elbow. She held out a glass. "Champagne?" Automatically, he took it, and she vanished into the crowd without a sound.

"Well, we'll credit the woman with being a genius in domestic matters," he growled. "But surely you haven't been taken in by her act, Pamela? She's an imposter!"

"That's as may be," said the lady with a flick of her fan. "But your imposter has just forgiven Virilio's debt to Buridan. It seems that with interest it would now be worth enough to out-fit a small fleet of merchant ships! And she's just erased it! Here, look! There's August Virilio himself, drinking himself into happy idiocy under that stallion statue."

Sarto stared. The limestone stallion appeared to be sneering over Virilio's shoulder at the small crowd of hangers-on he was holding forth to. He was conspicuously unmasked, like most of the other council representatives. The place was crowded with masked faces, though—some immediately identifiable, others un-familiar even to his experienced eye. "Who are all these people?" he wondered aloud.

"Debtors, apparently," said Lady Pamela with some relish. "And creditors . . . everyone who's taken care of Buridan's affairs or profited by their absence over the past two hundred years. They all look . . . happy, don't you think, Jacoby?"

Ennersin cleared his throat and leaned in to say, "Thrace-Guiles has clearly been doing her homework."

Despite himself, Sarto was impressed. This woman was contin-uing to confound his expectations. Was it possible that she might go on doing so? The thought was unexpected—and nothing un-expected had happened in Jacoby Sarto's life in a very long time.

He resisted where this line of thought led; after all, he had his instructions. Sarto dashed his champagne glass on the floor. Heads turned. "Let her enjoy her little party," he said in his dark-est voice. "Amandera Thrace-Guiles, or whatever her real name is, has about one hour of freedom left.

"And no more than a day to live."

VENERA STRODE THROUGH the crowd, nodding and smiling. She felt unsteady and vulnerable, and though her headache had finally faded she had to rein in an automatic cringe-reaction to bright lights and loud sounds. She felt hideously unready for the evening and had overdressed to compensate. Most of the people in Spyre wore dark colors, so she had chosen to dress in red—her corset was a glossy crimson inset with designs sewn in scarlet thread, with a wide-shouldered, open jacket atop that. She wore a necklace from the Anetene hoard. Her skin was recovering from the burns she'd suffered near Candesce, but the contrasts were still effective. To hide the scar on her chin she'd adopted one of the strange local skullcaps, this one of black feathers. It swept up behind her ears and down to a point in the middle of her forehead, where a single red Anetene gem glowed above her heavily drawn eyebrows—but it also thrust two small wings along her jawline. They tickled her chin annoyingly, but that was a small distraction compared with the sensations that the ankle-length skirt gave her. Dresses and skirts were considered obscene in most of Virga, where one might become weightless at any time. Back home, the prostitutes wore them. Venera wore a pair of breeches under the thing, which made her feel a bit better, but the long heavy drape still moved and turned like it had a mind of its own.

The one spot of white in her apparel was the fan she held before her like a shield. Nobody but Garth would know that its near side was covered with names and family trees, drawn in tiny spiked letters. She hadn't had time to read the complicated genealogies and financial records of Buridan and its dependents; this fan was her lifeline.

As she recovered from her migraine in the last day or so, the reconstruction work had caught up and the servants learned where everything was. To her relief Garth had orchestrated the ball without supervision, making sometimes brilliant decisions. Twenty years of pent-up social appetite, she supposed. The estate's pantries had been cleared of rats and spiders and re-stocked; the ancient plumbing system had been largely replaced (not without messy accidents) and the gas lines to the stoves re-connected.

In a way, she was grateful for having been distracted these past few days. This afternoon she'd had a brief moment with nothing to do, and into her mind had drifted memories of Chaison. Standing in her chambers, her hand half-lifted to her hair, she was suddenly miserable. Pain and anxiety had masked her grief until now.

She had to battle through it all—play her part. So now she marched up to a tight knot of masked nobles from the mysterious nation of Faddeste and bowed. "Welcome to my house. Speaking as someone who has seen few human beings in her life, outside her immediate family, I know how much it must cost you to attend a crowded event such as this."

"We find it . . . hard." The speaker could be a man or a woman, it was impossible to tell. Its accent was so thick she had to puzzle out the words. Tall and thickly robed, this ambassador from a ten-acre nation flicked a finger at the sweeping dancers now beginning to fill up the center of the hall. "Such frivolity should be banned. How are you so calm? Not raised to this, crowd should frighten."

Venera bowed. "I lived in my imagination as a girl." That much was true. "Lacking real people to talk to, I invented a whole court—a whole nation!—who followed me everywhere. I was never alone. So perhaps this isn't so strange for me."

"Doubtful. We don't believe you are of Buridan."

"Hmm. I could say the same—how do I know you're really from Faddeste?"

"Sacrilege!" But the robed figure didn't turn away.

"Whether either of us is who we say we are," said Venera

with a smug smile, "it remains a fact that Buridan owes Faddeste twenty thousand Spyre sovereigns. Imposter or not, I am willing to repay that debt."

Now she stepped in close, raising one black eyebrow and glancing around at the crowd. "Do you trust the pretenders in the crowd to do the same, if they acquire the title to Buridan? Think hard on that."

The ambassador reared back as though afraid Venera would touch it. "You have money?"

"Go see Master Flance." She pointed at Garth who, despite being masked, had characteristically surrounded himself with women young and old. All were laughing at some story he was telling. Seeing this, for a moment Venera forgot her worries and felt a pulse of warmth for the aging dandy. She turned back to the Faddestes, but they were already maneuvering across the dance floor like a frightened but determined flock of crows.

She blew out a held breath. Seven or eight more minor nations to bribe, and no time to do it. All the members of the Spyre council were here now, some clustered in little groups talking and pointing at her. It would all be decided soon, one way or another.

Before she could reach her next target a majordomo in the livery of the Spyre Council approached and bowed. "They are ready for you upstairs, madam," he said coolly.

She kept her gaze fixed on the top of his head as she bowed in return. All eyes were on her, she was certain. This was the moment when all would be decided.

As she clattered up the marble steps she tried to remember the lines and gambits she had crammed into her head over the past day or so. It hadn't been enough time, and the hangover of her migraine had interfered. She was not ready; she just had herself, the passing lanterns, the looming shadows above, and the single rectangle of light from a pair of doors in the upstairs hall. She told herself to slow down, control her breathing, count to ten—but finally just cursed and strode down the newly laid crimson carpet to pivot on one heel and step into the room.

Jacoby Sarto's leonine features crinkled into something like a smirk as he saw her. He was placing the final chair behind the long conference table in the high-ceilinged minor reception hall. Damn him, he'd moved everything! Where Venera had contrived a single long table with chairs along two sides, with her at the end, Sarto had turned the table sideways, crammed all the seats on one side of it (behind it, now), and left one solitary chair in the center of the carpet. What had been a conference room was now a court, with her as the defendant.

The rest of the council were standing around behind Sarto as the servants finished the new placement.

She had an overwhelming urge to pick a seat behind the table and put her feet up, then point to the solitary position and ask, "Who sits there?" Only memory of how badly her recent outbursts had gone stopped her.

Well, he had won this round, but she wasn't going to let him revel in it. Venera stopped one of the servants and said, "Bring me a side table, and a bottle of wine and a glass. Some cheese might be good too." She sat graciously in the exposed chair and draped her skirts as she'd seen the other ladies do. Then she locked eyes with Sarto and smiled.

The others began to take their places. There were twelve of them. Jacoby Sarto of Sacrus, who was rumored to be merely an errand boy to the true heads of the family, sat on the far left. The arch-conservative duke Ennersin, who had conspicuously arrived with Sarto, sat next to him, frowning in disapproval at Venera. She could count on those two to oppose her confirmation. Of the others . . .

Pamela Anseratte was smiling at something, but wouldn't meet Venera's eye. Principe Guinevera *was* trying to meet her eye and apparently attempting to wink; he took up two spaces at the table and his fleshy hands were planted on the tabletop as if he were, at any second, about to leap to his feet and proclaim something. Next to him sat August Virilio, who looked contented, half-asleep even—and probably was, after the heroic drinking he'd gotten up to after she forgave his nation's debt. These three were on her side—or so she hoped.

The other great families were represented by minor members and, in three cases, by ambassadors. Two of the ambassadors were cloaked and masked; the families in question, Garrat and Oxorn, were mysterious, isolate, and paranoid as only the ancients of Greater Spyre could be. Nobody knew what their nations produced—only that it went for fabulous prices and threat of death on exposure in the outside world.

Three out of twelve for sure. Maybe three others if her reckless divestment of Buridan's wealth had done what she hoped. But it was a big if. She was going to need every ounce of cunning and every resource to get through the evening free and intact.

The council all sat and waited while Venera's new servants placed decanters of wine and tall glasses on the table. Then Pamela Anseratte stood and smiled around the table. "Welcome, everyone. I trust the nations are well and that the hospitality of our host has been sampled and appreciated by all? Yes? Then let's begin. We're gathered here tonight to decide whether to reinstate Buridan as an active nation, in the person of the woman who here claims to be Amandera Thrace-Guiles, heir of said nation. I—"

"Why are you alone?" Duke Ennersin was speaking directly to Venera. "Why are we to take this one person's word for who she is? Where is the rest of her nation? Why has she appeared here, now, after an absence of centuries?"

"Yes, yes, we're going to get to those questions," soothed Lady Anseratte. "First, however, we have some formalities to clear away. Amandera Thrace-Guiles's claim is pointless and instantly void if she cannot produce documents indicating her paternity and ancestry, as well as the notarized deeds and titles of her nation, plus the key." She beamed at Venera. "You have all those things?"

Silently, Venera rose and walked to the table. She placed the thick sheaf of papers she'd brought in front of Anseratte. Then she unscrewed the heavy signet ring from her finger and placed it atop the stack.

This was her opening move, but she couldn't count on its effect.

"I see," said Lady Anseratte. "May I examine the ring?" Venera nodded, returning to her seat. Lady Anseratte took a flat box with some lights on it and hovered it over the ring. The box glowed and made a musical bonging sound.

"Duly authenticated," said the lady. She carefully placed the ring to one side and opened the sheaf. Many of its contents were genuine. Venera had found the deeds and titles in the tower. It had been the work of several careful days to extend the family tree by several centuries and insert herself at its end. She had intended to use her own not-inconsiderable talents at forgery but had been indisposed, and Garth had come through, displaying surprising skills. He was not just a gigolo in his previous life, evidently. As the papers were passed up and down the table Venera kept a bland expression on her face. She tried the wine and adjusted the fall of her skirt again.

"Convincing," said Jacoby Sarto after flipping through the papers. "But just because something is convincing that doesn't mean it's true. It's merely convincing. What can you do to establish the truth of your claim?"

Venera tilted her head to one side. "It would be impossible to do so to everyone's satisfaction, sir, just as it would be impossible for you to prove that you are, without doubt, Jacoby Sarto of Nation Sacrus. I rather think the onus is on this council to disprove my claim, if they can."

August Virilio opened one eye slightly. "Why don't we start with your story? I always like a good story after supper."

"Excellent idea," said Pamela Anseratte. "Duke Ennersin asked why it is that you are here before us now, of all times. Can you explain why your nation has hidden away so thoroughly for so long?"

Venera actually knew the answer to that one—it had been written in the contorted bodies of the soldiers inside the tower, and in the scrawled final confessions of the dead woman in the bedchamber.

Steepling her hands, Venera smiled directly at Jacoby Sarto and said, "The answer is simple. We knew that if we left Buridan Tower, we would be killed."

This was gambit number two.

The council members expressed various shades of surprise, shock, and satisfaction at her revelation. Jacoby Sarto crossed his arms and sat back. "Who would do this?" asked Anseratte. She was still standing and now leaned forward over the table.

"The isolation of Buridan Tower wasn't an accident," said Venera. "Or, at least, not entirely. It was the result of an attack— and the attackers were two of the great nations present at this table tonight."

August Virilio smiled sleepily, but Principe Guinevera leapt to his feet, knocking his chair over. "*Who?*" he raged. "Name them, fair lady, and we will see justice done!"

"I did not come here to open old wounds," said Venera. "Although I recognize that my position here is perilous, I had no choice but to leave the tower. Everyone else there is dead—save myself and my manservant. Some bird-borne illness took the last five of our people a month ago. I consigned their bodies to the winds of Virga, as we have been doing for centuries now. Before that we were dwindling, despite careful and sometimes repugnant breeding restrictions and constant austerity. . . . We lived on birds and airfish we caught with nets, and supplemented our diets with vegetables we grew in the abandoned bedrooms of our ancestors. Had I died in that place, then our enemies would truly have won. I chose a last throw of the die and came here."

"But the war of which you speak . . . it was centuries ago," said Lady Anseratte. "Why did you suppose that you would still be targeted after so long?"

Venera shrugged. "We had telescopes. We could see that our enemies' nations were thriving. And we could also clearly see that sentries armed with machine guns ringed the tower. I was raised to believe that if we entered the elevator and tried to reach Lesser Spyre, those machine gunners would destroy us before we rose more than a hundred meters."

"Oh, no!" Guinevera looked acutely distressed. "The sentries were there for your protection, madam! They were to keep interlopers out, not to box you in!"

"Well." Venera looked down. "Father thought so, but he also said that we were so reduced that we could not risk a single soul to find out. And isolation . . . becomes a habit." She looked pointedly at the ambassadors of Oxorn and Garrat.

Sarto guffawed loudly. "Oh, come on! What about the dozens of attempts that have been made to contact the tower? Semaphore, loudspeakers, smoke signals, for God's sake. They've all been tried and nobody ever responded."

"I am not aware that anyone has tried to contact us during my lifetime," said Venera. This was true, as she'd learned in the past days. Sarto would have to concede the point. "And I can't speak to my ancestors' motives for staying silent."

"That's as may be," Sarto continued. "Look, I'll play it straight. Sacrus was involved in the original atrocity." He held up a hand when Guinevera protested loudly. "But gentlemen and ladies, that was centuries ago. We are prepared to admit our crime and make reparations to the council when this woman is exposed for the fraud that she is."

"And if she's not?" asked Guinevera angrily.

"Then to the nation of Buridan directly," said Sarto. "I just wanted to clear the air. We can't name our coconspirators because, after all this time, the records have been lost. But having admitted our part in the affair, and having proposed that we pay reparations, I can now continue to oppose this woman's claim without any appearance of conflict."

Venera frowned. Her second gambit had failed.

If Sacrus had wanted to keep their involvement a secret, she might have had leverage over Sarto. Maybe even enough to swing his vote. As it was he'd adroitly sidestepped the trap.

Lady Anseratte looked up and down the table. "Is the other conspirator's nation similarly honorable? Will they admit their part?" There was a long and uncomfortable silence.

"Well, then," said Pamela Anseratte. "Let us examine the details of your inheritances."

From here the interview deteriorated into minutiae as the council members pulled out individual documents and points of law and debated them endlessly. Venera was tired, and every time she blinked to clear her vision, she worried that a new migraine might be reaching to crush her. Pamela Anseratte conducted the meeting as if she had boundless energy, but

Venera—and everyone else—wilted under the onslaught of detail.

Sarto used sarcasm, wit, guile, and bureaucracy to try to torpedo her claim, but after several hours it became clear that he wasn't making headway. Venera perked up a bit. *I could win this,* she realized—simultaneously realizing just how certain she'd been that she wouldn't.

Finally Lady Anseratte said "Any further points?" and nobody answered. "Well," she said brightly, "we might as well proceed to a vote."

"Hang on," said Sarto. He stood heavily. "I've got something to say." Everyone waited.

"This woman is a fraud. We all know it. It's inconceivable that this family could have sustained themselves and their retainers for centuries within a single tower, cut off from the outside world—"

"Not inconceivable," said the ambassador of Oxorn from behind her griffin mask. "Quite possible."

Sarto glared at her. "What did they do for clothes? For even the tiniest item of utility, such as forks or pens? Do you really believe they have an entire industrial base squirreled away in that tower?" He shook his head.

"It's equally inconceivable that someone raised in such total isolation should, upon being dropped into society and all its machinations, conduct herself like a veteran! Did she rehearse social banter with her *dolls?* Did she learn to dance with her rocking horse? It's preposterous on the face of it.

"And we all know why her claim has any chance of success. It's because she's bought off everyone who might oppose it. Buridan has tremendous assets—estates, ships, buildings, and industries here and on Greater Spyre that have been administered by other nations in absentia, for generations. She's promised to give those nations the assets they've tended! For the rest, she's proposing to beggar Buridan by paying all its debts here and now. When she's done Buridan will have nothing to its name but a herd of gangly equines."

"And this house," said Venera primly. "I don't propose to give that up." There was some stifled laughter around the table.

"It's a transparent fraud!" Sarto turned to glare at the other council members. "Forget about the formal details of her claim— in fact, let it be read that there's nothing to criticize about it. That doesn't matter. We all know the truth. She is insulting the name of a great nation of Spyre! Do you actually propose to let her get away with it?"

He was winning them over. Venera had one last hand to play, and it was her weakest. She stood up.

"Then who am I?" She strode up to the table and leaned across it to look Sarto in the eye. "If I'm a fraud I must have come from somewhere. Was I manufactured by one of the other nations, then? If so, which one? Spyre is secretive, but not so much so that we don't all keep tabs on one another's genealogies. Nobody's missing from the rosters, are they?

"And yet!" She turned to address the rest of the council. "Gaze upon me and tell me to my face that you don't believe I am noble born." She sneered at Sarto. "It's evident in my every gesture, in how I speak, how I address the servants. Jacoby Sarto says that he knows I am a fraud. Yet you know I am a peer!

"So then where did I come from?" She turned to Sarto again. "If Jacoby Sarto believes I did not come from Buridan Tower, then he must have some idea of where I did. What do you know, Sir Sarto, that you're not telling the rest of us? Do you have some proof that you're not sharing? A name, perhaps?"

He opened his mouth—and hesitated.

They locked eyes and she saw him realize what she was willing to do. The key to Candesce was almost visible in the air between them; it was the real subject of tonight's deliberations.

"Sacrus has many secrets, as we've seen tonight," she said quietly. "Is there some further secret you have, Sir Sarto, that you wish to share with the council? A name, perhaps? One that might be recognized by the others present? A name that could be tied to recent events, to rumors and legends that have percolated through the principalities in recent weeks?" She saw puzzled frowns on several faces—and Sarto's eyes widened as he heard her tread the edge of the one revelation Sacrus did not want made public.

He looked down. "Perhaps I went too far in my accusations," he said almost inaudibly. "I retract my statements."

Duke Ennersin leaned back in his chair, open-mouthed. And Jacoby Sarto meekly sat down.

Venera returned to her seat. *If I lose, everyone learns that you have the key,* she thought as she settled herself on the velvet cushion. She took a sip of wine and kept her expression neutral as Pamela Anseratte stood again.

"Well," said the lady in a cautious tone, "if there are no more outbursts . . . let us put it to a vote."

Venera couldn't help but lean forward a bit.

"All those who favor this young lady's claim, and who wish to recognize the return of Buridan to Spyre and to this council, raise your right hand."

Guinevera's hand shot up. Beside him, August Virilio languidly pushed his into the air. Pamela Anseratte raised her own hand.

Oxorn's hand went up. Then, Garrat's ambassador raised his.

That made five. Venera let out the breath she'd been keeping. It was over. She had failed—

Jacoby Sarto raised his hand.

His expression was exquisite—a mixture of distaste and resignation that you might see in a man who's just volunteered to dig up a grave. Duke Ennersin was staring at him in total disbelief and slowly turning purple.

Lady Anseratte's only show of surprise was a minute frown. "All those opposed?" she said.

Ennersin threw his hand in the air. Five others went up.

"And no abstentions," said Anseratte. "We appear to have a tie."

Jacoby Sarto slumped back in his chair. "Well, then," he said quietly. "I move we take the matter to the council investigative team. Let them visit the tower and conduct a thorough—"

"*Don't I get a vote?*"

They all turned to stare at Venera. She sat up straighter, clearing her throat. "Well, it seems to me . . ." She shrugged. "It's just that this meeting was called to confirm my identity and claim to being head of Buridan. Confirmation implies a presumption that I am who I say I am. I *am* Buridan unless proven otherwise. And Buridan is a member of the council. So I should have a vote."

"This is outrageous!" Duke Ennersin had had enough. He threw back his chair and stalked around the table. "You have the temerity to suggest that you—"

"She's right."

The voice was quiet and languid, almost indifferent—but it stopped Ennersin in his tracks. His head ratcheted around slowly, as if pulled by unwilling forces to look at the man who had spoken.

August Virilio was lounging back in his chair, his hands steepled in front of him. "Article five, section twelve, paragraph two of the charter," he said in a reasonable tone. "Identity is presumptive if there is no other proven heir. And Buridan is a member of the council. Its title was never suspended."

"A mere formality! A courtesy!" But Ennersin's voice had lost its certainty. He appealed to Pamela Anseratte, but she simply spread her hands and smiled.

Then, looking around him at Venera, she said, "It appears you are right, dear. You do get a vote. Would you care to . . . ?"

Venera smiled and raised her right hand. "I vote in favor," she said.

SHE WAS SURE you could hear Ennersin outside and down the street. Venera smiled as she shepherded her guests to the door. She was delirious with relief and was sure it showed in her ridiculous grin. Her soiree was winding down, though naturally the doors and lounges would be open all night for any stragglers. But the council members were tired; no one would criticize them for leaving early.

Ennersin was yelling at Jacoby Sarto. It was music to Venera's ears.

She looked for Garth but couldn't see him at first. Then—there he was, sidling in the entrance. He'd changed to inconspicuous street clothes. Had he been preparing to sneak away? Venera pictured him leaving through the wine cellar exit to avoid the council's troops. Then he could have circled around to stand with the street rabble who were waiting to hear the results of the vote. She smiled; it was what she might have done.

There went Ennersin, sweeping by Garth without noticing him. Diamandis watched him go in distaste, then turned and saw Venera watching him. He spread his hands and shrugged. She made a dismissive gesture and smiled back.

Time to mingle; the party wasn't over yet and her head felt fine. It felt good to reinforce her win with a gracious turn about the room. For a while everything was a blur of smiling faces and congratulations. Then she found herself shaking someone's hand (the hundredth, it must have been) and looked up to find it was Jacoby Sarto's.

"Well played, Ms. Fanning," he said. There was no irony in his voice.

She glanced around. They were miraculously alone for the moment. Probably a single glance from under Sarto's wiry brows had been enough to clear a circle.

All she could think of to say was, "Thank you." It struck her as hopelessly inadequate for the situation, but all her strategies had been played out. To her surprise, Sarto smiled.

"I've lost Ennersin's confidence," he said. "It's going to take me years to regain some allies I abandoned today."

"Oh?" The mystery of his reversal during the vote deepened. Not one to prevaricate, Venera said, "Why?"

He appeared puzzled. "Why did I vote for you?"

"No—I know why." The key was again unspoken-of between them. "I mean," she said, "why did you come out so publicly against me in the first place, if you knew I had that to hang over you?"

"Ah." It was his turn to look around them. Satisfied that no one was within earshot, he said, "I was entrusted with the safety of Sacrus's assets. You're considered one of them. If I could acquire you, I was to do that. If not, and you threatened to reveal . . . certain details . . . well, I was to contrive a murderous rage." He opened his jacket slightly and she saw the large pistol he had holstered there. "You would not have had a chance to say what you know," he said with a slight smile.

"So why didn't you . . ."

"It is useful to have an acknowledged heir of Buridan controlling that estate. This way we avoid a nasty succession conflict, which Sacrus would view as an unnecessary . . . distraction, right now. Besides." Sarto shrugged. "There are few moments in a man's life when he has the opportunity to make a choice on his own. I simply did not want to shoot you."

"And why tell me this now?"

His mouth didn't change from its accustomed frown, but the lines around Sarto's eyes might have crinkled a little bit—an almost-smile.

"It will be easy for me to tell my masters that the pistol was taken from me at your door," he said. "Without an opportunity to acquire or silence you, letting you win was the expedient option. My masters know that." He turned away, then looked back with a scowl. "I hope you won't give me reason to regret my decision."

"Surely not. And my apologies for inconveniencing you."

He laughed at the edge in her voice.

"You may think you're free," he said as the crowd parted to let him through, "but Sacrus still owns you. Never forget that."

Venera kept her smile bright, but his parting words worried at her for the rest of the evening.

11

MUSCLES ACHING, VENERA swung down from the saddle of her horse. It was two weeks since the confirmation and she had lost no time in establishing her rule over Buridan—which, she had decided, had to include becoming a master rider.

She'd knocked down two walls and sealed up the ends of one of the high-ceilinged cellar corridors, forming one long narrow room where her steed could trot. There were stalls at one end of this, and two workmen were industriously scattering straw and sand over the flagstones. "Deeper," Venera told them. "We need several inches of it everywhere."

"Yes, ma'am." The men seemed unusually enthusiastic and focused on their task. Maybe they had heard that the new foals were to arrive later today. Probably it was just being in proximity with the one horse now residing here. Venera hadn't yet met anyone who didn't share that strange, apparently ancient love for horses that seemed inbuilt in humans.

Venera herself wasn't immune to it. She patted Domenico and walked down the length of the long room, trailing one hand along the low fence that bisected it lengthwise. Her horsemaster stood at the far end, a clipboard clutched in his hand; he was arguing quietly with someone. "Is everything all right, gentlemen?" Venera asked.

The other man turned, lamplight slanting across his gnomish features, and Venera said "Oh!" before she could stop herself.

Samson Odess screwed his fishlike face up into a smile and practically lunged over to shake her hand.

"I'm honored to meet you, Lady Amandera Thrace-Guiles!" His eyes betrayed no recognition, and Venera realized that she was standing in heavy shadow. "Liris is honored to offer you some land to stable your horses. You see, we're diversifying and—"

She grinned weakly. It was too soon for this! She had hoped that the men and women of Liris would be consumed by their own internal matters, at least long enough for her new identity to become fixed. If Odess recognized her the news would be bound to percolate through the Fair. She didn't believe in its vaunted secrecy any more than she believed that good always triumphed.

She let go of Odess's hand before he could get entirely into his sales pitch, and turned away. "Charmed I'm sure. Flance! Can you deal with this?"

"Oh, but Master Flance was unable to resolve one little matter," said the horsemaster, stepping around Odess.

"Deal with it!" she snarled. She glimpsed a startled look in Odess's eye before she swept by the two men and into the outer hallway.

Well, *that* had been an unexpected surge of adrenaline! She laughed at herself as she strode quickly through the vaulted, whitewashed spaces. In the half-minute it took her to slow down to a stroll, Venera took several turns and ended up in an area of the cellars she didn't know.

Someone cleared their throat. Venera turned to find a man in servant's livery approaching. He looked only vaguely familiar but that was hardly surprising, considering the number of people she'd hired recently.

"Ma'am, this area hasn't been cleaned up yet. Are you looking for something in particular?"

"No. I'm lost. Where did you just come from?"

"This way." The man walked back the way they had both come. He was right about the state of the cellars; this passage hadn't been reconstructed and was only minimally cleaned. Black portraits still hung on the walls, here and there an eye glaring out from behind centuries of dust and soot. The lanterns were widely spaced and a few men visible down a side way were reduced to silhouettes, their backdrop some bright distant doors.

"Down this way." Her guide indicated a black stairwell Venera hadn't seen before. Narrow and unlit, it plummeted steeply down.

Venera stopped. "What the—" Then she saw the pistol in his hand.

"Move," grated the man. "Now."

She almost called his bluff. One of those quick sidesteps Chaison had taught her, then a foot sweep . . . he would be on the floor before he knew it. But she hesitated just long enough for him to step out of reach. Caught unprepared for once, Venera stumbled into the blackness with him behind her.

"YOU'RE IN A lot of trouble," she said.

"We're not afraid of the authorities." said her kidnapper contemptuously.

"I'm not talking about the authorities. I'm talking about *me*." The stairs had ended on a narrow shelf above an indistinct, dark body of water. It was dank and cold down here; looking left and right she saw that she was standing on the edge of a large tank—a cistern, no doubt.

"We've been watching you," said the shadowy figure behind

her. "I assure you we know what you're capable of." The pistol was in her back again and he was pushing her hard enough that she had trouble keeping her feet. Angrily she hurried ahead and emerged onto the flagstones next to the water. "I didn't know I had this," she commented as she turned right, toward the source of the light.

"It's not yours. This is part of the municipal water supply," said a half-familiar voice up ahead.

She eyed the black depths. Jump in? There might be a culvert she could swim through, the way heroes did in romance novels. Those heroes never drowned in the dark, though, and besides, even if she made it out of here her appearance, soaking wet, in the streets of the city was bound to cause a scandal. She did not need that right now.

There was an open area at the far end of the tank. The same tables and crates she'd seen in the wine cellar were set up here, and the same young revolutionaries were sitting on them. Standing next to a lantern-lit desk was the youth with straight black hair and oval eyes. He was dressed in the long coat and tails she'd seen fashionable men wearing on the streets of the wheel; with his arms crossed the coat belled out enough for her to see the two pistols holstered at his waist. She was suddenly reminded of Garth's apparel, which was like a down-at-heel version of the same costume.

"What's the meaning of this?" she snapped, even as she counted people and exits (there was one of the latter, a closed iron door). "You're not being very neighborly," she added more softly.

"Sit her down and tie her up," said the black-haired youth. He had a high tenor voice, not unmanly but refined, his words very precise. His eyes were gray and cold.

"Yes, Bryce." The man who'd led her here sat her down on a

stout wooden chair next to the table and, pulling her arms back, proceeded to tie a clumsy knot around her wrists.

Venera craned her neck to look back. "You obviously don't do this much," she said. Then, spearing this Bryce fellow with a sharp eye, she added, "Kidnapping is precision work. You people don't strike me as being organized enough to pull it off."

Bryce's eyebrows shot up, that same look of surprise he'd shown in the cellar. "If you'd been following our escapades you'd know what we're capable of."

"Bombing innocent crowds, yes," she said acidly. "Hero's work, that."

He shrugged, but looked uncomfortable. "That one was meant for the committee members," he admitted. "It fell back and killed the man who threw it. That *was* a soldier's death."

She nodded. "Like most soldiers' deaths, painfully unnecessary. What do you want?"

Bryce spun another chair around and sat down in it, folding his arms over its back. "We intend to bring down the great nations," he said simply.

Venera considered how to reply. After a moment she said, "How can kidnapping me get you any closer to doing that? I'm an outsider; I'm sure nobody cares much whether I live or die. And nobody will ransom me."

"True," he agreed with a shrug. "But if you go missing, you'll soon be declared a fraud and the title to Buridan will go up for grabs. It'll be a free-for-all, and we intend to make sure that it starts a civil war."

As plans went, it struck Venera as eminently practical—but this was not a good time to be smiling and nodding.

She thought for a while. All she could hear was the slow drip, drip of water from rusted ceiling pipes; doubtless no one would hear any cries for help. "I suppose you've been following my story," she said eventually. "Do you believe that I'm Amandera Thrace-Guiles, heir of Buridan?"

He waved a hand negligently. "Couldn't care less. Actually, I think you are an imposter, but why does it matter? You'll soon be out of the picture."

"But what if I *am* an imposter?" She watched his face closely as she spoke. "Where do you suppose I came from?"

Now he looked puzzled. "Here . . . but your accent is foreign. Are you from outside Spyre?"

She nodded. "Outside Spyre, and consequently I have no loyalty for any of the factions here. But I do have one thing—I've come into a great deal of money and influence, using my own wits."

He leaned back, laughing. "So what are you saying?" he asked. "That you're a sympathizer? More like an opportunist; so why should I have anything but contempt for that?"

"Because this power . . . is only a means to an end," she said. "I'm not interested in who governs or even who ends up with the money I've gained. I have my own agenda."

He snorted. "How vague and intriguing. Well, I'm sure I can't help you with this ill-defined 'agenda.' We're only interested in people who *believe*. People who know that there's another way to govern than the tyrannies we have here. I'm talking about emergent government, which you as a barbarian have probably never even heard of."

"Emergent?" Now it was Venera's turn to be startled. "That's just a myth. Government emerging spontaneously as a property of people's interactions . . . it doesn't work."

"Oh, but it does." He fished inside his jacket and came out with a small, heavily worn black book. "This is the proof. And the key to bringing it back." He held the book up for her to see; with her limited mobility, Venera could just make out the title: *Rights Currencies, 29th Edition.*

"It's the manual," he said. "The original manual, taken from the secret libraries of one of the great nations. This book explains how currency-based emergent government works and provides an example." He opened the book and withdrew several tightly folded bills. These he unfolded on the table where she could see them. "People have always had codes of conduct," said Bryce as he stared lovingly at the money, "but they were originally put together hit-or-miss, with anecdotal evidence to back them up, and using armies and policemen to enforce them. This is a system based on the human habit of buying and selling—only you can't use this money to buy *things.* Each bill stands for a particular *right.*"

She leaned over to see. One pink rectangle had the word JUDGEMENT printed on it above two columns of tiny words. "The text shows which other bills you can trade this one for," said Bryce helpfully. "On the flip side is a description of what you can do if you've got it. This one lets you try court cases if you've also got some other types of bill, but you have to trade this one to judge a trial. The idea is you can only sell it to someone who doesn't have the correct combination to judge and hopefully whoever they sell it to sells it back to you. So the system's not static; it has to be sustained through continual transactions."

She looked at another bill. It said GET OUT OF JAIL FREE. The book Bryce was holding, if it was genuine, was priceless. People had been looking for these lost principles for longer than they'd been trying to find the last key to Candesce. Venera had never believed they really existed.

Pointedly, she shrugged. "So?"

The young revolutionary snatched up the bills. "Currencies

like this can't just be *made*," he proclaimed, exhibiting a certain youthful zeal that she would have found endearing in other circumstances. "The rights, the classifications, number of denominations, who you can trade to—all of those details have to be calculated with the use of massive simulations of whole human societies. Simulate the society in a computing machine, and test different interactions . . . then compile a list of ratios and relations between the bills. Put them in circulation, and an ordered society emerges from the transactions—without institutions getting in the way. Simple."

"Right," said Venera. "And I'm betting that this book wasn't designed for a world like Virga, was it? Isn't this a set of rules for people who live on a flat world—a 'planet'? The legend says that's why the emergent systems were lost, because their rules didn't apply here."

"Not the old ratios, it's true," he admitted. "But the core bills . . . they're sound. You can at least use them to minimize your institutions even if you can't eliminate them completely. We intend to prove it, starting here."

"Well, that's very ambitious." Venera suddenly noticed the way he was looking at her. She was tied with her arms back and her breasts thrust at this young man and he was obviously enjoying her predicament. For the first time since being brought down here, she found herself genuinely off-balance.

She struggled to regain her line of thought. "Anyway, this is all beside the point. Which is, that I am in a greater position to help you as a free woman than as a social pariah—or dead. After all, this civil war of yours probably won't happen. As you say, the great nations have too big a stake in stability. And if it doesn't happen, then what? It's back to the drawing board, minus one hideout for you. Back to bombing and other ineffectual terrorist tactics."

Bryce closed the book and restored it to his jacket. "What of it? We've already lost this place. If the war doesn't happen there's no downside."

"But consider what you could do if you had an ally—a patroness—with wealth and resources, and more experience than you in covert activities." She looked him straight in the eye. "I've killed a number of men in my time. I've built and run my own spy organization. —No, I'm not Amandera Thrace-Guiles. I'm someone infinitely more capable than a mere heir to a backward nation on this backward little wheel. And with power, and wealth, and influence . . . I can help you."

"No deal." He stood up and gestured to the others to follow him as he walked to the metal door.

"A printing press!" she called after him. He looked back, puzzled. "In order for that money to work," she continued, "don't you need to mint thousands of copies of the bills and put them into circulation? It has to be used by everybody to work, right? So where's your printing press?"

He glanced at his people. "It'll happen."

"Oh? What if I offered you your own mint—delivery of the presses in a month—as well as a solid budget to print your money?"

Bryce appeared to think about it, then reached for the door handle.

"And what if you had an impregnable place to house the press?" she called, frantically reaching for the only other thing she could think to offer. "*What if Buridan Tower was yours?*"

One of his lieutenants put a hand on Bryce's arm. He glared at the man, then made a sour face and turned. "Why on Spyre would we trust you to keep your end of the bargain?"

"The tower contains proof that I'm an imposter," she said

quickly. "The council is going to want to visit it, I'm sure of it—but how can I clean it up and make it presentable? None of my new servants could be trusted with the secret. But you could—and you could take photographs, do what you need to do to assemble proof that I'm not the heir. So you'll have that to hold over me. You'll have the tower, you'll have money, and as much influence as I can spare for you."

He was thinking about it, she could tell—and the others were impressed as well. "Best of all," she added before he could change his mind, "if my deception is ultimately revealed, you may get your civil war anyway. What could be better?"

Bryce walked slowly back to her. "Again I say, why should we trust you? If there's proof as you say in Buridan Tower . . . if you'd even let us get there before the police descended on us . . . Too many ifs, Ms. Thrace-Guiles."

"I'll draft you a note right now," she said. "Made out to the night watch at the elevators, to let your people ride the elevator down to Buridan Tower. You can do it right now and release me after you're sure I'm right."

"And be trapped there when your charade is exposed?"

That was just too much for Venera. "Then forget it, you bastard!" she yelled at him. "Go on, get out! I'm sure you're far too busy playing the romantic revolutionary leader. Go and sacrifice the lives of a few more of your friends to convince the rest of them that you're actually doing something. Oh, and blow up a few women and babies for good measure. I'm sure that'll make you feel better—or start your damned war and kill ten thousand innocents, I don't care! Just get out of my sight!"

Bryce's face darkened with anger, but he didn't move. Finally he stalked over and scowled at her. Venera glared back.

"Bring this woman some paper," he said. "You'll write that

note," he said in a low voice, "and we'll see what we can find in Buridan Tower."

THE STREETS HAD not changed since his childhood. Garth Diamandis strode familiar ways, but after such a long absence it was as if he saw them with new eyes. His town-wheel, officially known as Wheel 3, had been called Hammerlong for centuries. Its riveted iron diameter spanned nearly a mile, and the inside surface on which the buildings were set was nearly half that wide. It had spun for five hundred years. In that time, the layout of Hammerlong's gargoyled buildings had been rearranged—or not where they accommodated stubborn holdouts—dozens of times. New edifices had hiked their buttresses over the shoulders of older ones as the population grew, then shrank, then grew again. The wheel had been fixed, reinforced, rejigged, and thrown out of whack by weight imbalances so often that its constant creaking and groaning was like background music to the citizens who lived there. The smell of rust permeated everything.

With finite space, the citizens of the wheel had jammed new buildings in between existing ones; corkscrewed them inward and outward from the rim; overgrown what was original with the new. Streamlined towers hung like knife blades below the rim, their bottom-most floors straining under nearly two gravities while the stacked apartments overhead converged to shadow the streets and a second layer of avenues, then a third, were built up where weight diminished. Ying-yang stairs, elevator cables, ancient rust-dribbling spokes, and leaking pipes all knotted together at the smoke-wreathed axis. Ships and shuttles clustered there like grazing flies.

Hammerlong seemed designed for skulking and the population did just that. Most were citizens of nations based on Greater

Spyre, after all, so they brought the paranoia of that realm with them to the city. Those born and raised in Hammerlong and the other wheels were more open, but they formed a separate class and had fewer rights in their own towns. Left to their own devices, they cultivated a second economy and culture in the alleys, air shafts, and crawlspaces of the layered city.

Garth was on a third-level street when the full force of nostalgia hit him. He had to stop, his imagination filling in gaps in the crowds that scurried to and fro like so many black-clad ants. He saw the young dandies of his youth, swaggering and hipshot to display their pistols; the young ingenues leaning on their balconies high above, their attention apparently elsewhere. He had walked or run or fled down these ways dozens of times.

Some of his old compatriots were dead, he knew, some had moved on to build prosperous families and deny their youths. Others . . . the prisons were still full, one of Venera Fanning's new carpenters had told him this morning. And, if one knew where to look, and how to read . . . there, yes, he saw a thin scrawl of graffiti on a wall ten feet beyond the parapet. Made with chalk, it was barely visible unless you knew to look for it. REPEAL EDICT 1, said the spiky letters.

Garth smiled. Ah, the naivete of youth! Edict 1 had been passed so long ago that most citizens of Spyre didn't even know it existed, nor would they have understood its significance if it were described to them. The hotheaded youth of Spyre were still political, it seemed, and still as incompetent at promoting their politics as in his day. Witness that appalling bomb attack the other day.

The memory chased all sentimentality out of Garth's mind. His mouth set in a stoic frown, he continued on down the street, digging his hands deep into his coat pockets and avoiding the glances of the few women who frequented the walkway. His aching feet carried him to stairs and more stairs, and his knees and hips began to protest at the labor. The last time he'd gone this way he'd been able to run all the way up.

Hundreds of feet above the official street level of Hammerlong, a bridge had been thrown between two buildings back in the carefree Reconstructionist period. Culture and art had flourished here before the time of the preservationists, even before the insular paranoia that had swallowed all the great nations.

The bridge was two stories tall and faced with leaded glass windows that caught the light of Candesce. It wasn't used by occupants of either tower; the forges of one had little use for the papermaking enterprise in the other. For decades, the lofting, sunlit spaces of the bridge had been used by bohemian artists—and the agitators and revolutionaries who loved them.

Garth's heart was pounding as he took the last few steps up a wrought-iron fire escape at the center of the span. He paused to catch his breath next to the wrought-iron curlicues of the door, and listened to the scratchy gramophone music that emanated from it. Then he rapped on the door.

The gramophone stopped. He heard scrambling noises, muffled voices. Then the door cracked open an inch. "Yes?" a man said belligerently.

"Sorry to disturb you," Garth said with a broad smile. "I'm looking for someone."

"Well, they're not here." The door started to close.

Garth laughed richly. "I'm not with the secret police, young pup. I used to live here."

The door hesitated. "I painted this iron about . . . oh, twenty years ago," Garth said, tracing his finger along the curves of metal. "It was rusting out, just like the one in the back bathroom. Do the pipes still knock when you run the water?"

"What do you want?" The voice held a little less harshness.

Garth withdrew his hand from the remembered metal. With difficulty he brought his attention back to the present. "I know she doesn't live here now," he said. "Too much time has passed. But I had to start somewhere and this was the last place we were together. I don't suppose you know . . . any of the former occupants of the place?"

"Just a minute." The door closed, then opened again, widely this time. "Come in." Garth stepped into the sunlit space and was overwhelmed by memory.

The factory planks paving the floor had proven perfect for dancing. He remembered stepping into and out of that parallelogram of sunlight—though there had been a table next to it and he'd banged his hip—while she sang along with the gramophone. That same gramophone sat on a windowsill now, guarded by twin potted orange trees. A mobile of candles and wire turned slowly in the dusty sunlight, entangling his view of the loft behind it. Where he'd slept, and made love, and played his dulcimer for years . . .

"Who are you after?" A young woman with cropped black hair stood before him. She wore a man's clothing and held a tattoo needle loosely in one hand. Another woman sat at the table behind her, shoulder bared and bleeding.

Garth took a deep breath and committed the name to speech for the first time in twenty years. "Her name is Selene. Selene Diamandis . . ."

12

SPYRE WAS AWE inspiring even at a distance of ten miles.
Venera held onto netting in a rear-facing doorway of the passenger liner *Glorious Dawn* and watched the vast blued circle recede in
the distance. First one cloud shot by to obscure a quadrant of
her view, then another, then a small team of them that whirled
slowly in the ship's wake. They chopped Spyre up into frag-
mented images: a curve of green trees here, a glint of window
in some tower (Liris?). Then, instead of clouds, it was blockhouses and barbed wire flicking by. They were passing the
perimeter. She was free.

She turned, facing into the interior of the ship. The velvet-
walled galleries were crowded with passengers, mostly visiting
delegations returning from the Fair. But a few of the men and
women were dressed in the iron and leather of a major nation:
Buridan. Her retainers, maids, the Buridan trade delegation . . .
she wasn't free yet, not until she had found a way to evade all of
them.

Now that she was undisputed head of the nation of Buridan,
Venera had new rights. The right to travel freely, for example; it
had taken only a simple request and a travel visa had been delivered to her the next day. Of course she couldn't simply wave
good-bye and leave. Nobody was fully convinced that she was
who she said she was. So, it had been necessary for her to invent

a pointless trade tour of the principalities to justify this trip. And that in turn meant that she could not be traveling alone.

Still, after weeks of running, of being captured by Liris and made chattel; after run-ins with bombers and bombs, hostile nobility, and mad botanists—after all of that, she had simply boarded a ship and left. Life was never like you imagined it would be.

And she could just keep going, she knew—all the way back to her home in Rush. The idea was tempting, but it wasn't why she had undertaken this expedition. It was too soon to return home. She didn't yet have enough power to undertake the revenge she planned against the Pilot of Slipstream. If she left now it would be as a thief, with only what she could carry to see her home. No, when she finally did leave Spyre, it must be with power at her back.

The only way to get that power was to increase her holdings here, as well as the faith of the people in her. So, like Liris and all the other nations of Spyre, Buridan would visit the outer world to find *customers*.

Her smile faltered as the last of the barbed wire and mines swept by to vanish among the clouds. True, if she just kept going she wouldn't miss anything of Spyre, she mused. Yet even as she thought this Venera experienced a little flash of memory: of Garth Diamandis laughing in sunlight, then of Eilen leaning on a wall after drinking too much at the party.

Last night Venera too had drunk too much wine, with Garth Diamandis. Sitting in a lounge that smelled of fresh paint and plaster, they had listened to the night noises of the house and talked.

"You're not kidding either of us," he'd said. "You're leaving for good. I know that. So let me tell you now, while I can, that you've stripped many years off my shoulders, Lady Venera Fanning. I hope you find your home intact and waiting for you." He toasted her then.

"I'll prove you wrong about me yet," she'd said. "But what about you? When all of this really is finished with, what are you going to do? Fade into the alleys of the town-wheels? Return to your life as a gigolo?"

He shook his head with a smile. "The past is the past. I'm interested in the future. Venera . . . I found her."

Venera had smiled, genuinely happy for him. "Ah. Your mysterious woman. Your prime mover. Well, I'm glad."

He'd nodded vigorously. "She's sent me a letter, telling where and when we can meet. In the morning, you'll head for the docks and your destiny, and I'll be off to the city and mine. So you see, we've both won."

They toasted one another, and Spyre and eventually the whole world before the night became a happy blur.

She kicked off from the ship's netting, almost colliding with one of the crew, and began hauling her way up the corridor to the bow of the ship. One of her new maids fell into formation next to her.

"Is there something wrong, lady?" The maid, Brydda, wrung her hands. Her normally sour face looked even more prudish as she frowned. "Is it leaving Spyre that's upset you so?"

Venera barked a laugh. "It couldn't happen soon enough. No." She kept hand-walking up the rope that led to the bow.

"Can I do anything for you?"

She shot Brydda an appraising look. "You've traveled before, haven't you? You were put onto my staff by the council, I'll bet. To watch me."

"Madam!"

"Oh, don't deny it. Just come with. I need a . . . distraction. You can point out the sights as we go."

"Yes, madam."

They arrived at a forward observation lounge in time for the ship to exit the cloud banks. The *Glorious Dawn* was a typical passenger vessel: a spindle-shaped wooden shell one hundred fifty feet long and forty wide, its surface punctuated with rows of windows and open wickerwork galleries. Big jet nacelles were mounted on short arms at the stern, their whine subdued right now as the ship made a scant fifteen miles per hour through the thinning clouds. The ship's interior was subdivided into staterooms and common areas and contained two big exercise centrifuges. With the engine sound a constant undertone, Venera could easily hear the clink of glassware in the kitchens, muted conversations, and somewhere, a string quartet tuning up. The lounge smelled of coffee and fresh air.

Such a contrast to the *Rook*, the last ship she had flown on. When she'd left it the Slipstream cruiser had stank of unwashed men, stale air, and rocket exhaust. Its hull had been peppered with bullet holes and scorched by explosions. The engines' roar would pierce your dreams as you slept and the only voices were those of arguing, cursing airmen.

The *Glorious Dawn* was just like every vessel she had traveled on prior to the *Rook*. Its luxuries and details were appropriate to one of Venera's station in life; she should be able to put the ship on like a favorite glove. In the normal course of affairs she would never have set foot on a ship like the *Rook*, much less would she have seen it through battle and boarding, pursuit and silent running.

Yet the quiet comforts of the *Glorious Dawn* annoyed her. Venera went right up to the main window of the lounge and peered out. "Tell me where we are," she commanded the maid.

There was distraction to be found in this view. Candesce lay ahead, its brilliance too intense to be looked at directly. Venera well knew that light; it had burned her as she'd fled from its embrace. She shielded her eyes with her hand and looked past it.

She saw the principalities of Candesce. Although she had spent a week in a charcoal-harvester's cabin perched on a burnt arm of the sargasso of Leaf's Choir, that place had been too close to Candesce; the white air cradling the Sun of Suns washed out any details that lay past it. Here, for the first time, she had a clear view of the nations that surrounded that biggest of Virga's artificial lights. And the sight was breathtaking.

Candesce lay at the center of the world, a beacon and a heart to Virga. Anything within a hundred miles of the Sun of Suns simply vanished in flame, a fact that the principalities exploited to dispose of trash, industrial wastes, and the bodies of their dead. This forbidden zone was completely empty, so Venera could see the whole inner surface of the two-hundred-mile-diameter bubble formed by it. On the far side of Candesce that surface was just a smooth speckled gray-green; in the middle distances Venera could make out dots and glitter, and individual beads of leaf color. As she turned to follow the curve of the material toward her the dots became buildings and the glints became the mirrored surfaces of house-sized spheres of water. The beads of green grew filigreed detail and became forests—dozens or hundreds of trees at a time with their roots intertwined around some buried ball of dirt and rocks.

Candesce presided at the center of a cloud of city whose inner extent was two hundred miles in diameter—and whose outer reaches could only be guessed at. The fog of habitations and farms receded into blue dimness, behind lattices of white cloud. Back in the darkening airs a hundred or two hundred miles away, smaller suns glowed.

"These are the principalities," said Brydda, sweeping her arm to take in the sight. "Sixty-four nations, countless millions of people moving at the mercy of Candesce's heat."

Venera glanced at her. "What do you mean by that? 'At the mercy of'?"

The maid looked chagrined. "Well, they can't keep station where they please, the way Spyre does. Spyre is fixed in the air, madam, always has been. But these—" she dismissed the principalities with a wave—"they go where the breezes send them. All that keeps them together as nations is the stability of the circulation patterns."

Venera nodded. The cluster of nations she'd grown up in, Meridian, worked the same way. Candesce's prodigious heat had to go somewhere, and beyond the exclusion zone it must form the air into Hadley cells: semistable up- and downdrafts. You could enter such a cell at the bottom, near Candesce, and be lofted a hundred miles up, then swept horizontally for another hundred miles, then down again until you reached your starting point. The Meridian Hadley cell was huge—a thousand miles across and twice that in depth—and nearly permanent. Down here in the principalities the heat would make the cells less stable, but quicker and stronger.

"So there's one nation per Hadley cell?" she asked. "That seems altogether too well-organized."

The maid laughed. "It's not that simple. The cells break up and merge, but it takes time. Every time Candesce goes into its night-cycle the heat stops going out and the cells falter. Candesce always comes back on in time to start them up again but not without consequence."

Venera understood what she meant by *consequence*. Without predictable airflow, whole countries could break apart, their provinces drifting away from one another, mixing with neighbors and enemies. It had happened often enough in Meridian, where the population was light and obstacles few. Down here, such an event would be catastrophic.

Brydda continued her monologue, pointing out border beacons and other sights of interest. Venera half-listened, musing at something she'd known intellectually but not grasped until this moment. She had been inside—had for one night been in control of—the most powerful device in the word. Whole cities rose and fell in a slow majestic dance driven by Candesce—as did forests, mists of green food crops and isolated buildings, clouds and ships and factories, supply nets a mile across, whale and bird paddocks. Ships and dolphins and ropeways and flapping, foot-finned humans threaded through it all.

She'd had ultimate power in her hands and had let it go without a thought. Strange.

Venera turned her attention back to Brydda. As the *Glorious Dawn* turned, however, she saw that Spyre lay in a kind of dimple in the surface of the bubble. The giant cylinder disrupted the smooth winds of the cells that surrounded it. Wrapped in its own weather, Spyre was an irritant, a mote in the gargantuan orb of the principalities.

"How they must hate you," she murmured.

SLIPSTREAM HAD AN ambassador at the Fitzmann States, an old and respected principality near Spyre. So it was that Buridan's trade delegation made its first stop there.

For two days Venera feted the local wealthy and talked horses—horses as luxury items, horses as tourist draws, as symbols of state power and a connection to the lost origins of Virga. She convinced no one, but since she was hosting the parties, her guests went away entertained and slightly tipsy. The arrangement suited everyone.

There was nothing scheduled for the third morning, and Venera awoke early with a very strange notion in her head.

Leave now.

She could do it. Oh, it would be so simple. She imagined her marriage bed in her chambers in Rush, and a wave of sorrow came over her. She was up and dressed before her thinking caught up to her actions. She hesitated, while Candesce and the rest of the capital town of Fitzmann still slept. She paced in front of her rented apartment's big windows, shaking her head and muttering. Every now and then she would glance out the window at the dark silhouette of the Slipstream ambassador's residence. She need only make it there and claim asylum and Spyre and all its machinations would lie behind her.

Slowly, as if her mind were on something else, she slipped a pistol into her bag and reached for a set of wings inside the closet. At that moment there came a knock on her door.

Venera came to herself, shocked to see what she had been doing. She leaned against the wall for a moment, debating whether to step into the closet and shut herself in it. Then she cursed and walked to the door of the suite. "Who's there?" she asked testily.

"It's Brydda, ma'am. I've a letter for you."

"A letter?" She threw open the door and glared at the maid, who was dressed in a nightgown and clutching a white envelope in one hand. She saw Brydda's eyes widen as she took in Venera's fully dressed state. Venera snatched the letter from her and said, "Lucky thing that I couldn't sleep. But how dare you come to disturb me in the middle of the night over this!"

"I'm sorry!" Brydda curtsied miserably. "The man who delivered it was very insistent that you read it now. He says he needs a signed receipt from you saying you've read it—and he's waiting in the foyer . . ."

Venera flipped the envelope over. The words *Amandera Thrace-Guiles* were written on it. There was no other seal or indication of its origin. Uneasy, Venera retreated into the room. "Wait there a moment." She went over to the writing desk; not seeing a letter opener anywhere handy, she slit the envelope open using the knife she'd been keeping in her vest. Then she unfolded the single sheet under the green desk lamp.

TO: *Venera Fanning*
FROM: ——
SUBJECT: *Master Flance, otherwise known as Garth Diamandis*

We have arrested your accomplice (above-named). As an exiled criminal he has no rights in Greater or Lesser Spyre. If you want him to continue living, you will return immediately to Spyre and await our instructions.

She swore and knocked over the writing desk. The lamp broke and went out. "My lady!" shouted Brydda from the doorway.

"Shut up! Get out! Don't disturb me again!" She slammed the door in the maid's face and began pacing, the letter mangled in her fist.

How dare they! This was obviously Sacrus asserting their hold over her—but in the most clumsy and insulting manner possible. There was a message in their bluntness and it was simple: they had neither the need nor the patience to treat her carefully. She would do as they asked, or they would kill Garth.

Like Garth, they must have thought she was going to run. So why not let her do it? They didn't appear to be concerned that she might alert Slipstream to the theft of the key to Candesce because they had let her get this far. That was odd—or not so odd, when you considered that the leaders of Sacrus must be as insular and decadent as any of the other pocket nations on the wheel. But why not just let her go?

They must have decided that they needed Buridan's stability. She probably shouldn't read too much into the decision. They could just as easily change their minds and have her killed at any moment.

Anyway, the reasons didn't matter. They had Garth—she had no reason to doubt that—and if she didn't return to Spyre immediately, his death would be her fault.

As her initial anger wore off, Venera sat down on a divan and, reaching into her jacket, brought out the bullet that nestled there. She turned it over in her hands for half an hour and then as Candesce began to ignite in the distant sky, she made her decision.

She slid the dagger back into her vest.

She took the wings from inside the closet and stepped into the hallway. Brydda was asleep in a wing chair under a tall leaded-glass window. Venera walked past her to the servant's stairs and headed for the roof.

Gold-touched by the awakening Sun of Suns, she took flight in the high winds and lower gravity of the rooftop.

Venera rose on the air, losing weight rapidly as the wind disengaged her from the spin of the town-wheel. High above the buildings, among turning cables and hovering birds, she turned her back on the apartment and on the trade delegation of Buridan. She turned her back on Garth Diamandis, and flew toward the residence of the ambassador of Slipstream.

VARIOUS SCENARIOS HAD played themselves out in her mind as she flew. The first was that she could pretend to be the estranged wife of one of the sailors on the Rook. Wringing her hands, she could look pathetic and demand news of the expedition.

Venera wasn't good at looking pathetic. Besides, they could legitimately ask what she was doing here, thousands of miles away from Slipstream.

She could claim to be a traveling merchant. Then why ask after the expedition? Perhaps she should say she was from Hale, not Slipstream, a distant relative of Venera Fanning needing news of her.

These and other options ran through her mind as Venera waited next to the tall scrolled doors of the ambassador's office. The moment the door lock clicked she pushed her way inside and said to the surprised secretary, "My name is Venera Fanning. I need to talk to the ambassador."

The man turned white as a sheet. He practically ran for the inner office and there was a hurried, loud conversation there. Then he stuck his head out the door and said, "You can't be seen here."

"Too late for that, if anyone's watching." She closed the outer door and walked to the inner. The secretary threw it open and stepped aside.

The ambassador of Slipstream was a middle-aged woman with iron-gray hair and the kind of stern features usually reserved for suspicious aunts, school principals, and morals crusaders. She glared at Venera and gestured for her to sit in one of the red leather wing chairs that faced her dark teak desk. "So you're alive," she said as she lowered herself heavily on her side.

"Why shouldn't I be?" Venera was suddenly anxious to the point of panic. "What happened to the others?"

The ambassador sent her a measuring look. "You were separated from your husband's expedition?"

"Yes! I've had no news. Just . . . rumors."

"The expeditionary force was destroyed," said the ambassador. She grimaced apologetically. "Your husband's flagship apparently rammed a Falcon dreadnaught, causing a massive explosion that tore both vessels apart. All hands are presumed lost."

"I see . . ." She felt sick, as though this were the first time she'd heard this news.

"I don't think you do see," said the ambassador. She snapped her fingers and her secretary left, returning with a silver tray and two glasses of wine.

"You've shown up at an awkward time," continued the ambassador. "One of your husband's ships did make it back to Rush. The *Severance* limped back into port a couple of weeks ago, and its hull was full of holes. Naturally the people assumed she was the vanguard of a return from the battle with Mavery. But no—the airmen disembarked and they were laughing, crying, claiming a great victory and waving away all talk of Mavery. 'No,' they say, 'we've beaten *Falcon*! By the genius of the Pilot and Admiral Fanning, we've forestalled an invasion and saved Slipstream!'

"Can the Pilot deny it? If Fanning himself had returned, with the other ships . . . maybe not. If the airmen of the *Severance* hadn't started throwing around impossible amounts of money, displaying rich jewels and gold chains and talking wildly about a pirate's hoard . . . Well, you see the problem. Falcon is supposed to be an *ally*. And the Pilot's been caught with his pants below his knees, completely unaware of a threat to his nation until after his most popular admiral has extinguished that threat.

"He ordered the crew rounded up on charges of treason. The official story is that Fanning took some ships on a raid into

Falcon and busted open one of their treasuries. He's being court-martialed in absentia as a traitor and pirate."

"Therefore," said Venera, "if I were to return now . . ."

"You'd be tried as an accessory, at the very least." The ambassador steepled her hands and leaned forward minutely in her chair. "Legally, I'm bound to turn you over for extradition. Except that should I do so, you'd likely become a lightning rod for dissent. After the riots—"

"What riots?"

"Well." She looked uncomfortable. "The Pilot was a bit . . . slow to act. He didn't round up all of the *Severance's* airmen quickly enough. And he didn't stem the tide until a good deal of money had flowed into the streets. Apparently these were no mere trinkets the men were showing off—and they're not treasury items either; they're plunder, pure and simple, and ancient to boot. And the people, the people believe the *Severance*, not the Pilot.

"Our last dispatch—that was two days ago—says that the bulk of the crew and officers made it back to the *Severance* and bottled themselves up in it. It's out there now, floating a hundred yards off the admiralty. The Pilot ordered it blown up, and that's when rioting started in the city."

"If you returned now," said the secretary, "there'd be even more bloodshed."

"—And likely your blood would be spilled as an example to others." The ambassador shook her head. "It gets worse too. The navy's refused the Pilot's command. They won't blow up the *Severance*. They want to know what happened. They're trying to talk the crew out and there's a three-way standoff now between the Pilot's soldiers, the navy, and the *Severance* herself. It's a real mess."

Venera's pulse was pounding. She wanted to be there, in the admiralty. She knew Chaison's peers, she could rally those men to fight back. They all hated the Pilot, after all.

She slumped back in her chair. "Thank you for telling me this." She thought for a minute, then glanced up at the ambassador. "Are you going to have me arrested?"

The older woman shook her head, half-smiling. "Not if you make a discreet enough exit from my office. I suggest the back stairs. I can't see how sending you home in chains would do anything but fan the flames at this point."

"Thank you." She stood and looked toward the door the ambassador had pointed at. "I won't forget this."

"Just so long as you never tell anyone that you saw me," said the ambassador with an ironic smile. "So what will you do?"

"I don't know."

"If you stay here in the capital, we might be able to help you—set you up with a job and a place to stay," said the ambassador sympathetically. "It would be below your station, I'm afraid, at least to start . . ."

"Thanks, I'll consider it. —And don't worry, if I see you again, I won't be Venera Fanning anymore." Dazed, she pushed through the door into a utilitarian hallway that led to gray tradesman's stairs. She barely heard the words "Good luck" before the door closed behind her.

Venera went down one flight then sat on a step and put her chin in her hands. She was trembling but dry-eyed.

Now what? The news about the *Severance* had been electrifying. She should board the next ship she could find that was headed for the Meridian countries and . . . but it might take weeks to get there. She would arrive after the crisis was resolved, if it hadn't been already.

There was one man who could have helped her. Hayden Griffin was flying a fast racing bike, a simple jet engine with a saddle. She'd last seen him at Candesce as the Sun of Suns blossomed into incandescent life. He was opening the throttle—racing for home—and surely by now he was back in Slipstream. If she'd gone with him when he offered her his hand, none of her present troubles would have happened.

Yet she couldn't do it. Venera had killed Hayden's lover not ten minutes before and simply could not believe that he wouldn't murder her in return if he got the chance.

She hadn't wanted to kill Aubri Mahallan. The woman had lied about her intentions; she had joined the Fanning expedition with the intention of crippling Candesce's defenses. She worked for the outsiders, the alien Artificial Nature that lurked somewhere beyond the skin of Virga. Had Venera not prevented it, Mahallan would have let those incomprehensible forces into Virga and nothing would now be as it was.

Once again Venera took out the bullet and turned it over in her fingers. She had killed the captain of the Rook and his bridge crew—shot them with a pistol—in order to save the lives of everyone aboard. Captain Sembry had been about to fire the Rook's scuttling charges during their battle with the pirates. She had shot several other people in battle and killed Mahallan to save the world itself. Just like she'd shot the man who had been about to kill Chaison, on the day they'd met. . . .

She had killed those people either because of a higher purpose or from naked self-interest. She could admit to being ruthless and callous, even heartless, but Venera did not see herself as fundamentally selfish. She had been bred and raised to be selfish, but she didn't want to be like her sisters or her father. That was the whole reason why she'd escaped life in Hale at her first opportunity.

Venera cursed. If she flew away from Garth Diamandis and the key to Candesce now, she would be admitting that she had killed Aubri Mahallan not to save the world but out of pure spite. She'd be admitting that she'd shot Sembry in the forehead solely to preserve her own life. Could she even claim to have been trying to save Chaison too?

All her stratagems collapsed. Venera returned the bullet to her pocket, stood, and continued down the steps.

When she reached the street she looked around until she spotted the apartment where at this moment Brydda and the rest of the Buridan trade delegation must be frantically searching for her. Leaden with defeat and anger, she let her feet carry her in that direction.

13

THERE WERE PLENTY of people waiting for Venera at the docks, but Garth was not among them. —Oh, she had accountants aplenty, maids and masters of protocol, porters and reporters and doctors, couriers and dignitaries from the nations of Spyre that had decided to conspicuously ally with Buridan. There was lots to do. But as she signed documents and ordered people about, Venera felt the old familiar pain radiating up from her jaw. Today's headache would be a killer.

She had to provide some explanation for why she'd returned early from the expedition, if only for the council representatives with their clipboards and frowns. "We were successful beyond expectations," she said, pinioning Brydda with a warning glare. "A customer has come forward who will satisfy all of our needs for quite some time. There was simply no need to continue with an expensive journey when we'd already achieved our goal."

This was far more information than most nations ever released about their customers, so the council would have to be content with it.

The return of the ruler of Buridan was a hectic affair, and it took until near dinnertime before Venera was able to escape to her apartment to contemplate her next move. There had been no messages from Sacrus, neither demands nor threats. They thought they had her in their pocket now, she supposed, so they could turn their attention to more important matters for a while. But those more important matters were her concern too.

She had a meal sent up and summoned the chief butler. "I do not wish to be disturbed for any reason," she told him. "I will be working here until very late." He bowed impassively and she closed and locked the door.

In the course of renovations some workmen had knocked a hole in one of her bedroom walls. She had chastised them roundly for it, then discovered that there was an airspace behind it—an old chimney, long disused. "Work in some other room," she told the men. "I'll hire more reliable men to fix this." But she hadn't fixed it.

Ten minutes after locking the door, she was easing down a rope ladder that hung in the chimney. The huge portrait of Giles Thrace-Guiles that normally covered the hole had been set aside. At the bottom of the shaft she pried back a pewter fireplace grate decorated with dolphins and naked women and dusted herself off in a former servant's bedroom that she'd recast as a storage closet.

It was easy to nip across the hall and into the wine cellar and slide aside the rack on its oiled track. Then she was in the rebels' bolt-hole and momentarily free of Buridan, Sacrus, and everything else—except, perhaps, the nagging of her new and still unfamiliar conscience.

THE INSANE ORGAN music from Buridan Tower's broken pipeworks had ceased. Not that it was silent as Venera stepped out of the filigreed elevator; the whole place still hummed to the rush and flap of wind. But at least you could ignore it now.

"Iron lady's here!" shouted one of the men waiting in the chamber. Venera frowned as she heard the term being relayed down the halls. There were three guards in the elevator chamber and doubtless more lurking outside. She clasped her hands behind her back and strode for the archway, daring them to stop her. They did not.

The elevator room opened off the highest gallery of the tower's vast atrium. It was also the smallest, as the space widened as it fell. The effect from here was dizzying: she seemed suspended high above a cavern walled by railings. Venera stood there looking down while Bryce's followers silently surrounded her. Echoes of hammering and sawing drifted up from below.

After a while there was a chattering of feet on the steps and then Bryce himself appeared. He was covered in plaster dust and his hair was disarrayed. "What?" he said. "Are they coming?"

"No," said Venera with a half-smile. "At least not yet. Which is not to say that I won't need to give a tour at some point. But you're safe for now."

He crossed his arms, frowning. "Then why are you here?"

"Because this tower is mine," she said simply. "I wanted to remind you of the fact."

Waving away the makeshift honor guard, he strode over to lean on the railing beside her. "You've got a nerve," he said. "I seem to remember the last time we spoke, you were tied to a chair."

"Maybe next time it'll be your turn."

"You think you have us bottled up in here?"

"What would be the use in that?"

"Revenge. Besides, you're a dust-blood—a noble. You can't possibly be on our side."

She examined her nails. "I haven't got a side."

"That *is* the dust-blood side," said Bryce with a sneer. "There's those that care for the people; that's one side. The other side is anybody else."

"I care for my people," she said with a shrug, then, to needle him, "I care for my horses too."

He turned away, balling his hands into fists. "Where's our printing press?" he asked after a moment.

"On its way. But I have something more important to talk to you about. Only to you. A . . . job I need done."

He glanced back at her; behind the disdain, she could see he was intrigued. "Let's go somewhere better suited to talking," he said.

"More chairs, less rope?"

He winced. "Something like that."

"YOU CAN SEE Sacrus from here," she said. "It's a big sprawling estate, miles of it. If anybody is your enemy, I'd think it was them."

"Among others." The venue was the tower's library, a high space full of gothic arches and decaying draperies that hung like the forelocks of defeated men from the dust-rimed window casements. Venera had prowled through it when she and Garth were alone here and who knew?—some of those dusty spines settling into the shelves might be priceless. She hadn't had time to find out; but Bryce's people had tidied up and there were even a few tomes open on the side tables next to several cracked leather armchairs.

Evening light shone hazily through the diamond-shaped windowpanes. She was reminded of another room, hundreds of miles away in the nation of Gehellen, and a gun battle. She had shot a woman there before Chaison's favorite staffer shattered the windows and they all jumped out.

Bryce settled himself into an ancient half-collapsed armchair that had long ago adhered to the floor like a barnacle. "Our goals are simple," he said. "We want to return to the old ways of government, from the days before Virga turned its back on advanced technologies."

"There was a reason why we did that," she said. "The outsiders—"

He waved a hand dismissively. "I know the stories, about this 'Artificial Nature' from beyond the skin of the world that threatens us. They're just a fairy tale to keep the people down."

Venera shook her head. "I knew an agent from outside. She worked for me, betrayed me. I killed her."

"Had her killed?"

"Killed her. With my sword." She allowed her mask to slip for a second, aiming an expression of pure fury at Bryce. "Just who do you think you're talking to?" she said in a low voice.

Bryce nodded his head. "Take it as read that I know you're not an ordinary courtier," he said. "I'm not going to believe any stories you tell without some proof, though. What I was trying to say was that our goal is to reintroduce computation machines into Virga and spread the doctrine of emergent democracy everywhere, so that people can overthrow all their institution-based governments, and emergent utopias can flourish again. We're prepared to kill anybody who gets in our way."

"I'm quite happy to help you with that," she said, "because I know you'll never be able to do it. If I thought you could do what you say . . ." She smiled. "But you might accomplish much, and on the way you can be of assistance to me."

"And what do you want?" he asked. "More power?"

"That would help. But let's get back to Sacrus. They—"

"They're your enemies," he said. "I'm not interested in helping you settle a vendetta."

"They're your enemies too, and I have no vendetta to settle," she said. "In any case I'm not interested in making a frontal assault on them. I just want to visit for an evening."

Bryce stared at her for a second, then burst into laughter. "What are you proposing? That we hit Sacrus?"

"Yes."

He stopped laughing. He shook his head. "Might as well just march everybody straight into prison," he said. "Or a vivisectionist's operating room. Sacrus is the last place in Spyre any sane person would go."

Venera just looked at him for a while. Finally she said, "Either you or one of your lieutenants works for them."

Bryce looked startled, then he scowled at her. "You've said ridiculous things before, but that one takes the prize. Why could you possibly—"

"Jacoby Sarto said something that got me thinking," she interrupted. "Sacrus's product is control, right? They sell it, like fine wine. They practice it as well; did you know that many, maybe most of the minor nations of Spyre are under their thumb? They make a hobby of pulling the strings of people, institutions—whole countries. I'm not so big a fool as to believe that a band of agitators like yours has escaped their attention. One of you works for them—for all I know, your whole organization is a project of theirs."

"What proof do you have?"

"My . . . lieutenant, Flance, whom you have yet to meet, has spent many nights walking the fields and plazas of Greater Spyre. He knows every passage, hedgerow, and hiding place on that decrepit wheel. But he's not the only one. There's others who creep about at night, and he's followed them on occasion. Many times, such parties either started or ended up at Sacrus."

Bryce scoffed. "I've seen a nation that was controlled by them," Venera continued. "I know how they operate. Look, they have to train their people somehow. To them, Greater Spyre is a . . . a paddock, like the one where I keep my horses. It's their school. They send their people out to take over neighbors, foment unrest, create scandals, and conduct intrigues. I'd be very surprised if they didn't do that up in the city as well. So, tell me I'm wrong. Tell me you're not working for them. And if not, look me in the eye and tell me that you're impervious to infiltration and manipulation."

He shrugged but she could tell he was angry. "I'm not a fool," he said after a while. "Anything's possible. But you're still speculating."

"Well I *was* speculating . . . but then I decided to do some research." She held up a sheaf of news clippings. "The news broadsheets of Lesser Spyre are highly partisan, but they don't disagree on facts. On the run-up to my party I spent a couple of afternoons reading news from the past couple of years. This gave me a chance to check on the places and properties that your group has targeted since you first appeared. Quite an impressive list, by the way. But every single one of these incidents has hurt a rival of Sacrus. Not one has touched them."

Bryce looked genuinely rattled for the first time in their brief acquaintance. Venera savored the moment. "I haven't been deliberately neglecting them," he said. "This must be a coincidence."

"Or manipulation. Are you so sure that you're the real leader of this rabble?"

Bryce began to look slightly green. "You don't think it's me."

Venera shook her head. "I'm not *totally* sure that you aren't the one working for them. But you're not"—she almost said *competent*, but turned it into—"ruthless enough. You don't have their style. But you don't make decisions without consulting your lieutenants, do you? And I don't know them. Chances are, you don't really know them either."

"You think I'm a puppet." He looked stricken. "That all along . . . So what—"

"I propose that we flush out their agent, if he exists."

He leaned forward and now there was no hesitation in his eyes. "How?"

She smiled. "Here, Bryce, is where your interests and mine begin to converge."

"I'LL SPEAK ONLY to Moss," said the silhouetted figure. It had appeared without warning on the edge of the rooftop of Liris, startling the night guard nearly out of his wits. As he fumbled for his long-neglected rifle, the shape moved toward him with a lithe, half-remembered step. "This is urgent, man!"

"Citizen Fanning! I—uh, yes, let me make the call." He ran over to the speaking tube and hauled on the bell cord next to it. "She's back—wants to talk to the botanist," he said. Then he turned back to Venera. "How did you get up here?"

"Grappling hook, rope . . ." She shrugged. "Not hard. You should bear that in mind. Sacrus may still hold a grudge."

Shouts and footsteps echoed up through the open shaft of the central courtyard. "Tell them to be quiet!" she hissed. "They'll wake the whole building."

The watchman nodded and spoke into the tube again. Venera walked over to look down at the tree-choked courtyard far below. She could see lanterns hurrying to and fro down there. Finally the iron-bound rooftop door creaked open and figures gestured to her to follow.

Moss was waiting for her in a gallery on the third floor. He was wrapped in a vast purple nightgown and his hair disheveled. His desperate, unfocused eyes glinted in the lantern light. "W-what is the m-meaning of this?"

"I'm sorry for rousting you out of bed so late at night," she said, eyeing the absurd gown. *We must look quite the couple,* she mused, considering her own efficient black and the sword and pistols at her belt. "I have something urgent to discuss with you."

He narrowed his eyes, then glanced at the watchman and soldiers who had escorted her here. "L-l-leave us. I, I'll be all right." With a slight bow he turned and led her to his chamber.

"You could have taken over Margit's apartments, you know," said Venera as she glanced around the untidy, tiny chamber with its single bed, writing desk, and wardrobe. "It's your right. You *are* the botanist, after all."

Moss indicated for her to take the single wooden chair; he managed one of his mangled smiles as he plunked himself down on the bed. "Wh-who says I w-w-won't?" he said. "H-have to get the sm-smell out first."

Venera laughed, then winced at the shards of pain that shot through her jaw and skull. "Good for you," she said past gritted teeth. "I trust you've been well since I left?" He shrugged. "And Liris? Made any new sales?"

"W-what do you want?"

Tired and in pain as she was, Venera would have been more than happy to come to the point. But, "First of all, I have to ask you something," she said. "Do you know who I am?"

"Of c-course. You are V-Venera F-Fanning, from—"

"Oh, but I'm not. —At least, not anymore." She grimaced at his annoyed expression. "I have a new name, Moss. Have you heard of Amandera Thrace-Guiles?"

His reaction was comically perfect. He stared, his eyes wide and his mouth open, for a good five seconds. Then he brayed his difficult laugh. "Odess was r-right! And h-here I thought he was m-mistaking every new face for s-somebody he knew." He laughed again.

Venera examined her nails coolly. "I'm glad I amuse you," she said. "But my own adventures hardly seem unique these days."

The grin left his face. "Wh-what do you mean?"

"Not that you have any obligation to tell me anything," she said, "but . . . surely you've seen that there are odd things afoot in Greater Spyre. Gangs of soldiers wandering in the dark . . . back-room alliances being made and broken. Something's afoot, don't you agree?"

He sat up straight. "Th-the Fair is full of rumors. Some of the l-lesser nations have been losing people."

"Losing them? What do you mean?"

"When the f-first of our people v-vanished, we assumed M-Margit's supporters were leaving. I th-thought it was o-only us. But others have also lost people."

"How many of yours have left?" she asked seriously.

He held up one hand, fingers splayed. Five, then. For a minia-ture nation like Liris, that was too many.

Moss stood up, walked to the door, and listened at it for a moment. Then he turned and leaned on it. "Sacrus," he said flatly.

"It can't be a coincidence," she said. "I came here to talk to you about them. They . . . they have one of my people. Moss, you know what they're capable of. I have to get him back."

Her words had a powerful effect on Moss. He drew himself up to his full height and for a moment his face lost its devastated expression; in that moment she glimpsed the determined, intel-ligent man who hid deep inside his ravaged psyche. Then his features collapsed back to their normal, woebegone state. He raised shaking hands and pressed his palms against his ears.

He said something, almost unintelligibly; after a moment Ven-era realized he'd said, "Are they toying with th-these recruits?"

"No," she countered hastily. "My man is a prisoner. The recruits or whatever they are . . . Moss, Sacrus has a reason to want an army of their own, possibly for the first time. They've finally discovered an ambition worth leaving their own doorstep." She said this with contempt, but in her imagination she saw the vast glowing bubble of nations that made up the principalities of Candesce. "They don't have the population to support what I think they're planning. But it wouldn't surprise me if they've been recruiting from the more secretive nations. Maybe they've always done it but never needed them all before. Now they're activating them."

Puzzlement spread slowly across Moss's face. "An a-army? What for?"

Venera took a deep breath, then said, "They believe they have the means to conquer the principalities of Candesce."

He stared at her. "A-and do they?"

"Yes," she admitted, looking at her hands. "I brought it to them."

He said nothing; Venera's mind was already racing ahead. "Their force must be small by my standards," she said. "Maybe two thousand people. They'd be overwhelmed in any fair fight but they don't intend to fight fair. If we could warn the principalities, they could blockade Spyre. But we'd need to get a ship out."

"Uh-unlikely," said Moss with a sour expression. "One thing I d-do know about Sacrus is that they have been buying ships."

"What else can we do?" she asked tiredly. "Attack them ourselves?"

"Y-you didn't come to ask me to h-help you do that?"

She laughed humorlessly. "Buridan and Liris against Sacrus? That would be suicidal."

He nodded, but suddenly had a faraway look in his eye. "No," Venera continued. "I came to ask you to help me break into Sacrus's prison and extract my man. I have a plan that I think will work. Margit told me where they keep their 'acquisitions.' I believe they view people as objects too, so he's likely to be in that place."

"Th-they guard their lands on the ground and a-above it," said Moss skeptically.

"I don't intend to come in by either route," she said. "But I need a squad of soldiers, at least a score of them. I have some of the forces I need, or I will." She half-smiled. "But I need others I can trust. Will your people do it?"

Now it was his turn to smile. "S-strike a blow against Sacrus? Of c-course! But once the other nations who've l-lost people find out it was S-Sacrus that stole them, y-you'll have more allies. A d-dozen at least."

Venera hadn't considered such a possibility. *Allies?* "I suppose we could count on one or two of the countries whose debts we forgave," she said slowly. "A couple of others might join us just out of devilment." She was thinking of Pamela Anseratte as she said this. Then she shook her head. "No—it's still not enough."

Moss gave his damaged laugh. "Y-you've f-forgotten the most important faction, Venera," he said. "And they have no l-love for Sacrus."

Venera rubbed her eyes. She was too tired and her head hurt too much to guess his meaning. "Who?" she asked irritably.

Moss opened the door and bowed slightly as he held it for her. "You c-came in s-secret. You should return before Candesce l-lights. We will assemble a force f-for you.

"And I will t-talk . . . to the preservationists."

14

"THIS IS THE window she was signaling from," said Bryce. He had his arms folded tightly to his chest and a muscle jumped in his jaw. Long tonguelike curls of wallpaper trembled over his shoulder in the constantly moving air. "I watched her send the whole message, clicking the little door of her lantern like she'd been doing light codes her whole life. She didn't even bother to encrypt it."

Venera had gotten the story out of him in fits and starts, as memory and anger distracted him in turn. Cassia had been one of Bryce's first recruits. They had argued with their foreheads together in the dark bars that peppered Lesser Spyre's red-light district, and defaced buildings and thrown rocks at council parades. It was her urging that had led him down the path to terrorism, he admitted. "And all along, I was a project of hers—some kind of entrance exam to the academy of traitors in Sacrus!" He slammed his fist against the wall.

"Well." Venera shaded her eyes with her hand and peered through the freshly installed glass. "In the end, you were the one who fooled her. And she's the one pent up in a locker downstairs."

He didn't look mollified. The false attack plan had been Venera's idea, after all; all Bryce had done was bring his lieutenants together to reveal the target of their next bombing, a Sacrus warehouse in Lesser Spyre. All three of the lieutenants had expressed enthusiasm, Cassia perhaps most of all. But as soon as the planning meeting broke up she had come down to this disused pantry midway up the side of Buridan Tower—and had started signaling.

Venera could see why she would have favored this room for more than its writhing, peeled wallpaper. From here you had a clear line of sight to the walls of Sacrus, which ran in uneven mazelike lines just past a hedge of trees and a preservationist siding. From the center of the vast estate, a single monolithic building rose hundreds of feet into the afternoon air. Venera imagined a tiny flicker of light appearing somewhere on the side of that edifice—the rapid blink-blink of a message or instruction for Cassia. Bryce was having the place watched round the clock, but so far Sacrus had not responded to Cassia's warning.

" 'Target is Coaver Street warehouse in two days,' she told them." Bryce shook his head in disgust. " 'Urge evac of assets unless I can change target.' "

"You've done well," said Venera. She turned and sat on the window casement. "Listen, I know you're upset—you feel unmanned. Fair enough, it's a humiliation. No more so than this, though." She held out a sheet of paper—a letter that had arrived for her this morning. She watched Bryce unfold it sullenly.

" 'Vote for Proposition forty-four at council tomorrow,' " he read. "What's that mean?"

She grimaced. "Proposition forty-four gives Sacrus control of the docks at Upper Spyre. Supposedly it's a demotion, since the docks aren't used much. Sacrus has modestly agreed to take that job and give up a plumb post in the exchequer that they've held for decades. Nobody's likely to object."

Bryce managed a grim smile. "So they're ordering you around like a lackey now?"

"At least they respected you enough to manipulate you instead," she said. "And don't forget, Bryce: your people follow you. Cassia recognized the leader in you, otherwise she wouldn't have singled you out for her attention. She may have been manipulating you all this time—but she was also training you."

He grumbled, but she could see her words had pleased him. At that moment, though, they heard rapid footsteps in the hall outside. Gray-haired Pasternak, one of Bryce's remaining two lieutenants, stuck his head in the doorway and said, "They're here."

Venera spared a last glance out the window. From up here the airfall was an insubstantial mesh of fabric where ground should be. Rushing clouds spun by beneath that faint skein, which she knew was really a gridwork of I-beams and stout cable—the tough inner skeleton of Spyre, visible now that the skin was stripped away. A small jumble of gantries and cranes perched timidly at the edge of the ruined land. The official story was that Amandera Thrace-Guiles was trying to build a bridge across the airfall to rejoin Buridan Tower to the rest of Spyre.

She followed Bryce out of the room. The truth was that the bridge site was a ruse, a distraction to cover up the real link between Buridan and the rest of the world. In the few days that had passed since Venera's conversation with Moss, a great deal of activity had taken place in the pipeworks that Venera and Garth had used to reach Buridan Tower the first time. A camouflaged entrance had been built near the railway siding a few hundred yards back from the airfall's edge. A man, or even a large group of men, could jump off a slow-moving train and after a sprint under some trees be in a hidden tunnel that led all the way to the tower. True, there were still long sections where men had to

walk separated by thirty feet or more lest the pipe give way . . .
but that would be fixed.

As she and Bryce strode down the long ramp that coiled from
the tower's top to its bottom, they passed numerous work sites,
each comprising half a dozen or more men and women. It was
much like the controlled chaos of her estate's renovation, except
that these people weren't fixing the plaster. They were assembling weapons, inventorying armor and supplies, and fencing in
the ballrooms. Bryce's entire organization was here, as well as
gray-eyed soldiers from Liris and exotics from allies of that
country. They had started arriving last night, after Bryce gave the
all-clear that he'd found his traitor.

Bryce's people were still in shock. They watched the new-
comers with mixed loathing and suspicion; but the shock of
Cassia's betrayal had been effective, and their loyalty to him still
held. Venera knew they would need something to do—and
soon—or their natural hatred of the status quo would assert itself. They were born agitators, cutthroats, and bomb builders,
but that was why they would be useful.

A new group was just tromping up from the stairs to the
pipeworks as Venera and Bryce reached the main hall. They wore
oil-stained leathers and outlandish fur hats. Venera had seen
these uniforms at a distance, usually wreathed in steam from
some engine they were working on. These burly men were from
the Preservation Society of Spyre, and they were sworn enemies
of Sacrus.

For the moment they were acting more like overawed boys,
though, staring around at the inside of Buridan Tower like they'd
been transported into a storybook. In a sense, they had; the
preservationists were indoctrinated in the history of the airfall,
which remained the greatest threat to Spyre's structural integrity
and which all now knew had been caused partly by Sacrus.

Buridan Tower had probably been a symbol to them for centuries of defiance against decay and treachery. To stand inside it now was clearly a shock.

Good. She could use that fact.

"Gentlemen." She curtsied to the group. "I am Amandera Thrace-Guiles. If you'll follow me, I'll show you where you can freshen up, and then we can get started."

They murmured amongst themselves as they walked behind her. Venera exchanged a glance with Bryce, who seemed amused at her formality.

The preservationists headed off to the washrooms and Venera and Bryce turned the other way, entering the tower's now-familiar library. Venera had ordered some of the emptied armor of the tower's long-ago attackers mounted here. The holed and burned crests of Sacrus and its allies were quite visible on breastplate and shoulder. As a pointed message, Venera'd had the suits posed like sentries around the long map table in the middle of the room. One even held a lantern.

Bryce's lieutenants were already at the table, pointing to things and talking in low tones with the commander of the Liris detachment. As the preservationists trooped back in, the other generals and colonels entered from a door opposite. Moss had exceeded Venera's wildest expectations: at the head of this group were generals from Carasthant and Scoman, old allies of Liris in its war with Vatoris—and they had brought friends of their own. Most prominent was the towering, frizzy-haired Corinne, princess of Fin. Normally Venera didn't like women who were social equals—in Hale they always represented a threat—but she'd taken an instant liking to Corinne.

Venera nodded around at them all. "Welcome," she said. "This is an extraordinary meeting. Circumstances are dire. I'm sure you all know by now that Sacrus has recruited an army, plundering its neighbors of manpower in the process. So far the council at Lesser Spyre is acting like it never happened. I think they're in a tailspin. Does anyone here believe that the council should be the ones to deal with the situation?"

There were grins round the table. One of the preservationists held up a hand. He would have been handsome were it not for the beard—Venera hated beards—that obscured the lower half of his face. "You're on the council," he said. "Can't you bring a motion for them to act?"

"I can, but the next morning I'll receive the head of my man Flance in the mail," she said. "Sacrus has him. So I'm highly motivated, though not in the ways that Sacrus probably expects. Still . . . I won't act through the council."

"Sacrus blocked one of our main lines," said the preservationist. "All of Spyre is in danger unless we can get a counterbalance running through their land. Beyond that, we don't give a damn who they conquer."

It was Venera's turn to nod. The preservationists were dedicated to keeping the giant wheel together. Most of their decisions were therefore pragmatic and dealt with engineering issues. They wouldn't care if they were ruled by the council or Sacrus itself, as long as the engineering was sound.

"Are you saying they could buy your loyalty by just giving you a siding?" she asked.

"They could," said the bearded man. There were protests up and down the table, but Venera smiled.

"I applaud your honesty," she said. "Your problem is that you'd need to give them a reason before they did that. They've never had any use for you and you've never been a threat to them. So you've come here to buy that leverage?"

He shrugged. "Or see them destroyed. It's all the same to us."

Bryce leaned out to look at the man. "And the fact that they used poison gas to kill twenty-five of your workers a generation ago . . . ?"

". . . Gives us a certain bias in the *destroy* direction. Who are you?" added the bearded man, who had been briefed on the identities of the other players.

With obvious distaste, Bryce said what they'd decided he would say: "Bryce. Chief of intelligence for Buridan." He nodded at Venera.

"You've a *spy network?*" The preservationist grinned at her ironically.

"I do, Mister . . . ?"

"Thinblood." It could have been a name or a title.

"I do, Mr. Thinblood—and *you've* got a secret warehouse full of artillery at junction sixteen," she said with a return smile. Thinblood turned red; out of the corner of her eye Venera saw Princess Corinne stifle a laugh.

"We are all to be taken seriously," Venera went on. "As is Sacrus. Let's return to discussing them."

"Hang on," said Thinblood. "What are we discussing? War?"

She shook her head. "Not yet. But clearly, Sacrus needs its wings clipped."

The lean, cadaverous general from Carasthant made a violent shushing gesture that made everyone turn to stare at him. "What can little guppies like us do?" he said in a buzzing voice that seemed to emanate from his bobbing Adam's appple. "Begging your pardon, Madam Buridan, Mr. Preservationist sir. Do you propose we take down a shark by worrying at its gills?"

His compatriot from Scoman waggled his head in agreement. The one tiny clock built into his armor clicked ahead a second. "Sacrus is bounded by high walls and barbed wire," he said over the quiet snicking of his clothing, "and they have sniper towers and machine-gun positions. Even if we fought our way in, what would we do? Piss on their lawn?"

That was an expression Venera had never heard before.

Venera had thought long and hard about what to say when this question came up. These men and women were gathered here because their homes had all been injured or insulted by Sacrus—but were they here merely to vent their indignation? Would they back down in the face of actual action?

She didn't want to tell them that she knew what Sacrus was up to. The key to Candesce was a prize worth betraying old friends for. If they knew Sacrus had it, half these people would defect to Sacrus's side immediately, and the other half would proceed to plan how to get it themselves. It might turn into a night of long knives inside Buridan Tower.

"Sacrus's primary assets lie inside the Grey Infirmary," she said. "Whatever it is that they manufacture and sell, that is its origin. At the very least, we need to know what we're up against, what they're planning to do. I propose that we invade the Grey Infirmary."

There was a momentary, stunned silence from the new arrivals. Princess Corinne's broad sunburnt face was squinched up in a failed attempt to hide a smile. Then Thinblood, the Carasthant general, and two of the minor house representatives all started talking at once.

"Impossible!" she heard, and "Suicide!" through the general babble. Venera let it run on for a minute or so, then held up her hand.

"Consider the benefits if it could be done," she said. "We could rescue my man Flance, assuming he's there. We could find out what Sacrus trades in—though I think we all know—but in any case find out what its tools and devices are. We might be able to seize their records. Certainly we can find out what it is they're doing.

"If we want, we can blow up the tower.

"And it *can* be done," she said. "I admit I was pretty hopeless myself until last night. We'd talked through all sorts of plans, from sneaking over the walls to shimmying down ropes from Lesser Spyre. All our scenarios ended up with us being machine-gunned, either on the way in or on the way out. Then I had a long talk with Princess Corinne, here."

Corinne nodded violently; her hair followed her head's motion a fraction of a second late. "We can get into the Grey Infirmary," she brayed. "And out again safely."

There was another chorus of protests and again Venera held up her hand. "I could tell you," she said, "but it might be more convincing to *show* you. Come." And she headed for the doors.

THE ROAR FROM the airfall was more visceral than audible here in the lowest of Buridan's pipes. Bryce's people had lowered ladders down here when they came to cut away the maddening random organ that had been created accidentally in Buridan's destruction. The corroded metal surface gleamed wetly, and as Venera stepped off the ladder she slipped and almost fell. She stared up at the ring of faces twenty feet above her.

"Well, come on," she said. "If I'm brave enough to come down here, you can be too."

Thinblood ignored the ladder and vaulted down, landing beside her with a smug thump. Instantly the surface under their feet began swaying and little flakes of rust showered down. "The ladder's here to save the pipe, not your feet," Venera said loudly. Thinblood looked abashed; the others clambered down the ladder meekly.

The ladder descended the vertical part of the pipe and they now stood where it bent into a horizontal direction. This tunnel was ten feet wide and who knew what it might originally have carried—horse manure, Venera suspected. Whatever the case, it now ended twenty feet away. Late afternoon sunlight hurried shadows across the jagged circle of torn metal. It was from there that the roar originated.

"Come." Without hesitation Venera walked to within five feet of the opening, then went down on one knee. She pointed. "There! Sacrus!"

They could barely have heard her over the roar of the thin air; it didn't matter. It was clear what she was pointing at.

The pipe they stood in thrust forty or fifty feet into the airstream below the curve of Spyre's hull. Luckily this opening faced away from the headwind, though suction pulled at Venera relentlessly and the air was so thin she was starting to pant already. The pipe hung low enough to provide a vantage point from which a long stretch of Spyre's hull was visible—miles of it, in fact. Way out there, near the little world's upside-down horizon, a cluster of pipes much like this one—but intact—jutted into the airflow. Nestled among them was a glassed-in machine-gun blister, similar to the one Venera had first visited underneath Garth Diamandis's hovel.

"That's the underside of the Grey Infirmary," she yelled at the motley collection of generals and revolutionaries crowding at her shoulder. Someone cupped hand to ear and looked quizzical. "Infirmary! In! Firm!" She jabbed her finger at the distant pipes. The quizzical person smiled and nodded.

Venera backed up cautiously and the others scuttled ahead of her. At the pipe's bend where breathing was a bit easier and the noise and vibration not so mind-numbing, she braced her rump against the wall and her feet in the mulch of rust lining the bottom of the pipe. "We brought down telescopes and checked out that machine-gun post. It's abandoned, like most of the hull positions. The entrance is probably bricked up, most likely forgotten. It's been hundreds of years since anybody tried to assault Spyre from the outside."

She could barely make out the buzzing words of Carasthant's general. "You propose to get in through that? How? By jumping off the world and grabbing the pipes as they pass?"

Venera nodded. When they all stared back uncomprehending, she sighed and turned to Princess Corinne. "Show them," she said.

Corinne was carrying a bulky backpack. She wrestled this off and plunked it down in the rust. "This," she said with a dramatic flourish, "is how we will get to Sacrus.

"It is called a *parachute*."

SHE HAD TO focus on her jaw. Venera's face was buried in the voluminous shoulder of her leather coat; her hands clutched the rope that twisted and shuddered in her grip. In the chattering roar of a four-hundred-mile-per-hour wind there was no room for distractions, or even thought.

Her teeth were clenched around a mouthpiece of Fin design. A rubber hose led from this to a metal bottle that, Corinne had explained, held a large quantity of squashed air. It was that ingredient of the air the *Rook's* engineers had called *oxygen*; Venera's first breath of it had made her giddy.

Every now and then the wind flipped her over or dragged her head to the side and Venera saw where she was: wrapped in leathers, goggled and masked, and hanging from a thin rope inches below the underside of Spyre.

All she had to do was keep her body arrow-straight and keep that mouthpiece in. Venera was tied to the line, which was being let out quite rapidly from the edge of the airfall. Ten soldiers had already gone this way before her so it must be possible.

It was night, but distant cities and even more distant suns cast enough light to silver the misty clouds that approached Spyre like curious fish. She saw how the clouds would nuzzle Spyre cautiously only to be rebuffed by its whirling rotation. They recoiled, formed cautious spirals, and danced around the great cylinder as if trying to find a way in. Dark speckles—flocks of piranhawks and sharks—browsed among them, and there in great black formations were the barbed wire and blockhouses of the sentries.

To be among the clouds with nothing above or below seemed perfectly normal to Venera. If she fell she only had to open her parachute and she'd come to a stop long before hitting the barbed wire. It wasn't the prospect of falling that made her heart pound—it was the savage headwind that was trying to snatch her breath away.

The rope shuddered and she grabbed it spasmodically. Then she felt a hand grab her ankle.

The soldiers hauled her through a curtain of speed ivy and into a narrow gun emplacement. This one was dry and empty, its tidiness somehow in keeping with Sacrus's fastidious attention to detail. Bryce was already here and he unceremoniously yanked the air line from Venera's mouth. —Or tried; she bit down on it tenaciously for a second, glaring at him, before relenting and opening her mouth. He shot her a look of annoyance and tied it and her unopened parachute to the line. This he let out through the speed ivy, to be reeled back to Buridan for its next user.

Princess Corinne's idea had sounded insane, but she merely shrugged, saying, "We do this sort of thing all the time." Of course, she was from Fin, which explained much. That pocket nation inhabited one of Spyre's gigantic ailerons, a wing hundreds of feet in length that jutted straight down into the airstream. Originally colonized by escaped criminals, Fin had grown over the centuries from a cold and dark subbasement complex into a bright and independent—if strange—realm. The Fins didn't really consider themselves citizens of Spyre at all. They were creatures of the air.

Over the years they had installed hundreds of windows in the giant metal vane as well as hatches and winches. They were suspected of being smugglers, and Corinne had proudly confirmed that. "We alone are able to slip in and out of Spyre at will," she'd told Venera. And, as their population expanded, they had colonized five of the other twelve fins by the same means they were using to break into Sacrus.

To reach Sacrus, one of Corinne's men had donned a parachute and taken hold of a rope that had a big three-barbed hook on its end. He had unceremoniously stepped into the howling airfall and was snatched down and away like a fleck of dust.

Venera had been watching from the tower and saw his parachute balloon open a second later. Instantly, he stopped falling away from Spyre and began curving back toward the hull. Down only operated as long as you were part of the spinning structure, after all; freed of the high speed imparted by Spyre's rotation, he'd come to a stop in the air. He could have hovered there, scant feet from the hull, for hours. The only problem was the rope he held, which was still connected to Buridan.

The big wooden spool that was unreeling it was starting to smoke. Any second now it would reach its end and the snap would probably take his hands off. Yet he calmly stood there on the dark air, waiting for Sacrus to shoot past.

As the pipes and machine-gun nest leaped toward him he

lifted the hook and, with anticlimactic ease, tossed it ahead of the rushing metal. The hook caught, the rope whipped up and into the envelope of speeding air surrounding the hull, and Corinne's man saluted before disappearing over Spyre's horizon. They'd recovered him when he came around again.

Now, brilliant light etched the cramped gun emplacement with the caustic sharpness of a black-and-white photograph. One of the men was employing a welding torch on the hatch at the top of the steps. "Sealed ages ago, like we thought," shouted Bryce, jabbing a thumb at the ceiling. "Judging from the pipes, we're under the sewage stacks. There's probably toilets above us."

"Perfect." They needed a staging ground from which to assault the tower. "Do you think they'll hear us?"

Bryce grimaced. "Well, there could be fifty guys sitting around up there taking bets on how long it'll take us to burn the hatch open. We'll find out soon enough."

Suddenly the ceiling blew out around the welder. He retreated in a shower of sparks, cursing, and a new wind filled the little space. Before anybody else could move Thinblood leaped over to the hole and jammed some sort of contraption up it. He folded, pulled—and the wind stopped. The hole the welder had made was now blocked by something.

"Patch hatch," said Thinblood, wiping dust off his face. "We'd better go up. They might have heard the pop or felt the pressure drop."

Without waiting he pressed against his temporary hatch, which gave way with a rubbery slapping sound. Thinblood pushed his way up and out of sight. Bryce was right behind him.

Both were standing with their guns drawn when Venera fought her way past the suction to sprawl on a filthy floor. She stood up, brushing herself off, and looked around. "It is indeed a men's room."

Or was it? In the weak light of Thinblood's lantern she could see that the chamber was lined in tiles that had once been white but which had long since taken on the color of rust and dirt. Long streaks ran down the wall to dark pools on the floor. Venera expected to see the usual washroom fixtures along the walls, but other than a metal sink there was nothing. She had an uneasy feeling that she knew what sort of room this was, but it didn't come to her until Thinblood said, "Operating theater. Disused."

Bryce was prying at a metal chute mounted in one wall. It creaked open and he stared down into darkness for a second. "A convenient method of disposal for body parts or even whole people," he said. "I'm thinking more like an autopsy room."

"Vivisectionist's lounge?" Thinblood was getting into the game.

"Shut up," said Venera. She'd gone over to the room's one door and was listening at it. "It seems quiet."

"Well, it is the middle of the night," the preservationist commented. More members of their team were meanwhile popping up out of the floor like Jacks-in-the-box. *Minus the windup music,* Venera mused.

Soon there were twenty of them crowded together in the ominous little room. Venera cracked the door and peered out into a larger, dark space full of pipes, boilers, and metal tanks. This was the maintenance level for the tower, it seemed. That was logical.

"Is everyone clear on what we're doing?" she asked.

Thinblood shook his head. "Not even remotely."

"We are after my man Flance," she said, "as well as information about what Sacrus is up to. If we have to fight, we cause enough mayhem to make Sacrus rethink its strategy. Hence the charges." She nodded at the heavy canvas bag one of the Liris soldiers was toting. "Our first order of business is to secure this level, then set some of those charges. Let's do it."

She led the soldiers of half a dozen nations as they stepped out of their bridgehead and into the dark of enemy territory.

15

EVERYTHING IN THE Grey Infirmary seemed designed to promote a feeling of paranoia. The corridors were hung with huge black felt drapes that swayed and twitched slightly in the moving air, giving the constant impression that there was someone hiding behind them. The halls were lit by lanterns fixed on metal posts; you could swivel the post and aim the light here and there, but there was no way to illuminate your entire surroundings at any point. The floors were muffled under deep crimson carpeting. You could sneak up on anybody here. There were no signs, doors were hidden behind the drapery, and all the corridors looked alike.

It reminded Venera unpleasantly of the palace at Hale. Her father's own madness had been deepening in the days before she succeeded in escaping to a life with Chaison. The Pilot had all the paintings in the palace covered, the mirrors likewise. He took to walking the hallways at night, a sword in his hand, convinced as he was that conspirators waited around every corner. These nocturnal strolls were great for the actual conspirators, who knew exactly where he was and so could avoid him easily. Those conspirators—almost entirely comprising members of his own family—would bring him down one day soon. Venera had not received any letters bragging of his downfall while she lived in Rush; but there could well be one waiting when or if she ever returned to Slipstream.

That was the madness of one man. Sacrus, though, had done more than generalize such paranoia: it had institutionalized it. The Grey Infirmary was a monument to suspicion and a testament to the idea that distrust was to be encouraged. "Don't pull on the curtains to look for doors," Venera cautioned the men as they rounded a corner and lost sight of the stairs to the basement. "They may be rigged to an alarm."

Thinblood scoffed. "Why do something like that?"

"So only the people who know where the doors are can find them," she said. "People trying to escape—or interlopers like us—set off the bells. Luckily there's another way to find them." She pointed at the carpet. "Look for worn patches. They signify higher traffic."

The corridor they were in seemed to circle some large inner area. Opposite the basement stairs they found the broad steps of an exit, and next to it stairs going up. It wasn't until they had nearly circled back to the basement stairs that they found a door letting into the interior. Next to a patch of slightly worn carpet, Venera eased the curtains to the side and laid her hand on a cold iron door with a simple latch. She eased the door open a crack—it made no sound—and peered in.

The room was as big as an auditorium, but there was no stage. Instead, dozens of long glass tanks stood on tables under small electric lights. The lights flickered slightly, their power no doubt influenced by the jamming signal that emanated from Candesce.

Each tank was filled with water, and lying prone in them were men—handcuffed, blindfolded, and with their noses and mouths just poking out of the water. Next to each tank was a stool and perched on several of these were women who appeared to be reading books.

"What is it?" Thinblood was asking. Venera waved at him impatiently and tried to get a better sense of what was going on here. After a moment she realized that the women's lips were moving. They were reading to the men in the tanks.

". . . I am the angel that fills your sky. Can you see me? I come to you naked, my breasts are full and straining for your touch."

Bryce put a hand on her shoulder and his head above hers. "What are they doing?"

"They seem to be reading pornography," she whispered, shaking her head.

". . . Touch me, oh touch me, exalted one. I need you. You are my only hope.

"Yet who am I, this trembling bird in your hand. I am more than one woman, I am a multitude, all dependent on you. . . . I am Falcon Formation, and I need you in all ways that a man can be needed . . ."

Venera fell back, landing on her elbows on the deep carpet. "Shut it!" Bryce raised an eyebrow at her reaction but eased the door closed. He twitched the curtain back into place.

"What was that all about?" asked Thinblood.

Venera got to her feet. "I just found out who one of Sacrus's clients is," she said. She felt nauseated.

"Can we seal off this door?" she asked. "Prevent anyone getting out and coming at us from behind?"

Bryce frowned. "That presents its own dangers. We could as easily trap ourselves."

She shrugged. "But we have *grenades*, and we're not afraid to use them." She squinted at him. "Are we?"

Thinblood laughed. "Would a welding torch applied to the hinges do the trick? We'll have to leave a tiny team behind to do that."

"Two men, then."

They went back to the upward-leading stairs. The second level presented a corridor identical to the one below. The same muffled silence hung over everything here. "Ah," said Venera, "such delicate decorative instincts they have."

Thinblood was pacing along bent over, hands behind his back. He stared at the floor mumbling "hmmm, hmmm." After a few seconds he pointed. "Door here."

Venera twitched back the curtain to reveal an ironbound door with a barred window. She had to stand on her tiptoes to see through it to the long corridor full of similar doors beyond. "This looks like a cell block." She rattled the door handle. "Locked."

"Hello?" The voice had come from the other side of the door. Venera motioned for the others to get out of sight, then summoned a laconic, sugary voice and said, "Is this where I can find my little captain?" She giggled.

"Wha—?" Two eyes appeared at the door, blinking in surprise at her. Just in time, Venera had yanked off her black jacket and shirt, revealing the strategic strappery that maximized her figure. "Who the hell are you?" said the man on the other side of the door.

"I'm your present," whispered Venera. "That is, if you're Captain Sendriks. . . . I'd like it if you were," she added petulantly. "I'm tired of tromping around these stupid corridors in nothing but my assets. I could catch a cold."

A moment later the latch clicked and seconds after that Venera was inside with a pistol under the chin of the surprised guard. Her men flowed around her like water filling a pipe; as she gestured for her new prisoner to kneel Thinblood said, "It's clear on this end, but there's another man around the corner yonder."

"Level a pistol at him and he'll fall into line." She watched one of the soldiers from Liris tying up her man, then said, "It is cold in here. Bryce, where's my jacket?"

"Haven't seen it," he said innocently. Venera glared at him, then went to collect it herself.

The corridor held a faint undertone of coughing and quizzical voices, which came from behind the other doors. This was indeed a cell block. Venera raced from door to door. "Up! Yes, you! Who are you? How long have you been here?"

There were men and women here. There were children as well. They wore a wide mix of clothing, some familiar from her days in Spyre, some foreign, perhaps of the principalities. Their accents, when they answered her hesitantly, were similarly diverse. All seemed well fed but they were haggard with fear and lack of sleep.

Garth Diamandis was not among them.

Venera didn't hide her disappointment. "Tell me where the rest of the prisoners are or I'll blow your head off," she told the guard. She had him on his knees with his face pressed against the wall, her pistol against the back of his head. "Bear in mind," she added, "that we'll find them ourselves if we have to, it'll just take longer. What do you say?"

He proceeded to give a detailed account of the layout of the tower, including where the night watch were stationed and when their rounds were. So far Venera hadn't seen any sign of watchmen; for a nation gearing up for war, Sacrus seemed extremely lax. She said so and her prisoner laughed, a tad hysterically.

"Nobody's ever gotten in or out of here," he mumbled against the plaster. "Who would break in? And from where?" He tried unsuccessfully to shake his head. "You people are insane."

"A common enough trait in Spyre," she sniffed. "Your mistake, then."

"You don't understand," he croaked. "But you will."

She had already noted that he wore armor that was light and utilitarian, and his holstered weapons had been similarly simple. This functionalism, which contrasted dramatically with the outlandish costumes of most of her people, made her more uneasy about Sacrus's abilities than anything he'd said.

They spent some time trying to get more out of him and his companion. Neither they nor the prisoners they spoke to knew what Sacrus's plan was—only that a general mobilization was underway. The prisoners themselves were from all over the principalities; some had recently gone missing within Spyre itself.

"They're enough evidence to haul Sacrus before the high court on crimes against the polity," crowed Bryce. "If we can just get some of these people out of here."

Venera shook her head. "They may be enough to get the rest of Spyre up in arms. But until we can come up with a decent plan for getting them out alive, they're safer where they are. Let them loose now and they'll give us away, and probably try to run the gauntlet of machine guns and barbed wire on their way to the outer walls. At least let's find them some weapons and a direction to run in."

Bryce and Thinblood exchanged glances. Then Bryce quirked his irritating smile. "I have an idea," he said. "Let's strike a compromise . . ."

THERE WERE PLENTY of cells in the block, but Garth was in none of them. While Venera searched for him, Thinblood took the bulk of the team to look for the night watch. Nearly fifteen minutes had passed before he reappeared.

Thinblood was jubilant. "Both floors are secure," he said. "We left the watchmen in a closet we found. And my welder has sealed off the main doors and a side entrance. He's a model of efficiency, that one."

Bryce put a hand on Venera's arm. "Your man doesn't seem to be here. We have to look to our other objectives."

She shrugged him off, gritting her teeth so as not to snap some withering retort. "All right, then," she said. "There's more to this tower upstairs. Let's find out what Sacrus is up to."

The next floor was different. Here the velvet-covered walls and darkness gave way to marble and bright, annoyingly uneven electric light. Venera heard the sound of voices and chatter of a mechanical typewriter coming from an open door about thirty feet to the left. Crouching under the lee of the steps with the others, she scowled and said, "The time for subtlety may be past."

"Wait." Thinblood pointed the other way. Venera craned her neck and saw the heavy vault-style door even as Thinblood said, "Sacrus is reputed to keep their most secret weapons in this place. Do you think . . . ?"

"I think I saw some of those weapons being made down-stairs," she said, thinking of the fish-tank room. "But you're right. It's just too tempting." The door was surrounded by big signs saying VALID PERSONNEL ONLY, and two men with rifles slouched in front of it. "How do we get past them?"

One of Corinne's men cleared his throat quietly. He drew something from his backpack and after a moment his companions did likewise. They strung the small compound bows with quick economical movements. Seeing this, Venera and the other leaders climbed back down and out of the way.

"Count of three," said the man at the top. "You take the one on the right, we'll do the one on the left. One, two—"

All four of Corinne's soldiers jumped out of the stairwell and rolled into crouches. Their shoulder muscles creased in unison as they drew back and Venera heard an intake of breath and "What the—" from off to the right and then they let loose.

There was a grunt, a thud, then another. The archers whirled around, looking for another target.

The sound of typing continued.

"Take out that office," Venera instructed the archers as she stepped into the hallway. "We'll go for the vault."

The heavy door had a thick glass window in it. Venera shaded her eyes with her hands and stared through for a few seconds. She whistled. "I think we've found the mother lode."

The chamber beyond was large—it took up most of this level. There were no windows and its distant walls were draped in black like the corridors downstairs. Its brick floor was criss-crossed by red carpets; in the squares they defined, pedestals large and small stood under cones of light. Each pedestal supported some device—brass canisters here, a fluted riflelike weapon there. Large jars full of thick brown fluid gleamed near things like bushes made of knives. There was nothing in there that looked innocuous, nothing Venera would have willingly wanted to touch. But all were on display as if they were treasures.

She supposed they were that; this might be the vault that held Sacrus's dearest assets.

The view was obscured suddenly. Venera found herself staring into the cold gray eyes of a soldier, who mouthed something she couldn't hear through the glass.

Deception wasn't going to work this time. "We've been seen," she said even as a loud alarm bell suddenly filled the corridor with jangling echoes.

"Can we blow this?" Thinblood was asking one of his men. The soldier shook his head.

"Not without taking time to figure out the vulnerable points . . . maybe doing some drilling . . ."

Thinblood looked at Venera, who shrugged. "It's going to be a firefight from now on," she said. "Better get downstairs and free those prisoners. Then we can—" Something bright and sudden flashed in her peripheral vision and there was a loud *clang!*

She stared in dumb surprise at the metal bars that now blocked the way to the stairwell. "Blow them!" she shouted, pulling out her preservationist-built machine pistol. "This is no time for subtlety!"

At that moment there was an eruption of noise from the far end of the corridor. Venera dove to the floor as impacting bullets sprayed marble dust and plaster at her. The others either flattened as well or staggered back against the wall. Blood spattered over the threaded stonework.

Now a smoke grenade was tumbling toward her, each end-over-end bounce sending a gout of black into the air. It stopped just outside the bars then disappeared in a growing pyramid of darkness. Past that Venera heard shouted orders, gunshots.

"You will lie facedown on the floor and put your hands behind your necks! Anyone we do not find in that position will be shot! You have five seconds and then we will shoot everything that sticks up more than a foot off the floor."

All she could hear after that was machine gun fire.

THE COMMANDANT HELD the mimeographed picture of Venera next to her head and compared the two. "You look older in real life," he said in apparent disappointment. She glared at him but said nothing.

"Really," he continued in apparent amazement, "what did you think you were going to achieve? Invading *Sacrus*? We've forgotten more tricks of incursion and sabotage than you people ever knew."

Twelve of Venera's people knelt around her on the floor of a storage room that opened off the third-floor corridor. Mops and brooms loomed over her; a single flickering bulb illuminated the three men with machine guns who were standing over the prisoners. Two more soldiers had been tying their hands behind their backs but the process had stalled out briefly as they ran out of rope. The commandant, who had at first seemed flustered and shocked, had soon recovered his poise and now appeared to be genuinely enjoying himself.

"You did a good job of sealing off the front doors, but my superiors were able to slip this through the crack." He waggled the mimeograph at Venera. He was a beefy man with an oddly asymmetrical face; one of his eyes was markedly higher than the other, and his upper lip lifted on the left, giving him a permanent look of incredulity. "They also slipped in some instructions on how we're to proceed while they cut through your welding job. It seems we had a—" He flipped the sheet over to read the back. "—A certain Garth Diamandis in our custody, as guarantor of your good behavior. Our arrangement was very clear. Should you fail to obey our orders, we were to kill this Diamandis. I'd say that your little incursion tonight constitutes disobedience, wouldn't you?"

Venera drew back her lips in a snarl. "Someday they're going to name a disease after you."

The commandant sighed. "I just wanted you to know that I've issued the order. He's being terminated, oh, even as we speak. And—" he laughed heartily "—I had an inspiration! The manner of his passing is quite hideous. You'll be impressed when you see—"

A soldier clattered to a stop at the door to the office. "The lower floors are secure, sir," he said. "They had tied up the night watch and the guards in the prison. In addition, we found ten of these in the basement." He handed the commandant one of the charges Venera's people had set.

Venera exchanged a glance with Bryce, whose hands were still untied.

"Well, look at this." The commandant knelt in front of Venera. "A little clockwork bomb. Why, it's so intricately made, I can only think of one place it might have come from." He arched an eyebrow at the knot of prisoners. "Are any of you from Scoman, by any chance?" He didn't wait for an answer, but turned the mechanism over under Venera's nose. "How does it work? Is it a timer?"

She said nothing; he shrugged and said, "I think I can figure it out. You turn this dial to give yourself . . . what? Ten minutes? If you don't reset it before it winds down to zero it explodes."

A muffled report sounded from somewhere in the building. A gunshot? The commandant glanced at his men; one turned and left the room. "I suppose one or two of your compatriots might still be loose," he admitted. "But we'll round them up soon enough."

He was just opening his mouth to add something else when the lights went out. The building rocked to a distant blast.

Instant pandemonium—somebody stepped on Venera and crumpled her to the floor while some sort of struggle erupted just to her right; one of the machine guns went off, apparently into the ceiling, lighting the space with a momentary red flicker. All she saw was people rearing up, falling down, tumbling like scattered chessmen. She strained but couldn't get free of the ropes that bound her hands behind her.

Another explosion, then another. How many of those bombs

had they said they'd found? She was sure they'd planted at least twelve.

Now somebody fell on her in a horrifyingly limp tangle and she screamed but nobody could hear her over the shouts, cries, and shots.

More machine gun fire, terrifyingly close but apparently directed out the door. Venera wormed out from under the wet body and found a corner to huddle in, hands jammed into the spot where walls and floor met. She cursed the dark and chaos and expected to receive a bullet in the head any second.

Silence and heavy breathing. Distant shouts. Somebody lit a match.

Bryce and Thinblood stood back to back. Each held a machine gun. Another gun lay under the body of the commandant, whose lopsided face was frozen in an expression of genuine surprise. The room was awash with men who were holding one another by the throat, or feet, or wrists, all atop the tiled bodies of the soldiers who were still tied up. Dark blood was spattered up the wall and over everybody. Venera looked down at herself and saw that her own clothes were glistening with the stuff.

"Get them untied!" Somebody flipped a knife into his hand and began bending and slashing at the ropes. When he reached Venera she saw that it was one of the archers. Venera leaned forward, knocking her forehead against the floor as he roughly grabbed her arms and cut.

"The prisoners are loose!" Bryce hauled her to her feet just as the match went out. "Somebody find a bloody lantern! We've got to get out of here!" They burst into the corridor just as the lights resumed a dim glow. There were bodies all over the place and bullet holes in the walls, and she heard shots and shouts coming from the stairwell.

"Good idea to leave those men in the cells," she said to Bryce. "A command decision."

He grinned. They had given two men some spare weapons and grenades and, out of sight of the tied-up guards, put them in a cell with a broken lock. They were to free the prisoners and arm them if the rest of the team didn't return in good time.

The soldiers recovered their guns and armor from a pile outside the storage room and one by one loped toward the T-intersection next to the stairwell. A firefight had broken out down there. Venera had her pistol in her hand but ended up in the rear, down on all fours as bullets sprayed overhead.

For a few minutes there was shouting and shooting. When it became clear that the men in the stairwell were of Sacrus, somebody threw a grenade at them, but more shots were coming from the side—the top right arm of the T from Venera's perspective. That was the direction the commandant's men had originally come from. The stairwell was at the very top of the T, the storage room behind her.

Now it was chaos and shooting again. Venera crawled to the left, to the spot where the metal cage had descended earlier. It was gone. She raised her head slightly and saw, through smoke and dim light, that the great metal door to the treasure room was open.

Bryce and the others had made it into the now-cleared stairwell but Venera had been too slow. Soldiers of Sacrus emerged from clouds of gunsmoke, faceless in the faint light. Venera scrambled to her feet, slipped on blood, and half-fell through the doorway into the treasure room. Her feet found purchase on the carpet and she pressed her whole body against the cold door. It slowly creaked shut, ringing from bullet impacts at the last instant.

She spun the wheel in the center of the portal and turned

around to lean on it. A sound hangover echoed through her head for a few seconds; or was she still hearing the battle, but muffled by iron and stone?

Stepping forward she lifted her arms, saw blood all over them. Something caught her foot and she stumbled. Looking down she saw that it was another body—a soldier of Sacrus, maybe the very one with whom she'd locked eyes through the little glass window in the door. He lay on his back, arms flung about and blood pooling behind his head.

His abdomen had been cut wide open and his entrails trailed along the floor.

A new wash of fear came over Venera. She backed against the door and brought up her pistol to check it. Wouldn't do to have a misfire due to blood in the barrel. For a few moments she stood perfectly still, listening and, finally, looking about at the place she had come to.

The huge square room was lit better than the hallway had been, by small electric spotlights that hung over dozens of pedestals. She had glimpsed those earlier, the canisters and boxes atop them now glowing in surreal majesty. There was nobody else in sight, but she thought she could see another door opposite the one through which she'd entered.

A woman chuckled somewhere; the chuckle turned into a laugh of childish delight.

Venera made her way around the room's perimeter in quick sprints, ducking from pedestal to pedestal. It was hard to tell where the laughter was coming from because sounds echoed off the high ceiling. Faintly, through the floor, she could still hear the noise of battle.

The laugh came again—this time from only a few yards away. Venera rounded a broad pedestal surmounted by some kind of cannon and stopped dead, pistol forgotten in her hand.

A big clockwork mechanism had been shoved off the next pedestal and now lay shattered on the floor. Little wisps of smoke rose from it. The pedestal itself was covered with the remains of a man.

Somebody was kneeling in the gore and viscera that dripped over the edges of the pedestal. It was a woman, completely nude, and she was bathing—no, wallowing—in the blood and slippery things she was hauling out of the man's torso. She stroked her skin with something, squeezing it as if it were a wet sponge, and gave a little mewl of delight.

Venera raised the pistol and aimed carefully. "Margit! What have you done?"

The former botanist of Liris cocked her head at Venera. She grinned, holding up two crimson hands.

"Don't you get it?" she said. "It's cherries! Red, red cherries, full and ripe."

"Wh-who—" Venera had suddenly remembered the commandant's boast. He had found a hideous death for Garth, he'd said. She stepped forward, staring past a haze of nausea at the few scraps of clothing she could recognize. Those boots—they were Sacrus army issue.

"They trusted me," said Margit as she lowered herself into the sticky mass she was massaging. "These two knew me—so they let me in. When the bombs went off, the wall and door parted a bit—the hinges sprung! I just pushed it open and ran right out of my little room! Nobody there to stop me. So I came here and brought him with me."

"Brought who?"

Margit raised a hand to point at something lying in the shadows of another pedestal. "The one they'd just given to me. My present."

"Garth!" Venera ran over to him. He was on his side, uncon-scious but breathing. His hands were tied behind his back. Ven-era knelt to undo the knots, putting her pistol down when she decided Margit was too far into her own delusions to notice.

Far gone she might be, but she'd killed at least two men in this room. "You must have ambushed them," said Venera, mak-ing it into a question.

"Oh yes. I was dressed oh-so respectably and had my pris-oner with me. They were staring out the window, you people were shooting and thrashing about somewhere out of sight, and I just popped up there in front of them. 'Let me in!' Oh, I looked so scared. As soon as their backs were to me I mowed them down."

"There were only two?"

Margit clucked reproachfully. "How many people do you put inside a locked vault? Two was overkill, but you see the doors don't open from the outside. That's a *precaution*." She enunciated the word cheerfully.

Venera slapped Garth lightly; he groaned and mumbled something, batting feebly at her hand.

She looked up at Margit again. "Why come here?"

Margit stood up, dripping. "You know why," she said, suddenly serious. "For *that*." She pointed, straight-armed, at something on the floor.

It was crimson now, but there was no mistaking the cylindrical shape of the key to Candesce. When Venera saw it she gasped and raised the pistol again, cocking it as she tried to haul Garth to his feet with her other hand.

Margit frowned. "Don't deny me my destiny, Venera. Behold!" She struck one of her poses, throwing her arms out in the spot-light. "You gaze upon the queen of Candesce!"

"V-Venera?" Garth blinked at her, then focused past her at Margit. "What the—"

"Quickly now, Garth." She half-carried him over to the blood-smeared stones where the key lay. She let go of him and reached to scoop it up, still keeping a bead on Margit.

The botanist simply stood there, awash in light and gore, and watched as Venera and Garth backed away.

She was still watching when they made it to the chamber's other door and spun the wheel to open it.

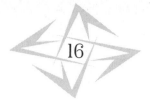

16

VENERA'S PARACHUTE YANKED at her shoulders vi-
ciously. All the breath drove out of her, the world spun, and then
a sublime calm seemed to ease into the world: the savage wind
diminished, became gentle, and the roar of gunfire faded.
Weight, too, slackened and in moments she found she had come
to a stop in dawn-lit air that was crisp but hinted at a warm day
to come.

All around her other parachutes had bloomed like night
flowers. There were shouts, screaming—but also laughter.
Corinne's people were taking charge; the air below Spyre was
their territory. "Catch this rope!" one of them commanded,
tossing a length at Venera. She grabbed it and he began to draw
her in.

The knot of people waited a hundred feet from the madly
spinning hull of Spyre. Twenty had arrived here in the early
morning hours, but more than seventy were leaving. There
hadn't been enough parachutes, but Sacrus had helpfully decorated its corridors with heavy black drapes. Many of these were
now held by former prisoners. Having belled with air to brake
them, the black squares were now twisting like smoke and were
starting to get in the way as people tried to grab one another by
wrist, fingertip, or foot.

She pulled herself up Garth's leg, hooked a hand in his belt, and met him at eye level. "Are you okay?" He still seemed disoriented and for a moment he just stared back at her.

"Did you come for me?" His voice was hoarse and she didn't like to think why. There were burn marks on his cheeks and hands and he looked thinner and older than ever.

Venera smoothed the backs of her fingers down the side of his face. "I came for you," she said, and was surprised to see tears start in his eyes.

Of course, she'd also gone in to find the key to Candesce— but now wasn't the politic time to say that.

"Listen up!" It was the leader of Corinne's troupe. "We've just passed Fin and I let out the signal flare. In a couple of minutes it's going to come by again and they'll have lowered a net! We're going to land in that net, all of us. Then we'll be drawn up into Fin. We need to stick together or people will get left behind."

"Isn't Sacrus going to pass us first?" somebody asked.

"Yes. So everybody with a gun get to the top. And unravel those drapes, we can use them to hide behind."

As Spyre rotated first Buridan, then Sacrus would go by before Fin came around again. The soldiers of Sacrus had been right on their heels as Venera's group crowded into the basement. Doubtless they would be bringing heavy machine guns down, or grenades or—it didn't bear thinking about because there was nothing to be done. For a few seconds at least, Venera and her people were going to be helpless targets pinioned in air.

"Ouch!" said a woman near Venera's feet. "I—ouch! Hey, ohmigod—" She screamed suddenly, a frantic yelp that grew into a wail.

Venera spun around to look. Dark shapes flickered around the woman's silhouette, half-seen but growing in number. "Piranhawks!" someone shouted.

A second later there were thousands of them, a swirling

cloud that completely enveloped the screaming woman. Her cries turned to horrible retching sounds and then stopped. Buzzing wings were everywhere, caressing Venera's throat and tossing her hair, but so far nothing had bitten her.

Nobody spoke. Nobody moved, and after a minute the cloud of piranhawks began to smear away into the air. They left behind a coiling cloud of black feathers and atomized red, at its heart a horrible thing bereft of blood and flesh.

"Brace yourselves! Here comes the airfall!" Venera looked up in time to see the latticework of girders that supported Buridan Tower flash past. In the next instant a fist of wind hit her.

Garth was nearly torn from her grasp by the pounding air. Two people who had refused to untie themselves from the black drapes were simply blown away, disappearing in moments into a distance blurred with barbed wire and mines. Others simply let go of their neighbors for a second and found themselves being drawn slowly, leisurely away as the airfall passed by and calmer air returned.

"Catch the rope! Catch it!" She watched the lines being tossed and frantic lunges to catch them; then one of the men who'd drifted a few yards away shuddered and spun. Dark lines stood in the air behind him for an instant before snapping and becoming thousands of red droplets. She heard machine gun fire.

"Sacrus! Return fire!" Everybody opened up on the small knot of pipes and the machine gun nest as it swept down and at them. Tracer rounds framed and dissected a vision of mauve cloud and amber sunlight. Venera blinked and couldn't see, waved her pistol hesitantly. Then Sacrus lofted up and away and the firing ceased.

"Get ready!"

Ready? Ready for what—the net caught her limp and unresisting and that probably saved Venera from a broken neck. As thin cords dug into her face and hands she was hauled into speeding air again, faster and faster until all breath was sucked out of her and spots danced in her eyes. Just as the howl and tearing fingers of the hurricane became intolerable it ceased so abruptly that she just lay for a while, staring at nothing. Gradually she made out voices, sounds of something heavy being shut as the wind sound cut out. Lantern light glowed below a metal ceiling where shadows of people hove to and fro. She rolled over.

Garth Diamandis was sitting up next to her. He probed at the back of his head carefully, then darted his eyes back and forth at the people who surrounded them. "Where are we?"

"Among friends," she said. "Safe. At least for now."

BLOOD SLID DOWN the drain, miniature rivers in the greater flow of water. After all that had happened, Venera was surprised to find that none of it was hers. By rights she should have been riddled with holes last night.

The facilities of Fin were primitive but the water was wonderfully hot. She dallied in the rusted metal cabinet that stood in for a shower, letting the stuff run over and off her in sheets, holding her face under it. Not thinking, though her hands still shook.

A loud banging startled her and she almost slipped. Venera flung open the sheet-metal door. "What?"

Bryce stood there. His glower turned to distraction as he took in her naked form. In a moment of reflected vision, she saw his gaze lower, pause, drop, pause again. Then he caught himself and met her eyes. "You're going to use up all the hot water," he said in a reasonable tone.

She slammed the door but it was too late; she could practically feel the line drawn down her body by his eyes. "So what if I use it all?" she said gamely. "You're a man—take yours cold."

"Not if I don't have to." She heard rattling around the side of the enclosure. "There's a master valve here, but I'm not sure whether it's for the cold or the hot. I'll give it a few turns . . ."

She threw the door open again and stalked past him to grab the rag they'd told her was her towel. Wrapping it around herself as best she could, she did a double take as she saw him watching her again. "Well?" she said. "What are you waiting for?"

"Huh?"

"Get in there." She crossed her arms and waited. Bryce turned his back to her as he undressed, but she didn't give him any relief. It was her turn to admire. With a sour glance that held more than a little humor, he stepped into the stall.

Venera leaned over to look at the side of the enclosure; there was the valve he'd mentioned. It was momentarily tempting to give a few turns—she could imagine his shouts quite vividly—but no. She was an adult, after all.

She left the enclosure and stepped gingerly over the grillwork floor to the little closet Fin had prepared for her. Despite the stares of those billeted in the hallway, she made her way to where Garth Diamandis lay. He was awake but listless. Still, he half-smiled as he saw her.

"Ah, that you should dress so for me," he murmured.

Venera smoothed the hair back from his brow. "What's wrong?"

He looked away, lips twisting. Then: "It was her. She betrayed me to them."

"Your woman? —Wife? Mistress?"

A heavy sigh escaped him. "My daughter."

Venera stepped back, shocked. For a moment she had no idea what to say, because her whole understanding of this man had been changed in one stroke. "Oh, Garth," she said stupidly. "I'm so sorry." *We daughters will do that*, she thought; but she didn't say it.

She held his hand for a minute until he gently disengaged it and turned on his side. "You must be cold," he said. "Go get some rest." So, reluctantly, she left him on his cot in the hallway.

She mused about this surprising new Garth as she threaded her way back to her sleeping station. It was hard navigating the place; the nation of Fin was less than thirty feet wide at its broadest point. Since it was literally a fin, an aileron for controlling Spyre's spin and direction, the place was streamlined and reinforced inside by crisscrossing girders. The citizens of the pocket nation had built floors and chambers all through the vertical wing and grudgingly added several ladder wells. Where Garth lay was not a corridor as such, however—just a more or less labyrinthine route between the rooms that were strung the length of the level. Privacy was to be had only within the sleeping chambers, where the ever-present roar of air just behind the walls drowned all other sounds.

Fin didn't have the capacity for an extra seventy or so people. Venera had been informed by an impatient Corinne that they must all leave by nightfall. That suited her fine—she had a meeting with the council later today in any case. But she needed to sleep first. So she was grateful for the little bed they'd prepared behind a set of metal cabinets. You had to squeeze around the last cabinet to get in here and there were no windows; still, it had an air of privacy. She rolled out of the towel and under the blanket.

Venera willed herself to sleep, but she was still a mass of

nerves from the events of the night. And, she had to admit, there was something else keeping her awake . . .

A blundering noise jolted her into sitting up. She groped for a nonexistent weapon. Somebody was blocking the light that leaked around the cabinets. "Who—"

"Oh, no! You!" Bryce stood there, his nakedness punctuated by the towel at his waist. His hands were on his hips.

Venera snatched up the blanket. "Don't tell me they put you in with me."

"Said there wasn't any room. Last good place was here." He crossed his arms. "Well?"

"Well what?"

"You've had at least fifteen minutes to sleep. My turn."

"Your—?" She reached for one of her boots and threw it at him. "Get out! This is my room!" Bryce ducked adroitly and stepped up, grabbing at her wrist. She rabbit-punched him in the stomach; the only effect was that his towel fell off.

He took advantage of her surprise to make a play for the bed. She managed to keep him from taking it but he did grab the blanket. She pulled it back; she kicked him and he toppled onto the mattress. He sprawled, laying claim to as much of it as he could, and pushed her to the edge.

"No you don't! My bed!" She tried to climb over him, aiming to reconquer the corner, but his hand was on her wrist then her shoulder and her breast and his other gripped the inside of her thigh. Bryce picked her up that way and would have thrown her off the bed if she hadn't squirmed her way loose. She landed straddling him and grabbed for the sheets on either side of his shoulders so when he pushed at her she had a good grip.

He was getting hard against her pubic bone and his hands were on her breasts again. Venera mashed her palm against his face and reared back but now his hands were on her hips and he was pulling her hard against him. They rocked together and she clawed at his chest.

Grabbing him around the shoulders she kissed him, feeling her nipples tease the hairs on his chest. All their movement was making him slide against her wetness and suddenly he was inside her. Venera gasped and reared up, pushing down on him with all her weight.

She leaned forward until they were nose to nose. "My bed," she hissed, grinning.

They were locked together now and each motion by one made the other respond. She had a hand behind his neck and his were behind her spreading her as they kissed and the bed shook and threatened to collapse. She bucked and rode him like the Buridan must have ridden their horses, all pounding muscle under her until wave after wave of pleasure mounted up her core and she came with a loud cry. Moments later he did the same, bouncing her up and nearly off of him. She held on and rode it out, then collapsed on the bellows of his chest.

"See?" he said. "You *can* share."

Well.

Venera wasn't about to dignify his statement with a response; but this was certainly going to change things. Now sleep really was coming over her, though, and she had no ability to think more about it. She nuzzled his shoulder.

Damn it.

THE SPYRE COUNCIL building was satisfyingly grandiose. It sprawled like a well-fed spider over an acre of town-wheel, with outbuildings and annexes like black-roofed legs half-encircling the nearby streets, plazas, and offices of the bureaucracy.

The back of the spider was an ornate glass and wrought-iron dome surmounted by an absurdly dramatic black statue of a woman thrusting a sword into the air. The statue must have been thirty feet tall. Venera admired it as she strolled up the broad ramp that led to the council chamber.

She was aware of many eyes watching her. Word had gotten around quickly of the events last night, and Lesser Spyre was quietly but visibly tense. Shops had closed early; people hurried through the streets. The architecture of the spider did not permit large assemblies—Spyre was not the sort of place to encourage mass demonstrations—but the people were a presence here nonetheless, standing in groups of two to ten to twenty on street corners and under the shadowy canopies of bridges. It was their presence, and not memory or reason, that convinced Venera that she had today done something highly significant.

Her own appearance must confirm that. She wore a high-collared black leather coat over a scarlet blouse, with her bleached shock of hair standing straight up and silver trefoil-shaped bangles the size of her hand hanging from her ears. Her makeup was dark—she'd redrawn her brows as two obsessively black lines. Trailing behind her in a V-formation like a flock of grim birds were two dozen people, all similarly startling to look upon. Some appeared pale and unsteady, their faces and exposed hands bearing bruises and burn marks. Others attended these souls, and marching behind like giant tin toys were soldiers of Liris and various preservationist factions. Venera knew that Bryce's people peppered the crowds, there to listen and give an alert if necessary.

"Do you think Jacoby Sarto brings his gun to council meetings?" she asked offhandedly. Corinne, who was walking beside her, guffawed.

"Here," she said, handing Venera a large black pistol, "try to take this in and see what happens. No, seriously. If they don't stop you, then he's probably got one too. You may need to get the drop on him."

"I can do that." She took the pistol and slipped it into her jacket, which promptly dragged down her right collar. She transferred it to the back of her belt.

"Not too obvious," said Corinne doubtfully.

A preservationist runner puffed to a stop next to her and saluted. "They're on the move, ma'am. Five groups of a hundred or more each were just seen exiting the grounds of Sacrus. They're in no-man's-land now but they have nowhere to go except through their neighbors. Of course, they own most of those estates . . ."

"What have they got?" she asked. "Artillery?"

He nodded. "We're moving to secure the elevator cables, but they're doing the same thing," he continued. "There's been no shots fired yet . . ."

"All right." She dismissed the details with a wave of her hand. "Let me see what we can do in council. We'll talk after that." He nodded and backed off.

The big front doors of the building were for council members only. The ceremonial guards there, with their plumed helmets and giant muskets, raised their palms solemnly to exclude the people following Venera. She turned and gestured with her chin for them to go around the side; she'd been told there was a second, more-traveled entrance there for diplomats, attachés, and other functionaries. She strode alone into the frescoed portico that half-circled the chamber itself.

The bronze council chamber doors were open and a small crowd was milling there. She recognized the other members; they were just filing in.

Jacoby Sarto was talking to Pamela Anseratte. He looked relaxed. She looked tense. He spotted Venera and, surprisingly, smiled.

"Ah, there you are," he said, strolling over to her. Venera glanced around to see what other people—or pillars or statues to hide behind—were nearby, and started to reach for the pistol. But Sarto simply took her arm and led her a bit to the side of the group.

"The preservationists and lesser countries are following you right now," he said. "But I can't see that continuing, can you? The only leverage you've got is the name of Buridan."

She extricated her arm and smiled back at him. "Well, that depends on the outcome of this meeting, I should think," she said. He nodded affably.

"I'm here to engineer a crisis," he said. "How about you?"

"I should have thought we were already in a crisis," she said cautiously. "Your troops are on the move."

"And we've seized the docks," he said. "But that may not be enough to serve either of our interests." She tried to read his expression, but Sarto was a master politician. He gave no sign that Spyre was balanced on the edge of its greatest crisis in centuries.

"Our interests aren't the same," he continued, "but they're surprisingly . . . compatible. You're after power, but not so much power as you'd have to have if you used the key again. It's difficult—you possess the ultimate weapon but no way to use it to get what you want. But the blunt fact is that as long as we hold the docks, the little trinket you stole from us last night is even worse than useless to you," he said. "It's an active liability."

She stared at him.

Apparently oblivious to her expression, Sarto continued as though he were discussing the budget for municipal plumbing contracts. "On the other hand, the polarization of allegiance you're generating is useful to us. I've been impressed, Ms. Fanning, by your abilities—last night's raid came as a complete surprise, advantageous as it's turned out to be. You got what you wanted, we get what we want, which is to flush out our enemies. The only matter of dispute between us, privately, is that ivory wand you took."

"You want it back?"

He nodded.

"Go fuck yourself!" She started to stalk toward the giant doorway but couldn't resist turning and saying, "You tortured my man Garth! You think this is a game?"

"The only way to win," he said so quietly that the others couldn't hear, "is to treat it as one." Now his expression was serious, his gray eyes cold as a statue's.

It was suddenly clear to Venera that Sacrus already knew what she had been planning to say and do here today—and they approved. She made an excellent enemy for them to rally their own forces around. If they had needed an excuse to extend martial law over their neighbors, she had provided it. If civil war came, they would have their justification for marshaling the ancient Spyre fleet. The civil war would provide a nice smokescreen behind which they could seize Candesce. It wouldn't matter then whether they won or lost back home.

She had given them the enemy they needed. Sarto's candid admission of the fact was a clear overture from him.

Venera hesitated. Then, deliberately clamping down on her anger, she walked back to him. They were now the only council members remaining in the hall. The others had taken their seats, and she saw one or two craning their necks to watch their confrontation.

"What do I get if I return the key?" she asked.

He smiled again. "What you want. Power. For the rest, take

your satisfaction by attacking us. We know you'll be sincere. We're counting on it. Only return the key, and at the end of the war you'll get everything you want. You know we can deliver." He held out his hand, palm up.

She laughed lightly, though she felt sick. "I don't have it with me," she said. "And besides, I have no reason to trust you. None at all."

Now Sarto looked annoyed. "We thought you'd say that. You need a guarantee, a token of our sincerity. My masters have . . . instructed me . . . to provide you with one."

She laughed bitterly. "What could you possibly give me that would convince me you were sincere?"

His expression darkened even further; for the first time he looked genuinely angry. Sarto spoke a single word. Venera gaped at him in undisguised astonishment, then laughed again. It was the bray of disdain she reserved for putting people down, and she was sure Sarto knew it.

However, he merely bowed slightly and turned to indicate that she should precede him into the chamber. The doors were wide, and so they entered side by side. As they did so Venera caught sight of Sarto's expression and was amazed. In a few seconds he had undergone a gruesome transformation from the merely dark expression he'd displayed outside to a mask of twisted fury. By the time they split up halfway across the polished marble floor he looked like he was ready to murder someone. Venera kept her own expression neutral, her eyes straight ahead of her as she climbed the red-carpeted steps to the long disused seat of Buridan.

The council members had been chatting, but one by one they fell silent and stared. Several of those were gazes of surprise; although they were masked, the ministers from Oxorn and Garrat were leaning forward in their seats as if unsure whether to run or dive under their chairs. August Virilio's usual expression of polite disdain was gone, in its place a brooding anger that seemed transplanted from an entirely different man.

Pamela Anseratte stood as soon as they were seated, and banged her gavel on a little table. "We were supposed to be gathering today to discuss the change of stewardship of the Spyre docks," she began. "But obviously—"

"She has started a war!"

Jacoby Sarto was on his feet before the echoes of his voice died out—and so were the rest of the ministers. For a long moment everyone was talking at once while Anseratte pounded her gavel ineffectually. Then Sarto held up one hand in a magisterial gesture. He gravely hoisted a stack of papers over his head. "I hold the signed declarations in my hand," he rumbled. "This is nothing less than the start of that civil conflict we have all been dreading— an unprovoked, vicious attack in the heartland of Sacrus itself—"

"To rescue those people *you* kidnapped," Venera said. She remained obstinately in her seat. "Citizens of sovereign states, abducted from their homes by agents of Sacrus."

"Impudence!" roared Sarto. Half the members were still on their feet; in the pillared gallery that opened up behind the council pew, the coteries of ministers, secretaries, courtiers, and generals that each council member held in reserve were glaring at one another and at her. Several clenched the pommels of half-drawn swords.

"I have a partial list of names," continued Venera, "of those we rescued from Sacrus's dungeon last night. They include," she shouted to drown out hecklers from the gallery, "citizens of every nation represented on this council, including Buridan. The council will not deny that I had every right to seek the repatriation of my own kinsman?" She looked around, locking eyes with the unmasked members.

Principe Guinevera's jowls quivered as he thunked solidly into his seat. "You're not going to claim that Sacrus stole one of my citizens? Surely—" He stopped as he saw her scan the list and then hold up her hand.

"Her name is Melissa Ferania," said Venera.

"Ferania, Ferania . . . I know that name . . ." Guinevera's brows knit. "It was a suicide. They never found a body."

Venera smiled. "Well, you'll find her right now if you turn your head." She gestured to the gallery.

The whole council craned their necks to look. People had been filing into the Buridan section of the gallery for several minutes; in the ruckus nobody on the council had noticed.

On cue, Melissa Ferania stood up and bowed to Guinevera.

"Oh my dear, my dear child," he said, tears starting at the corners of his eyes.

"I have more names," said Venera, eyeing Jacoby Sarto. Everyone else was staring into the gallery and he took the opportunity to meet her eye and nod slightly.

Venera felt a sinking sensation in the pit of her stomach.

She had stage-managed this confrontation for maximum effect, calling for volunteers from the recently rescued to attend the scheduled council meeting with her. Garth alone had refused to come; pale and still refusing to talk about his experience in the tower, he had remained outside in the street. But there were prisoners from Liris here as well as half a dozen other minor nations. As her trump card, she had brought people taken from the great nations of the council itself.

Sarto seemed more than unfazed at this tactic. He seemed *satisfied.*

She realized that a black silence had descended on the chamber. Everyone was looking at her. Clearing her throat, she said—her own words sounding distant to herself—"I move for immediate

censure of Sacrus and the suspension of its rights on the council
of Spyre. Pending, uh . . . pending a thorough investigation of
their recent activities."

For once, Pamela Anseratte looked out of her depth. "Ah . . .
what?" She pulled her gaze back from the gallery.

August Virilio laughed. "She wants us to expel Sacrus. A marvelous idea if I do say so myself—however impractical it may
be."

Venera rallied herself. She shrugged. "Gain a seat, lose a
seat . . . besides," she said more loudly, "it's a matter of justice."

Virilio toyed with a pen. "Maybe. Maybe—but Buridan forgot its own declaration of war before it invaded Sacrus. That nul-
lifies your moral high ground, my dear."

"It doesn't nullify them." She swept her arm to indicate the
people behind her.

"Yes, marvelous grandstanding," said Virilio drily. "No
doubt the majority of our council members are properly
shocked at your revelation. Yet we must deal with practicalities.
Sacrus is too important to Spyre to be turfed off the council for
these misdemeanors, however serious they may seem. In fact,
Jacoby Sarto was just now leveling some serious charges against
you."

There was more shouting and hand waving—and yet, for a
few moments, it seemed to Venera as though she were alone in
the room with Jacoby Sarto. She looked to him, and he met her
gaze. All expression had drained from his face.

When he opened his mouth again it would be to reveal her
true identity to these people: he would name her as Venera Fanning and the sound of her name would act like a vast hand, toppling the whole edifice she had built. Though most of her allies
knew or suspected she was an imposter, it had been neither polite

nor expedient for them to admit it. If forced to admit what they already knew, however, they would find her the perfect person to blame for the impending war. All her allies would desert her, or if they didn't at least they would cease listening to her. Sarto had the power to cast her out, have her imprisoned . . . if she didn't counter with her own bombshell.

This was the great gamble she had known she would have to take if she came here today. She had rehearsed it in her mind over and over: Sarto would reveal that she was the notorious Venera Fanning, who was implicated in dastardly scandals in the principalities. Opinion would turn against her and so, in turn, she would have to tell the people of Spyre another great secret. She would reveal the existence of the key to Candesce and declare that it was the cause of the coming war—a war engineered by Sacrus for its own convenience.

And now the moment had come. Sarto blinked slowly, looked away from her, and said, "I have here my own list. It is a list of innocent civilians killed last night by Amandera Thrace-Guiles and her men."

Braced as she was for one outcome, it took Venera some seconds to understand what Sarto had said. He had called her *Amandera Thrace-Guiles*. He was not going to reveal her secret.

And in return, he expected her not to reveal his.

The council members were shouting; Guinevera was embracing his long-lost countrywoman and weeping openly; August Virilio had his arms crossed as he stared around in obvious disgust. Swords had been drawn in the gallery and the ceremonial guards were rushing to do their job for the first time in their lives. Abject, shoulders slumped, Pamela Anseratte stood with gesturing people and words swirling around her, her hand holding a slip of paper that might have been her original agenda for the meeting.

It all felt distant and half-real to Venera. She had to make a decision, right now.

Jacoby Sarto's eyes were drilling into her.

She cleared her throat, hesitated one last second, and reached behind her.

17

TREBLE WAS A musician by day and a member of Bryce's underground by night. He'd always known that he might be called upon to abandon his façade of serene artistry and fight in the cause—though like some of the others in the secret organization, he was uneasy with the direction things had taken lately. Bryce was becoming altogether too cozy with the imposing Amandera Thrace-Guiles.

Not that it mattered anymore, as of this minute. Clinging to a knuckle of masonry high on the side of the Lesser Spyre Ministry of Justice, Treble was in an ideal position to watch the city descend into anarchy.

Treble had gained access to the building disguised as a petitioner seeking information about an imprisoned relative. His assignment was to plant some false records in a Ministry file cabinet on the twelfth floor. He evaded the guards adroitly, made his way up the creaking stairs with no difficulty, and had just ensconced himself in the records office when two things happened simultaneously: the staccato sound of gunfire echoed in through the half-open window; and three minor bureaucrats approached the office, talking and laughing loudly.

This was why Treble found himself clutching a rounded chunk of masonry that might once have been a gargoyle, and why he was staring in fascination at the streets that lay below and wrapped up and around the ring of the town-wheel. He hardly knew where to look. Little puffs of smoke were appearing around the Spyre docks directly overhead. The buildings there hovered in midair like child's toys floating in a bathtub and seldom moved; now several were gliding slowly—and ominously—on collision courses. Several ships had cast off. Meanwhile, halfway up the curve of the wheel, some other commotion had sprung up around the Buridan estate. Barnacled as it was by other buildings, he could never have identified the place had he not been familiar with the layout but it was clearly the source of that tall pillar of smoke that stood up two hundred feet before bending over and wrapping itself in a fading spiral around and around the inner space of the wheel.

People were running in the avenue below. Ever the conscientious spy, Treble shifted his position so that he straddled the masonry. He checked his watch, then pulled out a frayed notebook and a stub pencil. He dabbed the pencil on the tip of his tongue then squinted around.

Item one: at four-fourteen o'clock, the preservationists broke our agreement by attempting to prevent Sacrus from occupying the docks. At least, that was what Treble assumed was happening. The hastily scrawled note from Bryce that had mobilized the resistance told of arguments during the Sacrus raid last night, hasty plans made and discarded in the heat of the moment. Thrace-Guiles wanted to rally the nations of Greater Spyre that had lost people to Sacrus. The preservationists had their own agenda, which involved cowing Sacrus into letting them run a railway line through the middle of the great nation's lands. Sacrus itself was moving and activating its allies. So much was clear; but in the background of this fairly clear political situation, a greater upheaval was taking place.

Bryce had said on more than one occasion that Spyre was like the mainspring of a watch wound too tight. A single tap in the right place might cause a vicious uncoiling—a *snap*. Many in Spyre had read about the Pantry War with envy; over centuries a thousand resentments and grudges had built up between the pocket nations and it was glorious to watch someone else finally try to settle a score. Everyone kept ledgers accounting who had slighted whom and when. Nothing was forgotten and behind their ivy-and-moss-softened walls, the monarchs and presidents of nations little bigger than swimming pools spent their lives plotting their revenges.

The well-planned atrocities of the resistance were little triphammer blows on the watch's case, each one an attempt to break the mechanism. Tap the watch, shake it, and listen. Tap it again. That had been Bryce's strategy.

Sacrus and Buridan had hit the sweet spot. Shopfronts were slamming all over the place, like air-clams caught in a beam of sunlight, while gangs of men carrying truncheons and knives seemed to materialize like smoke out of the alleys. It was time for a settling of scores.

Item two: chaos in the streets. Maybe time to distribute currency?

Treble peered at the line of smoke coiling inside the wheel. *Item three: Sacrus seems to have had more agents in place in the city than we thought. They appear to be moving against Buridan without council approval. So . . . Item four: council no longer effective?*

He underlined the last sentence, then thought better and crossed it out. Obviously the council was no longer in control.

He leaned over and examined the flagstoned street a hundred feet below. Some of those running figures were recognizable. In fact . . .

Was that Amandera Thrace-Guiles? He shaded his eyes against Candesce's fire and looked again. Yes, he recognized the shock of bleached hair that surmounted her head. She was hurrying along the avenue with one arm raised to shoulder height. Apparently she was aiming a pistol at the man walking ahead of her. Oh that was definitely her then.

Around her a mob swirled. Treble recognized some of his compatriots; there were others, assorted preservationists, soldiers of minor nations, even one or two council guards. Were they escorting Thrace-Guiles or protecting someone else Treble hadn't spotted?

Item five: council meeting ended around four o'clock.

He sighted in the direction Thrace-Guiles's party was taking. They were headed for the Buridan estate. From ground level they probably couldn't tell that place was besieged. At this rate they might walk right into a crowd of Sacrus soldiers.

Treble could still hear voices in the room behind him. He tapped the file folder in his coat pocket and frowned. Then with a shrug he swung off his masonry perch and through the opened window.

The three bureaucrats stared at him in shock. Treble felt the way he did when he dropped a note in performance; he grinned apologetically, said, "Here, file this," and tossed his now-redundant folder to one of the men. Then he ran out the door and made for the stairs.

GARTH DIAMANDIS STAGGERED and reached out to steady himself against the wall of a building. He had to keep up; Venera Fanning was striding in great steps along the avenue, her pistol held unwaveringly to Jacoby Sarto's head. But Garth was confused; people were running and shouting while overhead even lines of smoke divided the sky. This was Lesser Spyre, he was sure of that. The granite voice of his interrogator still echoed in Garth's mind, though, and his arms and legs bellowed pain from the many burns and cuts that ribbed them.

He had insisted on coming today and now he regretted it. Once upon a time he'd been a young man and able to bounce back from anything. Not so anymore. The gravity here weighed heavily on him and for the first time he wished he was back on Greater Spyre where he could still climb trees like a boy. Alone all those years, he had reached an accommodation with himself and his past; there'd been days when he enjoyed himself as if he really were a youth again. And then the woman who now stalked down the center of the avenue ahead of him had appeared, like a burning cross in the sky, and proceeded to turn his solitary life upside down.

He'd thought about abandoning Venera dozens of times. She was self-reliance personified, after all. She wouldn't miss him. Once or twice he had gotten as far as stepping out the door of the Buridan estate. Looking down those half-familiar, secretive streets, he had realized that he had nowhere to go—nowhere, that is, unless he could find Selene, the daughter of the woman whose love had caused Garth's exile.

Logic told him that now was the time. Venera was bound to lose this foolish war she'd started with Sacrus. The prudent course for Garth would be to run and hide, lick his wounds in secret and then . . .

Ah. It was this *and then* that was the problem. He had found Selene, and she had turned him over to Sacrus. She was theirs—a recruit, like the ones Moss claimed had left many of Spyre's sovereign lands. Sacrus had promised Selene something, had lied to her; they must have. But Garth was too old to fight them and too old to think of all the clever and true words that might win his daughter's heart.

Selene, his kin, had betrayed him. And Venera Fanning, who owed him nothing, had risked her life to save his.

He pushed himself off from the wall and struggled to catch up to her.

A man ran down the broad steps of the Justice ministry. He waved his arms over his head. "Don't go that way! Not safe!"

Venera paused and glanced at him. "You're one of Bryce's."

"That I am, Miss Thrace-Guiles." Garth half-smiled at the man's bravado; these democrats refused to address people by their titles. Venera didn't seem to notice, and they had a hurried conversation that Garth couldn't hear.

"There you are." He turned to find the preservationist, Thinblood, sauntering up behind him. He grinned at Garth. "You ran off like a startled hare when she came out of the council chamber."

Garth grunted. Thinblood seemed to have decided he was an old man who needed coddling. It was annoying. He had to admit to himself that it was a relief to have him here, though. The rest of this motley party consisted mostly of Venera's other freed prisoners and they made for bad company, for much the same reasons as Garth supposed he did. They all looked apprehensive and tired. It didn't help that their presence at council didn't seem to have made a dent in Sacrus's support.

Garth and Thinblood had been talking under an awning across the street when Venera Fanning appeared at the official's entrance to the council chamber. She backed out slowly, her posture strange. As she emerged further it became clear that she was holding a gun and aiming it at someone. That someone had turned out to be Jacoby Sarto.

Before he knew it Garth was by her side. "What are you doing?" he heard himself shouting. She'd merely grimaced and kept backing up.

"Things didn't go our way," she'd said. Past Sarto, the council guards were lining up with their rifles aimed at her. At the same time, the commoner's doors around the long curve of the building were thrown open. A hoard of people spilled out, some of them fighting openly. Venera's supporters ran to her side as Bryce's agents appeared from nowhere to act as crowd control. And then a gasp went up from the watching crowd as Principe Guinevera and Pamela Anseratte pushed the council guards aside and came to stand at Venera's side.

"The lines have been drawn," Anseratte said to the council guards. "Sacrus is not on the council's side. Stand down."

Reluctantly, the guards lowered their rifles.

Garth leaned close to Venera. "Did he tell them your . . . se-cret?" But she shook her head.

Maybe it was having Thinblood's reassuring hand on his shoulder, but as Venera argued now with Bryce's spy, the fog of fatigue and pain lifted enough for Garth to begin to wonder about that. Jacoby Sarto had *not* told the council who Venera really was? That made no sense. Right now Amandera Thrace-Guiles was the darling of the old countries. She was the resurrected vic-tim of Sacrus's historical arrogance; she was a champion. If Sarto wanted to deflate Sacrus's opposition all he had to do was reveal that she was a fake.

"Why did she do it?" he wondered aloud. Thinblood laughed.

"You're trying to second-guess our Amandera?" He shook his head. "She's got too much fire in her blood, that's clear enough. Obviously she saw a chance to take Sarto and she went with it."

Garth shook his head. "The woman I know wouldn't see Sarto as a prize to be taken. She'd think him a burden and be happy to be rid of him. And if he's a prisoner why doesn't he seem more concerned?" Sarto was standing with his arms crossed, waiting patiently for Venera to finish her conversation. He seemed more to be *with* her than taken *by* her. Garth seemed to be the only who had noticed this.

"Attention!" Venera raised her pistol and for a moment he thought she was about to fire off a round. She already had the attention of everyone in sight, though, and seemed to realize it. "Buridan is under siege!" she cried. "Our ancient house is surrounded by Sacrus's people. We can't go back there."

Garth hurried over. "What are we going to do? They've moved faster than we anticipated."

She nodded grimly. "Apparently their ground forces are moving to surround the elevator cables. —The ones they can get to, that is."

"Most of our allies are on Greater Spyre," he said. If Sacrus isolated them up here in the city, they would have to rely on the preservationists, and a few clear-headed leaders such as Moss, to organize the forces down there.

For a moment that thought filled Garth with hope. If Venera was sidelined at this stage, she might be able to avoid being drawn into the heart of the coming conflagration. A checkmated Buridan might survive with honor, no matter who won.

Clearly Venera had no intention of going down that road. "We need to get down there," she was saying. "Sacrus doesn't control all the elevators. Pamela, your country's line, where is it?"

Anseratte shook her head. "It's two wheels away from here. We might make it, but if Sacrus already has men in the streets they've probably taken the axis cable cars as well."

Guinevera shook his head too. "Our line comes down about a mile from Carrangate. They're an old ally of Sacrus. They could use us for target practice on our way down."

"What about Liris?" It was one of Moss's men, standing alertly with a proud look in his eye. "Lady, we are the only nation in Spyre that has recently fought a war. There may not be many of us, but . . ."

She turned a dazzling smile on the man. "Thank you. Yes—but your elevator is above the Fair, isn't it?"

"And the Fair, m'lady, is six blocks up the wheel, that way." He pointed off to the left.

"This way!" Venera gestured for Sarto to precede her, then stalked toward the distant pile of buttresses and roofs that was the Fair.

Garth followed, but as the fog of exhaustion and pain slowly lifted from him he found himself considering their chances. It was folly for Venera to involve herself in this war. Sidelined, she might be safe.

Sacrus had known what to reveal about her to draw her fangs, but they had chosen not to reveal it. The only person on this side of the conflict who knew was Garth himself. If word got out, Venera would naturally assume that it was Sacrus's doing. It would be so simple . . .

Troubled but determined to follow this thought to its conclusion, Garth put an extra effort into his footsteps and kept up with Venera as she made for the Fair.

LIRIS PERCHED ON the very lip of the abyss. At sunoff the building's roof was soaked with light, all gold and purple and rose. The sky that opened beyond the battlement was open to all sides; Venera could almost imagine that she was back in the provinces of Meridian, where the town-wheels were small and manageable and you could fly through the free air whenever you chose. She leaned out, the better to lose herself in the radiance.

Tents had been set up on the rooftop behind her, and Moss was holding court to a wild variety of Spyre dignitaries. They came in all shapes and sizes, masked and unmasked, lords and ladies and diplomats and generalissimos. United by their fear of Sacrus and its allies, they were hastily assembling a battle plan while their tiny armies traveled here from across Greater Spyre. Venera had looked for those armies earlier—but who could spot a dozen men here or there making their way between the mazelike walls of the estates?

It would be an eerie journey, she knew. Garth had shown her the overgrown gates to estates whose windows were slathered with black paint, whose occupants had not been seen in generations. Smoke drifted from their chimneys; someone was home. The soldiers of her alliance might stop at one or two of those gateways and shout and rattle the iron, hoping to find allies within. But there would be no answer, unless it be a rifle shot from behind a wall.

For the first time in days, Venera found herself idle. She was too tired to look for something to do, and so as she gazed out at the endless skies that familiar deep melancholy stole over her. This time, she let it happen.

She wanted Chaison back. It was time to admit it. There were many moments every day when Venera longed to turn to him and grin, and say, "Look what I did!" or "Have you ever seen anything like it?" She'd had such a moment only an hour ago, as the first of the Dali horses were led into their new paddock in the far corner of Liris's lot. The spindly steeds had been trained to be ridden and she had mounted up herself and trotted one in a circle. Oh, she'd wanted to catch someone's eye at that moment! But she was Amandera Thrace-Guiles now. There was no one to appeal to, not even Garth, who had been making himself scarce since their arrival.

She heard a footstep behind her. Bryce leaned on the stones and casually reached out to take her hand. She almost snatched it back, but his touch awoke something in her. This was not the man she wanted; but there was some value in him wanting her. She smiled at him.

"All the pawns and knights are in play," he said. His thumb rubbed the back of her hand. "It's our opponent's move. What would you like to do while we wait?"

Venera's pulse quickened. His strong fingers were kneading her hand now, almost painfully.

"Uh . . . ," she said, then before she could talk herself out of it, "they've given me an actual room this time."

"Well." He smiled ironically. "That's an honor. Let's go try it out."

He walked toward the stairs. Venera hesitated, turning to look out at the dimming sky. No: the pang was still there, and no amount of time with Bryce was going to make it go away. But what was she to do?

Venera followed him down the stairs, her excitement mounting. Several people hailed her but she simply waved and hurried past. "This way," she said, grabbing Bryce's arm as he made to descend the main stairs. She dragged him through a doorway hidden behind a faded tapestry. This led to a narrow and dusty little corridor with several doors leading off of it. Hers was at the end.

She barely had time to open the door before his arms were around her waist. He kissed her with passionate force and together they staggered back to the bed under its little pebbled-glass window.

"Shut the door!" she gasped, and as he went to comply she undid her blouse. As he knelt on the bed she guided his hand under the silk. They kept their mouths locked together as they undressed one another, then she took his cock in her hands and didn't let go as they sank back onto the cushions.

Later as they sprawled across the demolished bed, he turned to her and said, "Are we partners?"

Venera blinked at him for a moment. Her mind had been entirely elsewhere—or, more exact, nowhere. "What?"

He shrugged onto his side and his hand casually fell on her hip. "Am I your employee? Or are we pursuing parallel interests?"

"Oh. Well, that's your decision, isn't it?"

"Hmm." He smiled, but she could tell he wasn't satisfied with that reply. "My people have been acting as your spies for the past few days. They're not happy about it. Truth to tell, Amandera, I'm not happy about it."

"Aaahhh . . ." She stretched and leaned back. "So the past hour was your way of softening me up for this conversation?"

"Well, no, but if there's going to be a good strategic moment to raise the issue, this has got to be it." She laughed at his audacity. He was no longer smiling, though.

"You'd be mistaken if you thought I was picking sides in this war," he said. "I don't give a damn whether it's Sacrus or your faction that wins. It's still titled nobles and it'll make no difference to the common people."

Now she sat up. "You want your printing press."

"I *have* my printing press. I forged your signature on some orders and it was delivered yesterday. Those of my people who aren't in the field right now are running it. Turning out bills by the thousands."

She examined his face in the candlelight. "So . . . how many of your people really *are* in the field?"

"A half-dozen."

"You told me they were all out!" She glared at him as a spasm of pain shot up her jaw. "A half-dozen? Is this why we had no warning that the estate was being attacked? Because you were keeping a handful of people where they'd be visible to me? —So I'd think they were all out?"

"That's about the size of it, yes."

She punched him in the chest. "You lost me my estate! My house! What else have you given to Sacrus?"

"Sacrus is not my affair," he said. Bryce was deadly earnest now. Clearly she had misjudged him. "Restoring emergent democracy in Virga is my only interest," he said. "But I don't want you to die in this war, and I'm sorry about your house if it's any consolation. But what choice did I have? If everything descends into chaos, when am I going to get my ink? My paper? When were you going to do what I needed you to do? Look me in the eye and tell me it was a priority for you."

Venera groaned. "Oh, Bryce. This is the worst possible time . . ."

"—The only time I have!"

"All right, all right, I see your point." She glowered at the plaster ceiling. "What if . . . what if I send some of my people in to run the press? We don't need trained insurgents to do that. All I want is to get your people out in the field! I'll give you as much ink and paper as you want."

He flopped onto his back. "I'll think about that."

There was a brief silence.

"You could have asked," she said.

"I did!"

Venera was trying to think of some way to reply to that when there was a loud bang and she found herself inside a storm of glass, shouting in surprise and trying to jump out of the way, banging her chin while shards like claws scrawled up her ribs and along her thigh.

Scratched and stunned, she sat up to find herself on the floor. Bryce was kneeling next to her. The candle had gone out and she sensed rather than saw the carpet of broken glass between her and her boots. The little window gaped, the leading bent and twisted to let in a puff of cold night air. "What was . . ." Now she heard gunfire.

"Oh shit." Bryce stood up and reached down to draw her to her feet. "We've got to get out there.

"Sacrus has arrived."

18

THERE WAS STILL a splinter in the ball of her foot but Venera had no time to find it and dig it out. She and Bryce raced up the stairs to the roof as shouts and thundering feet began to sound on the steps below.

They reached the roof and Bryce immediately ran off somewhere to the right. "I need to get to the semaphore!" he shouted before disappearing into the gloom. All the lanterns had been put out, Venera realized; she could just see the silhouettes of the tents where her people had been meeting. The black cutout shapes of men roved to and fro and she made out the gleam of a rifle barrel here and there. It was strangely quiet, though.

She found the flap to the main tent, more by instinct than anything else, and stepped in. Lanterns were still lit here, and Thinblood, Pamela Anseratte, Principe Guinevera, Moss, and the other leaders were all standing around a map table. They all looked over as she entered.

"Ah, there you are," said Guinevera in a strangely jovial tone. "We think we know what they're up to."

She moved over to the table to look at the map. Little counters representing Sacrus's forces were scattered around the unrolled rectangle of Greater Spyre. A big handful of tokens was clustered at the very edge of the sheet, where Liris had its land.

"It's an insane amount of men," said Thinblood. He appeared

nervous. "We think over a thousand. Never seen anything like it in Spyre."

Guinevera snorted. "Obviously they hope to capture our entire command all at once and end the war before it begins. And it looks like they stand a good chance of succeeding. What do you think, Venera?"

"Well, I—" She froze.

They were all staring at her. All silent.

Guinevera reached into his brocaded coat and drew out a sheet of paper. With shocking violence he slammed it down on the table in front of her. Venera found herself looking at a poor likeness of herself—with her former hairstyle—on a poster that said, WANTED FOR EXTRADITION TO GEHELLEN, VENERA FANNING.

"So it's true," said Guinevera. His voice was husky with anger, and his hand, still flattening the poster, was shaking.

She chewed her lip and tried to stare him down. "This is hardly the time—"

"This *is* the time!" he bellowed. "*You have started a war!*"

"Sacrus started it," she said. "They started it when they—"

But he struck her full across the face and she spun to the floor.

She tasted blood in her mouth. Where was Bryce? Why wasn't Moss rushing to her defense?

Why wasn't Chaison here?

Guinevera reared over her, his dense mass making her flinch back. "Don't try to blame others for what you've done! You brought this catastrophe on us, imposter! I say we hang her over the battlement and let Sacrus use her for target practice." He reached down to take her arm as Venera scrambled to get her feet under her.

Light knifed through the tent's entrance flap and then miraculously the whole tent lifted up as though tugged off the roof by a giant. The giant's cough was still echoing in Venera's ears as the tent sailed into the permanent maelstrom at the edge of the world and was snatched away like a torn kerchief.

Another bright explosion, and everyone ducked. Then they were all running and shouting at once and soldiers were popping up to fire their blunderbusses then squatting to refill them as trails of smoke and fire corkscrewed overhead. Venera's ears were still ringing, everything strangely aloof as she stood up and watched the big map on the table lift in the sudden breeze and slide horizontally into the night.

Who had it been? she wondered dimly. Had Moss turned on her? Or had Odess said something injudicious? Probably some soldier or servant of Liris had spoken out of turn . . . But then, maybe Jacoby Sarto had become bored of his confinement and decided to liven things up a bit.

Venera was half-aware that the squat cube of Liris was surrounded on three sides by an arcing constellation of torches. The red light served to illuminate the grim faces of the soldiers rushing past her. She raised her hand to stop one of them, then thought better of it. What if Guinevera had remembered to order her arrest? —Or death? As she thought about her new situation, Venera began to be afraid.

Maybe she should go inside. Liris had stout walls, and she still had friends there—she was almost sure of that. She could, what—go chat with Jacoby Sarto in his cell?

And where was Bryce? Semaphore, that was it; he'd gone to send a semaphore. She forced herself to think: the semaphore station was over there . . . where a big gap now yawned in the side of the battlement. Some soldiers were laying planks across it.

"Oh no." No no no.

Deep inside Venera a quiet snide voice that had always been

there was saying, "Of course, of course. They all abandon you in the end." She shouldn't be surprised at this turn of events; she had even planned for it, in the days following her confirmation. It shouldn't come as a shock to her. So it seemed strange to watch herself, as if from outside, as she hunkered down next to the elevator mechanism at the center of the roof, and wrapped her arms around herself and cried.

I don't do this. She wiped at her face. *I don't.*

Maybe she did, though; she couldn't clearly remember those minutes in Candesce after she had killed Aubri Mahallan and she had been alone. Hayden Griffin had pulled Mahallan's body out of sight, leaving a few bright drops of blood to twirl in the weightless air. Griffin was her only way out of Candesce, and Venera had just killed his lover. It hardly mattered that she'd done it to save the world from Mahallan and her allies. No one would ever know, and she was certain she would die there; she had only to wait for Candesce to open its fusion eyes and bring morning to the world.

Griffin had asked her to come with him. He had said he wouldn't kill her; Venera hadn't believed him. It was too big a risk. In the end she had snuck after him and ridden out of Candesce on the cargo net he was towing. Now the thought of running to the stairs and throwing herself on the mercy of her former compatriots filled her with a similar dread. Better to make herself very small here and risk being found by Guinevera or his men than to find out that even Liris now rejected her.

"There they are!" Someone pointed excitedly. Staccato runs of gunfire sounded in the distance—they were oddly distant, in fact. If Venera had cared about anything at that moment she might have stood up to look.

"We're gonna outflank them!"

Something blew up on the outskirts of Liris's territory. The orange mushroom lit the whole world for a moment, a flicker of estates and ornamental ponds overhead. Her ground forces must have made it here just after Sacrus's.

Well. Not my forces, she thought bitterly. *Not anymore.*

"There she is!" Venera jerked and tried to back up but she was already pressed against the elevator platform. A squat silhouette reared up in front of her and something whipped toward her. She cringed. Nothing happened; after a moment she looked up.

An open hand hovered a few inches above her. A distant flicker of red lit the extended hand and behind it, the toadish features of Samson Odess. His broad face wore an expression of concern. "Venera, are you hurt?"

"N-no . . ." Suspiciously, she reached to take his hand. He drew her to her feet and draped an arm across her shoulder.

"Quickly now," he said as he drew her toward the stairs. "While everyone's busy."

"What—" She was having trouble finding words. "What are you doing?"

He stopped, reared back, and stared at her. "I'm taking you home."

"Home? Whose home?"

"Yours, you silly woman. Liris."

"But why are you helping me?"

Now he looked annoyed. "You never ceased to be a citizen of Liris, Venera. And technically, I never stopped being your boss. You're still my responsibility, you know. Come on."

She paused at the top of the steps and looked around. The soldiers who had crowded the roof all seemed to be leaping off one side, in momentary silhouetted flashes showing an arm brandishing a blunderbuss, another waving a sword. There was fighting down in the bramble-choked lot that surrounded Liris. Farther out, she glimpsed squads of men running back and forth, some piling up debris to form barricades, others raising archaic weapons.

"Venera! Get off the roof!" She blinked and turned to follow Odess.

They descended several levels and Venera found herself entering, of all places, the apartments of the former botanist. The furniture and art that had borne the stamp of Margit of Sacrus was gone, and there were still burn marks on the walls and ceiling. Someone had moved in new couches and chairs, and one particularly charred wall was covered with a crepuscular tapestry depicting cherry trees shooting beams of light all over an idealized tableau of dryads and fairies.

Venera sat down under a dryad and looked around. Eilen was there with the rest of the diplomatic corps. "Bring a blanket," said Odess, "and a stiff drink. She's in shock." Eilen ran to fetch a comforter and somebody else shoved a tumbler of amber liquid into Venera's hand. She stared at it for a moment, then drank.

For a few minutes she listened without comprehension to their conversation; then as if a switch had been thrown somewhere inside her, she realized where she must be and she understood something. She looked at Odess. "This is your new office," she said.

They all stopped talking. Odess came to sit next to her. "That's right," he said. "The diplomatic corps has been exalted since you left."

Eilen laughed. "We're the new stars of Liris! Not that the cherry trees are any less important, but—"

"Moss understands that we need to open up to the outside world," interrupted Odess. "It could never have happened under Margit."

Venera half-smiled. "I suppose I can take some credit for making that possible."

"My dear lady!" Odess patted her hand. "The credit is all yours! Liris has come alive again because of you. You don't think we would abandon you in your hour of need, do you?"

"You will always have a place here," said Eilen.

Venera started to cry.

"WE WOULD NEVER have told," Odess said a few minutes later. "None of us."

Venera grimaced. She stood at a mirror where she was dabbing at her eyes, trying to erase the evidence of tears. She didn't know what had come over her. A momentary madness; at least it was only the Lirisians who had witnessed her little breakdown. "I suppose it was Sarto," she said. "It hardly matters now. I can't show my face up there without Guinevera putting a bullet in me."

Odess hmmphed, wrapping his arms around his barrel chest and pacing. "Guinevera has impressed no one since he arrived. Why should any of your other allies listen to him?"

She turned, raising an eyebrow. "Because he's the ruler of a council nation?"

Odess made a flicking motion. "Aside from that."

With a shake of her head Venera returned to the divan. She could hear gunfire and shouting through the opened window, but it was filtered through the roar of the world-edge winds that tumbled above the courtyard shaft. You could almost ignore it.

In similar fashion, Venera could almost ignore the emotions overflowing her. She'd always survived through keeping a cool head and this was no time to have that desert her. It was inconvenient that she felt so abandoned and lost. Inconvenient to feel so grateful for the simple company of her former coworkers. She needed to recover her poise, then act in her own interests as she always had before.

There was a commotion in the corridor, then someone burst through the doors. He was covered in soot and dust, his hair a shock, the left arm of his jacket in tatters.

Venera leaped to her feet. "Garth!"

"There you are!" He rushed over and hugged her fiercely. "You're alive!"

"I'm—oof! Fine. But what happened to you?"

He stepped back, keeping his hands on her arms. Garth had a crazed look in his eye she'd never seen before. He wouldn't meet her gaze. "I was looking for you," he said. "Outside. The rest of them, they're all out there, fighting around the foot of the building. Sacrus has ringed us, they want something here very badly, and our relief force is trying to break through from the outside. So Anseratte and Thinblood are leading the Liris squads in an attempt to break out—make a corridor . . ."

Venera nodded. The irony was that this fight was almost certainly about her, but Anseratte and the others wouldn't know it. Sacrus wanted the key and they knew Venera was here. Naturally they would throw whatever they had at Liris to get it.

If Guinevera had thrown her over the walls half an hour ago, the battle would already be over.

Garth toyed with the ripped fringe of his coat for a moment, then burst out with, "Venera, I am so, so sorry!"

"What?" She shook her head, uncomprehending. "Things aren't so bad. Or do you mean . . . ?" She thought of Bryce, who might be lying twisted and broken at the foot of the wall. "Oh," she said, a twisting feeling running through her.

He had just opened his mouth—doubtless to tell her that Bryce was dead—when the noises outside changed. The gunfire, which had been muffled with distance and indirection, suddenly sounded loud and close. Shouts and screams rang through the open windows.

Venera ran over, and with Odess and Eilen craned her neck to look up the shaft of the courtyard. There were people on the roof.

She and Odess exchanged a look. "Are those our . . . ?" she started to say, but the answer was clear.

"Sacrus is inside the walls!" The cry was taken up by the others and everyone ran for the doors, streaming past Garth Diamandis, who was speaking but inaudible through the jumble of shouts.

Venera paused long enough to shrug at him, then grabbed his arm and hauled him after her into the corridor.

The whole population of Liris was running up the stairs. They carried pikes, kitchen knives, makeshift shields, and clubs. None had on more than the clothing they normally wore, but that meant they were formidably armored. There were one or two soldiers in the mix—probably the men who had been guarding Jacoby Sarto. They were frantically trying to keep order in the pushing mass of people.

Garth stared at the crowd and shook his head. "We'll never get through that."

Venera eyed the window. "I have an idea."

As she slung her leg over the lintel Garth poked his head out next to her and looked up. "It's risky," he said. "Somebody could just kick us off before we can get to our feet."

"In this gravity, you're looking at a sprained ankle. Come on." She climbed rapidly, emerging from the stairs into the light of flares and the sound of gunfire. Half the country was struggling with something at the far end of the roof. Venera blinked and squinted, and realized what it was: they were trying to dislodge a stout ladder that had been swung against the battlements. Even as that came clear to her, she saw the gray cross-hatch of another emerge from the darkness to thud against the stonework.

Withering fire from below prevented the Lirisians from getting near the things. They were forced to crouch a few feet back and poke at them with their pikes.

A third ladder appeared and now men were swarming onto the roof. The Lirisians stood up. Venera saw Eilen raise a rusted old sword as a figure in red-painted iron armor reared above her.

Venera raised her pistol and fired. She walked toward Eilen, firing steadily until the man who'd threatened her friend fell. He wasn't dead—his armor was so thick that the bullets probably hadn't penetrated—but she'd rattled his skull for sure.

She was five feet away when her pistol clicked empty. This was the gun Corinne had given her; she had no idea whether it took the same caliber of bullets as anything the Lirisians used. Examining it quickly, she decided she didn't even know how to breech it to check. At that moment two men like metal beetles surmounted the battlement, firelight glistening off their carapaces.

She tripped Eilen and when the woman had fallen behind her Venera stepped between her and the two men. She drop-kicked the leader and he windmilled his arms for a moment before falling back. The force of her kick had propelled Venera back ten feet. She landed badly, located Eilen, and shouted, "Come on!"

Moss straight-armed a pike into the helmet of the other man. Beside him Odess shoved a lighted torch at a third who was stepping off the ladder. Gunfire sounded and somebody fell but she couldn't see who through the press of bodies.

She grabbed Eilen's arm. "We need guns! Are there more in the lockers?"

Eilen shook her head. "We barely had enough for the soldiers. There's that." She pointed.

Around the corner of the courtyard shaft, the ancient, filigreed morning gun still sat on a tripod under its little canopy.

Venera started to laugh but the sound died in her throat. "Come on!"

The two women wrestled the weapon off its stand. It was a massive thing and though it weighed little in this gravity it was difficult to maneuver. "Do we have shells?" Venera asked.

"Bullets, no shells," said Eilen. "There's black powder in that bin."

Venera opened the gun's breech. It was of a pointlessly primitive design. You poured black powder into it and then inserted the bullet and closed the breech. It had a spark wheel instead of a percussion trigger. "Well, then, come on."

Eilen grabbed up the box of bullets and a sack of powder and they ran along the inner edge of the roof. In the darkness and confusion Eilen stumbled, and Venera watched as the bullets spilled out into the air over the courtyard. Eilen screamed in frustration.

One bullet spun on the flagstones at Venera's feet. Cradling the gun, she bent to pick up the metal slug. A wave of cold prickles swept over her shoulders and up her neck.

This bullet was identical to the one that nestled inside her jacket—identical save for the fact that it had never been fired.

The bullet she carried—that had sailed a thousand miles through the airs and clouds of Virga, avoiding cities and farms, adeptly swerving to avoid fish and rocks and oceanic balls of water—this bullet that had lined up on Slipstream and the city of Rush and the window in the admiralty where Venera stood so innocently; had smashed the glass in a split-second and buried itself in her jaw, spinning her around and nailing a sense of injured outrage to Venera forever—it had come from here. It had not been fired in combat. Not in spite. Not for any murderous purpose, but for tradition, and to celebrate the calmness of a morning like any other.

Venera had fantasized about this moment many times. She had

rehearsed what she would say to the owner of the gun when she finally found him. It was a high, grand, and glorious speech that, in her imagination, always ended with her putting a bullet in the villain. Cradling this picture of revenge to herself had gotten her through many nights, many cocktail parties where out of the corner of her eye she could see the ladies of the admiralty pointing to her scar and murmuring to one another behind their fans.

"Huh," she said.

"Venera? Are you all right?"

Venera shook her head violently. "Powder. Quick!" She held out the gun and Eilen filled it. Then she jammed the clean new bullet into the breech and closed it. She lofted the gun and spun the wheel.

"Everybody down!" Nobody heard her but luckily a gap opened in the line at the last second. The gun made a huge noise and nearly blew Venera off the roof. When the vast plume of smoke cleared she saw nearly everybody in sight recovering from having ducked.

It might not be powerful or accurate, but the thing was loud. That fact might just save them.

She ran toward the Lirisians. "The cannons! Start shouting stuff about cannons!" She breeched the smoking weapon and handed it to Eilen. "Reload."

"But we lost the rest of the bullets."

"We've got one." She reached into her jacket pocket. There it was, its contours familiar from years of touching. She brought out her bullet. Her fingers trembled now as she held it up to the red flare-light.

"Damn you anyway," she whispered to it.

Eilen glanced up, said, "Oh," and held up the gun. There was no time for ceremony; Venera slid the hated slug into the breech and it fit perfectly. She clicked it shut.

"Out of my way!" She crossed the roof in great bounding steps, dodging between fighting men to reach the battlement where the ladders jutted up. The gunfire from below had stopped; the snipers didn't want to hit their own men as they topped the wall. Venera hopped up onto a crenelation and sighted nearly straight down. She saw the startled eyes of a Sacrus soldier between her feet, and half a dozen heads below his. She spun the spark wheel.

The explosion lifted her off her feet. Everything disappeared behind a ball of smoke. When she staggered upright some yards away Venera found herself surrounded by cheering people. Several of Sacrus's soldiers were being thrown off the roof and for the moment no more were appearing. As the smoke cleared she saw that the top of the ladder she'd fired down was missing.

"Keep filling it," she said, thrusting the gun at Eilen. "Bullets don't matter—as long as it's bright and loud."

Moss's grinning face emerged from the gloom. "They're hesitating!"

She nodded. Sacrus didn't have so many people that they could afford to sacrifice them in wave attacks. The darkness and confusion would help; and though they had probably heard it every day of their lives, the thunderous sound of the morning gun at this close range would give pause to the men holding the ladders.

"It's not going to keep them at bay for long, though," she said. "Where are the rest of our people?"

Now Moss frowned. "T-trapped, I fear. Guinevera l-led them into an ambush. Now they have their backs to the open air." He pointed toward the edge of the world and the night skies beyond.

Venera hopped up on the edge of the elevator platform and

took a quick look around. Sacrus's people were spread in a thin line around two of the approaches to Liris. On their third side ragged girders and scoured metal jutted off the end of the world. And on the fourth—behind her—a jumble of brambles, thornbushes, and broken masonry formed a natural barrier that Sacrus wasn't bothering to police.

In the darkness beyond, hundreds of torches lit the contours of an army small by Venera's standards but huge for Spyre. There might be no more than a thousand men there, but that was all the forces that opposed Sacrus on this world.

Spreading away behind that army was the maze of estates that made up Greater Spyre. Somewhere out there was the long low building where the hollowed bomb hung, with its promise of escape.

She turned to Moss. "You need to break through Sacrus's lines. Otherwise, they'll overwhelm us and then they can turn and face our army with a secure fortress behind them."

He nodded. "But all our leaders are t-trapped."

"Well, not all." She strode across the roof to the battlements that overlooked the bramble-choked acres. He came to stand at her side. Together they gazed out at the army that lay tantalizingly out of reach.

"If the semaphore were working—" She stopped, remembering Bryce. Moss shook his head anyway.

"S-Sacrus has encircled the t-tower. They would read every letter."

"But we need to coordinate an attack—from outside and inside at the same time. To break through . . ."

He shrugged. "Simple matter. If we c-can get one p-person through the lines."

She speculated. If she showed up there among the brambles,

would the generals of that army have her arrested? How far had news of her deceptions spread?

"Get them ready," she said. "Everyone into armor, everyone armed. I'll be back in two minutes." She headed for the stairs.

"Where are you g-going?"

She shot him a grim smile. "To check in on our bargaining chip."

VENERA RAN THROUGH empty halls to the old prison on the main floor.

As she'd suspected, the guards had deserted their posts when the roof was attacked. The main door was ajar; Venera slowed when she saw this. Warily, she toed it open and aimed her pistol through. There was nobody in the antechamber. She sidled in.

"Hello?" That was Jacoby Sarto's voice. Venera had never heard him sound worried, but he was clearly rattled by what was happening. *He's never been in a battle before,* she realized—nor had any of these people. It was shocking to think that she was the veteran here.

Venera went on her tiptoes to look through the door's little window into the green-walled reception room. Sarto was the sole occupant of a bench designed to seat thirty; he sat in the very center of a room that could have held a hundred. He squinted at the door, then said, "Fanning?"

She threw open the door and stepped in. "Did you tell them?"

He appeared puzzled. "Tell who what?"

She showed him her pistol; he wouldn't know it was empty. "Don't play games, Sarto. Someone told Guinevera who I really am. Was it you?"

He smiled with a trace of his usual arrogance. He stood up and adjusted the sleeves of the formal shirt he still wore. "Things not going your way out there?"

"Two points," said Venera, holding up two fingers. "First: I'm holding a gun on you. Second: you're rapidly becoming expendable."

"All right, all right," he said irritably. "Don't be so prickly. After all, I came here of my own free will."

"And that's supposed to impress me?" She leaned on the doorjamb and crossed her arms.

"Think about it," he said. "What do I have to gain from revealing who you are?"

"I don't know. Suppose you tell me?"

Now he scowled at her, as if she were some common servant girl who'd had the temerity to interrupt him while he was talking. "I have spent thirty-two years learning the ins and outs of council politics. All that time, becoming an expert—maybe the expert—on Spyre, learning who is beholden to who, who's ambitious, and who just wants to keep their heads down. I have been the public face of Sacrus for much of that time, their most important operative, because for all those years, Spyre's politics were all that mattered. But look at what's happening." He waved a hand to indicate the siege and battle going on beyond Liris's thick walls. "Everything that made me valuable is being swept away."

This was not what Venera had been expecting to hear from him. She came into the room and sat down on a bench facing Sarto. He looked at her levelly and said, "Change is inconceivable to most people in Spyre; to them a catastrophe is a tree falling across their fence. A vast political upheaval would be somebody snubbing somebody else at a party. That's the system I was bred and trained to work in. But my masters have always known that there's much bigger game out there. They've been biding their time, lo these many centuries. Now they finally have in their grasp a tool with which to conquer the world—the *real* world, not just this squalid imitation we're standing in. On the scale of Sacrus's new ambitions, all of my accomplishments count for nothing."

Venera nodded slowly. "Spyre is having all its borders redrawn around you. Even if they never get the key from me, Sacrus will be facing a new Spyre once the fighting stops. I'll bet they've been grooming someone young and malleable to take your place in that new world."

He grimaced. "No one likes to be discarded. I could see it coming, though. It was inevitable, really, unless . . ."

"Unless you could prove your continuing usefulness to your masters," she said. "Say, by personally bringing them the key?"

He shrugged. "Yesterday's council meeting would otherwise have been my last public performance. At least here, as your, uh, guest, I might have the opportunity to act as Sacrus's negotiator. Think about it—you're surrounded, outgunned; you're approaching the point where you have to admit you're going to lose. But I can tell you the semaphore codes to signal our commanders that we've reached an accommodation. As long as you had power here, you could have functioned as the perfect traitor. A few bad orders, your forces ordered into a trap, then it's over the wall for you and me, the key safely into my master's hands, you on your way home to wherever it is you came from."

Venera tamped down on her anger. Sarto was used to dealing in cold political equations; so was she, for that matter. What he was proposing shouldn't shock her. "But if I'm disgraced, I can't betray my people."

"Your usefulness plummets," he said with a nod. "So, no, I didn't tattle on you. You're hardly of any value now, are you? All you've got is the key. If your own side's turned against you, your only remaining option is to throw yourself on the mercy of Sacrus. Which might win me some points if I'm the one who brings you in, but not as much, and—"

"—And I have no reason to expect good treatment from them," she finished. "So why should I do it?"

He stood up—slowly, mindful of her gun—and walked a little distance away. He gazed up at the room's little windows. "What other option do you have?" he asked.

She thought at first that he'd said this rhetorically, but something about his tone . . . It had sounded like a genuine question.

Venera sat there for a while, thinking. She went over the incident with the council members on the roof; who could have outed her? Everything depended on that—and on when it had happened. Sarto said nothing, merely waited patiently with his arms crossed, staring idly up at the little window.

Finally she nodded and stood up. "All right," she said. "Jacoby, I think we can still come to an . . . accommodation. Here's what I'm thinking . . ."

19

AS SOMETIMES HAPPENED at the worst of moments, Venera lost her sense of gravity just before she hit the ground. The upthrusting spears of brush and stunted trees flipped around and became abstract decorations on a vast wall she was approaching. Her feet dangled over sideways buildings and the pikes of soldiers. Then the wall hit her and she bounced and tumbled like a rag doll. Strangely, it didn't hurt at all—perhaps not so strangely, granted that she was swaddled in armor.

She unscrewed her helmet and looked up into a couple dozen gun barrels. They were all different, like a museum display taken down and offered to her; in her dazed state she almost reached to grab one. But there were hands holding them tightly and grim men behind the hands.

When she and Sarto had reached the rooftop of Liris they found a theatrical jumble of bodies, torn tenting, and brazier fires surrounded by huddling men in outlandish armor. At the center of it all, the thick metal cable rose up and out of sight into the turbulent mists; that cable glowed gold now as distant Candesce awoke.

She had spotted Moss and headed over, keeping her head down in case there were snipers. He looked up, lines of exhaustion apparent around his eyes; glancing past her, he spotted Sarto. "What's this?"

"We need to break this siege. I'm going over the wall, and Sarto is coming with me."

Moss blinked, but his permanently shocked expression revealed none of his thoughts. "What for?"

"I don't know whether the commanders of our encircling force have been told that I'm an imposter and a traitor. I need to bring Jacoby Sarto in case I need a . . . ticket, I suppose you could call it . . . into their good graces."

He nodded reluctantly. "And how do you p-propose to reach our force? S-Sacrus is between us and them."

Now she grinned. "Well, you couldn't do this with all of us, but I propose that we jump."

Of course they'd had help from an ancient catapult that Liris had once used to fire mail and parcels over an enemy nation to an ally some three miles away. Venera had seen it on her second day here; with a little effort, it had been refitted to seat two people. But nobody, least of all her, knew whether it would still work. Her only consolation had been the low gravity in Spyre.

Now Venera had two possible scripts she could follow, one if these were soldiers of the council alliance, one if they owed their allegiance to Sacrus. But which were they? The fall had been so disorienting that she couldn't tell where they'd ended up. So she merely put up her hands and smiled, and said, "Hello."

Beside her Jacoby Sarto groaned and rolled over. Instantly another dozen guns aimed at him. "I think we're not that much of a threat," Venera said mildly. She received a kick in the back (which she barely felt through the metal) for her humor.

A throb of pain shot through her jaw—and an odd thing happened. Such spasms of pain had plagued her for years, ever since the day she woke up in Rush's military infirmary, her head bandaged like a delicate vase about to be shipped via the postal system.

Each stab of pain had come with its own little thought, whose content varied somewhat but always translated roughly to either *I'm all alone* or *I'm going to kill them.* Fear and fury, they stabbed her repeatedly throughout each day. The fierce headaches that often built over the hours just added to her meanness.

But she'd taken the bullet that struck her jaw and blown it back out the very same gun that had shot her. So, when her jaw cramped this time, instead of her usual misery Venera had a flash of memory: the morning gun going off with a tremendous explosion in her hands, bucking and kicking and sending her flying backward into the Lirisians. She had no idea what the feeling accompanying that had been, but she liked it.

So she grinned crookedly and stood up. Dusting herself off, she said with dignity, "I am Amandera Thrace-Guiles, and this is Jacoby Sarto of the Spyre Council. We need to talk to your commanders."

"YOU HAVE A reputation for being foolhardy," said the army commander, his gray moustaches waggling. "But that was ridiculous."

It turned out that they'd nearly overshot both Sacrus and Council Alliance positions. Luckily several hundred pairs of eyes had tracked their progress across the rolled-up sky of Spyre and it was her army that had gotten to Venera and Jacoby first. Sarto didn't seem too upset about the outcome, which was telling. What was even more significant was that everyone was calling her "Lady Thrace-Guiles," which meant that word of her deceptions hadn't made it out of Liris. Here, Venera was still a respected leader.

She preened at the commander's back-handed compliment. He stood with his back to a brick wall, a swaying lamp nodding shadows across the buttons of his jacket. Aides and colonels bustled about, some shoving little counters across the map board, others reading or writing dispatches.

Venera smelled engine oil and wet cement. The alliance army had set up its headquarters in a preservationist roundhouse about a mile from Liris; these walls were thick enough to stop anything Sacrus had so far fired. For the first time in days, Venera felt a little safe.

"I wouldn't have had to be foolhardy if the situation weren't so dire," she said. It was tempting to upbraid this man for hesitating to send his forces to relieve Liris; but Venera found herself uninterested anymore in taking such familiar pleasures. She merely said, "Tell me what's been happening out here."

The commander leaned over the board and began pointing at the little wooden counters. "There've been engagements all across Greater Spyre," he said. "Sacrus has won most of them."

"So what are they doing? Conquering countries?"

"In one or two cases, yes. Mostly they've been cutting the preservationist's railway lines. And they've taken or severed all the elevator cables."

"Severed?" Even to an outsider like her this was a startling development.

One of the aides shrugged. "Easy enough to do. They just use them for target practice. Except for the ones at the edge of the world, like Liris. The winds around those lines deflect the bullets."

She raised her eyebrows. "Why don't they just use more high-powered guns on them?"

The aide shook his head. "Ancient treaty. Places limits on muzzle velocities. It's to prevent accidental punctures of the world's skin."

"—Not significant, anyway," said the commander with an

impatient gesture. "The war will be decided here on Greater Spyre. The city will just have to wait it out."

"No, it can't wait," she said. "That's what this is all about. Not the city, but the docks."

"The docks?" The commander stared at her. "That's the last thing we're going to worry about."

"I know, and Sacrus is counting on that." She glared at him. "Everything that's happening down here is a diversion from their real target. Everything except . . ." She nodded at Liris.

Now they were looking at each other with faintly embarrassed unease. "Lady Thrace-Guiles," said the commander, "war is a very particular art. Perhaps you should leave such details to those who've made it their careers."

Venera opened her mouth to yell at him, thought better, and took a deep breath instead. "Can we at least be agreed that we need to break Sacrus's hold on Liris?"

"Yes," he said with a vigorous nod. "We need to ensure the safety of our leadership. For that purpose," he pointed at the table, "I am advocating a direct assault along the innermost wall."

A moment of great temptation made Venera hesitate. The commander was proposing to go straight for the walls and leave the group trapped at the world's edge to its fate. He didn't know that his objective was actually there. They'd made themselves her enemies and Venera could just . . . forget to tell him. Leave Guinevera and the others to Sacrus's mercy now that she had the army.

She couldn't claim not to have known, though, unless the Lirisians went along with it. And she was tired of deceptions. She sighed and said, "Liris is a critical objective, yes, but the rest of our leadership is actually trapped with the Lirisian army at the edge of the world." There were startled looks up and down the table. "Yes—Master Thinblood, Principe Guinevera, and

Pamela Anseratte, among others, are among those pinned down in the hurricane zone. I'm sure you were concerned for the safety of that group, but they're even more important than you probably knew."

The commander frowned down at the map. On it, Liris was a square encircled by red wooden tokens representing Sacrus's army. This circle squashed a knot of blue tokens against the bottom edge of the map: the Lirisian army, trapped at the edge of the world. Left of the encirclement was a no-man's-land of tough brush that had so far resisted burning. Left of that, the preservationist siding and army encampment where they now stood.

"This is a problem," said the commander. He thought for a moment, then said, "There are certain snakes that coil around their victims and choke them to death." She raised an eyebrow, but he continued, "One of their characteristics, so I've been told, is that if you try to remove them they tighten their grip. Right now Sacrus has both Liris and our leaders in its coils, and if we try to break through to one they will simply strangle the other."

To relieve the Lirisian army, they would have to force a wedge under Liris, with the edge of the world at their right side. To do this they would trade off their ability to threaten Sacrus along the inner sides of Liris—freeing those troops up to assault the walls of Liris. Conversely, the best way to relieve Liris would be to come at it from the inner side, which meant swinging the army away from the world's edge—thus giving Sacrus a free hand against the trapped force.

Venera examined the map; it didn't tell her anything she didn't already know. "We have to fool them into making the wrong choice," she said.

"Yes, but how are we going to do that?" He shook his head. "Even if we did, they can maneuver just as fast as we can. They have less ground to cover than we do to redeploy their forces."

"As to how we'll fool the snake into uncoiling," she said, "it helps to have your own snake to consult with." She turned and waved to some figures standing a few yards away. Jacoby Sarto emerged from the shadows; he was a silhouette against klieg lights that pinioned a pair of hulking locomotives in the center of the roundhouse. He was accompanied by two armed soldiers and a member of Bryce's underground.

The commander bowed to Sarto but then said, "I'm afraid we cannot trust this man. He is of the enemy."

"Lord Sarto has seen the light," said Venera. "He has agreed to help us."

"Pah!" The commander sneered. "Sacrus are masters of deception. How can we trust him?"

"The politics are complex," she said. "But we have very good reasons to trust him. I do. That is why I brought him."

There were more glances thrown between the colonels and the aides. The commander twitched a frown for just a moment, then said, "No. I understand the dilemma we're in, but my sovereign and commanding officer is Principe Guinevera, and he's in danger. Politically, saving our leadership has to be the priority. I'll not countenance any plan that weakens our chance of doing that."

Jacoby Sarto laughed. It was an ugly, contemptuous sound, delivered by a man who had spent decades using his voice to whither other men's courage. The commander glared at him. "I fail to see the humor in any of this, Lord Sarto."

"Forgivable," said Sarto drily, "as you're not aware of Sacrus's objectives. They want Liris, not your management. They haven't crushed the soldiers pinned down at the world's edge because they're dangling them as bait."

"What could they possibly want with Liris?"

"Me," said Venera, "because they surely think I'm still there. —And the elevator cable. They need to cut it. All they have to do is capture me or make it impossible for me to leave Greater Spyre. Then they've won. It will just be a matter of time."

Now it was the commander's turn to laugh. "I think you vastly overrate your own value and underrate the potential of this army," he said, sweeping his arm to indicate the paltry hundreds gathered in the cavernous shed. "You alone can't hold this alliance together, Lady Thrace-Guiles. And I said it before, the elevator cables are of little strategic interest."

Venera was furious. She wanted to tell him that she'd seen more men gathered at circuses in Rush than he had in his vaunted army. But, remembering how she had thrown a lighted lamp at Garth in anger and his gentle chiding after, she bit back on what she wanted to say and instead said, "You'll change your mind once you know the true strategic situation. Sacrus wants—" She stopped as Sarto touched her arm.

He was shaking his head. "This is not the right audience," he said quietly.

"Um." In an instant her understanding of the situation flipped around. When she had walked in here she had seen this knot of officers in one corner of the roundhouse and assumed that they were debating their plan of attack. But that wasn't what they were doing at all. They had been huddling here, as far as possible from the men they must command. They weren't planning; they were hesitating.

"Hmmm . . ." She quirked a transparently false smile at the commander. "If you men will excuse me for a few minutes?" He looked puzzled, then annoyed, then amused. Venera took Sarto's arm and led him away from the table.

"What are you going to do?" he asked.

She stopped in an area of blank floor stained over the decades by engine oil and grease. At first Venera didn't meet Sarto's eyes. She was looking around at the towering wrought-iron pillars, the tessellated windows in the ceiling, the smoky beams of light that intersected on the black backs of the locomotives. A deep knot of some kind, loosened when she cried in Eilen's arms, was unraveling.

"They talk about places as being our homes," she mused. "It's not the place, really, but the people."

"I'm sure I don't know what you mean," he said. His dry irony had no effect on Venera. She merely shrugged.

"You were right," she said. He cocked his head to one side, crossing his arms, and waited. "After the confirmation, when you said I was still Sacrus's," she went on. "And in the council chamber, even when we talked in your cell earlier tonight. Even now. As long as I wanted to leave Spyre, I was theirs. As long as they've known what to dangle in front of me, there was nothing I could do but what they wanted me to do."

"Haven't I said that repeatedly?" He sounded annoyed.

"All along, there's been a way to break their hold on me," she said. "I just haven't had the courage to do it."

He grumbled, "I'd like to think I made the right choice by throwing in with you. Takes you long enough to come to a decision, though."

Venera laughed. "All right. Let's do this." She started to walk toward the locomotives.

"*There you are!*" Venera stumbled, cursed, and then flung out her arms.

"Bryce!" He hugged her, but hesitantly—and she knew not to display too much enthusiasm herself. No one knew they were lovers; that knowledge would be one more piece of leverage against them. So she disengaged from him quickly and stepped back. "What happened? I saw the semaphore station blown up. We all assumed you were . . ."

He shook his head. In the secondhand light he did look a bit disheveled and soot-stained. "A bunch of us got knocked off the roof, but none of us were hurt." He laughed. "We landed in the brambles and then had to claw our way through with Sacrus's boys firing at our arses all the way. Damn near got shot by our own side as well, before we convinced them who we were."

Now she did hug him and damn the consequences. "Have you been able to contact any of our—your people?"

He nodded. "There's a semaphore station on the roof. The whole Buridan network's in contact. Do you have orders?"

As Venera realized what was possible, she grinned. "Yes!" She took Bryce by one arm and Sarto by the other and dragged them across the floor. "I think I know a way to break the siege and save the other commanders. You need to get up there and get Buridan to send us something. Jacoby, you get up there too. You need to convince Sacrus that I'm ready to double-cross my people." She pushed them both away.

"And what are you going to do?" asked Bryce.

She smiled past the throbbing in her jaw. "What I do best," she said. "I'll set the ball rolling."

Venera stalked over to the black, bedewed snout of a locomotive and pulled herself up to stand in front of its headlamp. She was drenched in light from it and the overhead spots, aware that her pale face and hands must be as bright as lantern flames against the dark metal surrounding her. She raised her arms.

"It is tiiiiiime!"

She screamed it with all her might, squeezed all the anger and the pain from her twisted family and poisonous intrigues of her youth, the indifferent bullet and her loss of her husband Chaison, the blood on her hands after she stabbed Aubri Mahallan, the smoke from her pistols as she shot men and women alike, all of it into that one word. As the echoes subsided everyone in the roundhouse came to their feet. All eyes were on her and that was exactly right, exactly how it should be.

"Today the old debts will be settled! Two hundred years and more the truth has waited in Buridan Tower—the truth of what Sacrus is and what they have done! Nearly too late, but not too late, because you, here today, will be the ones to settle those debts and at the same time prevent Sacrus from ever committing such atrocities again!

"Let me describe my home. Let me describe Buridan Tower!" Out of the corner of her eye she saw the army commanders running from their map table, but they had to shoulder their way through hundreds of soldiers to reach her, and the soldiers were raptly attentive to her alone. "Like a vast musical instrument, a flute thrust into the sky and played on by the ceaseless hurricane winds of the airfall. Cold, its corridors decorated with grit and wavering, torn ribbons that once were tapestries. Wet, with nothing to burn except the feathers of birds. Never silent, never still as the beams it stands on sway under the onslaught of air. A roaring tomb, that is Buridan Tower! That is what Sacrus made. It is what they promise to make of your homes as well, make no mistake.

"That's right," she nodded. "You're fighting for far more than you may know. This isn't just a matter of historical grudges, nor is it a skirmish over Sacrus's kidnapping and torture of your women and children. This is about your future. Do you want all of Spyre to become like Buridan, an empty tomb, a capricious playground for the winds? Because that is what Sacrus has planned for Spyre."

The officers had stopped at the head of the crowd. She could see that the commander was about to order her to be taken off her perch, so Venera hurried on to her main point. "You have not been told the truth about this war! Before we leave this place you need to know why Sacrus has moved against us all. It is because they believe they have outgrown Spyre the way a wasp outgrows its cocoon. Centuries ago they attacked and destroyed Buridan to gain a treasure from us. They failed to capture it but never gave up their ambition. Ever since Buridan's fall they have bided their time, awaiting the chance to get their hands on something Buridan has guarded for the sake of Spyre since the very beginning of time." She was really winding herself up now and for the moment the officers had stopped, curious no doubt about what she was about to say.

"Since the creation of Spyre my family has guarded one of the most powerful relics in the world! It was for the sake of this trust that we kept to Buridan Tower for generations, not venturing out because we feared Sacrus would learn that the tower is not the empty shell they believed—afraid they would learn that it can be entered. The thing we guarded is so dangerous that my brothers and sisters, my parents, grandparents, and their grandparents, all sacrificed their lives to prevent even a hint of its existence from escaping our walls.

"Time came when we could no longer sustain ourselves," she said more softly, "and I had to venture forth." Dimly, Venera wondered at this grand fib she was making up on the spot; it was a rousing story, and if it proved rousing enough then nobody would believe Guinevera if he survived to accuse her of being an imposter.

"As soon as I came forth," she said, "Sacrus knew that Buridan had survived, and they knew why we had stayed hidden. They knew that I carried with me the last key to Candesce!"

She stopped, letting the echoes reverberate. Crossing her arms, she gazed out at the army, waiting. Two seconds, five, ten, and then they were muttering, talking, turning to one another with frowns and nods. Some who prided themselves on knowing old legends told the men standing next to them about the keys; word began to spread through the ranks. In the front row, the officers were looking at one another in consternation.

Venera raised a hand for silence. "That is what this war is about," she said. "Sacrus has known of the existence of this key for centuries. They tried to take it once, and Buridan and its allies resisted. Now they are after it again. If they get it, they will no longer need Spyre. To them it is like the hated chrysalis that has confined them for generations. They will shed it, and they don't care if it unravels in pieces as they fly toward the light. At best, Spyre will prove a good capital for the world-spanning empire they plan—once they've scoured it clean of all the old estates, that is. Yes, this cylinder will make a fine park for the palace of Virga's new rulers. They'll need room for the governors of their new provinces, for prisoners, slaves, treasure houses, and barracks. They might not knock down all the buildings. But you and yours . . . well, I hope you have relatives in one of the principalities, because rabble like us won't be allowed to live here anymore."

The soldiers were starting to argue and shout. Belatedly the officers had realized that they weren't in control anymore; several darted at the locomotive but Venera crouched and glared at them, as if she was ready to pounce on them. They backed away.

She stood up, onto her tiptoes as she flung one fist high over her head. "We have to stop them! The key must be protected, for without it Spyre itself is doomed. You fight for more than your lives—more than your homes. You are all that stands between Sacrus and the slow strangulation of the very world!

"Will you stop them?" They shouted yes. "*Will* you?" They screamed it.

Venera had never seen anyone give a speech like this, but she'd heard Chaison work a crowd and had read about such moments in books. It all took her back to those romantic stories she'd devoured as a little girl in her pink bedroom. Outrageous theatricality, but none of these men had ever seen its like either; few had probably ever been in a theater. For most this roundhouse was the furthest they had ever been from home, and the looming locomotive was something they had only ever glimpsed in the far distance. They stood among peers who before today had been dots seen through telescopes and they were learning that however strange and foreign they were, all were united in their loyalty to Spyre itself. Of course the moment made them mad.

Fist still raised, Venera smiled down at the commander who shook his head in defeat.

Bryce and Jacoby Sarto clambered along the side of the locomotive to join her. "What's the news?" she asked over the roar of the army at her feet.

Bryce blinked at the scene. "Uh . . . they're on their way."

Sarto nodded. "I semaphored the Sacrus army commander. Told him you realize your situation is hopeless, that you're going to lead your army into a trap."

She grinned. "Good." She turned back to the crowd and raised her fist again.

"It! Is! Tiiiiiiiiiiime!"

20

THE SOUND OF bullets hitting Liris's walls reminded Garth
Diamandis of those occasional big drops that fall from trees
after a rain. Silence, then a *pat* followed in this case by the distant sound of a shot. From the gunslit where he was watching
he could see the army of the Council Alliance assembling next to
the rust-streaked roundhouse. In the early morning light it
seemed like a dark carpet moving, in ominous silence, in the
direction of Liris. Little puffs of smoke arose from the Sacrus
line but the firing was undisciplined.

"Come away from there," said Venera's friend Eilen. They stood
in a musty closet crammed with door lintels, broken drawers,
cracked table legs: useless junk, but impossible for a tiny nation
like Liris to throw away. Lantern light from the corridor shone
through Eilen's hair. She could have been attractive, a habitual
part of his mind noted. At one time, he could have helped her
with that.

"I have a good view of the Sacrus camp," he said. "And it's
too dangerous to be on the roof right now."

"You'll get a bullet in the eye," she said. He grunted and
turned back to the view, and after a moment he heard her leave.

He couldn't tell her that he had recognized one of the uni-
formed figures moving down there. Maybe two of them, he
couldn't be sure. Garth was sure that Eilen would tell him he was

suffering an old man's delusions if he said he'd recognized his daughter among the hundreds of crimson uniforms.

He could be imagining it. He'd had scant moments to absorb the sight of her before she'd signaled her superiors and Sacrus's thugs had moved in on him. Yet Garth had an eye for women, was able to recall the smallest detail about how this or that one moved or held herself. He could deduce much about character and vulnerability by a woman's stance and habitual gestures; and he damned well knew how to recognize one at a distance. That was Selene standing hipshot by that tent, he was sure of it.

Garth cursed under his breath. He'd never been one to probe at sore spots, but ever since they'd thrown him into that stinking cell in the Grey Infirmary, his thoughts had pivoted around the moment of Selene's betrayal.

He had told her that he was her father, just before she betrayed him. In the seconds between, he'd seen the doubt in her eye—and then the mad-eyed woman with the pink hair had come to stand next to Selene.

"He said he's my father," Selene murmured as the soldiers cuffed Garth. The pink-haired woman laughed.

"And who knows?" Selene had said. "He might well be." She had laughed again, and Garth had glimpsed a terrible light in his daughter's eye just before he was hauled out of her sight.

There it was again, that mop of blossom-colored hair poking out from under a gray army cap. She was an officer. The last time Garth had seen her had been in a bizarre fever dream where Venera was whispering his name urgently. This woman had been there, among glass cases, but she was naked and laved with crimson from head to toe. Venera had spoken her name then, but Garth didn't remember it.

The sound of firing suddenly intensified. Garth craned his neck to look in the direction of the roundhouse. Sacrus's forces were moving out to engage the council troops on the inside of Liris. Behind him, though, he could see an equally large contingent of Sacrus's soldiers circling back around the building. Headed toward the edge of the world.

Garth had some inkling of what the council army was doing. They were pressing up against the no-man's-land of thorn and tumbled masonry, a scant hundred yards from the walls of Liris. From there they could turn left or right—inward or toward the world's edge—at a moment's notice. Sacrus would have to split their forces into two to guard against both possibilities.

It was an intelligent plan and for a moment Garth's spirits lifted. Then he saw more of Sacrus's men abandon their positions below him. They were leaving a noisy and smoke-wreathed band of some two hundred men to defend the inward side while the rest of their forces marched behind Liris and out of sight from the roundhouse. They clearly expected the council army to split right and try to relieve Guinevera and Anseratte at the hurricane-wracked world's edge. But how did they know what the council was planning?

He cursed and jumped down off the ancient credenza he'd been perched upon. The corridors were stuffed with armed people, old men and women mostly (strange how he thought of other people his age as old, but not himself). He elbowed his way through them carelessly. "Where the hell is Moss?"

Someone pointed down a narrow, packed hallway. Liris's new botanist was deep in discussion with the only one of Bryce's men left inside the walls. "I need semaphore flags," Garth shouted over two shoulders. "We have to warn the troops what Sacrus is doing!"

To his credit, Moss didn't even blink. He raised a hand, pointed to one man, then held up two fingers. "Forward stores," he said. He pointed to another man and then at Garth. "Go with."

It took precious minutes for Garth and his new helper to locate the flags. Then they had to fight their way to the stairs. They emerged outside to the mind-numbing roar of the winds and an almost continual sound of gunfire. Ducking low, they ran for the edge of the roof.

"THEY EXPECT YOU to act as if you don't know about the key," Venera was explaining for the tenth time. She was surrounded by nervous officers and staffers; the gray-mustachioed army commander stood with his arms crossed, glowering as she drew on the ground with a stick. "If you don't know about it, then the obvious strategic goal is to relieve Guinevera's force. Jacoby Sarto has told them that we are going to do that. This frees Sacrus to take Liris, their real objective."

The commander nodded reluctantly. A bullet whined past somewhere too near for comfort. They stood behind a screen of brush on the edge of no-man's-land. An arc of soldiers surrounded them, far too few for Venera's taste. This force would hardly qualify as a company in Chaison's army. Yet Sacrus didn't have much more.

"So," she continued. "We feint right then strike left. I humbly suggest that we start with sustained fire into Sacrus's position on the edge-side of no-man's-land."

There was some talk among the officers—far too much of it to suit her—then the commander said, "It's too risky. And I remain skeptical about your story."

He didn't believe the key was real. Venera was tempted to take it out and show it to him, but that might backfire. Who could believe a whole war would be fought over an ivory wand?

While she and the commander were scowling at one another

Bryce ran up, puffing. "They're here!" Venera turned to look where he pointed.

She turned back, grinning broadly. "Commander, would you be more amenable to my plan if you had a secret weapon to help with it?"

The commander and all the officers fell silent as they saw what was approaching. Slowly, the commander began to smile.

"DAMN IT, THEY'RE ignoring us!" Garth ducked as another volley of fire from below raked the edge of the roof. His assistant slumped onto the flagstones next to him, shaking his head.

"Maybe they don't see us," he said.

"Oh, they see us all right. They just don't believe us." Garth risked a glance over the stones. The council army was pressing hard against the barricades hastily thrown up by Sacrus on the inward side of Liris. The bulk of their army was hovering on the far side of the building, ready to speed toward the edge as soon as they were given the word.

Another ladder thunked against the wall. That made four in as many seconds. Garth pushed his companion. "Back to the stairs!" Sacrus were moving to take Liris. There was nothing anyone could do to stop them.

Garth stood up to run and hesitated for just a second. He couldn't stop himself from looking down through the gunfire and smoke to find his daughter. The ground around Liris was boiling with men; he couldn't see her.

Something hit him hard and he spun around, toppling to the flagstones. A bullet—was he dead? Garth clawed at his shoulder, saw a bright scar on the metal of his armor but no hole.

"Sir!" Damn him, his helper was running back to save him.

"No, get to the stairs, damnit!" Garth yelled, but it was too late. A dozen bullets hit the man and some of those went right through his armor. He fell and slid forward, and died at Garth's feet.

Garth had never even learned his name.

Up they came now, soldier after soldier hopping onto Liris's roof. One loped forward, ignoring rifle fire from the stairs, and pitched a firebomb into the central courtyard. The cherry trees were protected under a siege roof, but a few more of those and they would burn.

Swearing, he tried to stand. Something hit him again and he fell back. This time when he looked up, it was to see the black globe of a Sacrus helmet hovering above him, and a rifle barrel inches from his face.

Garth fell back, groaning, and closed his eyes.

"WE'VE LOST OUR momentum," said Bryce. He and Venera were crouched behind an upthrust block of brickwork from some ancient, abandoned building. A hundred feet ahead of them, men were dying in a futile attack on the Sacrus barricade.

She nodded, but the council officers were already ordering a retreat. For a few seconds she watched the soldiers scampering back under relentless fire. Then she cocked an eyebrow at Bryce and grinned.

"*We've* lost our momentum? When did you decide this was your fight?"

"People are dying," he said angrily. "Anyway, if what you say is true, there's far more at stake than any of us knew." She shrugged and glanced again at the retreat, but then noticed he was staring at her.

"What?"

"Who are you, really? Surely not Amandera Thrace-Guiles?"

Venera laughed. He hadn't been there for her moment of humiliation at the feet of Guinevera—had, in fact, been flying through the air over brambles and scrub just about then.

She stuck out her hand for him to shake. "Venera Fanning. Pleased to meet you."

He shook it, a puzzled expression on his face, but then a new commotion distracted him. "Look! Your friends . . ."

Through the drifting smoke she could see a dozen spindly ladders wobbling against the building's walls. Men were swarming up them and there was fighting on the roof. In seconds she could lose the people who had become most precious to her. "Come on!"

They braved rifle fire and ran back. The army commander was crouched over a map. He looked up grimly as Venera approached. "Can you feel it?" When she frowned, he pointed down at the ground. Now she realized that for some time now, she had been feeling a slow, almost subliminal sensation of rising and falling. It was the kind of faint instability of weight that you sometimes felt when a town's engines were working to spin it back up to speed.

"I think Sacrus cut one too many cables."

"Let the preservationists deal with it when we're finished," she said. "Right now we need to cut down those ladders."

He shook his head. "Don't you understand? This is more than just a piece or two falling off the world. Something's happened. It—we . . ." She realized that he was very, very frightened. So were the officers kneeling with him.

Venera felt it again, that long slow waver, unsettling to the inner ear. Way out past the smoke, it seemed like the curving landscape of Spyre was crawling, somehow, like the itchy skin of a giant beast twitching in slow motion.

"We can't do anything about that," she said. "We have to focus on saving lives here and now! Look, I don't think there's
more than three dozen men on those barricades. The rest of
their men are waiting on the far side for us to try to relieve
Guinevera."

With an effort he pulled himself together. "Your plan . . . Can
you do it?"

"They'll start to pull back as soon as they realize we're con-
centrating here," she said. "When they do, we'll have them."

"All right. We have to . . . do something." He got to his feet
and began issuing orders. The frightened officers sprinted off in
all directions. Venera and Bryce ran back in the direction of the
roundhouse and as they passed the fringe of the no-man's-land
she saw scores of men standing up from concealment in the
bushes. Suddenly they were all bellowing and as more popped
up from unexpected places Venera found herself being swept
back by a vast mob of howling armored men. She and Bryce
fought their way forward as hundreds of bodies plunged past
them. She had no time to look back but could imagine the
Sacrus barricades being overwhelmed in seconds; the ladders
would tremble and fall, and when they rose again it would be
council soldiers climbing them.

A small copse of trees stood at the end of no-man's-land;
bedraggled and half-burnt, they still made a good screen for
what hid behind them. Venera smelled the things before she saw
them, and her spirits soared as she heard their nervous snorting
and stamping.

With murmurs and an outstretched hand, she approached
the Dali horse. A dozen others stood huddled together, flanks
twitching, their heads a dozen feet off the earth. All were sad-
dled and some of the horsemen were already mounted.

Bryce stopped short, a wondering expression on his face.

Venera put her hand on the rope ladder that led up to her beast's saddle, then looked back at him. "See to your people," she said. "Run your presses. If I live, I'll see you after."

He smiled and for a moment looked boyishly mischievous. "The presses have been running for days, and I've sent my messages. But just in case . . . here." He dug inside his jacket and handed her a cloth-wrapped square. Venera unwrapped it, puzzled, then laughed out loud. It was a brand-new copy of the book *Rights Currencies*. She raised it to her nose and smelled the fresh ink, then stuffed it in her own jacket.

She laughed again as Bryce stepped back and the rest of her force mounted up behind her. Venera turned and waved to them, and as Bryce ran back toward the roundhouse and safety, she yelled, "Come on! They're not going to be expecting this!"

GARTH COULD SEE it all. They'd tied his hands behind him and stood him near the body of the man who'd come with him to the roof. From behind him came the sounds of Sacrus's forces mopping up on the lower floors of Liris. Prisoners were being led onto the roof under the direction of Margit, who had climbed up the ladder with ferocious energy a few minutes before.

Garth had turned away when his daughter stepped onto the roof behind her.

Turning, he saw what was developing under the shadow of the building, and despite all the tragedy it made him smile.

A dozen horses, each one at least ten feet tall at the shoulder, were stepping daintily but rapidly through no-man's-land. The closely packed thornbushes and tumbled masonry were no barrier to them at all. Each mount held two riders except the one in the lead. Venera Fanning rode that one, a rifle held high over her head. Garth could see that her mouth was wide open—mother of Virga, was she howling some outlandish battle cry? Garth had to laugh.

"What's so funny, you?" A soldier cuffed him on the side of his head. Garth looked him in the eye and nodded in Venera's direction.

"That," he said.

After he finished swearing, the man ran toward Margit, shouting, "Sir! Sir!" Garth turned back to the view.

Sacrus had taken Liris with a comparatively small force and were now depleted on the Spyre side of the building. The bulk of the council army was wheeling in that direction, pushing back the few defenders on the barricades. They'd take the siege ladders on that side in no time. It shouldn't have been a problem for Sacrus; they now held the roof and could lower ladders, ropes, and platforms to relieve their own forces from the other side of the building. Now that they knew where the council army was going, their ground forces had started running back in that direction from the world's edge. This seemed safe because they had a large force below no-man's-land to block any access from the direction of the roundhouse.

But Venera's cavalry had just crossed over no-man's-land and were now stepping into the strip of cleared land next to the building. Without hesitation they turned right and galloped at the rear of the Sacrus line. Simultaneously those council troops fronting the roundhouse assaulted them head-on.

A hysterical laugh pierced the air. Garth turned to see Margit perched atop the wall. She was staring down at the horses with a wild look in her eye. "I'm seeing things in broad daylight now," she said, and laughed again. "This is a strange dream, this one. Things with four legs . . . taller than a man . . ."

Selene reached up to take Margit's arm but the former botanist batted her hand aside. Stepping back, her face full of doubt, Selene looked around—and her eyes met Garth's. He frowned and shook his head slowly.

Angrily, she turned away.

The twelve horses stepped over a barricade while their riders shot the men behind it. The horses were armored, Garth saw, although he was sure it wouldn't prove too effective under direct fire. Sacrus's men weren't firing, though. They were too amazed at what they were seeing. The beasts towered over them, huge masses of muscle on impossibly long legs, festooned with sheet metal barding that half-hid their giant eyes and broad teeth. The monsters were overtop and past and wheeling before the defenders could organize. And by then bullets and flicking hooves were finding them, and they all fell.

Margit stood there and watched while the commanders on the ground shouted and waved. The other men on the rooftop stared at the fiasco unfolding below them, then looked to Margit. The seconds dragged.

In that time the horses reached a point midway between the bottled-up council leadership and the Sacrus force below no-man's-land. Now they split into two squads of six. Venera led hers in a thunderous charge directly at the men who had pinned down Guinevera and the Liris army.

Selene jumped onto the wall beside Margit. She stared for a second, then cursed, and whirling, shouted, "Shoot! Shoot, you idiots! They're going to—"

Margit seemed to wake out of her trance. She stepped grandly down from the wall and frowned at the line of prisoners that had been led onto the roof. She strolled over, loosening a pistol at her belt.

"Where is Venera Fanning?" she shouted.

A sick feeling came over Garth. He watched Margit walk up

and down the line, saw her pause before Moss, sneer at Samson Odess, and finally stop in front of Eilen.

"You were her friend," she said. "You'll know where she is." She raised the pistol and aimed it between Eilen's eyes.

Garth tried to run over to her but a soldier kicked his legs out from under him and only the light gravity saved him from breaking his nose as he fell. "She's right there!" Garth hollered at Margit. "Riding a horse! You were just looking at her."

Margit glanced back. Her eyes found Garth lying prone on the flagstones.

"Don't be ridiculous," she said with a smile. "Those things weren't *real*."

She shot Eilen in the head.

Venera's friend flopped to the rooftop in a tumble of limbs. The other captives screamed and quailed. "Where is she?" shrieked Margit, waving the pistol. Now, too late, Selene was running to her side. The younger woman put her hand on Margit's arm, spoke in her ear, tugged her away from the prisoners.

As she led Margit away Selene glanced over at Garth. It was his turn to look away.

There was a lot of running and shouting then, though little shooting because, he supposed, the men on the roof were afraid of hitting their own men. Garth didn't care. He lay on his stomach, with his cheek pressed against the cold stone, and cried.

Someone hauled him to his feet. Dimly he realized that a great roaring sound was coming from beyond the roof's edge. Now the men on the roof did start firing—and cursing, and looking at one another helplessly.

Garth knew exactly what had happened. Venera had broken the line around Guinevera's men. They were pouring out of their defensive position and attacking Sacrus's force beneath no-man's-land. That group was now itself isolated and surrounded.

He wouldn't be surprised if Venera herself had moved on, perhaps circling the building to connect up with the main bulk of the council army. If she did that, then none of the ladders and elevator platforms to this roof would be safe for Sacrus.

"Come on." Garth was hauled to his feet and pushed to the middle of the roof. He coughed and realized that black smoke was pouring up from the courtyard. The prisoners were wailing and screaming.

Margit's soldiers had set the cherry trees alight.

"Get on the platform or I'll shoot you." Garth blinked, and saw that he was standing next to the elevator that climbed Liris's cable. Margit and Selene were already on the platform, with a crowd of soldiers and several Liris prisoners, including Moss and Odess.

He climbed aboard.

Margit smiled with supreme confidence. "This," she said as if to no one in particular, "is where we'll defeat her."

VENERA LOOKED DOWN from her saddle at Guinevera, who stared at her with his bloody sword half-raised. "You spoke out of turn, Principe," she called down. "Even if I wasn't Buridan before, I am now."

He ducked his head slightly, conceding the point. "We're grateful, Fanning," he said.

Venera finally let herself feel her triumph and relief, and slumped a bit in her saddle. Fragmentary memories of the past minutes came and went; who would have thought that the skin of Spyre would *bounce* under the gallop of a horse?

Scattered gunfire echoed around the corner of the building, but Sacrus's army was in full retreat. Their force below no-man's-land had surrendered. No one had any stomach for fighting anyway; Sacrus and council soldiers stood side by side, exchanging uneasy glances as another long slow undulation moved through the ground. Council troops were swarming up the sides of Liris, but there was no sound from up there and an ominous flag of black smoke was fluttering from the roofline.

Seeing that, Venera's anxiety about her friends returned. Garth, Eilen, and Moss—what had become of them during Sacrus's brief occupation? Her eyes were drawn to the cable that stretched from Liris up to Lesser Spyre. It seemed oddly slack, and somehow that tiny detail filled her with more fear than anything else she'd seen today.

Closer at hand, she spotted Jacoby Sarto walking, unescorted, past ranks of huddling Sacrus prisoners. He looked up at her, his face eloquently expressing the unease she too felt.

Another undulation, stronger this time. She saw trees sway, and a sharp crack! echoed from Liris's masonry wall. Some of the soldiers cried out.

Guinevera looked around. Ever the dramatist, his florid lips quivered as he said, "This should have been our moment of triumph. But what have we won? What have we done to Spyre?"

Venera did her best to look unimpressed, though she was worried too. "Look, there's no way to know," she said. That was a lie: she could feel it, they all could. Something was wrong.

A captain ran up. He saluted them both but it was almost an afterthought. "Ma'am," he said to Venera. "It's . . . they're waiting for you. On the roof."

A cold feeling came over her. For just a second she remembered lying on the marble floor of the Rush admiralty, bleeding from the mouth and sure she would die there alone. And then, curled around herself inside Candesce, feeling the Sun of Suns come to life, minutes to go before she was burnt alive. She'd almost lost it all. She could lose it all now.

She flipped down the little ladder attached to her saddle and climbed down. Her thighs and lower back spasmed with pain, but there was no echo from her jaw. She wouldn't have cared if there had been. As a tremor ran through the earth Jacoby Sarto reached to steady her. She looked him in the eye.

"If you come with me," she said, "whose side will you be on?"

He shrugged and staggered as the ground lurched again. "I don't think sides matter anymore," he said.

"Then come." They ran for the ladders.

21

ALL ACROSS SPYRE, metal that had been without voice
for a thousand years was groaning. The distant moan seemed
half-real to Venera, here at the world's edge where the roar of
the wind was perpetual; but it was there. Spyre was waking,
trembling, and dying. Everybody knew it.

She put one hand over the other and tried to focus on the
rungs above her. She could see the peaked helmets of some of
Guinevera's men up there and was pathetically glad that she
wouldn't have to face this alone.

Sarto was climbing a ladder next to hers. Even a month ago, the
very idea of trusting him would have seemed insane to her. And
anyway, if she were some romantic heroine and this were the sort
of story that would turn out well, it would be her lover Bryce of-
fering to go into danger at her side—not a man who until recently she would have been perfectly happy to see skewered on a
pike.

"Pfah," she said, and climbed out onto the roof.

Thick smoke crawled out of the broad square opening in the
center of the roof. Black and ominous, it billowed up twenty
feet and then was torn to ribbons by the world's-edge hurri-
canes. The smoke made an undulating black tapestry behind
Margit, her soldiers, and their hostages.

The elevator platform had been raised six feet. It was closely ringed by council troops whose weapons were aimed at Margit and her people. Venera recognized Garth Diamandis, Moss, and little Samson Odess among the captives. All had gun muzzles pressed against their cheeks.

A young woman in a uniform stood next to Margit. With Garth's face hovering just behind her own Venera could be in no doubt as to who she was; she had the same high cheekbones and gray eyes as her father.

Her gaze was fixed on Margit, her face expressionless.

"Come closer, Venera," called Margit. She held a pistol and had propped her elbow on her hip, aiming it casually upward. "Don't be shy."

Venera cursed under her breath. Margit had managed to corral all of her friends—no, not all. Where was Eilen? She glanced around the roof, not seeing her among the other newly freed Lirisians. Maybe she was downstairs fighting the fires; that was probably it. . . .

Her eye was drawn despite herself to a huddled figure lying on the roof. Freed of life, Eilen was difficult to recognize; her clothes were no longer clothes but some odd drapes of cloth covering a shape whose limbs weren't bent in any human pose. She stared straight up, her face a blank under the burnt wound in her forehead.

"Oh no . . ." Venera ran to her and knelt. She reached out, hesitated, then looked up at Margit.

Black smoke roiled behind the former botanist of Liris. She smiled triumphantly. "Always wanted an excuse to do that," she said. "And I'd love an excuse to do the same to these." Her pistol waved at the prisoners behind her. "But that's not going to happen, is it? Because you're going to . . ." She seemed to lose the thread of what she was saying, staring off into the distance for a few seconds. Then, starting, she looked at Venera again and said, "Going to give me the key to Candesce."

Venera glanced behind her. None of the army staff who knew about the key were here. Neither was Guinevera nor Pamela Anseratte. There was no one to prevent her from making such a deal.

Margit barked a surprised laugh. "Is this your solution? You thought to do a trade, did you?" Jacoby Sarto had stepped into view, paces behind Venera. Margit was sneering at him with undisguised contempt.

"That man-shaped thing might have been valuable once, but not anymore. It's not worth the least of these fools." She flipped up the pistol and fired; instantly hundreds of weapons rose across the roof, hammers cocking, men straining. Venera's heart was thudding painfully in her chest; she raised a hand, lowered it slowly. Gratefully, she saw the council soldiers obey her gesture and relax slightly.

She ventured a look behind her. Jacoby Sarto was staring down at a hole in the rooftop, right between his feet. His face was dark with anger, but his shoulders were slumped in defeat. He had nothing now, and he knew it.

"Your choice is clear, oh would-be queen of Candesce," shouted Margit over the shuddering of the wind. "You can keep your trophy, and maybe even use it again if you can evade us. Maybe these soldiers will follow you all the way to Candesce, though I doubt it. But go ahead: all you have to do is give the order and they'll fire. I'll be dead—and so will your friends. But you can walk away with your trinket.

"Or," she said with relish, "you can hand it to me now. Then I'll let your friends go—well, all save one, maybe. I need *some* guarantee that you won't have us shot on our way up to the docks. But I promise I'll let the last one go when we get there. Sacrus keeps its promises."

Venera played for time. "And who's going to use the key when you get to Candesce? Not you."

Margit shrugged. "They are wise, those that made me and healed me after you . . ." Her brows knit as though she were trying to remember something. "You . . . Those that made me— yes, those ones, not this one and his former cronies." She nodded to Sarto. "No, Sacrus underwent a . . . change of government . . . some weeks ago. People with a far better understanding of what the key represents, and who we might bargain with using it, are in charge now. Their glory shall extend beyond merely cowing the principalities with some show of force from the Sun of Suns. The bargain they've struck . . . the forces they've struck it with . . . well, suffice it to say, Virga itself will be our toy when they're done."

An ugly suspicion was forming in Venera's mind. "Do these forces have a name? Maybe—Artificial Nature?"

Margit shrugged again, looking pleased. "A lady doesn't tell." Then her expression hardened. She extended her hand. "Hand it over. Now. We have a lot to do, and you're wasting my time."

The rooftop trembled under Venera's feet. Past the pall of smoke, Spyre itself shimmered like a dissolving dream.

She'd almost had the power she needed; power to take revenge against the Pilot of Slipstream for the death of her husband. Enough wealth to set herself up somewhere in independence. Maybe she was even growing past the need for vengeance. It was possible she could have stayed here with her newfound friends, maybe in the mansion of Buridan in Lesser Spyre. Such possibilities had trembled just out of reach ever since her arrival among these baroque, ancient, and inward-turned people. It had all been within her grasp.

And Margit was right: she could still turn away. The key was hers and with it untold power and riches if she chose to exercise it. True, she would have to move immediately to secure her own safety, else the council would try to take it from her. But she was sure she could do that, with Sarto's help and Bryce's. Maybe Spyre would survive, if they spun its rotation down in time and repaired it under lesser gravity. She could still have Buridan, her place on the council, and power. All she had to do was sacrifice the prisoners who stood watching her now.

The Venera Fanning who had woken in Garth Diamandis's bed those scant weeks ago could have done that.

She reached slowly into her jacket and brought out the slim white wand that had caused so much grief—and doubtless would be the cause of much more. Step by step she closed the distance between herself and Margit's outstretched hand. Venera raised her hand and Margit leaned forward, but Venera would not look her in the eye.

Selene Diamandis put her foot in Margit's lower back and pushed.

As the former botanist sprawled onto Venera, bringing them both down, Selene pulled her own pistol and aimed it at the face of the man whose gun was touching Garth's ear. "Father, jump!" she cried.

Margit snarled and punched Venera in the chin. The explosion of pain was nothing compared to the spasms she usually got there so Venera didn't even blink. She grabbed Margit's wrist and the two rolled over and away from the platform.

"Lower your guns," Selene was shouting. Venera caught a confused glimpse of men and women stepping out of the way as she and Margit tumbled to the edge of the roof by the court-yard. Nobody moved to help her—if anyone laid a hand on either her or Margit, everyone would start shooting.

Margit elbowed Venera in the face and her head snapped back. She had an upside-down view of the courtyard below; it was an inferno.

"That red looks good on the trees, don't you think?" Margit muttered. She struck Venera again. Dazed, Venera couldn't recover fast enough and suddenly found Margit standing over her, pistol aimed at her.

"The key," she said, "or you die."

A shadow flickered from overhead. Margit glanced up, said, "What—," and then Moss collided with her and the two of them sailed off the roof. In the blink of an eye they were gone, disappearing silently into the smoke.

No one spoke. On her knees, gazing into the fire, Venera realized that she was waiting like everyone else for the end: a scream, a crash, or some other evidence that Margit and Moss had landed. It didn't come. There was only the dry crackle of the flames. Someone coughed and the spell was broken. Venera took a proffered arm and stood up.

It was Samson Odess who had helped her to her feet. A short distance away Garth Diamandis was hugging his daughter fiercely as the remaining Sacrus troops climbed down from the platform. The building was swaying, its stones cracking and grinding now. The whole landscape of Spyre was transforming as trees fell and buildings quivered on the verge of collapse. Soldiers and officers of both sides looked at one another in wonder and terror. Their alliances suddenly didn't matter.

Odess pointed to the grandly spinning town-wheels miles overhead. "Come on," he said. "Lesser Spyre will survive when the world comes apart. It'll all fall away from the town-wheels."

Venera followed his gaze, then looked around. The little elevator platform might hold twelve or fifteen people; she could save her friends. Then what? Repeat the standoff she'd just undergone, this time at the docks? Sacrus's leaders were there. They probably held the entire city by now.

"Who are you going to save, Samson?" she asked him. "These are your people now. You're the senior official in Liris—you're the new botanist now, do you understand? These people are your responsibility."

She saw the realization hit him, but the result wasn't what she might have expected. Samson seemed to stand a little taller. His eyes, which had always darted around nervously, were now steady. He walked over to where Eilen lay crumpled. Kneeling, he arranged her limbs and closed her eyes so that it looked like she was sleeping with her cheek and the palm of one hand pressed against the stones of Liris. Then he looked up at Venera. "We have to save them all," he said.

It seemed hopeless, if the very fabric of Spyre was about to come apart around them. Even burying the dead in the thin earth of their ancestral home seemed pointless. In hours or minutes they would be emptied into the airs of Virga. The alternative for the living was to rise to the city, to probably become prisoners in Lesser Spyre.

The air . . .

"I know what to do," Venera said. "Gather all your people. We might just make it if we go now."

"Where?" he asked. "If the whole world's coming apart—"

"Fin," she shouted as she ran to the edge of the roof. "We have to get to Fin!"

SHE MOUNTED HER horse and led them at a walk. At first only a trickle of people followed, just those who had been on the rooftop, but soon soldiers of Liris and Sacrus threw down their weapons and joined the crowd. Their officers trailed them.

Guinevera and Anseratte appeared, but they were silent when anyone asked them what to do.

As they passed the roundhouse Bryce emerged with some of his own followers. They fell into step next to Venera's horse but, while their eyes met, they exchanged no words. Both knew that their time together had ended, as certainly as Spyre's.

In the clear daylight, Venera was able to behold the intricacies of Greater Spyre's estates for the first and last time. Always before she had skulked past them at night or raced along the few awning-covered roads that were tolerated by this paranoid civilization. Now, atop a ten-foot-tall beast striding the narrow strip of no-man's-land between the walls, she could see it all. She was glad she had never known before what lay here.

The work of untold ages, of countless lives, had gone into the making of Spyre. There was not a square inch of it that was untouched by some lifetime of contemplation and planning. Any garden corner or low stone wall could tell a thousand tales of lovers who'd met there, children who built forts or cried alone, of petty disputes with neighbors settled there with blood or marriage. Time had never stopped in Spyre, but it had slowed like the sluggish blood of some fantastically old beast, and now for generations the people had lived nearly identical lives. Their hopes and dreams were channeled by the walls under which they walked—influenced by the same storybooks, paintings, and music as their ancestors—until they had become gray copies of their parents or grandparents. Each had added perhaps one small item to Spyre's vast stockpile of bric-a-brac, unknowingly placing one more barrier before any thoughts of flight their own children might nurture. Strange languages never spoken by more than a dozen people thrived. Venera had been told how the lightless inner rooms of some estates had become bizarre shrines as beloved patriarchs died and because of tradition or fear no one could touch the body. More than one nation had died too as its own mausoleum ate it from the inside, its last inhabitants living out their lives in an ivy-strangled gatehouse without once stepping beyond the walls.

Now the staggered rows of hedge and wall were toppling. From half-hidden buildings came the sound of glass shattering as pillars shifted. Doors unopened for centuries suddenly gaped revealing blackness or sights that seared themselves into memory but not the understanding—glimpses, as they were, of cultures and rituals gone so insular and self-referential as to be forever opaque to outsiders.

And now the people were visible, running outside as the ground quaked and the metal skin of Spyre groaned beneath them. They were like grubs ejected from a wasp's nest split by some indifferent boy; many lay thrashing on the ground, unable to cope with the strangeness of the greater world they had been thrown into. Others ran screaming, or tore at themselves or one another, or stood mutely or laughed.

As a many-veranda'd manor collapsed in on itself Venera caught a glimpse of the people still inside: the very old, parchment hands crossed over their laps as they sat unmoved beneath their collapsing ceilings; and the panicked who stood staring wide-eyed at open fields where walls had been. The building's floors came down one atop the other, pancaking in a wallop of dust, and they were all gone.

"Liris's cable has snapped," someone said. Venera didn't look around. She felt strangely calm; after all, what lay ahead of them all but a return to the skies of Virga? She knew those skies, had flown in them many times. There, of course, lay the irony: for those who fell into the air with the cascading pieces of the great wheel, this would not be the end, but a beginning. Few, if any, could comprehend that. So she said nothing.

And for her? She had saved herself from her scheming sisters and her father's homicidal court by marrying a dashing admiral. In the end he had lived up to her expectations, but he had also died. Venera had been taught exactly one way to deal with such crises, which was through vengeance. Now she patted the front of her jacket, where the key to Candesce nestled once again in its inner pocket. It was a useless trinket, she realized; nothing worthwhile had come of using it and nothing would.

For her, what was ending here was the luxury of being able to hide within herself. If she was to survive, she would have to begin to take other people's emotions seriously. Lacking power, she must accommodate.

Glancing affectionately at Garth, who was talking intensely with his red-uniformed daughter, Venera had to admit that the prospect wasn't so frightening as it used to be.

It became harder to walk as gravity began to vary between nearly nothing and something crushingly more than one g. Her horse balked and Venera had to dismount; and when he ran off, she shrugged and fell into step next to Bryce and Sarto, who were arguing politics to distract themselves. They paused to smile at her, then continued. Slowly, with many pauses and some panicked milling about as gaps appeared in the land ahead, they made their way to Fin.

They were nearly there when Buridan finally consigned itself to the air. The shouting and pointing made Venera lift her eyes from the splitting soil, and she was in time to see the black tower fold its spiderweb of girders around itself like a man spinning a robe over his shoulders. Then it lowered itself in stately majesty through the gaping rent in the land until only blue sky remained.

She looked at Bryce. He shrugged. "They knew it might happen. I told them to scatter all the copies of the book and currency to the winds if they fell. They're to seed the skies of Virga with democracy. I hope that's a good enough task to keep them sane for the next few minutes; and then, maybe, they'll be able to see to their own safety."

The tower would quickly disintegrate as it arrowed through the skies. Its pieces would become missiles that might do vast harm to the houses and farms of the neighboring principalities; much more so would be the larger shreds of Spyre itself when it all finally went. That was tragic; but the new citizens of Buridan, and the men and women of Bryce's organization, would soon find themselves gliding through a warm blue sky. They might kick their way from stone to tumbling stone and so make their way out of the wreckage. And then they would be like everyone else in the world: sunlit and free in an endless sky.

Venera smiled. Ahead she saw the doors of the low bunker that led to Fin, and broke into a run. "We're there!"

Her logic had been simple. Fin was a wing, aerodynamic like nothing else in Spyre. Of all the parts that might come loose and fall in the next little while, it was bound to travel fastest and farthest. So, it would almost certainly outrun the rest of the wreckage. And Venera had a hunch that Fin's inhabitants had given thought, over the centuries, about what they would do when Spyre died.

She was right. Although the guards at the door were initially reluctant to let in the mob, Corinne appeared and ordered them to stand down. As the motley collection of soldiers and citizens streamed down the steps she turned to Venera and grinned, just a little hysterically. "We have parachutes," she said. "And the fin can be detached and let drop. It was always our plan of last resort if we ever got invaded. Now . . ." She shrugged.

"But do you have boats? Bikes? Any means of traveling once

we're in the air?" Corinne grinned and nodded, and Venera let out a sigh of relief. She had led her people to the right place.

Spyre's final death agony began as the last were stumbling inside. Venera stood with Corinne, Bryce, and Sarto at the top of the stairs and watched a bright line start at the rim of the world, high up past the sedately spinning wheels of Lesser Spyre. The line became a visible split, its edges pulling in trees and buildings; and Spyre peeled apart from that point. Its ancient fusion engines had proven incapable of slowing it safely—it might have been the stress they generated as much as centripetal force that finally did in the titanium structure. The details didn't matter; all that Venera saw was a thousand ancient cultures ending in one stroke of burgeoning sunlight.

A trembling shockwave raced around the curve of the world. It was beautiful in the blued distance but Venera knew it was headed straight for her. She should go inside before it arrived. She didn't move.

Other splits appeared in the peeling halves of the world and now the land simply shredded like paper. A roar like the howl of a furious god was approaching and a tremble went through the ground as gravity failed for good.

Just before Bryce grabbed her wrist and hauled her inside, Venera saw a herd of Dali horses gallop with grace and courage off the rim of the world.

They would survive, she was sure. Kicking and neighing, they would sail through the skies of Virga until they landed in the lap of someone unsuspecting. Gravity would be found for them, somewhere; they were too mythic and beautiful to be left to die.

Then Corinne's men threw the levers that detached Fin from the rest of Spyre. Suddenly weightless, Venera hovered in the open doorway and watched a wall of speed ivy recede very quickly and disappear behind the clouds.

Nobody spoke as she drifted inside. Hollow-eyed men and women glanced at one another, all crowded together in the thin antechamber of the tiny nation. They were all refugees now; it was clear from their faces that they expected some terrible fate to befall them, perhaps within the next few minutes. None could imagine what that might be, of course, and seeing that confusion, Venera didn't know whether to laugh or cry for them.

"Relax," she said to a weeping woman. "This is a time to hope, not to despair. You'll like where we're going."

Silence. Then somebody said, "And where is that?"

Somebody else said, "Home."

Venera looked over, puzzled. The voice hadn't been familiar, but the accent . . .

A man was looking back at her steadily. He held one of Fin's metal stanchions with one hand but otherwise looked quite comfortable in freefall. She did recognize the rags he was wearing, though—they marked him as one of the prisoners she had liberated from the Grey Infirmary.

"You're not from here," she said.

He grinned. "And you're not Amandera Thrace-Guiles," he said. "You're the admiral's wife."

A shock went through her. "What?"

"I only saw you from a distance when they rescued us," said the man. "And then lost sight of you when we got here to Fin. Everyone was talking about the mysterious lady of Buridan. But now I see you up close, I know you."

"Your accent," she said. "It's *Slipstream.*"

He nodded. "I was part of the expedition, ma'am—aboard the *Arrest.* I was there for the big battle, when we defeated Falcon Formation. When your husband defeated them. I saw him plunge the *Rook* into the enemy's dreadnought like a knife into another man's heart. Had time to watch the bastard blow up,

before they netted me out of the air and threw me into prison."
He grimaced in anger.

Venera's heart was in her throat. "You saw . . . Chaison die?"

"Die?" The ex-airman looked at her incredulously. "*Die*? He's
not dead. I spent two weeks in the same cell with him before
Falcon traded me to Sacrus like a sack of grain."

Venera's vision grayed and she would have fallen over had she
been under gravity. Oblivious, the other continued: "I might'a
wished he were dead a couple times over those weeks. It's hard
sharing your space with another man, particularly one you've
respected. You come to see all his faults."

Venera recovered enough to croak, "Yes, I know how he can
be." Then she turned away to hide her tears.

The giant metal wing shuddered as it knifed through the air.
Past the opened doorway, where Bryce and Sarto were silhouetted, the sky seemed to be boiling. Cloud and air were being torn
by the shattering of a world. The sound of it finally caught up
with Fin, a cacophony like a belfry being blown up that went on
and on. It was a knell that should warn the principalities in time
for them to mount some sort of emergency response. Nothing
could be done, though, if square miles of metal skin were to
plow into a town-wheel somewhere.

To Venera, the churning air and the noise of it all seemed to
originate in her own heart. He was alive! Absurdly, the image
came to her of how she would tell him this story—tell him
about Garth rescuing her, about her first impressions of Spyre as
seen from a roofless crumbling cube of stone; about Lesser
Spyre and Sacrus and Buridan Tower. Moments ago they had
been mere facts, memories of a confused and drifting time.
With the possibility that she could tell him about them, they
suddenly became episodes of a great drama, a rousing tale she
would laugh and cry to tell.

She turned to Garth, grinning wildly. "Did you hear that? He's alive!"

Garth smiled weakly.

Venera shook him by the shoulders. "Don't you understand? There is a place for you, for all of you, if you've the courage to get there. Come with me. Come to Slipstream, and on to Falcon, where he's imprisoned. We'll free him and then you'll have a home again. I swear it."

He didn't move, just kept his grip on his daughter while the wind whistled through Fin and the rest of the refugees looked from him to Venera and back again.

"Well, what are you scared of?" she demanded. "Are you afraid I can't do what I say?"

Now Garth smiled ruefully and shook his head. "No, Venera," he said. "I'm afraid that you can."

She laughed and went to the door. Bracing her hands and feet on the cold metal, she looked out. The gray turbulence of Spyre's destruction was fading with the distance. In its place was endless blue.

"You'll see," she said into the rushing air. "It'll all work out. I'll make sure of it."